PRAISE ... **AY**

"A labyrinth of rich suspense, *Blown Away* by Shane Gericke explodes across the page in a nerve-tingling tale of cops and a baffling serial killer. Fascinating, intense, the novel is utterly gripping. Shane Gericke writes with the clear eye of a hard-nosed reporter and the sweet soul of an artist. The power of *Blown Away* is visceral and unforgettable—you won't want to miss this gem."
　—Gayle Lynds, *New York Times* best-selling author of *The Last Spymaster* and *The Coil*

"Blast off! Shane Gericke's *Blown Away* is a rambunctious, devious novel full of chutzpah, high energy and surprises. Forget roller coaster; this one reads like a rocket."
　—John Lutz, *USA Today* best-selling author of *Darker Than Night,* winner of the Edgar and Shamus awards

"The ultimate 'game' of cat and mouse."
　—Alex Kava, international best-selling author of *A Necessary Evil*

"Shane Gericke's smart and suspenseful book will keep you turning the pages . . . then get you up in the morning, hiding your board games away. A remarkably strong first novel; I can't wait for the next!"
　—Deborah Blum, Pulitzer Prize–winning author of *Bad Karma: A True Story of Obsession and Murder*

"Move over, Elmore Leonard, there's a new sheriff in town! Real cops, terrific action, a twisted plot that will keep you awake at night and a tough-gal detective who makes it all happen. More please!"
　—Roy Huntington, editorial director, *American Cop* magazine

"As a veteran cop who's also female, I approach such thrillers with a jaded eye. But *Blown Away* didn't let me down! It's one of the rare books where the female lead isn't only a cop, she's smart, savvy and tough, too. We need more of this!"

—Suzanne Huntington, police officer, San Diego Police Department

"Watch out, V.I. Warshawski, there's a new detective in town. Shane Gericke's new thriller will keep you on the edge of your seat as some sharp cops take on a serial killer with a huge ego and deadly grudge. Here's the beach book for the summer."

—Howard Wolinsky, author of *Serpent on the Staff*

"A quickening series of savage clues suck rookie cop Emily Thompson and her fellow law-enforcement officers into a grisly guessing game—a game whose rules only the twisted killer knows. With insightful grace, Shane Gericke weaves vivid characters and nonstop action into a compelling page-turner. He emerges as a rising star of the police-thriller genre."

—Peter Haugen, author of *World History for Dummies*

"Shane Gericke's first novel is a fast-moving police procedural of the highest order. From the chilling opening chapter to the stunning conclusion, Gericke weaves a tale of a police hunt for a serial killer in which the cops and the criminal are compelling and realistic."

—Tim West, *Sun Newspapers*

"*Blown Away* tightens the plot around detective Emily Thompson like a terrifying noose. From the opening pages, Shane Gericke's characters race to stop serial killings that are based on a pattern both diabolical and seemingly innocent. The quiet Midwestern city of Naperville has never before seen a police thriller like this one."

—Thomas Frisbie, author of *Victims of Justice,* the Jeanine Nicarico murder

BLOWN
AWAY

SHANE GERICKE

PINNACLE BOOKS
Kensington Publishing Corp.
http://www.kensingtonbooks.com

PINNACLE BOOKS are published by

Kensington Publishing Corp.
850 Third Avenue
New York, NY 10022

All Kensington Titles, Imprints, and Distributed Lines are
available at special quantity discounts for bulk purchases for
sales promotions, premiums, fund-raising, and educational
or institutional use. Special book excerpts or customized print-
ings can also be created to fit specific needs. For details, write
or phone the office of the Kensington special sales manager:
Kensington Publishing Corp., 850 Third Avenue, New York,
NY 10022, attn: Special Sales Department, Phone: 1-800-
221-2647.

Pinnacle and the P logo Reg. U.S. Pat. & TM Off.

First Pinnacle Books Printing: May 2006

10 9 8 7 6 5 4 3 2 1

Printed in the United States of America

To Jerrle, who brings out the best in everyone

ACKNOWLEDGMENTS

My deep appreciation to those who helped wrench this story from my overly caffeinated brain.

Foremost is my editor, Michaela Hamilton, of Kensington Publishing. I wrote this novel, but she brought it to life. Thanks, Michaela.

After that come my superb agent, Bill Contardi, of Brandt & Hochman Literary Agents, manuscript readers Bill and Jan Page, photographer Ellen Newman, firearms consultant Roy Huntington, and my family and friends, whose unflagging encouragement over the years meant so much.

Finally, the women and men of the Naperville Police Department, who allowed me to observe, inquire, ride along, and otherwise learn what they do. They are Chief David Dial, Captains David Hilderbrand and Raymond McGury, Sergeants Elizabeth Brantner Smith and Michael Brian, Detective Nick Liberio, Officers Ann Quigley and Christopher Cali, Crime Prevention Specialist Marita Manning, and Investigations Specialist Kris Stockwell. May you all stay safe.

PROLOGUE

"911, where is your emergency?" Bertha Pruitt repeated. No reply.

"Come on, caller, talk to me. This is Boston 911—oh Jesus!" The howl on the other end was so loud that several operators snapped their heads her way. Bertha waved them off. "Talk to me, caller, please!" she said. "Where is your—"

"Actually, Boston," a silky male voice interrupted, "the proper question is, 'What is your emergency?' not 'Where is your emergency?' Understand?" His tone turned to disgust. "Or maybe you're just too stupid to understand my rules. Not uncommon with inferiors."

Bertha's computer display started whirling and blipping like a slot machine. "Just what I need," she muttered as numbers and street names danced and disappeared. "A caller ID crash." She punched the alert button and watched Trout Lips, the shift supervisor, run for a headset. Normally, the E-911 software displayed the caller's location till the dispatcher finished sending cops, fire, Con Ed, or other personnel. Now the location changed every time she blinked—downtown Boston,

Southie, Amherst, Cape Cod, downtown again, a nonexistent address in Boston Harbor. She shook her head. She'd have to keep the loony talking till the techs fixed the problem or the loony gave it up. Normally, she enjoyed playing Beat the Techs. Today, 911 calls were stacked thanks to the nor'easter slamming the coast. Which meant she'd wind up pulling another shift. She blew out her breath. She'd been looking forward to spending Christmas with her husband, five daughters, three sons-in-law, and eleven grandchildren. The first time in ages the entire family was home for the holidays . . .

Enough whining.

"Sir, I'm sorry if I sound stupid," Bertha began in her most sincere voice. "I'm just trying to help. What was that scream? Do you have an emergency to tell me about?" No reply. "Or did you call me just to talk, see if we can figure things out?"

"I don't have an emergency, Boston. But a friend of mine certainly does."

"A friend of mine," Bertha repeated. Mirroring the caller's words often speeded the process. "Is that who screamed? Your friend?"

"Yes."

"Does your friend need my help?"

"He needs somebody's, Boston."

"OK, then," Bertha said. "Where do I send my ambulance so I can help—"

"It won't work, Boston," the caller interrupted.

Damn. "Work? What won't work, sir?" Bertha said, all innocence.

"You want my address. So you can stop the screaming. It won't work." The man coughed. "Here's the thing, Boston. My friend is a police officer. He's badly hurt. He might die." A low chuckle. "Correction, he will die. Because in a few minutes I'm going to saw out his heart."

She shuddered. In twenty-seven years of dispatching, she'd

never heard anything more cold. "Sir, you don't mean that," she said, knuckles whitening. No answer. "Are you still there?"

"Still here. Still mean it."

Her head began pounding. "Sir, tell me what you're talking about. Please."

A sigh from the other end. "Well, Boston, it's like this . . . You know, I really hate that."

"Hate what?"

"Calling you 'Boston.' It's so impersonal. What's your name?"

"I can't tell you that," Bertha said as Trout Lips shook his head. "It's against departmental policy to identify ourselves to callers."

"That's a fine rule, Boston," he replied. "But why don't you tell me, anyway?"

"I can't, sir, I really—"

The bloodcurdling shrieks erupted again. "Come on, Boston, say it," the wacko cajoled. "Be a good little girl and play along with my—"

"It's Bertha," she said, hating him for it.

The howls trailed off. "No fooling?"

"Come down to the police station, and I'll show you my birth certificate."

"Cute, Bertha." Pause. "Bertha Bertha Bo-Bertha. Remember that old novelty song? Where you set names to music?"

"Yes," she said cautiously.

"Why don't you finish yours for me?"

She stared at the computer. "Sing? My *name?*"

"Yes, Boston. It'll be fun! Here, I'll start. Bertha Bertha Bo-Bertha . . ."

She hated to participate in this maniacal karaoke, but another scream convinced her. She sang fast, clenching her fists. The screaming faded.

"Very good," the wacko said. "Bertha what?"

Trout Lips shook his head and waved his arms, his mouth a grim line. Bertha debated furiously with herself. *Yes, save the poor officer. No, don't risk your family.*

"I can't go further than Bertha, sir," she tried. "Honest to God! It's for our own safety. And it would mean my job. My boss has warned me twice about no last names"—Trout Lips nodded at the exaggeration—"and if I tell you, I'll get fired." She closed her eyes, fearing the next sound.

"Well, we can't have that," the wacko said, surprising her. "I know how tough it is to get a job these days, with health insurance and all. I just appreciate that you didn't lie about your first name, my dear—"

"How do you know that, pal?" Bertha spat, incensed at his endearment. "You have ESP?"

"Who'd make up 'Bertha?'" A slight pause. "Mine's John."

"John," she repeated. "That wouldn't be John Doe by any chance?"

He laughed delightedly. "Hey, you aren't stupid, are you?"

She ignored that, glancing at Trout Lips, who was growling into his phone, "Dammit to hell, my cop's in deep! Get off your ass and fix this!"

She rolled her eyes. If cussing could fix the problem, she'd have done it already. It wouldn't. She had to talk to John Doe. Listen. Talk some more. Coax, wheedle, flatter, threaten, tap-dance. Anything to keep him on the line.

"Now that we're clear on names, Mr. Doe," she said, "can we get back to the issue at hand?"

"*Mister* Doe?" he repeated, amused. "No need for formality, this isn't exactly black-tie."

"OK . . . John," she said. "Let's get back to the—"

"Dead cop walking?"

"That's exactly who I mean, John," Bertha said. "What

are you doing to this officer, John, and why are you doing it?"

"Very good questions, Bertha," he replied. "Thanks for asking them, Bertha."

She shook her head in frustration. The repetition of her name wasn't a variation on "my dear." This man knew the cop playbook and wouldn't fall for any of her caller-bonding techniques.

"Would you like the officer to tell you, Bertha?"

She blinked at the surprise offer. "Yes! I would!" Abducted cops were trained to shout their location to anyone within earshot. If they didn't know, then they'd describe what they smelled, heard, or felt. Stinking fish might mean a harbor. Train whistles or heavy rumbles, a freight yard. She hoped this officer was coherent enough to try. "Would you really allow me to speak with him?"

"Hey, darlin', anything for you," John Doe said breezily. "Hang on while I hold the phone to his ear. He's kind of tied up. Ha-ha." A short silence, then Bertha heard raw, wet breathing, skidding on every exhale. She willed herself to relax. Tension made you miss the critical subtleties. "Hello?" she ventured. "Am I speaking to the officer?"

"Yes . . . I . . . I don't . . . know where I am," a boyish voice said.

"That's OK, Officer," Bertha said. "We'll figure it out together. My name is Bertha. I'm a senior 911 operator with the Boston Police Department, and I'm going to get you out of there."

"I . . . I hope so. . . ."

"I promise. Can you tell me your name?"

"Timothy O'Brien. Massachusetts State Police. I'm—" He loosed an unearthly howl.

"What's that lunatic doing to you?" Bertha shouted. "Timothy, speak to me!" No reply, just wild screams. Then he was back. "He cut me . . ." Ohhh, it hurts. . . ." Gelatinous sobbing, fast and deep. "I was driving my car . . . Bertha, this hurts so awful. . . ."

"Your car, Timothy?" she interrupted, glancing at the growing mob of bosses in the 911 room. "Do you mean your police cruiser?"

"No . . . personal car. Driving . . . home."

"From where?"

"Barracks. After work."

Bertha nodded. The 7,838 square miles of the Bay State were divided into thirty-nine state police districts called barracks. It was a yawning cop-to-acreage ratio, one she dared not think about right now. "What time did you leave the barracks, Timothy?"

"I think 8 . . . no . . . 8:15 . . . night . . . last night."

"At 8:15 last night, good! What direction did you drive?" No answer. "You know, after you left the barracks?" Still no answer. Too much for his terrorized brain. Break it into pieces. "What direction?"

"Huh?" he said.

"What direction?" Bertha repeated. "Which way did you drive? North? East?"

"When?"

"After you left the barracks."

"Uh, I don't know."

"Toward or away from the ocean?"

"Oh. I, uh, well . . ."

"Was the sun in your eyes?"

"Yes. Setting. It was red. Big. Pretty."

"You drove west, Timothy. Good. What happened after you started driving west?"

Long pause. "I stopped."

"To do what?"

No answer.

"C'mon, Timmy, I need to know," Bertha cajoled. "I want

to help you." Still no answer. "Answer me!" she roared in Full Metal Sergeant, drawing a startled glare from a boss. "I'm giving you a direct order, Trooper O'Brien! Tell me why you stopped your car last night!"

"To . . . help . . . a man change a flat tire," he replied, the logjam breaking. "Yeah! Highway 143, east of Chesterfield, next to the river bridge." Trout Lips typed the location into the statewide emergency network. In seconds, every cop in a hundred miles would mash gas toward the tiny town in western Massachusetts. "I squatted to work the jack," the trooper continued. "He slugged me on the head. When I woke up, I found myself handcuffed. To this operating table."

"When did you wake up?" Bertha asked. No reply. "How long have you been awake?"

"Hour."

"One hour? Are you sure?"

"Been counting minutes."

She glanced at her watch. John Doe had had him fifteen hours. Subtract one for the time on the table and . . .

Sigh. They could be right here in Boston. Or down along the Cape. Holed up on a coastal island. Or stuffed in a spider hole in the Florida Panhandle. Maybe even in Canada, though she believed this abductor was too smart to risk Homeland Security sniffer dogs. She shook her pounding head. "You said an operating table, Timothy?" she asked. "Can you describe it for me?" Any little clue could jog a local constable's memory.

The trooper groaned. "I'm in an operating room. Handcuffed to a table, so I can't move. There's a large overhead light with a reflector. Two big air tanks. A metal tray with tools. Hammer, scalpels, pliers. The room is small. The walls are . . . breathing." Before she could ask what that meant, his voice became deeper, more defiant. "He's dressed in surgical scrubs, Bertha. Rubber gloves. A bag over his head. Holes for his eyes. Another for his mouth. His lips are painted a girly cherry red so he can hide even that much. Hey! You! Take off these handcuffs, and fight me like a man—"

"Forget that! Tell me everything else!" Bertha interrupted. "Height? Weight? Eye color? Tattoos? C'mon, you know the drill." She was amazed the abductor hadn't stopped this conversation already.

"He's tall. Almost seven feet. Mirrored sunglasses. Can't see his eyes." The trooper sounded much weaker. "The damn walls keep breathing . . . What . . . what's your name again?"

"Bertha," she said. "It's Bertha. Timothy. What do you mean the walls are—"

"He cuts me, Bertha," he gasped. "With the tools. Ankle, throat, ribs, hands. Hurts so much—"

"I've been carving on the lad since he woke, my dear," the kidnapper interrupted. "Just surface cuts. In exactly the right places, of course. He's not bleeding much." Serene chuckle. "Not yet."

Bertha thought of her father, who'd worn a Boston shield for thirty-two years before retiring happily to the golf course. Not one injury all those years, not one wacko whispering death in his ear. "What did Timothy do to make you hate him?" she tried.

"Nothing."

"Nothing?" she said, genuinely curious. "Then why are you doing this to him?"

"I needed to know."

She glared at the lead technician, who shook his head in exasperation, as if to say, "Hell, lady, I don't know what the hell's wrong." She went back to the caller. "Need to know what, John?"

"If I could do it," he replied. "It's one thing to dream about executing a cop, Bertha. You can plan and rehearse all you want, and that's fun. It's another thing to actually, you know, do it." He was extremely calm. Robotic. No, that wasn't it, not exactly. *Unsure.* As if he needed to talk himself into this.

"Soda," she croaked, throat parched. "Hurry." Trout Lips ran for one. Her supervisor was a good guy, but stunningly inept at his job. He survived because he was the mayor's cousin. That guaranteed him two things—a city paycheck and a catty nickname. His came from his enormously fat lips, which stuck so far out they resembled a trout's.

The soda can hit her desk. She drank fast, sorting options. John Doe was approaching the center of the high wire, not sure if he should keep going, and risk falling, or walk back to the stability of the platform. Forward, victory, backward, safety. She could play with that. Ask about his life, his dreams, what bothered him so much he'd execute another human being in cold blood. Let him unburden his soul if he had one. In return, she'd tell him about herself, provide her full name. She owed that much to the brave young man on the table.

But John Doe was no longer tentative. "I drove ahead of the trooper, flattened my own tire, and waited for him to come by," he was crowing. "I brained him, threw him in the trunk, drove here, handcuffed him to the operating table, and I'm carving him like a Christmas goose! I'm going to kill your cop in cold blood, Bertha, and there's nothing you can do to stop—"

"You bastard!" Bertha screamed, praying that cursing John Doe would work better than cursing the malfunctioning computer. "No-guts, yellow-belly coward! You stop hurting that boy right now, you goddamn lunatic!"

"Phew, honey, you eat with that mouth?" Cheerful, not the least bit offended.

"Sorry, John," she mumbled, tossing him the apology for delaying the kill. "You frustrate me, that's all." Trout Lips slapped the trooper's personnel record next to her soda, and she scanned it for a counterattack. Timothy was twenty-four years old, several months out of the academy. Like all newly minted troopers, he patrolled the boondocks, where Massachusetts kissed New York. He lived thirty-one miles from his barracks, with wife, son, daughter, three greyhounds, and a pony. Bertha wanted John Doe to know every one of those facts before he finished his terrible obsession. "John, his nickname is Legs!"

"Legs?" he asked. "What on earth for?"

She studied the fax. It wasn't there. "I don't know," she admitted. "Basketball star? Ballet dancer? What I do know is he's got two darling children, Alyssa and T.J., Timothy Junior. They're twins, just a year old. Today's their birthday, in fact." It wasn't—not for another two days—but she decided to risk that one lie. "Do you really want to butcher their daddy on their birthday?" she continued. "Make those angels cry on their special day for the rest of their lives?"

"Hey!" he snapped. "I've got nothing against kids!"

"Of course, you don't," Bertha said. "No real man does. So why don't you let him go?"

He blew out his breath. "I'm disappointed, Bertha. I thought you were taking me seriously."

"I am, John," she assured. "I heard Timothy's screams. They're real. They tell me you'll go all the way." She shook her head as if he could see. "But you don't have to actually commit the murder. The fact that you can do it is enough, isn't it?" No answer. "Knock Timothy cold, and dump him at a truck stop. We'll find him. You'll get away clean since he can't identify you, and we certainly have no idea what you look like."

"But you're figuring out where I am, Bertha," Doe countered. "SWAT boys are closing in on me even as we speak, aren't they?"

"No," she said forlornly, eyeing the techs. "I'm trying to

track you, sure. A young man I care about is in the tall weeds, and I want to find him. But I can't."

"Certain about that, Bo-Bertha?"

She cocked her head. For the first time the man's tone and words didn't match. It was subtle, but unmistakable—John Doe didn't sound as surprised as he should have at the "joyous" news the cops couldn't track his location.

"Yes, I'm sure," Bertha said. "You know why, John? Because my caller ID's busted!" She ground her knuckles into her throbbing forehead. "Ten-million-dollar piece of junk!"

"There's never a cop when you need one," Doe said. "Cyber or otherwise."

Bertha's heart lifted a fraction. A joke was a good sign. "What's equally important is you haven't committed murder," she said. "Only assault."

"And kidnapping, Bertha," he said. "Or did you repeal that particular felony when I wasn't looking?"

"Let Timothy go, and you won't be charged with anything."

Silence. "Now that's interesting," he said. "Tell me more."

"You release Timothy without further harm. In return, we give you a get-out-of-jail card that exempts you from all prosecution in this matter. The chief of police has already confirmed it with the governor, and the feds are on board." Trout Lips rolled his eyes. She shrugged.

Doe laughed. "No prosecution? After I tortured a cop?"

"We want Timothy alive more than we need you in jail."

"Huh. Might be worth considering at that. I did prove my point."

She gripped her chair. "Yes, you did. So get out. Now. Caller ID will be fixed any minute, and the first copper that finds you will—"

"Shoot first and ask questions later?"

"You bet! When the Staties arrive, you'll be shot 3,000 times for resisting arrest!" Bertha barked. "So escape while you can! Timothy has those two darling babies, and he's never done you any harm—"

"Pay attention when I talk!" Doe interrupted angrily. "I told you I've never met the man."

"Then why do this?" Bertha asked. "Why torture this innocent—"

Doe's chuckle was so low and evil, she knew he'd never intended to stop. This entire conversation had been an amusement for him. "It's simple, Bo-Bertha," he said brightly. "Practice makes perfect."

"Please, John, don't. I'm begging you."

"It's unfortunate your trooper has to die, because I honestly have nothing against him," he said. "But I need to know. For her. Anything less than perfection isn't worthy of her."

"Her?" Bertha said. "Her who?" But John Doe was away from the phone. Tools clanged. Handcuffs ratcheted. Timothy whimpered. John sang.

Then he was back.

"There's nothing you could have said to stop what's happening," he said. "I called you because I wanted a live audience for this dress rehearsal. The only phone answered twenty-four hours a day is 911." His laugh slashed like broken glass. "You're a nice lady, Bertha. Clever. If anybody could have convinced me to stop, it would have been you. But it wasn't in the cards. Sorry you got stuck."

"I don't feel stuck, John, not at all. I just want you to stop. Please stop. I'll conference in the chief right now, John. Please, I'm begging you. Listen, here, here, my last name is Pruitt—"

"There's no way you could have known about the false-number generator I attached to my cell phone to scramble your caller ID. Or the digital voice changer that lets me sound like anyone I want. For all you know, I could be a woman." She heard a hand slap flesh. "Oops! There go my trade secrets! You wormed it out of me, Bertha. Hope your chief gives you a nice raise—"

"Pruitt, Bertha Pruitt, born right here in Boston as Bertha Bridget—"

"And last but not least, because you finally told me your name, I'll let you be Timothy's escort to the hangman. Just like I'll be hers." He cackled. "Merry Christmas, Bo-Bertha."

Frantic screaming assaulted Bertha's ears. "He's slicing me!" Timothy cried. "With the scalpel! Cutting my chest . . . Please, Bertha, help. . . ." The heavy whine of a power tool kicked in. "Oh my Christ it's a circular saw! Don't do this, mister. My wife, my sweet precious babies . . ."

The whirling steel hit home, and Timothy's hideous shriek couldn't mask the industrial butchering of muscle and bone. Bertha smashed the blinking computer display with her soda can till both broke, then collapsed in her chair, head exploding. "Sweet Jesus, he's sawing out my heart!" Timothy gurgled, to the room's utter horror. "You promised, Bertha, you promised to save me! You promised . . ."

CHAPTER 1

Monday, 6 A.M.
Seventy-two hours till Emily's birthday

Emily Thompson exploded off her back porch, ready to sweat. Buried in overtime the past three weeks as flu knocked down more and more of her colleagues, she'd shoved her daily run to the back burner. That was stupid, she knew—six miles every morning provided the clear head she needed for her job. *Keeps my thighs in check, too!* But when she was under the gun, she tended to replace sensibility with the Four Horsemen—caffeine, sugar, fat, and sitting around. She'd vowed last night to rectify the situation, so here she was, running fast under the French vanilla sky heralding dawn.

Her war whoops panicked spring's first robins into flight as she sailed down her steep backyard hill toward the Du-Page River. Like an Olympic hurdler, she cleared the drainage ditch—exactly twenty-nine strides from her porch—and the long, low stack of seasoned firewood—forty-two strides—enjoying the burn in her knotted calves. The dank smell from the river sparked her adrenaline, and she reveled in the sensation of flight as Canada geese flapped so low, she could practically rub their ivory bellies. She plunged into the narrow dirt path through the trees and tall weeds at the hill's bottom and emerged a minute later at the Naperville Riverwalk, the redbrick walking trail that edged the DuPage like eyeliner.

"Aw, man! I can't believe it," Emily grumbled as warm liquid splashed on her legs. She glanced at the sky and waggled her finger. "Hey! You can't give me one day without mud puddles?" *Apparently not.* If the fresh-from-the-box Nikes had been black, or even navy, it would have been months before she crudded them up. But, no, they only came in white. *Sigh.* She untied the left shoe, stripped the sock, wrung it like a dishrag . . . then wondered why there was a puddle in the first place. It hadn't rained since March 1. Today was April 28. In the Chicago area, spring without rain was so unheard-of, the TV anchors were already chanting, "Dust Bowl! Dust Bowl!" Puzzled, she looked closer at the sock.

The wet spots were pink.

She dropped her eyes to the puddle.

It was red.

Her pulse quickened. She knelt, sniffed. A coppery scent of old pennies. She dipped two fingers, rubbed them together. Thick. Slippery.

Blood.

"What on earth is going on?" Emily whispered. She shook her chestnut hair off her face and listened. Rippling from the river. Gnats buzzing in her ears. Faint crashing in the underbrush. Raccoon? Beaver? No, heavier, a deer perhaps. Honks from distant cars, ducks quacking, doves mourning, squirrels scampering, geese flapping. Then even those hushed, leaving no sound but her breathing.

She stood, spun around. Nothing amiss. In front of her

flowed the DuPage, the hip-deep river that divided the city of Naperville north and south. To her left was downtown. To her right, wooded parkland. Across the river, houses and more park. Behind her, atop the north river crest, the two-story log home her husband, Jack, built as his wedding present to her. The back of their home looked down on the river. The front faced Jackson Avenue, which started at their driveway, paralleled the river to downtown, and dead-ended at Washington Street, the main north-south arterial of Chicago's biggest suburb.

She turned back to the river to see a V of geese landing on the whitecaps at the precise angle Mother Nature spent millions of years perfecting. She shook her head. Except for the blood, there was nothing wrong with this picture—

Whoa.

Twenty feet ahead. At the edge of the maroon paver bricks. Two lumps.

Before they'd looked like matted leaves. Now they didn't. She walked toward them, stomach lurching. There weren't two lumps, she realized, but three. One big, the others smaller. They had no color but radiated an emotional intensity so fierce, they couldn't be anything but . . .

"Dead babies!" Emily gasped. She clawed her 9-millimeter Glock from under her Ramones T-shirt, front sight wobbling from the adrenaline tsunami slamming her body. She crept toward the lumps, trying to look everywhere at once. *If the perp's watching, he can kill you, too,* she reminded herself. *Keep your head moving and your trigger finger cocked.*

She dropped her arms and rolled her eyes, glad nobody could see her flush of embarrassment. The lumps weren't human after all.

The big one was a goose. The little ones, ducks. So freshly dead, they steamed.

"Dummy," Emily chastised herself as her heart sank back into her chest. "They're animals!" She tried to recall the recent memo on Riverwalk predators. There were foxes. Owls. Coyotes. Dogs wandering around off-leash. The occasional bobcat, forced onto human turf because subdivisions stole its natural habitat. Any of them could have killed these birds.

She picked up a winter-burned pine branch and turned over the first bird to see if she could guess the predator from the bite pattern. She stared, flipped the others. "The heads are gone," she breathed. Lopped cleanly at the base of each graceful neck. With a knife. An ax. A machete, possibly, or . . . hedge clippers? Could a human have done this instead of an animal?

"No way," she said, dismissing the notion. "Nobody brings a Lawn Boy to the Riverwalk. A coyote killed these geese, plain and simple."

Correction, Princess, the familiar voice of her husband whispered in her head. *One goose, two ducks!*

"Oh, Jack," she murmured back. "Why did you have to leave me?"

Biting off the thought, she pitched the carcasses into the underbrush so the stroller moms arriving later wouldn't have to see them. Then she blew out her breath and loped toward downtown. She smiled as the river scent sharpened. If Proust had his madeleines, she had her moss—the muddy-dog aroma that triggered delicious remembrance of her childhood on Chicago's Southwest Side. Specifically, the dank basement of their yellow-brick bungalow, where her parents stored the board games they broke out every Saturday night for the "Thompson Family Game and Ice Cream Festival."

She kept running.

She rounded the curve near the old limestone quarry that served as Naperville's municipal beach, her bloodstained Nikes pounding cadence. Several minutes later she dipped under the Main Street Bridge, where her foot slaps echoed hollowly off the concrete.

She closed her eyes and imagined being at this spot two

centuries ago, when a thunderous flood ripped the guts out of the spanking new town. She smiled. Her husband, Jack Child, a local history buff, was forever taking her on the grand tour of Naperville's ghosts. "Here lies the Pre-Emption House," he'd cry as they quick-marched through downtown. "Oldest tavern west of the Alleghenies! Where Abe Lincoln guzzled beer and Grover Cleveland snored away the night!" He'd wave at the far north end of Main Street. "Yonder lies the Stenger Brewery, built 1848, bulldozed 1956! Its underground cooling tunnels are still there today, buried deep underground!"

Just like Jack . . .

God! Where is all this melancholy reminiscence coming from? "Stupid birds," she hissed. "It's your fault." She left the Riverwalk and sprinted south along Washington Street. Next stop Naperville Cemetery, the halfway point of her Jack-to-Jack Fun Run. For ten years she'd made this trip from the house that Jack built to where he now made his eternal rest, and she hadn't yet found a reason to stop.

"Hi, baby," she wheezed as she pulled up to his grave. The lawn was shaggy here and there, the grass finally unknotting itself from long winter hibernation. "How are you today?" Bending to straighten the roses and baby's breath she'd placed here Friday, she traced Jack's name in the tombstone, marveling at how well the deeply chiseled channels were holding up to the elements. Today being Monday, the flowers were pecked ragged—the crows had undoubtedly gotten to them. She leaned against the chilly stone and told her husband about the birds, the coyotes, the blood puddle.

She flinched at the shrill noise emanating from her belly. Straightening, she unclipped the departmental pager from the gun belt that girdled her hips.

555-7428. 911.

Captain Hercules Branch, the Naperville Police Department's chief of detectives. The "911" meant "call back immediately." But the fun run was the only occasion when she didn't carry a cell phone. She hated interruptions when talking to Jack. The cemetery office didn't open till nine, and she was south of the business district. *Let's see, who's awake this early?*

Exactly 622 strides later—she always counted when she ran, a good practice for estimating distances at traffic accidents—Emily flashed her badge at the emergency-room receptionist at Edward Hospital. "Police officer," she panted. "Just got paged. Use your phone?"

"Sure!" the receptionist said. "Anything for our boys in . . . well, gals in blue, too! This way."

A minute later Emily was alone, having politely shooed her escort. She punched in Branch's number. Mid third ring she heard a series of clicks, then a silky male voice.

"Bambi!"

Emily stared daggers at the phone. "Am I ever going to live that down?"

"Not if I can help it," Branch said. "I take it from the delay that you're back running?"

"Yes, Mother," she said. "You can stop nagging now."

"Hey, it worked, didn't it? Where are you?"

"Edward Hospital," Emily said. "Closest phone to the cemetery. What's up?"

"You familiar with Vermont Cemetery?"

"Yes."

"Good. Come join me."

"Now?" Emily frowned. Driving there and back guaranteed being late for work. She wanted that as much as a root canal. Chief of Police Kendall Cross hated her enough as it was. He was always nitpicking and criticizing, constantly demanding she "shape up or ship out." Even a second's tardiness would rekindle his animosity. "Branch, I don't have enough time before—"

"I already spoke to Ken," Branch interrupted. "He knows you're gonna be late, and he's not gonna give you any grief."

None? This must be important! She hastily calculated her time. "I'll run home, shower, and drive right over," she said. "Figure an hour."

"Twenty minutes," Branch said. "And forget the shower. It's better you stay smelly for this."

CHAPTER 2

Monday, 7 A.M.
Seventy-one hours till Emily's birthday

Emily drove fast as dawn hardened into morning. The Vermont Cemetery was located in a farm area southwest of Naperville, and she knew the trip would take longer than Branch's allotted twenty minutes. She tried, anyway, pushing her car through every gap in traffic. She finally saw the flashing lights that heralded a major crime scene and slowed for the turn onto Normantown Road, the north-south arrow of blacktop that ran past the cemetery.

"Captain Branch ordered me here," she explained, flashing her badge at the roadblock.

The sheriff's deputy pointed to a patch of cornfield. "Park there," he said. "Your boss is a hundred feet up the road." Emily locked her car and went to find him, noting the knot of deputies around the silver Porsche convertible inside the cemetery's chain-link fence. The car was wrecked and rested on a tombstone. One of the deputies bent so far into the passenger side, only his waist and legs showed. Another snapped photos. A third took notes. Her excitement grew.

"You needed my help for a traffic accident?" she asked when close enough.

Branch smiled, made a show of looking at his watch, a Guy Special with the huge bezel and multiple knobs. "What kept you?" he asked. "Bambi's mother get in your way?"

Emily made a face, shaking her head. The day she graduated the police academy, she bought one of those red flashing lights TV cops used in their cars. She listened to her radio scanner when off-duty, figuring she could check out interesting calls. An opportunity came a few weeks later, a bank robbery near Fox Valley Mall. She slapped the "Kojak" flasher on her roof, mashed the accelerator—and slammed into a deer leaping from the shadowed tree line. The impact totaled both deer and forest green Saturn, but Emily was merely shaken, thanks to air bags.

The first responder to her 911 call was a Joliet patrol officer she liked. He checked her for damage, found none, then wagged his finger at the deer. "Next time, buddy, move right for sirens and light."

"Very funny," Emily shouted over the howl of approaching fire engines. "Don't tell anyone at my shop about this, OK? I'll never hear the end of it."

"Course I won't," the officer assured her. "Your secret's safe with me."

The next night she walked into roll call for the pre-shift briefing and found, propped in her chair, a set of deer antlers bolted to a junkyard fender. "Bambi" and "Thumper" from a child's coloring book were skewered on the tips. "Oh, no!" Emily shrieked, touching the Rust-Oleum "blood" as her face turned equally scarlet. "I'll get him for this, no matter how long it takes!" The grinning cops sprang to their feet and, led by the shift commander, chanted, "Bambi! Bambi! Bambi!" Her friend Annie Bates, a patrol sergeant and lead sharpshooter on the department's SWAT team, put out the word the next day to knock it off. "'Cause it's pathetic," she explained when Emily asked why. "Roadkill? Deerslayer? Cool nicknames. But Bambi?" Annie shook her head in disgust. "I told the boys to cease and desist or I'd Thumper 'em." Branch still loved to tease her about it.

Emily gave as good as she got, though, and fired back, "I might be a stone-cold killer, Captain, but at least I'm properly groomed."

Branch scratched his salt-and-pepper stubble. "I was running, too, when Marty called," he said, fishing through his fanny pack. He pulled out a long green cigar that was frayed on both ends. "Happy birthday," he said, tossing it her way.

Emily grabbed it midair and looked at him, puzzled. Branch knew her birthday—the big Four-O—was still three days away. He also knew she detested cigars.

"The stogie's only half your present," he said. "The other half is the homicide we're gonna help Marty investigate. The body's inside the car."

Emily got excited even as her legs turned to ice. "Homicide? Wow!" she said, surprised at her mixed feelings. She'd been telling Branch for months she wanted to work a "big crime." Now that he'd made that possible, she didn't know if she was up to it. She decided to cover with bravado. "I'm ready. That fatal crash on Valentine's Day? The drug overdose by the river? I handled those with no problem."

Branch shook his head. "This is a homicide, not a death. Complete with rotting corpse. That's what the cigar is for. The stink keeps you from losing breakfast." He glanced at the big black flies dive-bombing the car. "With this one, we'll need all the help we can get."

The strain in his voice intrigued her. Branch worked hundreds of murder investigations in New Jersey before Bell Laboratories transferred his wife, Lydia, an engineer, to Naperville. Branch came along for the ride, tired of Garden

State politicians big-footing his cases for their elections. Chief Kendall Cross took one look at his resume and appointed him chief of detectives, the first outsider to win that coveted post. The troops griped but eventually fought to get on his squads because he was good and backed his people completely. *If Branch needs a cigar,* she told herself, *who am I to argue?*

She accepted the match proffered by a young deputy. This was the county sheriff's jurisdiction, as the cemetery was a whisker outside Naperville's city limits. She nodded her appreciation, puffed till the end flamed yellow . . . then coughed till her eyes flooded.

"Well, it is a fifty-cent cigar," Branch said. "It's gonna taste a little rough."

Emily hacked till the burning eased. "Haven't you heard life's too short to smoke cheap cigars?"

"Whoever said that never drew no chalk line round no dead body," Branch observed. "These things taste like dead perch, but man they generate a stink. A trait you'll appreciate when you meet the deceased." Branch handed her a pair of white latex gloves.

Emily eyed the convertible, then took a more tentative puff. "What do you want me to do?"

"Look over the crime scene. Start here at the road, and examine everything you see. Don't forget to listen and smell."

"Why?"

"Clues aren't always visual."

Emily tugged on the gloves and smoothed the air lumps between her fingers. Even counting the "headline" murders—Marilyn Lemak poisoning and smothering her three young children to repay her husband for suggesting divorce, a psycho abducting little Jeanine Nicarico from her home in broad daylight, then dumping her broken body on a nearby walking trail—homicides were exceedingly rare in upper-middle-class Naperville. Making a cop's chances of working one accordingly slim. She was glad Branch called. Even if it made her uneasy. "Then what?"

Branch hopped the drainage ditch separating the road from the cemetery. "Find me when you're ready, and we'll compare notes." He walked away, shoving his hands in his pockets.

She looked down on Normantown Road. The asphalt was new, its coal black surface still sheeny with oil. Maybe some rubbed onto the killer's shoes. Be sure to mention that to Branch. Beyond the east ditch sat the tiny, fenced-off cemetery. Beyond the west ditch ran the Elgin, Joliet & Eastern Railway, a freight line that cinched Chicago's outermost suburbs in a 110-mile iron belt.

Next to the tracks was a concrete pylon with a *W* mortised into the top. It looked like a grave marker. "How appropriate," Emily murmured, though she knew it told the engineer to whistle for Wolf's Crossing Road a half-mile north. West of the tracks was an industrial park filled with jeans-and-flanneled truck drivers gawking at the flash-flash. She smiled. Not that long ago she'd been doing the same. Surrounding everything was cornfield, though that was changing fast—Naperville was expanding like Jiffy Pop. It was the rare farmer who turned down eight figures to grow houses instead of corn. In two years this field would sprout million-dollar condos.

She walked toward the cemetery, skirting a puppy sprawled lifelessly on the shoulder. Judging from the smear of blood around her mouth, the Scottish terrier had lost a game of tag with a car. Emily's heart went out to the unmoving pile of fur. She loved dogs—all animals, in fact, even the crazy deer that totaled her car. She couldn't afford tears, though. She'd look weak to the other cops. So she bade the pup silent good-bye and leaped the ditch in one graceful bound, drawing admiring whistles from a knot of deputies, along with a hammy drawl from a fat, crew-cutted sergeant. "Hey, honey, I'll jump in yer ditch anytime!"

Emily turned. If it had just been the whistles, she would have curtsied, been a good sport. "Jump in yer ditch" was obscene, and she couldn't let it pass. She raised her middle finger and growled just loud enough for them to hear, "Jump this, Doughboy."

The sergeant's eyebrows knitted as his pals hooted with laughter. "No call to talk like that," he said, forcing a smile. "I was kiddin' around."

That was a crock, she knew, but there was little to gain from dragging this out. "Fine, Sergeant," she said. "Apology accepted."

That he didn't like. He worked his jaw like he wanted to take it to the next level, but nothing happened. She shrugged, started to walk away.

"Cunt," he spat at her back.

"What did you call me?" Emily demanded, whirling. The last person to throw that vile slur at her had ended up on the pea gravel behind St. Mary's Elementary with a split lip and two black eyes. The nuns were sympathetic—"nice upper-cut, dear," Sister Bethany had whispered as she hauled insult slinger Brady Kepp away for iodine and bandages—but the principal suspended her the rest of the week for fighting. Mama canceled the Saturday night family game festival as punishment. "Violence never settles anything, Emily Marie, and you need to learn that," she lectured as Daddy peeked over the *Chicago Daily News,* with a small, proud grin. Emily had no regrets. No one called her names again.

Still no reply from the sergeant. "What did you call me?" Emily repeated.

"Nothing, missy," he said, all innocence. "Didn't say a thing, did I, boys?"

The deputies shook their heads. But they didn't grin

back, either. It told her they weren't happy with what he was doing but wouldn't interfere. Tribal law. She was on her own.

"Gol-ly, Sarge, you're not afraid of a girl, are you?" Emily jeered, striding to the edge of the ditch opposite him, flapping her arms like a chicken. "A big strong hunk like you? No way!"

"Lady," he sputtered, face turning cranberry. "You oughta think real hard about shuttin' up—"

"Honey, cunt, missy, lady," Emily interrupted. "And you still can't get it right. Maybe you're a moron." She tapped her badge. "For future reference, my name is 'Officer.'"

"Fuck you!" he growled.

"No, thanks. If you and a goat were the last two men on Earth, I'd pick the goat."

His nostrils flared, and his belly shook like a paint mixer. "Gonna have to teach you some respect, little girl," he hissed, stomping down into the ditch. She shifted her weight to knee him. But the most grizzled of the deputies caught her eye, shook his head microscopically, and grabbed the sergeant's shoulder. "Why don't we let this go, Sarge?" he said quietly. "Your uncle don't need this crap in an election year."

The sergeant huffed and puffed but let himself be talked into giving up. "Yeah, all right," he muttered. "Better things to do, anyway, than argue with some play-cop." He wheeled toward the road, clapped his puffy hands. "Look alive, people!" he barked. "Double-check the tracks and ditches to make sure we haven't missed any evidence! Move it!"

Emily glued her hands to her sides so no one would see them tremble. She'd been willing to fight the man but certainly didn't want to—he outweighed her by 150 pounds. Even if she won, she'd hurt for a month. She turned and jogged toward Branch, who was walking along the fence. He gave no sign he'd noticed the exchange. "I'm back," she said. "I saw—"

"Not yet," Branch said, eyes everywhere, planting his shoes in others' footprints. "The victim isn't going anywhere. So go slow. Weigh everything. Weather, for instance. It hasn't rained in weeks. What does that tell you about, say, tire tracks? *Then* tell me what you see."

Emily nodded, resumed scanning.

The sky was azure. The breeze smelled sweet as towels from the dryer. The cheerful chirps of robins and cardinals were undercut by the eerie moan from the galvanized steel fence. The chain-link aria rose and fell with the breeze, prickling the hairs on her neck. Purple shadows from the links formed a quilt of triangles on the crime scene investigators swarming the weedy ground inside. The fence line was clogged with a winter's worth of debris—yellow newspapers, blown tires, cracked transmissions, trash bags, beer cans, lumps of desiccated somethings, paper plates, a harvest gold refrigerator door, two sump pumps, and a Michael Jordan *Space Jam* cup so faded from the sun Michael was white. Tire ruts in the surrounding cornfield indicated the convertible had left the road, circled through the crushed stalks of last fall's harvest, and freight-trained through the back fence. The impact ripped a jagged hole in the links, and the car came to rest atop the black granite tombstone. The ruts, she noted, were shallow because the ground was hard from lack of rain.

Twenty minutes later she'd absorbed everything she could and rejoined Branch. They traded observations as they ducked into the cemetery, careful not to cut themselves on the broken links. "Helluva desecration," he murmured.

Emily nodded. The cemetery contained the remains of the shovel-faced farmers who fled Vermont after the American Revolution to wrest life from the wilderness. The plants she was now trampling were the great-great-great-grandchildren of a vast heartland prairie tamed into row crops and, now, subdivisions. Pioneer cemeteries were scattered like diamonds around Naperville. This one was the most isolated. Where she'd been with Jack, the most prominent. She swung her attention to the car with the cops with the corpse with the flies.

"Watch out," Branch warned.

Emily froze, looked down. She'd nearly stepped on the tiny boot peeking from the animal burrow in the milkweeds. "Sorry," she said, guiding her foot to a less harmful spot.

"Murder scenes are overwhelming," he said, waving it off. "Easy to get distracted."

Emily stuck the cold cigar in her mouth. "You don't," she said, relighting as several deputies walked past. "Why? Experience?"

Branch smiled. "Fear. When I was at my first murder scene as a new detective, I roamed that ground like a fullback. Gonna find me a clue, yessir, gonna make me a big name. I did all right. I stepped on a shard of glass. It was hidden in the weeds, just like that boot." He rolled his eyes. "Turned out to be the murder weapon—the guy's throat was slashed—and I'd crunched it into a jillion pieces. Destroyed its value as evidence."

"Ow. What happened?"

"The killer confessed, so I didn't get busted back to patrol for my mistake. I treated the next crime scene like a minefield, where one little misstep could make me a soprano. Still do." He flagged a CSI. "My keen police instincts tell me this boot's too new to be garbage. Is our corpus delicti missing one?"

"Nah, it's wearing both shoes," the CSI grunted as she walked over. "Geez, maybe you found a clue or something."

"First time for everything." Branch made introductions. The CSI nodded, then whistled across the graveyard. "Yo! Commander! Take a look!"

A giant in a tailored charcoal suit trotted over. From the road he'd looked fat, Emily thought, but up close, the bulk was solid muscle. He was a serious weight lifter. He bent from the waist and eyeballed the boot from wide, rounded toe to horizontal treads on the sole to pull-loop in back. He told the CSI to take pictures, then bag it for the lab. Finally, he tilted his face up at Branch and grinned. "If *you* found this, there must have been a sign saying *X* MARKS THE SPOT."

Branch grinned back, jerked his head at Emily. "Actually, my colleague here found it."

"Good thing someone did. I'd like to wrap this up already." He straightened to six-foot-six, casting Emily into shadow. "Hi. I'm Commander Martin Benedetti. Sheriff's chief of detectives."

"Officer Emily Thompson," she replied, accepting his hand, which was so big it enveloped hers in warmth. She was pleased to find he didn't shake limp-fingered as so many men did with women. "Actually, Commander, I didn't—"

"Call me Marty," Benedetti urged. "All my friends do." He squinted at Branch. "You, on the other hand, should keep calling me commander."

"That might be interpreted as a sign of respect," Branch said. "So I'll call you nothing." His square face tightened. "I still think you're wrong. But you're gonna do what you want, anyway, so let's get it over with."

"Fine by me," Benedetti said. He pulled handcuffs from under his suitcoat. "Emily Thompson, you're under arrest," he said, motioning for her wrists. "For the murder of Lucille Crawford, shot dead this morning in a silver Porsche. You have the right to remain silent. . . ."

EMILY AND BRADY

Chicago, Illinois
January 1965

"There she is, Miss America!" Dwight Kepp sang to the nurse's aide clipping barrettes into Alice's raven hair. "Doctor says you've been taking good care of my wife." He tipped his fedora. "I thank you and intend to mention your fine attitude to your superiors."

The young aide beamed. "Every patient should be so easy to care for," she said, patting Mrs. Kepp's paper white hand. "All this woman suffered without a word of complaint."

"I've nothing to complain about, dear," Alice said, gazing up from the hospital bed at her handsome, perfectly groomed man. "I've got a wonderful husband, a lovely home, and a new son. What's a little pain compared to all those blessings?"

Little pain, indeed, the aide thought, marveling at how stoically Mrs. Kepp bore her ordeal. Their boy was thirteen pounds, nine ounces, of elbows and knees turned sideways in the birth canal. Doctor struggled two hours to pull the boy out—doctor was so pious about natural childbirth!—but finally ordered Mrs. Kepp into surgery when he spotted the umbilical cord around the boy's neck. Thirty minutes later baby entered the world, pink, healthy, and howling. But Mrs. Kepp paid a terrible price—this child would be her last. The aide wasn't sure if Mr. Kepp knew that yet, but it wasn't her place to tell him. That was doctor's job. She shook off the negative thoughts. "Mr. Kepp, would you like to meet your new son?"

"I've waited nine months to answer that," Dwight said, face glowing. "It's yes, emphatically."

"Then I'll fetch him from the nursery. I won't be long." As she left, Dwight gently took Alice's hand and bent to whisper in her ear.

"Your papa's wonderful," the aide told the sleepy infant as she plucked him from the warmed blankets. "Handsomer than Cary Grant! Thoughtful! Attentive! Devoted to mother. You're a lucky one to have such a fine dad!"

Mrs. Hoffmeyer, head nurse of the maternity ward, asked jokingly whether Mr. Wonderful just happened to have a twin brother who wanted to take an unmarried nurse's aide to dinner and dancing. The aide eagerly told her about the handsome couple. "He took his wife's hand to whisper in her ear," she finished. "It was so romantic—they looked just like Jackie and our president before . . . you know."

"God rest his soul," Mrs. Hoffmeyer said, crossing herself.

"God rest," the aide agreed, clutching the boy to her bosom and finger-whisking blanket fuzz off his unusually large ears. "Let's go see your folks, darling," she cooed. "I'll bet Daddy is telling Mommy right now how much he loves her for bringing you into his world. Oh, someday I'll have a husband so handsome and fine, just you wait and see."

"No more children?" Dwight whispered through his frozen smile. "Is that some kind of joke?"

"It's not my fault, darling," Alice whimpered, tears welling from the pain of his thumb on her incision. "He was so turned around inside me—"

"You knew I wanted sons," Dwight hissed. "Plural. Sons are the measure of a man. Thanks to this, I'm stuck with one. One!" His breathing was shallow, his eyes bright. "Pray to the Blessed Goddamn Virgin he's a good one. I will not tolerate a loser. Ah, here he is now!" His sour demeanor turned sunny as he took the infant from the aide. "I name you Brady Maurice Kepp," he cooed, waltzing him around the room. "After your great-grandfather, who came to America penniless and built a good life with his own two hands." He planted a kiss on Brady's furrowed forehead. "Let's walk down the hall and get to know each other a little. Then we'll come back and introduce ourselves formally to Mother and her friend."

The aide turned to Alice as they trotted away. "You're so lucky, Mrs. Kepp. Your husband's one in a million." She frowned at the pallor of her patient's face. "Are you all right? Should I get Mrs. Hoffmeyer?"

"No," Alice breathed, patting the aide's hand. "The incision hurts a bit, that's all. Get me an aspirin, and I'll make do just fine." She watched her husband and son disappear. "It's a wife's job to make do."

CHAPTER 3

Monday, 9 A.M.
Sixty-nine hours till Emily's birthday

"Very funny," Emily said. "You sing and dance, too?"

Benedetti looked sourly at Branch. "This was your idea. You said she'd laugh. Thanks for getting her mad at me."

Branch grinned. "What are friends for?"

"Yeah, yeah." Benedetti tugged at the bulletproof vest under his suitcoat. "All right, here's what we know so far. It's 3 A.M. Some kid's out party hopping, stops by the cemetery to drain the lizard. He notices the wrecked race car and calls 911. Then skedaddles 'cause, well, he's DUI and doesn't need the hassle." The look on his face said he was still trying to sort these cards. "Sheriff rousts me out of a sound sleep, and here I am."

Emily nodded, recalling Branch was telephoned by someone named Marty. "But why us, Commander? What do we bring to the party?"

"I found something puzzling," Benedetti replied. "I needed somebody to tell me what it means. Nobody smart was available, so I called Branch." His grin showed even white teeth. "We've got history."

"Working undercover on joint task forces, among other things," Branch explained, touching the thin gray scar that half-mooned his jaw. "That's where I got this beauty mark. You should have seen the other guy when Marty got through kicking his ass . . . uh . . ." Embarrassed at the hint of emotion he'd let show, Branch steered back to business. "Marty buzzed me, I took a look, then called you."

"So what did you find, Commander?" Emily said, impatient at the maddeningly slow answers.

"Your police card," Benedetti said. "In the dead gal's purse."

Emily felt like she'd touched a live wire. Modeled on the Pokemon types so popular with kids, the wallet-size police cards displayed an officer's photograph, career highlights, vital statistics, and hobbies. They came in boxes of 1,000 and were showered on the public like confetti. Officers routinely lectured at churches, schools, homeowners associations, scout meetings, and Safety Town, the miniature Naperville that sat kitty-corner from the police station, and they handed out their cards to promote a positive image. She'd handed out hundreds of her own in her eleven months on the job. "You're kidding," she said, for lack of anything better.

"Nope. She knew you. Or planned to talk to you. Or . . ." The thought trailed off, and he thumbed through his notebook. "Vic's name is Lucille Crawford," he said. "Goes by Lucy. She lives—lived—in Fox Valley Villages. Know the place?"

North of here, near the mall . . . "Sure," Emily said. "But I've never heard of a Lucille Crawford, from there or anywhere else." She paused to think—cops ran across a lot of names in the course of their work—but decided she'd never heard this one. "That last 'or' implies a third possibility," she continued. "What is it?"

Benedetti's lips formed an O as he sucked in air. "Your card wasn't mixed up with the hair spray and Juicy Fruit at the bottom of her purse," he said. "It was right on top, in plain sight. Lucy may have put it there to keep it handy." Pause. "Or it could have been planted by her killer."

Emily took a step back. "Planted? You mean as in framing me?"

Benedetti shrugged. "More a message, I think," he said. "To you. Or about you."

Emily shook her head so vigorously, her chestnut hair danced. "Kill someone to send me a message? That's a little, uh, extreme, don't you think?" Her arrests were numerous but dull—speeders, burglars, Peeping Toms, drunks, and check-kiters. Not killers! And she only had a handful of stalkers, the lonely social inepts who dropped by the station with undying professions of love. They were harmless, and a minute or two of chitchat was all they really wanted. The one stalker who grabbed her got busted hard and fast by the desk officers. But the man never vowed vengeance. As Annie explained one night over salsa and chips washed down by margaritas, "The guy loved it. Handcuffing is the ultimate 'I love you' for a stalker." Emily glanced back at the wreck and felt electricity drip down her backbone. *What's this all about, Lucy?* she wondered.

"Want me to roust Emily's jailbirds?" Branch was saying. "Run down her stalkers and see what they're up to?"

Benedetti shook his head. "I didn't bring you guys here to work. Just wanted to size up my clue in person, see if anything rang a bell." He turned to Emily. "How many stalkers do you have, anyway?"

"Seven," she replied. "That I know of. Five men, two women. I can call later with names."

Benedetti nodded. "Do that. Probably won't amount to anything. Stalkers are usually lovers, not fighters." He thumbed a page, cleared his throat. "Lucy lived on Prancing Pony Lane. Jesus, where do they come up with these silly goddamn names, huh? Worked as a mechanic."

"Auto?" Branch asked.

"Truck."

"Where?"

"Mall," Benedetti said. "Night supervisor at Great Lakes Engines. Four to midnight. Last two hours by herself, doing paperwork and setting up the computer for the next day. Boss can't praise her enough. She's hardworking, dependable. Just got a double-digit raise."

"She still doesn't sound familiar. What else do we know about her?" Emily said.

"Recently divorced," Benedetti said. "Ex lives in Los Angeles. Got his name from the address book in her purse. I talked to him an hour ago. Also talked to their son, who runs the London branch of a New York brokerage firm. He was in his flat—that's Brit for apartment—an hour ago." He added details from Lucy's driver's license, explaining he'd pulled it from her purse on the backseat. Along with a Visa, Master-Card, and $147.30 in cash, all of which ruled out robbery. "Anything ring a bell?"

"No," Emily said. "I've never heard of this woman."

Benedetti closed his notebook. "So much for doing this the easy way. Ready to meet her?"

Emily clenched her jaw and nodded, neck hairs stiffening in protest. She marched toward the convertible, stopped abruptly as her nose recoiled from a horrid smell. "Branch?" she said, holding the cigar out to her side like half a crucifix. "My, um, gas mask went cold. I need a light."

Branch roasted the tip till Emily was shrouded in a thick blue fog.

Then all three went to see Lucy Crawford.

CHAPTER 4

Monday, 10 A.M.
Sixty-eight hours till Emily's birthday

Bile rose in Emily's throat as the odor of the decomposing body penetrated her cigar smoke. "Come here often, Commander?" she joked, noticing Benedetti had no tobacco. Nor were his nostrils plugged with cigarette filters or Vicks Vapo-Rub, two other cop-tested odor blockers.

"Sure," Benedetti said, crinkling his wide-set hazel eyes. "Unlike you Goody Two-shoes in Naperville, there's loads of murderous citizens in my jurisdiction."

"How do you deal with it?"

"Death?" he said. "Like anything else in this business, you get used—"

"No. The stink."

Benedetti tapped his camel's-back nose. "A few years back my basement flooded in that eighteen-inch thunderstorm. I cleaned it up real nice with bleach and elbow grease, but that damn black mold kept reappearing. Smart me decided battery acid was just the ticket."

Emily stared. "You washed your basement in battery acid?"

"Seemed like a good idea at the time," Benedetti said. "Worked great, too. The acid cleaned that concrete down to the white." His expression turned rueful. "But I was too manly to wear one of those sissy respirators. Only a paint mask. The fumes burned away my sense of smell."

Emily wrinkled her nose in sympathy. "I'm sorry. That must be terrible."

Benedetti's shrug said, "Whaddaya gonna do?" "Has its advantages. I couldn't smell Lucy if I picked her up for a polka. On the other hand, everything I eat tastes like cardboard. I'd give anything to enjoy my famous jalapeno pork chops again." He nodded at the Porsche. "Time you two got acquainted."

Emily worked up a huge cloud of smoke and began her examination of Lucille Crawford.

The middle-aged woman's hair was long. Strawberry blond. Neatly trimmed, held in a ponytail by a spangled purple scrunchie. Emily looked for signs of dye. Nope, Lucy was real to the roots. Pale blue eyes, widely spaced. Broad shoulders just this side of butch. No jewelry except a thin gold wedding band on her left ring finger. Interesting that a divorcée still wore it. Carpenter-style blue jeans with a bit more room in the seat, sopping from the release of her bladder and bowels at the moment of death. Red-striped work shirt with "Lucy" embroidered over the left breast. A support bra—Emily could see the wide, heavy strap through the more faded of the stripes—and steel-toe shoes laced tightly to her feet. She estimated Lucy's weight and smiled. Nice to know one other person lies on her driver's license! Flies dive-bombed the stiff body.

She worked up more smoke, then ran a latexed finger down Lucy's left cheek. Blemish-free and smooth as varnished teak, the pores fine and clear. The skin of a supermodel, someone used to pampering. But Lucy's hands were horned with scarred yellow calluses. She humped engine blocks for a living. Nobody had pampered her for a long time. Her expression in death seemed much like the Scottie pup's—utter disbelief at the situation she'd found herself in. All in all, Emily decided, Lucy was an ordinary, hardworking, pleasant-looking woman.

As pleasant as anyone with two extra holes in her head.

Emily's gaze shifted to the handgun on the passenger seat. "The victim was shot with a Glock," Benedetti recited from his notes. "A 9-millimeter Model 17."

Emily nodded, staring at the mirror image of the pistol she pulled on the birds just hours ago. The 17 was the most popular sidearm in law enforcement because it was light, reliable, ergonomic, inexpensive, and held lots of bullets. It had a chunky black plastic frame and a carbon steel slide. Just like hers. Glow-in-the-dark night sights. Just like hers. Skateboard tape wrapped around the handle to keep wet fingers from slipping . . .

Just like mine. Weird. She thought back on how weightless her pistol felt when she aimed it at the decapitated birds. Was it as light in Lucy's hand? Or did it weigh a ton, a crushing anvil of hopelessness and despair? She shook her head. "The only thing I know for certain is Lucy's gun is the spitting image of mine, down to the homemade tape job."

"Say what?" Benedetti said.

"Oh!" Emily yipped, flustered she'd said it aloud. "I carry the same pistol, that's all." She stuck out her right hip so he could see it, eliciting a grunt. "You were saying, Commander?"

"One round was fired. Straight into her head, as you can see."

Emily nodded, swallowing the fresh rise of bile. The entry

hole in Lucy's right temple was the size of a pencil eraser. The surrounding flesh was a charred sunburst, indicating the muzzle had been near the head. The hole in the opposite temple was the exit wound. It was ragged and crusty, the size of a quarter. Emily followed the trajectory to the gore on the driver's window. It was mealy, like cold oatmeal, and shot through with whitish grit. Lucy's brains and blood, blended with skull fragments. Emily tried to imagine the moment the supersonic tip of the bullet pierced Lucy's flash-roasted skin—Pain? Panic? Regret for life unlived?—but couldn't. Even ten years after Jack's death, such imaginings were too exquisitely painful to dwell on. She shook her head, praying Jack died instantly.

Uh, I mean Lucy.

"Sexual?" Branch asked.

"Jeans were zipped and belted, shirt buttoned," Benedetti said. "That's all I can tell right now. Coroner hasn't shown yet to authorize moving the body."

Branch looked at his watch, surprised. "You called him, right?"

"Twice. He's sorting a twenty-car pileup at the Joliet Arsenal. I'll be lucky if he shows by supper." He looked at Emily. "For what it's worth, I'm betting no sexual assault."

"Good," she said, relieved. Even a dead woman should keep that dignity. "Was there a farewell note?"

"Suicide?" Branch asked, brows arching in surprise. "Rather than murder?"

Emily nodded.

"Explain."

She puffed to combat the odor. "There was a single shot. A professional killer would pull the trigger at least twice to guarantee her death. Someone killing out of fury or revenge would have emptied the gun, then beat her with it." Branch nodded, and she kept going. "A Glock's the kind of pistol a civilian might buy—familiar, something she's seen on a mil-

lion TV shows. She probably bought it for self-protection."
She pursed her lips at the irony. "I know the ex was home
when you called. But there's hourly service between O'Hare
and LAX. I presume he has an alibi?"

Benedetti nodded.

"OK." She pointed to the Glock. "The gun is still in the
car. A killer would have taken it. The position on the passenger seat is consistent with falling from her hand after a self-
inflicted gunshot. Did you find the ejected shell casing?"

"Wedged at the bottom of the windshield," Branch said.
"Next?"

Emily pointed at the right temple. "The bullet entered the
skull there. Meaning she held the gun in her right hand.
That's consistent with being right-handed."

"We don't know she's a rightie," Benedetti objected.

"She's got bigger calluses on her right fingers, and the
palm and nails are more heavily worn. She uses that hand
much more often. Making her right-handed."

Benedetti looked impressed. "What else?"

Emily took a drag of her cigar. It tasted like burnt rope.
"Her money and credit cards were intact, so it wasn't robbery. She's intact, so it wasn't rape. She works nights, the
last few hours by herself, which explains her having the gun.
As for opportunity, Lucy had it 24/7."

"So we've got means and opportunity," Benedetti said.
"But what's her motive? Why would this lady kill herself?"

"The divorce."

Both detectives blinked at the bald assertion.

"It's not a crisis with the kids," Emily explained. "Her
son's grown and doing well. It's not about work. She got a
nice raise in a down economy. She looks healthy. Well, except
for *that*," she said in answer to Benedetti's smirk. "So unless
she had some incurable disease, that leaves her marriage."
She stopped to play the argument through and, satisfied, continued. "I don't care how common divorce is nowadays. It's

still an emotional nightmare. Especially for middle-aged women who grew up believing marriage is till death do us part. No matter who wanted the divorce and for what reason, Lucy thinks it's her fault the marriage ended. Her fault she was abandoned."

The word brought the familiar catch in her throat.

"It ate at Lucy, made her sick with loneliness," she said. "She couldn't take it anymore and decided to call it a life." She shook her head at the sadness of Lucy's decision. "Murder just doesn't make sense in this case, guys. It's too risky. The killer would have had to overpower a blue-collar worker surrounded by power tools, stuff her in that tiny trunk, and drive to the cemetery in the middle of the night. What's he going to say if a bored cop pulls him over for a safety check? 'Gee, Officer, I thought she seemed a little quiet tonight.'" She shooed flies from Lucy's crotch, looked at Benedetti. "So I think suicide. But you're calling it homicide. Why?"

"Suicides *are* homicides," Benedetti replied. "So we treat 'em that way till proven otherwise. But, yeah, I'm ready to rule this suicide, too."

"You are?" Emily said, wishing she hadn't wasted all that time laying out connections he'd already made on his own. "Why didn't you say so, save me from running my big mouth?"

"'Cause I wanted to hear what you thought," Branch answered. "I didn't call you here only for my bad joke. As it happens, we agree with you. Lucy's a suicide."

"Though I'd like to see her farewell note," Benedetti said.

"If she bothered to write one," Branch warned. "Sometimes they don't."

Benedetti wagged a finger north. "A team is searching Lucy's town house. So let's discuss our next problem." He thumped the Porsche's macerated hood. "These wheels were borrowed."

"Stolen?" Emily said.

"Yeah. Last night, from the mall parking lot. Lady had primo taste in race cars."

Emily agreed. Leather galore, triple-digit horsepower, the deep polished silver, which looked so elegant on a powerful vehicle. But its racing days were over. Granite does not forgive its trespassers. "But why bother stealing a car?" she asked. "Lucy had one already—"

"Commander!" shouted the grizzled deputy from the ditch.

Benedetti squinted through the chain links. "Yeah?"

"Boys just found the suicide note."

"Excellent! Where?"

The deputy spoke into his cell phone, then back at Benedetti. "In an e-mail."

"Christ on a crutch, a *cyber*-cide?"

"Appears so. The e-mail was in her computer at work."

Benedetti stared. "The engine place? Where I sent Luerchen?"

The deputy grinned. "Sergeant Luerchen made dynamic entry into the building. The office computer was on, and the screen indicated e-mail. Sergeant Luerchen investigated."

Benedetti groaned like he'd stubbed his toe. "What'd he do?"

"Clicked on the mail folder. Saw the suicide note. It was written but not sent."

"Gimme the Cliff's version."

"'Hubby dumped me for a trophy wife, so I'm outta here. Tell my son I love him.'"

Benedetti nodded. "OK. Thanks. Tell Luerchen, uh, good job." Under his breath, "For a fat, lazy bastard who'd be pawing through Lucy's panty drawers if I'd been retarded enough to send him to the town house." Louder, to the deputy, "Call LAPD, ask 'em to confirm the ex's alibi. Likewise Scotland Yard for sonny."

The deputy nodded. Benedetti turned back. "If that don't

beat all," he complained. "Rayford Luerchen doing smart police work."

"Who's Rayford Luerchen?" Emily said.

Benedetti looked like he'd bitten into a worm. "Just the stupidest man I've ever met in my entire life," he said. "He's cocky, mean, and lazy, and the only badge he's fit to wear says Mattel. He's also the sheriff's wife's son from her first marriage, which makes him untouchable." He shook his head. "I send him to the garage 'cause he can't step on his dick there, and he goes and finds the suicide note that closes this case. I'll probably have to give the jerk a commendation." He made a little smirk at Emily. "Course, maybe I shouldn't be telling you this."

"Why not?"

"I hear you like ol' Rayford."

Emily couldn't imagine where that came from. Luerchen sounded like someone she'd just as soon shoot as talk to! "What do you mean, like him?"

"Well, you know, that pet name you've got for him." The smirk widened. "Doughboy?"

The sergeant from the ditch! She looked around, didn't see him, and felt her face flush hot with embarrassment. "You weren't supposed to hear that."

"Us chiefs of detectives hear everything," Benedetti said. "Don't we, Branch?"

Branch nodded. "Course, it helps that Ray's deputies like him about as much as you do, and one of them 'accidentally' thumbed his radio so we could enjoy the show."

Emily shook her head. "Cops."

"Cops," Branch agreed. He looked at his watch and frowned. "Let's finish up, Marty."

"Yeah, I know you've got that meeting," Benedetti said, slapping his notebook in his palm. "The farewell clears up a lot of doubt about suicide. But not all."

"Meaning?" Emily asked.

"Gun suicides are a guy thing. Women almost always choose something less violent, like carbon monoxide or sleeping pills."

"Lucy was a mechanic," Branch countered. "She's comfortable in a male world. And her gun was right there with her."

"Something to be said for convenience," Benedetti agreed. "But then there's Emily's question. Why steal a car when her own is fifty feet away?"

Emily glanced at Lucy's wedding ring and felt a small, sad certainty. "How recent was the divorce?"

"Ex walked out a year ago. Final court papers came through last week."

"It took a year?" Branch said. "With no minors to fight over?"

Benedetti shrugged. "According to her boss, Lucy had three decades invested and wasn't handing him to some bimbo without a battle."

Emily nodded. That information only cemented her conviction. "What kind of car did she own?"

"Cadillac. Brand-new. Heated leather seats, satellite radio, the whole megillah."

"When did she buy it?"

Benedetti consulted his notes. "Two weeks before the old man bailed."

Bingo. "That car was the last significant purchase of her marriage, Commander. Maybe she just didn't want to ruin the upholstery." Emily noticed his disbelief and added, "Look, maybe it's not how you or Branch might react. But it's exactly how I would. The fact she's still wearing her wedding ring after all this time proves it—she carried her man's flame to the end. Have Luerchen examine that Cadillac. He'll find it as clean as the day Lucy bought it. As well preserved as she wanted her marriage to be."

Benedetti thought about that. "Old man dumps Lucy for a

race car . . ." She's crazy with loneliness . . . knows how to hot-wire a car . . . Mall lots are easy pickings . . . Final papers push her buttons, so she steals a Porsche—I'll show *you* a trophy, asshole!—and drives around working up her nerve . . . sees the cemetery, gun's in the purse, tire tracks fit the Porsche . . ."

The satisfaction in his voice pleased her. She'd handled her first homicide OK.

"So I think we can put this one to bed. Assuming the crime lab doesn't run across inconsistent fingerprints or trace evidence."

"Or footprints," Branch said, nodding to the perimeter. "Any you can't account for?"

Benedetti grimaced. "You know how cops react to homicide calls, Branch. A dozen guys ran all over this field looking for a shooter, like the mope's gonna hang around to confess. It'll take weeks to match all the footprints we found with the deputies' shoes."

"Well, you've got your suicide note," Branch said. "Written on the computer the victim used every day. Ballistics consistent with a self-inflicted wound. She lives and works locally and would know about this cemetery. She's got her money and credit cards, and so forth. What's still bothering you?"

Benedetti raised two fingers "The boot you guys found— trash or clue? And where does Emily's police card fit in? Message from a killer? Did Lucy want to see her? If so, why?" He snorted. "Or is it just a goofy damn coincidence designed to drive me batty?"

Emily wondered that herself. Benedetti and Branch began brainstorming solutions to the boot—some kid tossed it during a drunken joyride, raccoons stole it from the industrial park and dragged it to their nest—but she couldn't add anything useful. So she squatted, curious to see how much undercarriage survived the encounter.

"Not much," she muttered. The tombstone acted like the

bullet, ripping out everything in its path, then drenching itself in bodily fluids—brake, transmission, lubrication, coolant. Sheet-metal shards glittered like tinsel. Remembering how she'd traced her husband's name just a few hours ago, Emily thumbed the mess from this inscription.

KINLEY

WILLIAM KINLEY 1784–1878.

WIVES ANN ALLEN 1802–1840

ELIZABETH ASHLEY 1784–1884

Emily sucked in her breath so hard, Branch broke off a sentence. "Hey, you OK?" he asked.

She pointed to the chiseled lettering. "An interesting . . . coincidence," she breathed, fighting off light-headedness. "The name on the tombstone is Kinley."

"So?" Benedetti said.

"That's her husband's name," Branch explained. "Kinley Jack Child."

"Late husband," Emily murmured, rocking on her heels. Something else was at play here. She glanced around—street, fence, Scottie, train tracks, boot, stolen Porsche—but nothing grabbed her.

"Late?" she heard Benedetti say. "As in dead?"

Emily nodded.

Benedetti stared at her left hand, where the hammered-pewter wedding ring tented her latex glove. Shot Branch a look that said, "Thanks for telling me, pal." Then looked at Emily, bewilderment washing his face. "Sorry for my surprise, but the way you talk about him in the present tense . . . and the ring . . . I just assumed your husband was, well, you know, alive."

He is *alive, Commander!* she thought furiously. *In here!* But she didn't say it. The words would sound as ridiculous to him as "life goes on" and "you're still young" and "you'll fall in love again" did to her at Jack's funeral. She stood, slapped grass off her knees, cleared her throat. "Jack was killed a decade ago," she said. "By person or persons unknown throwing rocks from a highway overpass." Blinded by flying glass, Jack had lost control of his Jeep Cherokee and had crashed into a concrete viaduct on Interstate 88, halfway home from a business meeting at Northern Illinois University in DeKalb. "I've got far better things to do on your thirtieth birthday than sell telephone equipment to eggheads, Princess," he'd vowed to her at breakfast. "I'll be home as soon as I can." She skipped the part about how she'd raced to the front door in a green lace teddy, intending to deliver a grand thank-you for the matching emerald earrings she'd found in her underwear drawer after her shower. But the peephole revealed two Illinois State Police troopers wearing Smokey the Bear hats and grim expressions. Alarmed, she jerked on the knee-length jacket she used for yard work and opened the door. The troopers doffed their hats and asked if they could come in. . . .

"That was your husband?" Benedetti asked, interrupting her reverie. He sounded genuinely distressed. "I remember that case. Troopers never did catch the scumbags, did they?"

Emily shook her head, remembering the official conclusion that Jack was a random victim of kids throwing rocks. Youngsters had played "rock hockey" with cars since the Model T, and the overpass sidewalk was littered with rocks, as was the interstate below. "The deceased has no known enemies," the official report droned. "Solid bank account and investments, lifestyle reflective of income. No gambling, drugs, adultery, or other vices. No criminal record. Significant community involvement. Highly regarded at work. Solid relationship with Emily Thompson, wife of one year. Ms. Thompson possesses airtight alibi. She was talking with Lydia Branch, wife of the Naperville Police Department's chief of detectives, at the moment of the wreck, according to phone company records. Vehicle not tampered with." And so on. The private eye Emily hired to double-check the state investigation agreed—tragedy, not murder. Because the rocks were too rough and dirty to hold fingerprints, the kids had never been caught.

"That's the worst part of it, Commander," Emily said, shaking off the gloom that came from telling the story. "Jack died without knowing why." She smiled to herself. Her oh-so-logical husband would have detested not knowing the exact details of his fate. It was a loose end. Jack hated loose ends. He liked life as neat and tidy as his beloved engineering flowcharts.

She considered saying more, because Benedetti looked like he wouldn't mind hearing it. She quickly squelched the notion. He had bigger priorities than her pain. More important things to worry about than what Jack was thinking when the upside-down viaduct filled his windshield. She'd always hoped he was thinking of her. Prayed it so many times she'd lost count. But she didn't know. That was the worst part for her—the utterly unbreachable wall separating her from Jack's last moment on earth. But it was also her problem, not Benedetti's, not Branch's. Why waste time speaking of things that didn't matter anymore and couldn't be changed even if they did? It was time to concentrate not on her memories, but on one victim she might actually be able to do something about.

Lucy Crawford.

She examined her cigar stub and found herself hoping Branch had a spare. Despite its foul taste, working without tobacco right now wasn't high on her list of priorities. "If I can scrounge another smoke," she said finally, "maybe we can get back to work."

EMILY AND BRADY

Chicago
May 1965

"Congratulations, friend," doctor announced to the grubby redhead slumped in the corner of the waiting room. "You're a father!"

Gerald Thompson lifted his bloodshot eyes from the cigarette-burned floor tile, nodded.

"You should be happy," doctor prodded, annoyed this lout wasn't thanking him. Respect the white coat, if not the man wearing it! "Your daughter's in with your wife. Do you want to see them?"

"Yes," Gerald grunted. He got to his feet, weaving a bit. He brushed crud off his jeans, prompting the other new dads to lean away. He ignored them, stomping his boots, wiping sweat salt off his stubbled cheeks, tucking a work shirt that smelled like unwashed armpits. "I'm ready," he said, pulling a flat jewelry box from his pocket and staring at it. Doctor nodded, walked him to Room 313, and stepped inside. Gerald took his elbow, leaving grungy fingerprints on the white cotton. "Just the three of us," he said.

Doctor struggled to keep his expression professional. "I suppose that's all right, Mr. Thomas. I'll be at the nurses' station"—he pointed—"if you have questions."

Gerald went inside without replying.

"The state should require parenting licenses," doctor grumbled to the nurse filling out paperwork. "Not everyone's fit to have children, you know."

"Who are you talking about?" Mrs. Hoffmeyer said, looking up.

He nodded at the closed door. "Mr. Thomas."

"Thompson," Mrs. Hoffmeyer corrected. She'd had no use for this idiot since the day he lectured the maternity nurses saying, "I don't know how other doctors handled you, but my team gives a full day's work for a day's pay. I'll tolerate nothing less." Like they didn't work hard already! Arrogance came with the territory with doctors, she knew after thirty-four years of working with them, but this one was so beyond the pale that several nurses were thinking of joining the Teamsters. Besides, he was too young and inexperienced to be making such harsh judgments. "His wife, Alexandra, is lovely," she said. "Why do you think her husband isn't fit to be a father?"

"His appearance says it all, Nurse," doctor snapped, reading a chart through his mother-of-pearl half glasses. "The man couldn't bother to bathe or shave. And those clothes! Anyone knows you wear something clean and pressed to meet a newborn. Just because a man's poor doesn't mean he can't have pride in himself."

"Pride," Mrs. Hoffmeyer repeated. "In himself."

"Correct. The man also weaved as he walked. It's shameful, drinking this time of morning. This Thomas fellow gives fatherhood a bad name."

Mrs. Hoffmeyer pursed her lips. "Well, I don't know

about all that, Doctor. I didn't go to Harvard like you. But it might interest you to know, I was in the emergency room at dawn. You weren't here yet."

"I know what time I arrived, Nurse," he said. "Your point?"

"There was a terrible accident at Chicago Steel and Wire," she replied, setting aside her paperwork to gaze at him. "A cauldron cracked as it was being pulled from the oven. Two thousand gallons of molten steel spilled onto the work floor. Have you ever worked in a mill, Doctor?"

Doctor wrinkled his nose.

"Didn't think so. Well, a spill is the worst thing that can happen to a steel man. That bubbling metal melts his flesh clean off, then roasts his bones for the devil's soup. Leaves nothing for his widow to bury but his sainted memory." She noted the doctor's flinch. "Those steel men ran for their lives when the alarm sounded. All except one—Tommy Lutz, the son of a steel widow I know from the neighborhood. His boot got caught in a floorboard, trapping him. Mr. Thompson heard Tommy screaming and ran back to the cauldron room. He wrapped his legs in asbestos fire blankets and walked into that river to free his friend." Mrs. Hoffmeyer shook her head. "The inhalator squad brought the casualties to our emergency room, where Tommy Lutz died. In Mr. Thompson's arms."

Doctor remained silent.

"I stayed with Mr. Thompson after the morgue boys wheeled Tommy away," Mrs. Hoffmeyer continued. "I listened to how they'd fished and hunted the North Woods, up in Wisconsin. Then I escorted him to our maternity waiting room. The shift foreman told him just moments before the accident that his wife was going into labor and he should meet her here." She fixed doctor a stony glare. "Mr. Thompson didn't have time to wash his face or put on nice clothes like he would have preferred, Doctor. He had more important things to do."

Crying erupted in Room 313. Yowls of a newborn mingled with the baritone gasping of a big male. Mrs. Hoffmeyer smiled.

"Don't confuse those with tears of sorrow, Doctor," she said. "Mr. Thompson's all cried out for Tommy Lutz. Those are tears of joy for his newborn daughter, along with the children Tommy won't ever have." Doctor shifted his gaze to the wall clock. "If that man isn't good enough be a father, Doctor, then God himself wouldn't have qualified for baby Jesus."

CHAPTER 5

Monday, noon.
Sixty-six hours till Emily's birthday

Tongue still numb from the third cigar, Emily slipped her key in the front door. The more she thought about Benedetti's "suggestion" that Lucy's suicide was some kind of message to her, the funnier it got. The look on his face when he dreamed up the "gotcha" must have been priceless. She wished she'd seen it. She couldn't put her finger on why she liked Marty Benedetti. She'd spent, what, five hours in his company, and most of that looking for clues. Still, there was an undefined something in how he watched her. That she didn't mind looking back when his head was turned said something, too.

She grinned at the bellowed "Arooooooof!" from the end of the driveway. It was Shelby, the yellow Labrador retriever who lived down the street. He had the voice of a cattle wrangler, the fur of a worn-out broom, and the endearing personality of his master, an elderly widower who baked snickerdoodles for the neighbors when he wasn't out skydiving. She turned to see Shelby's enormous tongue lick the air like an invisible ice cream cone. How she'd managed to miss him she didn't know—Shelby was a baby moose. But she'd make up his favorite way. "Come here, sweetie!" she cried, flinging her arms apart. "Hugs 'n' kisses, come and get 'em!"

The Lab danced but stayed near the mailbox. *That's unusual*, Emily thought. Her invitation always set off a rump wiggle and mad gallop into her arms. This prancing seemed to say, "C'mere, c'mere, I gotta show ya something!"

Normally, she'd oblige. She'd wanted a pack of beagles after settling into the new house, but Jack wasn't keen on the idea. "We'd spend forever cleaning hair off my suits, and it'd be difficult to travel." Engineer logic. She finally bowed to it. Marriage is the art of compromise, right? A year after the funeral, the hollowness of life alone prompted her to build a pet flap in her kitchen door, with every intention of adopting a fuzzy-faced pup from the city pound. But Saturday dawned, and she put off the search till next weekend, Jack's objections fresh on her mind. Ten years later she was still putting it off till next weekend.

"I'd love to play, but I'm running late!" Emily said, envisioning Chief Cross pulling into the driveway while they romped. "Tonight after supper, I promise! Now run home so you don't get hit by a car!" Shelby quit prancing but didn't vamoose, either. "Home! Git!"

Shelby hung his head and whined. Emily waved goodbye and walked into the foyer, breathing deep the burntspice aroma from the back of the house. *Excellent!* In the mad dash to the Vermont Cemetery, she'd forgotten all about the French roast on the warmer. She trotted into the knottypine kitchen to pour her second cup—the first was drunk pre-run—into a coconut-size mug handpainted with the Three Little Pigs. It was a graduation gift from Annie Bates, who taught shooting tactics at the police academy, where they'd met and become fast friends. Each grinning pig wore a badge with Emily's number—103201—waved a nightstick drawn suspiciously like a penis, and chased a fleeing Big Bad Wolf. Her good humor deepened, and she headed up the stairs.

The master suite at the landing was large enough for a king-size cannonball bed, triple dresser, two nightstands, armoire, lounging chair, and wide-screen TV. Floors and ceiling beams were crafted from the same knotty pine as the kitchen. She tossed her purse and gun belt on the bed and eagerly tuned the clock radio for news of Lucy's suicide. A cold snap reduced Florida's orange crop to pulp. Terrorists blew up a bus of schoolkids. An industrial psychologist named Marwood—she didn't catch the first name, Trellis, Nellis, something like that—talked about his role in the hunt for the lunatic who'd kidnapped and torture-murdered a Massachusetts state trooper last Christmas. A dozen commercials, Newsradio jingle, traffic, weather, sports, more commercials, a "medical moment" on spring allergies.

Nothing about Lucy.

Disappointed, Emily kicked off her shoes and walked into the bathroom. *Creak.* She glanced at the floor, made a sour face. The pine planks were bowed from humidity, and she hadn't had time to get them fixed. Or the inclination. She'd rather just rip the noisy things out. Along with the eagles and cannonballs and lace curtains and stupid, rustic, ancient, depressing . . .

Yo, Em, chill! The decor isn't the problem! Well, actually, it was. She disliked Early American and its coffinlike woodiness, so she nearly bit off her tongue when Jack told her about the "surprise" he'd had constructed as his wedding gift to her—a high-end custom log home overlooking the Riverwalk. "It's authentic Early American, honey," he'd said. "Down to the milk paint and puffball curtains." He'd been so excited that she couldn't bring herself to say she preferred more contemporary architecture, airy, colorful, carefree. At times like this, though, she wished they'd met halfway.

Too many dead animals today! she told herself. *That's your problem!* She flipped on the shower, stripping her clothes as cold water turned steamy. She opened the shower door and hopped in quick lest all that delicious steam escape.

"Yeah, baby," she moaned, staccato Newsradio updates fading to background burble. She'd gotten a chill at the Vermont, and this was melting it out of her bones, off her skin, down the drain. She crick-cracked her neck to ease the stiffness, her mind drifting to a long-ago morning in this very bedroom suite, where she and Jack had Done It so much, she thought she'd never stand again. Delightfully sleepless as dawn spilled in, she'd wobbled into the shower for a pick-me-up. Moments later Jack did, too. Then Branch's wife called, alarmed because her pal always got to his desk precisely at 7 A.M., and he was two hours overdue. Emily cracked up watching Jack drip all over the floor, stammering out an appropriate fib.

She closed her eyes, trembling from the unusually vivid memory. Jack's sweet face faded to the penetrating eyes of Martin Benedetti.

"No!" Emily squeaked. She hopped out and toweled till the heat left. Then dried her hair. She wore a News 'Do, the hairstyle of practically every female TV news anchor on the planet. Short in front, off the ears and plunging to the shoulders in back, the News 'Do had just enough sweep and undercurl to say, "Professional and perky." She chose it because the police academy required short hair, or at least pinnable under a cap. At the time her hair hung to her waist. When she test-pinned it, her head looked like a twist of chocolate softserve. So she hacked off the tresses the night before reporting to the academy, naked as a jaybird and singing with

Sting as she piled the bathroom sink high. She truly hated to part with her hair. Every strand was a cherished memory of Mama, who'd loved combing, teasing, primping, and untangling the chestnut mess after her daughter's bath, occasionally Dippety-do-ing it into something so wacky—flower, surfboard, teeter-totter—they'd collapse in giggles. But rules were rules, chardonnay made the snipping easier, and she'd donated the mound to a charity that turned hair into wigs for cancer kids.

Finally dry, she hung the damp brown towel over the bar, lining up the embroidered gold eagles, glancing at the mirror from the corner of her eye. "Is our belly sagging?" the reflection asked. Emily pressed her pale abs. False alarm. Still a washboard. *Whew. Better safe than sorry, though. Do a hundred more sit-ups before bed, swallow one less spoon of ice cream at breakfast. More sweat, less sugar, yeah, that's the ticket.*

She examined the rest while she was at it and found herself with the usual mixed feelings. She had a good behind— high, round, well-defined, no sag or dimples. It topped a pair of strong legs, the lower half of which pleased her no end. Her thighs . . . well, they were a preoccupation, if not exactly a problem, the former because of her daily intake of French vanilla ice cream and the latter because she ran six miles a day to make up for it. Her arms were well-defined from push-ups, which camouflaged the fact they were unusually long for her height. Her face was classically oval, with a sturdy jaw and wisdom lines around the large emerald eyes. "Or maybe they're crow's-feet," she murmured. Her chin was strong, her neck slim.

Her chest was a little too small for her taste. Other people seemed to like it fine, though. The constant stares told her what she needed to know about that. Careful tweezing kept her thick eyebrows from being too Brooke Shields. Her skin was cream with a splash of coffee, limiting her make-up requirements to lipstick. Her teeth gleamed when she smiled, which she did easily and often. All in all, she told herself, the Total Emily, while far from perfect, had been good enough to hook a great guy like Kinley Jack Child.

"All right, all right," she scolded her reflection. "The nuns said too much self-admiration makes you go blind. Let's go catch some desperados." The reflection winked, then vanished as Emily walked into the bedroom to lay out her uniform and equipment. *Everything's here*, she noted. *Good*. She never violated her dressing ritual. Part of it was her need for order in her life, which intensified after Jack's death. The rest was life insurance. The tools of her trade had to be in the same place every time so she could grab them without thinking. Quarter-seconds counted in a fight for your life.

Starting to shiver now that she was dry, she donned thong panties and a navy blue sports bra. She slipped a tiny slashing knife inside the left cup, a last-ditch survival tool she'd deploy if a bad guy took everything else. She slid on a T-shirt, athletic socks, bulletproof vest, navy uniform shirt and trousers, then clipped her seven-pointed badge to her chest.

Time for the third cup of French roast.

She double-timed back up the stairs, slopping on the sixth tread. *Add it to the spring cleaning list!* Movement in the large octagon window overlooking her front yard caught her eye. It was Shelby, clawing at her mailbox. "Geez Louise!" she said, shaking her head. "You just won't go home till I see what's up, will you?"

The Lab looked up and barked. Emily saluted. "You win. Soon as I'm done dressing."

Shelby dipped his head as though he were nodding and went back to clawing.

Emily sat on the bed, swaddled her feet in steel-toed boots, knotted the laces, and wiped dirt spots off the leather. One less thing for Cross to complain about. She dreaded what came next, the twenty-odd pounds of equipment that street cops toted around their waists. The Mule Train, Annie called it. She sighed, then snapped, buckled, clipped, and Velcroed a gun belt, "garter" straps that married it to the trouser belt underneath, a Glock pistol, four spare magazines holding seventeen bullets apiece, a carrier for the two-way radio she'd sign out at the station, handcuffs, a collapsible baton, a folding knife, two flashlights, extra batteries, pepper spray, latex gloves, cut-resistant search gloves, an all-in-one tool with pliers, file, saw, knife blades, screwdrivers, wrenches, awl and scissors, lock picks, a pager, a cell phone, and a steel ring with eleven keys. Into various pockets went pens, a notebook, a ticket book, sunglasses, a key to unlock the handcuffs, a spare handcuff key, a third taped to her left ankle just in case, Kleenex, red-and-white Starlight Mints for coffee breath, a tube of lipstick in the muted cherry she liked. . . .

"Now I know how Atlas felt," Emily groaned as the gear dug into her hips. No matter how many miles she ran or sit-ups she knocked out, her lower back ached like grandma's bunions by shift's end. And it wasn't even winter yet, with its hats, coats, gloves, boots, and cold tablets.

She shadowboxed into the bathroom and skipped rope on the way out, making sure everything was locked down. The badge rattled. She fixed it, then removed the bayonet from her nightstand. She kissed it for luck and slipped it into the scabbard inside her left boot. Every cop needed backup weapons. Many packed a second pistol, but she preferred this battered steel bayonet. It had accompanied Daddy on the killing beaches of D-day, then on hundreds of deer hunts and fishing trips to the North Woods.

Fully mule-trained, she hustled down to the kitchen and threw back the final cup. She rinsed the Three Little Pigs, gulped cranberry juice, a Power Bar, and three tablespoons of French vanilla—*I'll cut back tomorrow*—then headed for the driveway. Ten minutes to the station, ten more to sign out a police cruiser and radio, then out on the street, where she belonged.

"What are you still doing here?" Emily blurted. Despite their "conversation" on the landing, she never dreamed Shelby would stay this long. The lively Lab never gathered moss when there was somebody to play with somewhere. He barked, then started head-butting the post holding up the mailbox. Whatever was prompting this behavior must really be something.

That's when she noticed the flies dive-bombing the box.

"Christ on a crutch," Emily muttered. "You hitch a ride from the cemetery?" She shooed them from the mailbox door, pulled it open, stared slack-jawed.

Goose head. Duck heads. Black with crusting blood. Eyes milky and staring back into hers.

The three missing pieces from the Riverwalk.

Each with a familiar white card slipped between its bill.

She opened her mouth but nothing came out. *I fell asleep after my shower, and this is a bad dream, right?* She closed her eyes, pinched her inner thigh, slowly reopened.

No dream.

"That's what you were trying to tell me, wasn't it?" she said, light-headed. Shelby thumped his tail but, seeming to sense Emily didn't need more distractions right now, made no other move.

Emily punched her cell phone's redial. "Branch," the familiar voice boomed.

"Remember how we decided Lucy wasn't a message to me?" she said without preamble.

"Emily?" Branch said. "Where are you? What's the matter—"

"Remember?" Emily persisted.

"Yes," Branch said.

"We were wrong. I just found three heads in my mailbox." Her voice was steady, thought processes efficient. Which surprised her, because at the moment she was frightened half to death. "Two ducks and a goose. They belong to three decapitated birds I found on the Riverwalk this morning during my run."

Long pause. "There's something else, isn't there?"

"Yes. Each beak contains one of my police cards. Like Lucy had at the cemetery."

Longer pause. "You still home?"

"Yes."

"Stay out by the street. Don't touch anything. I'll be there in six minutes."

CHAPTER 6

Monday, 1 P.M.
Sixty-five hours till Emily's birthday

"All this for a bunch of birds?" Emily groaned. Her lawn was as crowded as Easter church with cops, detectives, bomb dogs, CSIs, and firefighters. Even a sawhorse team from Public Works to keep rubbernecks at bay. Yellow tape was everywhere. It was monumentally embarrassing.

"Let's talk," Branch rumbled from behind.

Emily turned, saw he'd changed. At the cemetery he was detached—fascinated, certainly, but ultimately a bystander, like her. Here, on his home turf, Branch was Alpha Wolf, protecting his pack from marauders. His expression was harder, lips flatter, eyes wide and darting, looking for the scat and broken twigs that signified the presence of the Other. A warmth washed over her. Even though she could take care of herself, she was happy to see the department bare its teeth on her behalf. "Did you find those three . . . uh, bodies?"

"In the bushes, right where you threw 'em. We need to talk about that." He answered his ringing cell phone. "Hey, Marty, good timing. I was just gonna call you. What? Geez, he's a tricky scumbag. OK, sure, I'll go first." He peered into Emily's mailbox as he sketched the crime scene, then listened to Benedetti. "Thanks, amigo. Hang on." He handed Emily the phone.

"Hello?" she said, feeling her heart speed up.

"You all right?" None of the lighthearted banter from the cemetery.

"Yes," she said, nodding, happy to hear his voice. "I guess our crimes are related."

"So it seems. I filled Branch in on what's going on here. He'll give you the details. I just called to . . . I wanted to make sure you weren't hurt."

"No, not at all. Thanks, Commander."

"Sure thing."

"You need Branch again?"

"No. I'll talk to you both when I have anything else. Make sure he tells you what I said."

"Got it." She closed the phone and handed it to Branch, raising an expectant eyebrow.

"Lucy's left-handed," Branch said.

Emily didn't understand. Then, "Left-handed! The gun was fired from her right side! Which means she couldn't have shot herself!"

Branch nodded. "CSI found steel shavings by the hole in the fence. Lucy's killer cut the links first so he wouldn't hurt his precious self getting the car inside."

Emily fumed. "He staged that entire scene, didn't he?"

Branch worked his chin side to side. "Yup. Marty's changing the call to murder. Given the connection between our crime scenes, he ordered a fresh evidence team to the cemetery to make sure nothing's overlooked."

"A leftie," Emily muttered. "And I swore it was suicide."

"That's why investigations take so long. Everything's tentative till you prove it. In this case, the ex confirmed Lucy was a southpaw."

She cocked her head, puzzled. "Out of everything a husband could say about his dead wife, why would he bring up what hand she uses?"

"Marty asked."

"Why would he?" she pressed. "He seemed so convinced I was right."

"He was. But Marty subscribes to the old newspaper credo 'If your mother says she loves you, check it out.' So he did."

Emily shook her head, dismayed at how she'd misread the evidence. "Then what about the calluses and chipped nails?" she tried, making one final attempt to resuscitate her ego.

"Lucy played lead guitar in a rockabilly band."

"Let me guess," Emily said. "Right-handed."

Branch nodded. "Only thing she did that way. Everything else was leftie."

She looked at her feet. "Some lousy detective I am," she said.

"Don't beat yourself up, kiddo. Only TV cops solve crimes in an hour." A grumpy stare replaced his sympathy. "What you ought to feel shitty about is not telling me about those dead birds," he said, pointing at her backyard hill. "That crime scene was pristine a few hours ago. Now it's useless. Something ate the goose. The ducks are pecked apart. Blood puddle's halfway to China—"

"I know, I know." Emily hoisted her arms in surrender. "My first reaction to seeing those lumps was 'Where's the bad guy? Where's the bad guy?' I pulled my Glock on them like some stupid rookie!"

"You *are* a rookie," Branch pointed out.

"Thanks for leaving out stupid," she said, smiling wanly. "Then I saw they were birds, and they were headless, and . . .

I mean, what human would go to all that trouble? I was convinced a coyote killed them." She looked at the mailbox. "We're dealing with a wacko, aren't we?"

"Certainly. Nobody sane would pull this kind of"—Branch squeezed her arm—"Ah, Bambi, don't let it worry you too much. Wackos always do something stupid, like calling to brag without canceling their caller ID. We'll get this one before he does you any harm."

"I hope so."

Branch studied her house. "Nothing's missing? No dust bunnies out of place?"

He'd already asked that twice. "Everything's exactly where it should be," she reassured him. She'd walked the house with Branch and the first two responding uniforms, Glock welded into her fist, every creak in the floorboards a bomb exploding. Nobody inside. She spotted a fresh swarm of cruisers heading up Jackson and pointed with her head. "Is this really necessary?"

"You've been targeted, Emily. I take that seriously." Branch answered the cell phone, looked at her when done. "Chief does, too. He wants to see you ASAP."

"Why?" Emily said, wary.

"He probably wants to make sure you're all right. He'll meet you in roll call." He grinned at Emily's doubtful expression. "If there's more, you'll find out quick enough. Ken doesn't beat around the bush when something's on his mind."

"No kidding."

He winked. "Where's your car?"

"In the VFW lot down the street," Emily said. "CSI cleared it, so I moved it out of the way. One of the patrol guys is standing guard."

Branch nodded. "Why don't you head to the station then?"

Emily nodded, gazed at her house, then walked away.

CHAPTER 7

Monday, 3 P.M.
Sixty-three hours till Emily's birthday

Emily turned the corner to roll call, keeping a firm grip
on her emotions for her one-on-one with the chief. She saw
Annie Bates in the hallway ahead, arms swinging, toes tapping, burning off anxious energy. "Branch told me what
happened," Annie called, opening her arms when Emily got
close. "Thank God you're all right!" They embraced, and
then Annie stepped away, looking hard into her friend's eyes.
"You *are* all right?"

"Of course," Emily replied. Then, in a small voice, "No."

Annie pushed her into an interrogation room. She closed
the door, sat Emily in the suspect chair, and squatted next to
her. "How bad was it?"

"Horrible," Emily said, breaking down. "That dead
woman had flies all over her. Flies! And those heads in my
mailbox were so revolting. . . ." Tears splashed down her
face, and Annie hugged her again. "It's OK, sweetie," she

soothed. "Don't worry about it. Even Branch gets scared sometimes, and he's the toughest person I know."

"I wish I was as tough as him. Or you," Emily snuffled. The terrors eased, and she disengaged. Annie tousled Emily's hair. "Feel better?"

Emily sniffed, wiped her eyes.

"Good," Annie said. "So you're not scared anymore, right?"

"Heck, no."

"Yeah, me neither."

Emily asked why she was so muddy. "We were crawling through drainpipes," Annie replied. "Training exercise. We got the alert for your house. Halfway there Branch called us off, so we came here." She raised an eyebrow. "If you're not up to the chief, I can make excuses—"

"No," Emily interrupted. "I'm OK. I should get this over with."

Annie grinned. "So what's keeping you?"

Emily wiped her face with her palms, got to her feet, and opened the door. "By the way," she heard Annie add, "Your tush is fine today."

"Excellent," Emily said, running a hand over her behind. She'd been getting all kinds of unexpected looks there lately and wondered why. She asked Annie yesterday. "Hmm. You buy new underwear?" the sergeant said after checking. "Heavier material than normal?"

"Yes," Emily said, unsure why that mattered. "My regular ones wear out too fast. Why?"

"These uniform trousers are 100 percent polyester, girl," Annie said, slapping her own. "Polyester never lies about what's underneath, so the boys can see every stitch and bump in your panty line. Fevers their little imaginations no end."

"What do I do about it?"

"Floss your butt like the rest of us."

Emily scowled. "I hate thongs."

"Who doesn't? But it's that or stares," Annie said. "The initial looks don't stop, thank God for men and their wonderfully dirty minds. But if they don't see panty lines, their attention turns elsewhere. . . ."

Emily came back to the present, more relaxed. "Thanks," she tossed back. Annie waved and headed for the locker room.

Soon she was at roll call, peeking through the tall, narrow window in the door.

The rectangular room was spacious and low-ceilinged, with maroon-and-beige floor tile and fluorescent lighting that turned everyone's skin off-color. Its walls were plastered with crime bulletins, duty rosters, vacation schedules, department memoranda, union notices, family photos, newspaper clippings, Dilbert cartoons, and grating "motivational" posters of cartwheeling seagulls ("Soar like a bird!") and impossibly perfect sunrises ("Make someone's life glow bright!"). The riser in the front held a lectern, desk, and chair for the watch commander, the lieutenant who ran each shift. A side table held a Bunn brewer with several glass pots of cop coffee—scorched, dense, shiveringly acidic. Roll call, where cops and bosses gathered to trade gossip, intelligence, and observations before hitting the streets, was the beating heart of patrol operations.

Emily's smile carbonized. *Let's get it over with.* She took a breath and pushed through the door. "Captain Branch said you wanted to see me, sir," she announced, reminding herself again to keep her temper in check. "May I ask what it's about?"

"Something for which you're not ready," Chief of Police Kendall Cross replied as he rose, banging his chair off the wall so hard the whiteboards thundered. "Not remotely." He limped her way, stopping just outside the personal zone she'd pepper-spray a perp for violating. He put his hands on his hips and glared, brass and leather gleaming, every strand of sun-bleached blond hair in place, lips pressed into unyielding flatness. She smelled his citrus aftershave and felt her anger mount.

"Your badge is smudged with fingerprints, Officer," he said. "Your holster is an inch out of optimum position, Officer. Your left bootlace is loose, Officer. . . ."

Emily glanced down. It was tied, knotted, and tied again. She was about to correct him, then noticed the bottommost rappelling wasn't taut across the tongue. Loose, even. She glanced back into Cross's hard gray eyes and listened to the rest.

" . . . and your gun's probably dirty."

"Wrong, sir," Emily snapped. "I cleaned it last night."

"Oh? Let's see."

Suppressing the urge to fling it, she pulled the Glock, ejected the magazine, and cleared the firing chamber. She watched as he aimed the weapon at the nearest light. "There's crud in this barrel!" he barked, handing it back. She looked herself. Sure there were a few specks of burnt gunpowder, but she *did* blast it thoroughly with Gun Scrubber. . . .

"It's good enough for government work, right?" Cross continued. "Nobody can be expected to clear every flake of dirt? Well, you're incorrect about that. There's nothing wrong with your weapon that five more minutes of work wouldn't fix." His voice was low, but the tone cut like a whip. "A clean weapon is a malfunction-free weapon. You've been here long enough to know that! I shouldn't have to remind you, especially after this morning. Shape up or ship out!"

Emily felt her temper push deep into the red zone. "Enough already, Ken!" she hissed. "What did I ever do to deserve your hatred—" She cut it off, slapping herself mentally. Challenging the chief—by his first name yet!—could be construed as insubordination, a capital offense in the paramilitary world of policing. Daddy had warned that her big mouth would bite her someday, and he was right. She waited for the nuke to go off.

Instead, his lips twisted into something resembling a smile. "You think I hate you, Officer?"

"Seems that way to me, sir," Emily replied, focusing on a spot several inches over his broad shoulders. Like Marty, Cross was a weight lifter. She'd seen him in the gym off the locker rooms, punching barbells so huge he needed three spotters to complete his sets. Cross also ran. Long, hard, and every day, pumping through his limp even when he looked beyond exhaustion. That single-mindedness was one of the reasons Cross was so good at his job, she supposed. He juggled cops, citizens, suspects, vendors, politicians, equipment, security, budget, everything, down to how often to wash the cruisers. If that wasn't enough, he personally made sure every rookie officer adjusted as quickly as possible to life in uniform. Not through win-win management techniques—empathy, encouragement, coaching for success—but the old way, nagging, picking, and damning imperfections. Branch respected him immensely, though, which counted for a lot. Other veterans she admired said Cross was a scream when you got enough drinks into him—his Jerry Lewis imitation, one said, would set the most somber Frenchman howling. He probably would be fun to share a beer with sometime after work. If he wasn't such a jerk . . .

"You're always criticizing me," Emily continued. "Obsessing over things like my badge is smudged, when there's much bigger fish to fry."

Cross stepped an inch forward. "You think being involved in a homicide gives you permission to be sloppy, Officer Thompson?"

Emily felt her face burn. "No, not at all. What I do think is that you should lighten up. I'm a good cop, and I bust my butt for this department. Life's too short—"

"That's the point," Cross interrupted. "Life *is* too short. I'll be damned if you'll shorten it more by sloppiness." Another inch forward. "A smudged badge isn't just a smudge. It's a symptom. Of inattention to detail. Which will get you killed." Another inch. "You will not die on my watch, Officer Thompson. Repeat, not. If that means ragging you every single day, forcing you to shape up or ship out, then, by God, I'll nag and you'll listen!"

She'd never heard such emotion from Cross—his lectures were normally delivered in measured tones, Jack-ish in their logical precision. "I'm a good cop, Chief," she repeated, refusing to yield ground. "Just because you hate me doesn't make me think any less of myself or my abilities."

"That's the second time you've said that," Cross said. "I don't hate you. I hate your imperfections because they'll make you as dead as Lucille Crawford." A curious little cloud passed across his face, and he glanced at her neck. "Did you tape on that key?"

Emily winced. After the Massachusetts trooper's slaying, Cross had urged those with long enough hair to tape a handcuff key to the hollow at the base of the skull. Hidden by hair, it would be another way for an overpowered, handcuffed cop to escape. At the time she'd thought it a good idea, but the urgency faded as time passed. Now, adding even a quarter ounce to The Mule Train was more than her aching back could bear. "Uh, no, sir," she admitted. "I forgot."

Cross sighed. "I won't order you to do it, Officer. But it's smart. There's body-colored tape in both locker rooms for just that reason." He frowned at the clock. "But let's talk about why you're here. I'm transferring you to Branch's command."

Emily blinked. "You're making me a detective?"

"Temporarily."

"Why?"

"To catch this serial killer."

Emily threw up her hands. "Whoa, Chief! It's just kids playing around!"

Cross shook his head. "By themselves the heads in your mailbox could be a prank. But your police card in their beaks? The three carcasses outside your home? Your card in Lucille Crawford's purse? No, officer, this is a statement— 'I'm after *you*, Emily Thompson.'" He let that sink in. "The FBI won't declare a serial until three bodies are found. Human bodies." Brief grin. "But I'll stake my reputation that this is the opening round of a serial spree. One that will get quite ugly. We need to find this Unsub fast."

Emily cocked her head at the unfamiliar term.

"FBI term for unidentified subject," he explained. "Everyone else uses John Doe, but the FBI loves its fedspeak."

"Why not Jane?" she said, unable to resist jabbing the sexism.

"Statistics show 99 percent of all serial killers are male, Officer."

"Oh," she said, chastened. "So how does my becoming a detective help catch this guy?"

"It makes you instantly available to Branch. He can ask questions as they occur, rather than radioing you into the station every time."

"Ask me what, Chief?" Emily said. "I don't know anything about this wacko!"

His frown reappeared. "Get that word out of your vocabulary. What took place this morning required intelligence and planning. That makes the Unsub a skilled criminal, not a wacko. He may indeed be psychopathic—we won't know till we catch him—but calling him 'wacko' or 'loony' only makes you underestimate him. Do that and you're dead."

Emily shivered. "Got it. What happens now?"

Cross looked at her. "You've got some vacation time coming. I certainly wouldn't object if you wanted to take it. Don't worry. Nobody will think you're chicken."

Well, I am *chicken*, she thought. But she needed a brave front. As much for herself as for Cross. "No, sir, I'm staying," she said. "If this Unsub has targeted me and I disappear, he might take out his frustration on innocent people."

A faint smile tugged at Cross's mouth. "That's what I thought you'd say. Unfortunately, I agree. Do you want the rest of the day off, start fresh tomorrow?"

"I'd rather work, if that's all right."

"Go ahead then. Another officer will ride shotgun, and I've already put a car in your driveway. Report to Branch first thing in the morning." He headed for the desk. "Stop by the locker room first," he reminded over his shoulder. "Fix those problems I noted."

She'd forgotten all about the nit-picking that had started this, and annoyance bubbled up faster than she could swallow. "Right away, sir," she said. "I'll go shine my badge and tighten my shoelaces. I know they're very important in finding serial killers."

Cross whirled. "You've been a cop less than a year!" he shouted. "You don't know jack about what's important! Assuming you do gets you killed in a heartbeat!" Then he shrugged, thunderstorm passed. "But I can't live your life for you. Just don't get hurt finding out."

"I can take care of myself, Chief," Emily said, patting her sidearm.

Cross's smile was without humor. "Yes, Miss Crawford's weapon certainly kept her safe, didn't it? Now get going. Service calls are stacked to kingdom come, thanks to that little incident at your house."

"Ten-Four, Chief," Emily said. She walked out of roll call with head held high, then ran for the bathroom with as much dignity as a newly minted detective could muster.

EMILY AND BRADY

Chicago
November 1967

"These are dice, honey," Gerald Thompson said, shaking his fire-engine hair out of his eyes. "We roll them to see how many spaces we move our game pieces." He handed the ivory-colored cubes to Emily, who squealed happily. Alexandra Thompson laughed and took them away before her two-year-old decided they were gum balls. Emily's pink cheeks blew up like little basketballs, followed by caterwauling and bouncing around in her high chair.

"Princess hates to lose," Gerald said. "She was born to play games."

"Good thing in this family," Alexandra said, moving his pewter race car seven spaces while he cheered Emily with funny faces. "Speaking of losing, you just landed on Boardwalk." She slapped her hands to her cheeks in fake astonishment. "And it contains two of my hotels."

"Gloat while you can, woman," Gerald grumbled, forking

over half his Monopoly dollars. "I've got four on Park Place. Land there and you're bankrupt."

"What a terrible example to set for our precious girl, thinking her mother can't handle money," Alexandra replied, licking a finger and slowly running it down her husband's cheek. "Perhaps you'd take my IOU instead?"

Gerald arched an eyebrow. "Sure. If you provide sufficient collateral."

Alexandra smiled, rubbing her bare toes on his. "I've got plenty of assets for you to examine. Just as soon as Emily falls asleep—"

Gerald jumped to his feet and snatched his daughter. "Bedtime!" he announced to the startled child, rushing her to the pink-and-blue nursery and tucking her in with favorite doll and blanky. "The Three Little Pigs kicked the Big Bad Wolf's ass and lived happily ever after," he said. "The End." He heard Alexandra laugh from the master bedroom. He never tired of that tinkling sound. "Sorry the story isn't longer, Princess," he whispered, kissing her cheeks and forehead, then turning on her Donald Duck night-light. "But your mama needs some very personal banking."

CHAPTER 8

Monday, 8 P.M.
Fifty-eight hours till Emily's birthday

The patrol proved uneventful, and Emily headed home. She started thinking of Jack, Mama, and Daddy on the way, and became so emotional she pulled over twice to sob. The SWAT cop following her didn't jump out the second time to check.

The emotions also triggered an inexplicable longing to play her board games. So she locked the car in her garage, checked in with the driveway team, and thanked her understanding escort. She showered and changed, gobbled down some leftover deep-dish pizza, then descended the padded stairs to her cold, dry basement, debating whether she really wanted to open the boxes again after so many years.

"Yes," she said to no one there.

She lifted the blanket covering them and flapped off ten years of dust. She cleared her parents' old game table of detergent and dryer sheets, then picked up the Monopoly box, thrilling at the familiar rattle of parts. She walked it to the table, unfolded the game board, and centered it on the green felt Daddy glued to the tabletop so many years ago. She withdrew property cards, dice, and pewter-colored game pieces from their cardboard cradles, arrayed the ersatz money, doled out property from B&O to Boardwalk, set out little green houses and larger red hotels.

"Whoops! A job worth doing is worth doing well!" she said, turning back to the stairs. Daddy liked to slip such life lessons into playtime, certain his little Princess wouldn't pick up on his clever moral turnips. She saw through it but never let on. Her girlfriends thought his lessons were sweet and wanted to hear what he came up with each week.

She returned with a soup spoon and carton of French vanilla ice cream. She pulled a card chair to the table, kicked off her shoes, engaged her rich imagination, and began.

"What shall we play today?" Emily asked, carefully studying Mama's narrow face. A bit more drawn than yesterday. Insomnia? Bedsores? Back spasms from the merciless tag team of bed and wheelchair? She'd talk to the charge nurse, see what she thought. Then arrange for the hairstylist to visit. Emily tripled the woman's usual fee to do them both in Mama's nursing home room. Their shared hour of snipping and curlers let them both escape to their giggly days at the bathroom sink of the family bungalow. "Operation? Do you want to play Operation?"

Blink-blink.

"No, huh? How about I Spy?"

Blink-blink.

"Clue?"

Blink-blink.

"Timebomb?"

Blink.

"Maybe next time," Emily said, grinning. As physical games were behind Mama forever, she was pleased to see her play along with the dark humor. "Monopoly?"

Long pause.

Blink . . .

Yes . . .

Emily found herself blinking tears as she rolled in the warm memory. She loved games, having learned in diapers the addictive joy of bouncing dice and shuffling cards. Not from brothers or sisters, as she was an only child, but from her parents. Every Saturday night they crowded around the wobbly game table to argue about rules, form alliances, plot strategies, and eat French vanilla. She adored the ritual. When Mama asked how she wanted to celebrate her tenth birthday—Pony ride? Bowling? Pizza?—she'd squealed, "Game party!" She pecked out the invitations on the family typewriter, colored them with her Crayolas—the cool sixty-four pack with built-in sharpener—pasted on construction-paper cakes and candles, and delivered them at school the next day. Three dozen classmates arrived two Saturdays later and spent her birthday playing Operation, Monopoly, Duck Duck Goose, Boggle, Clue, Chutes and Ladders, I Spy, and Timebomb. But the magic of game playing came to a horrifying end just ten years later.

"Emily?" the caller had said.

"Speaking," Emily shouted over the high-volume Black Sabbath, impatient to go out. She was finishing her junior year at the University of Wisconsin-Madison, and friends were taking her out for her twentieth birthday.

"It's Goldie Abrams. Your parents' next-door neighbor."

"Oh right!" Emily said, kicking the dorm room door shut. Mrs. Abrams had been her favorite neighbor when she was growing up. At the Sweet Sixteen party Emily's parents threw, the regally dressed woman had told the wide-eyed teen that "since you're a woman now, call me Goldie instead of Mrs. Abrams." Emily had always cherished that. "How are you, Goldie?"

"Can you come home? Right now?"

Emily clutched the phone, eyes widening. "Why?"

"They . . . there's been an accident. Your folks. Police are here. You need to come home."

Emily made the two-hour drive in eighty-six minutes, abandoning her thirdhand Mustang at a fire hydrant. Goldie intercepted her. "Your father so missed you being home for this milestone birthday," she said, "that he rounded up the neighbors for an impromptu party." Mama would take home movies so when Emily came home for the summer, she could see everyone eating, waving, and singing "Happy Birthday!" They hung streamers in the family room, strolled to the corner store for extra film and French vanilla ice cream. They invited the Polish owner to stop by after closing—he agreed happily—then headed back. A pickup truck jumped the curb right in front of the bungalow, drove over them, and took off. "I heard screams and ran outside," Goldie choked. "The streetlight's out, and I couldn't get the license. No one did. Mr. Czerwinski chased him but couldn't catch up." She shuddered. "I'm so sorry to have to tell you, darling, but your father's dead. Mama's in the hospital. We'll take you right now. . . ."

The doctors pronounced Mama "lucky." Emily found the word obscene. With a crushed spine, Mama couldn't walk or talk, move head or limb, scratch her feet, or lick her thumb. She could breathe, blink, take nutrition through one tube and release it out another. That was as good as it would get.

Emily buried Daddy three days later—Mama couldn't attend her own husband's funeral—then welded rebar around her heart so she could attend to Mama's needs without mushing out. She moved home and talked Northern Illinois University into accepting her credits. She spent her senior year commuting to DeKalb—an hour west of Chicago via the same Interstate 88 that ran through Naperville—and taking care of Mama. First at the hospital, then at the nursing home when the insurance company decided she'd never get any better.

From seven to nine every night, they discussed the news of the day—Mama's brain was unaffected, she just couldn't move or speak—decided Daddy could eat as much French vanilla as he liked without getting fat, otherwise what's a heaven for, and played a game from the Thompson Family Game and Ice Cream Festival, Mama blinking instructions and Emily moving game pieces. One blink meant yes, two blinks no. Mama had tried "semaphoring"—five blinks for *E*, thirteen for *M*, nine for *I*, and so on—but her eyelid muscles went spastic around *G*. So daughter asked yes-and-no questions, and mother answered one blink or two. When Alexandra Thompson's heart gave out, two weeks short of her daughter's graduation, Emily packed the games away for what she assumed would be forever.

Then she married Jack and moved to his hometown, Naperville, in the western suburbs. She watched the storage carton segue from cellar to basement and found herself longing to at least see the games again. She wouldn't play— too many dreadful memories in those game pieces—but the colorful boxes perked up her spirits on lousy days. Jack built a shelf large enough to display the games, and she spread them out so she could eye them when doing laundry. When Jack died, she covered them with a tattered old army blanket and never looked again.

Till tonight.

She reengaged her imagination and patted Mama's hair into place. "Which game piece do you want?" she asked, feeling a little ridiculous talking to thin air. The muse, however, demanded it. "The Scottish terrier?"

Blink.

Yes.

Emily set Mama's favorite game piece on GO—"collect $200.00 salary as you pass"—and picked up her own favorite, a cowboy riding a bucking horse. She eased into the chair, yipping when her back touched the cold brown metal. She doled out $1,500 in Monopoly money, rolled snake eyes for herself and a six for Mama. "You always win the first toss," she complained. She thought she saw Mama smile. But that was impossible, as this entire conversation was ersatz. Sighing, she nibbled some French vanilla, put the carton on the dryer, and tap-tap-tap-tap-tap-tapped the Scottie dog to Oriental Avenue. "One hundred dollars," she announced. "Want to buy it?"

Blink.

Emily paid the bank, slid the baby-blue card to Mama's side, rolled herself a twelve. Electric Company, a $150 utility. She laid her money down. . . .

"You don't have to worry, you know," Emily said an hour later as she galloped toward Free Parking. "We'll get this Unsub long before he hurts me." She froze above New York Avenue. "Oh my God," she whispered as Mama vanished. "That's it!" Her knee caught the table as she leapt, raining game pieces, hotels, and Chance cards. She sprinted for the phone, pacing as it rang. Finally, she heard, "This is Branch."

"I know what the message is!" Emily shouted. "I know!"

"What are you talking about?"

"The crime scenes!" she answered. "I know what the killer's telling us! Come over and—"

"Slow down," Branch interrupted. "Compose your thoughts."

Emily took a deep breath. "The Unsub left us messages. At the cemetery and the house. I know what they mean. I can't explain over the phone. You've gotta see it."

A chair leg scraped. "All right. I'll shake loose for awhile."

"Thanks," she said. "Should I call Marty, have him meet us? This involves Lucy, too."

"Right here, Ossifer," Benedetti said, cutting in with an affectionate twist on "Officer." "Or should I say 'defective' now that you've been promoted?"

"Hi," Emily said, startled. "What are you doing on Branch's phone?"

"We're in his office, writing case notes. I heard it was you and conferenced in."

"Can you come over?"

"We're leaving now."

"Terrific," Emily said.

"You want Rayford to tag along? I'd like to hear that goat thing again—"

"See you in fifteen, Commander," she said. She uprighted the table, recentered the Monopoly board, and grouped the six pewter game pieces inside Community Chest. She piled the property cards on Go To Jail, picked houses off the concrete floor, and rinsed the hotel that had landed in the ice cream. She walked to the game shelf and lifted a much smaller box, put it on the table next to the Monopoly board, then sagged against the clothes dryer, spent.

CHAPTER 9

Monday, 9 P.M.
Fifty-seven hours till Emily's birthday

The ringing phone startled Emily from her doze. She glanced at her watch—twenty minutes since she'd telephoned. It took six to drive here with lights and siren, twelve without. *Where are you?* she wondered, picking up the ivory handset.

"Where are you, Emily?" Branch demanded. "We've been knocking for a couple minutes. The driveway guys are ready to kick the door."

Emily groaned, slapped her head. "I didn't hear you. I fell asleep in the basement. Be right up."

"So Rip Van Winkle isn't a fable," Benedetti said, clomping inside.

Emily looked away, embarrassed. "I'll put on coffee."

"No time," Branch said. His face edges were soft with weariness. "Half of patrol called in sick. We're still trying to cover the midnight shift. Show us what you've got."

Emily led them downstairs, held up the smaller box. "This is it."

"Is what?" Branch asked.

"Duck Duck Goose," Emily said, rattling it. "The board game." She looked for a big "aha!" but saw only "huh?"

"I don't get it," Branch said.

"It's a board game," she repeated, feeling foolish. "And so is . . . uh . . . well . . ."

"Spit it out already," Benedetti groaned.

"So are the murders."

Branch's eyebrows jumped.

"Remember that shock I had under the Porsche?" Emily continued, words spilling fast now. "When I saw Jack's name on the tombstone? The harder I tried to figure it out, the worse it . . . ow!" She kicked the stray red hotel toward the water heater, mentally cursing the pain in her foot. "Getting away from it these last few hours let my mind sort things out. Those crime scenes were staged all right, Branch. The killer set them up as games."

Branch looked at her doubtfully.

Emily refused to retreat. "If you don't think I can support my theory, gentlemen, you're wrong."

"Good," Branch said. "I'd hate to be here for nothing." He drummed his fingers on his chest, pointed to the smaller box. "If I understand what you're saying, this Duck Duck Goose game represents the decapitated birds on the River-walk."

"Along with the heads in my mailbox, right," Emily said. She grabbed the pewter tokens from the Monopoly board. "And these represent Lucille Crawford's murder."

"The game pieces?" Benedetti said.

Emily nodded. "My Monopoly game has six of them. Boot. Wheelbarrow. Race car. Flatiron. Cowboy riding a horse. And a dog." Anger fizzed as she recalled the Scottie's squashed face. "Each represents a separate part of Lucy's murder scene."

Branch unfolded a chair. "The race car represents the wrecked Porsche? That sort of thing?"

Emily nodded, handing him the car. Branch remarked that both game piece and Porsche were the same shade of silver, handed it to Benedetti. "What's next?" he asked.

"The boot," she said, pinching it between thumb and forefinger. "This is like the one we found in the weeds."

Branch stroked his chin. "We never did come up with a good explanation for that, did we, Marty?"

"We knew the boot wasn't Lucy's because she wore shoes," Benedetti agreed, hopping up on the dryer. His weight made the sheet metal boom. "Having no bootlace was even more puzzling."

Emily cocked her head.

"The boot didn't have one, remember?" Benedetti said. "Nobody disposes of a boot but keeps the lace. It's got to mean something—"

"It does!" Emily said, waving her game piece. "This doesn't have one, either!" She gave it to Benedetti. "The rest is identical too—pull-up loop in back, rounded toe, horizontal treads."

"Instead of the more common lugged sole," Branch said, his expression interested. "OK, race car and boot make two matching points. What's the third?"

"The dead puppy," Benedetti ventured. "It was relatively fresh, wasn't it? Not the usual dried-out roadkill?"

Emily nodded, tossed the piece at her boss. "Look carefully at the breed."

"It's a Scottish terrier. Just like our dead pooch!" Branch noted. He fingered the paintbrush face, handed it to Benedetti. "That's three. What about the wheelbarrow?"

Emily wobbled her hand to indicate this is a stretch. "The Porsche was stolen. Another way of putting that is—"

Benedetti snapped his fingers, craggy face lighting up with understanding. "What I said back at the cemetery. *Wheels borrowed*. Wheelbarrow!"

"Exactly."

"Wheels borrowed, wheelbarrow," Branch repeated. "A little iffy. Marty?"

"I buy it."

"Me, too. What's left?"

"Flatiron," Benedetti said, surveying the table from his perch.

"And the horse," Emily sighed, bouncing them in her cupped hand. "I know these fit, but I can't say how. A flat-iron. A cowboy on a horse. Flatiron, cowboy riding a horse. Flatiron, cowboy, horse—"

"Iron horse," a familiar voice said from the staircase.

Emily jumped, whirling toward the short blue apparition.

"You left the front door ajar," Cross said. "You need to be careful with that."

"How long have you been standing there?"

"Long enough to hear this cockamamie idea of yours."

Emily flushed. "It's not cockamamie," she said. "I just can't prove it yet."

Cross regarded her, then shifted his gaze to Branch. "I worked out the personnel changes. See if they make sense to you." He handed over a sheaf of papers. "Hello, Marty. How's it going?"

"Shit, Ken, I think I know how Custer felt with all those Indians," Benedetti said. "What's that about an iron horse?"

Cross leaned against the bumpy concrete wall, still perfectly uniformed but looking even blearier than Branch. "Iron horse. It's an archaic term for a railroad."

"The EJ&E tracks!" Emily said.

"Yes. Flatiron plus horse equals iron horse. Accounting for your last two game pieces."

Branch blew out his breath. "Which also means the Unsub is tying his murders to Emily's games specifically."

"How do we know they're hers?" Cross asked. "Why not just games in general?"

Branch waved at the table. "The Monopoly set my kids play with at home contains nine game pieces. These six plus a thimble, a top hat, and a bag of money."

Emily scratched her head. "I dropped those down a heating vent when I was a kid. So my folks and I always played with six game pieces. The Unsub has to be using my games."

Cross nodded, convinced. "How many games do you have, Detective?"

"Eight," Emily said, pointing to the shelf. "Operation, Monopoly, Duck Duck Goose, Boggle, Clue, Chutes and Ladders, I Spy, and Timebomb."

"We're only on two," Benedetti said. "There's a lot more blood coming our way."

Branch looked even more glum. "I'll tell CSI to dust for prints, see if he touched anything."

"Sure he did. And I've got a bridge to sell you," Benedetti snorted. "Any idea how this bozo knew the games were in the basement?"

Emily shook her head. "I always lock the house when I leave. I've never been burglarized."

"Maybe you leave a window open," Benedetti suggested. "Upstairs. Those big trees around your house, he could have climbed up while you were at work."

She considered that. "I do leave my bedroom window cracked year-round. I like fresh air. As for finding evidence the Unsub was here, though, my cleaning lady is very thorough."

"Do you use a service?" Benedetti asked.

"No. One woman. She has a key. I've used her for years. I trust her."

Branch scribbled notes. "Maybe she's got helpers you don't know about. Or saw something that'll give us a lead. I'll kick her to the top of the interview list."

Emily turned to Benedetti. "Speaking of evidence, there's no way that dog died accidentally."

"I'll get it autopsied," Benedetti agreed. "The asshole probably snapped her neck and left her for us to find. Can't wait to return the favor."

They traded ideas for a few minutes, and then Cross caught Emily's eye. "Detective, you've had a long, draining day. But it'll be impossible to cover the midnight shift without you. Would you volunteer—"

"Jesus Christ, Ken!" Benedetti sputtered, jumping off the dryer. "You think that's smart? Sending Emily out with that bastard on the loose?"

Cross looked at him. "I don't like it, either. But there's 140,000 citizens to protect and no officers to—"

"Let me send some deputies to fill—"

"Already asked the sheriff, but the flu's affecting your people, too."

"Call the goddamn State Police—"

"I can use the overtime, Chief," Emily interrupted, touched at Marty's concern, but not about to let the Unsub dictate the terms of her existence. She looked at Branch, who was watching the interplay with faint amusement. "I'll be safe enough for tonight, don't you think?"

Branch thought about it, nodded. "Serial killers are obsessed with foreplay. He'll let the suspense build a few days before delivering the next game."

"Then I'll see you at midnight, Chief."

Cross looked relieved, then reapplied his poker face. "Thank you, Detective. I'll show myself out." He headed up the stairs.

"Goddamn you, Halfass," Benedetti muttered. "Putting Emily in harm's way like it's nothing."

Branch patted his shoulder. "You've done it yourself, pal. The public's welfare comes first."

"Yeah. But I don't have to like it." Benedetti stretched. "You warned everyone to keep this police-card connection to themselves, right?"

"Yeah," Branch said. "But it's already the buzz at the station. It'll make TV the first time a reporter buys his favorite cop a drink." His expression turned conspiratorial. "Only four of us know about these games, however. Any objection to keeping it that way?"

"Fine by me," Benedetti said. "Just be careful. The politicians will scalp you if they find out you kept them out of the loop."

Branch snorted. "Speaking of politicians, I need to hit the john."

"Meet you at the car."

Emily turned to Benedetti when they reached the driveway. "I appreciate your concern for my safety, Commander," she said, with extra emphasis on his rank. "But I'm perfectly capable of deciding whether to work an extra shift."

Benedetti winced. "I wasn't being sexist, Emily."

"Yes, you were."

He shook his head. "You probably see it that way. But it's more that I like you and don't want to see any harm come to you unnecessarily."

Emily considered that. "If harm becomes necessary, though?"

"Hey, take the bullet with my blessings," he insisted. "Absolutely! No problem!"

She laughed. "In that case, I'm glad you said what you did . . . Marty."

Benedetti grinned. "As long as I'm around, Ossifer,

you're never gonna wind up like that deer. See you on the street."

Branch reappeared and they sped away. Emily watched till their taillights disappeared, then headed inside to prepare for the long night ahead.

EMILY AND BRADY

Chicago
December, 1969

"What are you doing, Daddy?" said Brady Kepp, padding into the kitchen. He loved being with his father, and it was just the two of them till Mommy came back from the store.

"Finishing my model airplane," Dwight Kepp answered, dabbing paint on the gossamer wings of the World War I biplane. "This is what your grandfather flew against Kaiser Bill."

"What's a Kaiser Bill?" Brady asked, walking to the table where his father worked.

"He's a who, not a what," Dwight corrected. "Way back before you were born, Kaiser Bill was the leader of a country we now call Germany." He tousled Brady's hair, happy to encourage his son's interest in history. He was a helluva smart kid for four! "His subjects loved him because he was very strong and took good care of them."

"He sounds like you, Daddy," Brady said. "Maybe you're a kaiser, too!"

"Thank you, son. That's a nice compliment," Dwight said, touched. Brady beamed and took the chair next to Daddy, careful not to touch anything.

Dwight went back to the biplane, humming. He'd been detailing this one for six months, having found model building the perfect relaxation from long days of selling insurance. His job was to correct the negative thinking of those who didn't want his policies—make the ignorant understand what was good for them. Something at which he was so gifted, he'd been promoted to senior vice president, "with much more to follow if you keep up those numbers," his boss had promised with a hearty thump on the back. He made good money, owned a nice house in one of Chicago's best neighborhoods, married a beautiful woman who understood he was the head of the family and what he said went. Better yet, she bore him a strong boy who worshipped his old man. Other than the fact that she couldn't give him more sons—those damnable butchers at the hospital!—life was good. "Hand me that yellow paint, would you, buddy?" he said. "Just one more detail to paint and we can put this in the display case."

"Sure, Daddy!" Brady enthused. He picked up the open tube and thrust it Daddy's way. A bright snake squirted from its round mouth, marking the top wing with a fat, runny squiggle.

"Son of a bitch!" Dwight roared, leaping to his feet. He pinched the mess with tissue, which only smeared it further. His thumb punched through the gossamer. Furious, he turned on his wide-eyed son. "You idiot! You ruined it!" he raged. "Why aren't you more careful?"

"I'm sorry!" Brady blubbered. His tummy was sick. Daddy worked so hard providing nice things for him and Mommy. This was an awful thing to do to him. "It was an accident! I didn't mean to hurt the airplane, honest I didn't. No, Daddy, not the belt! Not again! It hurts too much!"

"Maybe this will teach you to be more careful with my things," Dwight said, spread-eagling Brady across the ruined project, ripping down his footed pajamas, and flailing his buttocks with his thick leather trouser belt. Brady screeched, and Dwight put his face to the boy's ear. "No son of mine cries while being corrected," he warned. "Shut your little mouth, and take it like a man."

"Yes, Daddy," Brady whimpered.

CHAPTER 10

Tuesday, 2:44 A.M.
Fifty-one hours till Emily's birthday

"Patrol Unit Five is back in service," Emily radioed her dispatcher buddy Jodi. She tapped the last drop of coffee on her tongue. Shivered violently. At three in the morning the overcooked roll-call brew was a violent slush of acid and caffeine. She normally avoided it. But she was so zonked from the adrenaline blasts of the past twenty-one hours, she choked it down. "I'm heading back downtown."

"Affirmative, Patrol Five," Jodi replied. "Stand by for mail."

Emily arched an eyebrow. She'd just filed her paperwork from the hospital run and hadn't even left the parking lot behind the station.

JUST FIVE HOURS TO GO, read the car's cellular computer. STAY SAFE.

Emily nodded gratefully. Everyone was looking out for

her. She and her shotgun rider, who felt lousy from flu but came to work, anyway, started the shift by breaking up a bar fight. She split a thumbnail and purpled a bicep but made four arrests. They rolled into a shoutathon among husband, wife, and teenage son, which they defused with stern warnings. Then her rider's sweating got so heavy, Emily took him to the Edward Hospital emergency room. A replacement wasn't immediately available—everyone not out sick was handling a 911—so the shift commander reassigned her to the downtown business district, the quietest sector this time of night. Emily cruised the empty streets, looking for open doors and windows. The shift commander made her check in every ten minutes. Branch drove by three times, Annie twice. Marty phoned from a stakeout. "I'm bored, Detective," he'd said. "How about you?"

"Yep," she'd said.

"Keep it up," he'd said.

She clicked her microphone twice—"Thanks, Jodi"—and typed a quick reply—"I'll bring you guys doughnuts if you don't tell Cross." She put the black-and-white in gear and drove out of the lot, feeling for the lump at the base of her skull. Handcuff key firmly attached. And since she'd "dressed" her neck in the locker room, that was where she'd do it each and every time. Silly, she supposed, this superstition about continuing routines where she began them. But she bowed to its comfort nonetheless. Smiling at how Marty might react to this bit of voodoo, she finger-combed her thick hair in place, turned east at Safety Town, and sped toward downtown. Halfway there, a siren burped from a side street. Emily looked over to see Annie Bates waving "over here." She pulled window to window, rolled hers down.

"Hubby dropped off some real coffee," Annie said, handing over a commuter cup of French roast. "I figured you could use some about now."

"God, yes!" Emily drank deep. "Oh, that's good. Reward that man handsomely."

"I always do," Annie said with a wink. "How are you holding up?"

"I'm gonna die from boredom, not the Unsub."

Annie reached across the gap to pat her elbow. "That's the spirit! We'll turn you into a SWAT yet." They gossiped about who was genuinely sick and who was faking for free time off. Then Emily asked as casually as she could manage, "You know Martin Benedetti, right?"

"Marty? Yeah, sure. Good guy. Smart, funny, best pitcher their softball team ever had till his shoulder got funky." Annie managed the NPD team and knew talent. "The troops like him. He goes out of his way to mentor the few women the sheriff deigns to hire. Has an MBA from the University of Chicago yet puts away beer and bratwurst like any regular Joe. Why?"

Emily drank some more. "I met him this morning at the cemetery," she said, licking her lips. "He treated me square, and I wondered if he's like that with everyone."

Annie's face lit up. "You slut! You like him!"

"No, no," Emily protested, waving her hands. "Nothing like that."

"Don't lie to me, girly," Annie said, delighted. "Your eyes sparked when you said his name."

Emily sighed. "So is he . . . available?"

Annie scratched her blond ringlets. "Off my radar since he quit softball. He *was* married, that I know for sure. Probably divorced by now. Most of the old-timers are. I can sniff around."

Emily nodded. "Discreetly, please. I don't know yet if I want to pursue this."

Annie punched her arm. "Why not? You're a great catch. Besides, you really need to get laid." She cackled as Emily rolled her eyes, then grabbed the radio mike. "Patrol Eleven. Go ahead."

"Respond to a disturbance," Jodi said. "Sunny Acres Retirement Village, Unit 722."

Annie blew raspberries into the mike. "Those two at it again?"

"Apparently. Neighbors report shouting and glass breaking."

"Understood. I'll be there in seven minutes." Then, to Emily, "He's always honked off about something, and she won't take his crap. The dishes pay the price." She shook her head in wonder. "They're eighty-nine years old. Why aren't they in bed, with their teeth in a glass?"

Emily laughed and put her car in gear.

"We'll catch up later. I want all the juicy details about you and Marty," Annie said. "Consider it payment for drinkable coffee." She flipped on her roof lights and accelerated for the Far Southeast Side. Emily drove the remaining half mile to Washington and Jefferson, the heart of downtown, which was deader than the proverbial doornail at 2:59:59.

"What was that?" she gasped as a deep-pitched explosion shook her windows. A dozen burglar alarms erupted. She stuck her head out, looked around. Stars twinkled, so it wasn't thunder. Plane crash? Train derailment? The radio burped, and she turned up the volume.

"All units, be advised," Jodi announced as fire sirens from neighboring communities wailed. "Explosion at Neuqua Valley High School. Fire department responding Code 3." Lights, sirens, ignore the speed limit. "Stand by for assignments."

Emily slapped the dashboard. With its diving pools, recording studios, and boutique gymnasiums, Neuqua High was the most luxurious public school in America, resembling the dungeon she'd attended in Chicago as much as The Four Seasons looked like Motel 6. Maybe the crew replacing the school's natural-gas mains over the past few weeks had nicked one, and it ignited. "How serious?" she radioed.

"Patrol Five, switch to tactical channel two."

It was the shift commander, a good guy who'd led the cheers in her "Bambi" escapade. Emily switched to the encrypted special-operations frequency. "Patrol Five on tac two," she said, champing to get moving. "Where do you want me?"

"Sorry, Emily, no fire for you. We've got to cover 911s and this fire till State Police backups arrive from Chicago. We're shifting to emergency plan Charlie." A drawn-out mutter. "Till further notice, we respond only to dire emergencies. You'll handle calls north of 75th Street. Patrol Fourteen will handle calls south of 75th. Understood?"

"Aw, Lieutenant, I'd rather work the fire."

"Understood?"

"Ten-Four," Emily said. She flipped back to the general patrol channel. "Dispatch, I'm at Washington and Jefferson," she radioed. "Anything you want me to do?"

"Continue routine patrol—Ah, stand by."

Emily clicked to the fire frequencies as she waited, flooding the car with sirens, horns, and firefighters shouting over the roar of the American LaFrance diesels under their rubber feet. "Looks like a nuke went off!" one yelled. "Mobilize reserves, off-duties, and mutual aid! Everything!" Emily craned her head to the southwest sky. The inferno jiggled and erupted over the downtown streetlights. She could practically smell charring blackboards, hear the bell tower jangling in cindered collapse.

"Patrol Five, respond to disturbance," Jodi crackled. "Nichols Library, main parking lot. Neighbors report naked man screaming."

Emily raised an eyebrow—*dire emergencies only?*—and pushed transmit. "I'm on it."

"Patrol Five, meet me on tac two." Shift commander again.

"Go."

"Patrol Fourteen is responding to a multiple injury crash," he said. "I'm sending Sergeant Bates to back you up. She's responding to your location Code 13."

The last two words jolted her like a cattle prod. Code 13 was shorthand for "cop in mortal danger, death imminent." Why would a weenie-wagger rate Code 13? "Copy that transmission," she said, covering her anxiety with copspeak. "Can you advise particulars?"

"Subject is screaming your name," he replied.

Emily's fingers sought the reassurance of her Glock. "Hope you're paying attention out there, Marty," she murmured. Then, into the microphone, "ETA thirty seconds."

"Scout it out, but take no action till your backups arrive," he ordered. "Annie's en route, and a sheriff's car is breaking away from a stakeout."

I guess he was *listening!* "Understood," Emily responded as she laid a black ribbon of Goodyear on Jefferson Avenue, roof flashers licking downtown with red and blue tongues. She crested the hill at Eagle Street and saw the subject baying at the full moon.

With a full moon.

"You're gonna love this, Marty," she muttered, looking for weapons as she barreled into the lot. None. Nowhere to hide them, anyway. As Daddy used to say, the young man was "nekked as a jaybird." Her floodlight lit up his pale body—skater hair, narrow chest, muscled legs, no wrinkles, shriveled johnson—as she skidded to a halt. She popped out, leading with her Glock. "Police!" she barked. "Put your hands on top of your head!"

A jaunty grin broke across the boy's whitewashed features. "Emily?"

"Put your hands on your head!"

"You *are* Emily!" the kid cried. "You're the one I'm supposed to talk to!"

"Put your hands on your head!" she bellowed, each word distinct in case the kid was stoned. No good—he bounced and wriggled like a puppy. "Sir, if you don't obey my orders, I'll get in my car and run you over."

His stubby fingers wove together and grabbed his head. "I'm unarmed!" the kid shouted, squinting against the eye-busting glare. "I'm just supposed to talk to you!"

"We'll get to that in a minute," Emily replied. "First you need to get on your knees."

"On the asphalt?" the kid complained. "Aw, shit, c'mon, it's full of gravel!"

"On your knees. Now."

He complied.

"Very good," Emily said. "Now lie facedown, and clasp your hands behind your back."

"All right." Then in a muffled voice, "Then can we talk, Emily?"

"Absolutely." She shuffle-stepped to ensure she didn't lose her balance. Forget the Unsub. If she fell on top of a naked guy, she'd never hear the end of it. "I'm going to handcuff you," she said when close enough. "Don't fight me, OK?"

"God no!" the kid squealed, and she whiffed the stale beer. *Phew!* This guy didn't want to fight. He had to take a leak! "I'm just supposed to deliver a message, Emily. The dude said taking off my clothes was part of it. I'm not a pervert, you know." It seemed important she acknowledge that, so she made appropriate murmurs. "Do whatever, Emily. I won't fight."

"Thank you, sir. I appreciate it," she said, cuffing his bony wrists behind his back and his ankles to each other. She bunny-hopped him to the car, locked him in the caged backseat. "Situation is under control, dispatch," she reported. "Tell backups to slow down."

"All units, cancel Code 13," Jodi said. A moment later, "Patrol Five, what did I tell you about waiting for help?"

"Sorry, sir, couldn't be helped," Emily said. "The subject insisted on surrendering." She glanced around the lot, saw movement. "Civilians are gathering. I didn't want them endangered if the subject changed his mind and ran. So I double-cuffed and locked him in my unit."

"Understood, Five. Sounds like the correct call. But we'll review your actions later."

Which meant he agreed but would chew her out, anyway, make sure it got around. He needed to wave that flag for anyone who might be tempted, for less credible reasons, to "misinterpret" his orders.

She could live with that.

"So what's this all about, kid?" Emily asked. "Some kind of fraternity stunt?"

He shook his head. "I was watching the Bulls game at the Lantern. You know, the downtown tavern?"

She nodded.

"This old dude walked up and says hello."

"Old?"

"Ancient. At least forty."

Hey! Wait till you're *two days away!* "What'd this man look like?"

"A dude," the kid said, shrugging. "You know."

"I don't know. I wasn't there. Was he white?"

"Uh-huh, he—"

"Tall?"

"Yeah, pretty big, I guess—"

"How was he dressed?"

"I need to tell you the message, OK?" the kid said. "It's part of his deal."

"All right, but hurry it up."

He nodded. "Me and the dude are talking sports. He buys a round. Cool. Then asks if I'd do him a favor. He's buying, so I said, 'Yo, dude, if I can.'" He paused.

"And?" Emily prompted.

"Says he's planning a birthday joke for his girl. If I help, he'll pay me five hundred."

Emily blinked. "Dollars?"

"I thought he was yankin' my chain, too," the kid said. "Then he shows me the wad. I put down my beer and say, 'For that kinda dough, who do I gotta kill?' Dude laughs, says naw, his girl's a Naperville cop, and he wants to deliver her birthday card in a way she'll never forget. He's willing to pay 'cause the deal's pretty loopy."

"Tell me exactly what he wanted you to do."

"Get here at 3 A.M. Ditch my clothes and scream your name. When you show up, hand you the envelope and say, 'Happy Birthday, Bambi!'"

The use of her work nickname made her stomach loop the loop. "Where's the envelope?"

"Wallet pocket of my jeans."

"Do you have the money?"

The kid looked as indignant as a naked teenager could look. "Well, duh. Think I'd do something this stupid without seeing the green first?"

"Of course not," Emily lied. "I'll check it out. You stay here and . . . well . . ." The kid was standing a lot taller than a moment ago, and she bit her lip to not laugh. "Want to cover up?"

He looked down. "Uh, yeah, that sounds good."

She grabbed a blanket from her trunk and tented it across

his lap. Then hustled to the clothes. T-shirt and shoes were clean. No underwear—kid went commando. She rifled the Levis and found the cash, along with keys, condoms, and peanut shells. Finally, she fished out a large white envelope. The outside was blank except for a single, manually type-written sentence.

to bambi on her big four-o

Cursing the tremble in her hands, Emily pulled her fold-ing knife and slit the envelope down the side, preserving the flap for DNA testing. She worked carefully, not wanting to nick herself and bleed on the evidence.

The card inside was ordinary Xerox paper, folded twice. Construction-paper candles and cakes adorned the front. Under them was a message handwritten in red crayon. She sniffed to ensure it wasn't blood—heavy, waxy, nope, it's Crayola—and read the words aloud.

that you made it this far, dear emily

She opened cautiously to the inside, half expecting it to blow up in her face.

does so Boggle the mind! happy birthday!

"Oh God," she whispered. The *B* wasn't lowercase, but capital. The only capital on the card. Therefore, not boggle as in overwhelmed with amazement, but Boggle as in the game.

"Dispatch!" she radioed. "Send chief of detectives to this location Code 13."

"Already en route," Jodi radioed back.

Back to the card. No signature. Left side blank. On the right side, under the "Boggle" scrawl, a small envelope was taped at the corners. She unstuck one end, tugged out the glossy cardboard inside. Flinched at the oval face smiling back.

"Emily! Hey!"

She whirled to see the kid banging his forehead on the

window. She rushed over, flung the door wide, waved her police card in his face. "What kind of sick game are you playing—"

"He said your present's inside the library!"

Her mouth dried up.

"That's the last part of the message," he explained. "For the five bills, I had to hand you the envelope, let you read what's inside, then say your birthday present's in the library."

She blinked rapidly, trying to think. "What would you have said if another officer had arrived first?"

"That I have a message for Emily Marie Thompson, and I'd deliver it when you arrived. Dude said Bambi's your nickname and Child's your hubby's name, but your real name is Thompson, so don't get confused." His grin turned sly. "Scuse me for saying so, but isn't this a little too, you know, public? For a married lady? What if your husband finds out?"

She grabbed the radio mike.

"The subject is a delivery man," she told the shift commander. "The Unsub paid him $500 to deliver a birthday card." She provided details, relieved to see the sheriff's car bounce into the lot. Marty's protectiveness was definitely welcome now. "Do you agree with my assessment?"

"Yes," he said. "Has backup arrived?"

"Sheriff just pulled in."

"OK, I'm sending you inside to find out," he said. "Annie's four minutes out. I've mobilized SWAT, the canine unit, and the county bomb squad."

"I'm only guessing, boss," Emily warned. "I might be wrong."

"You might be right, too," he replied. "Which is why you need to get inside. But watch yourself. No unnecessary heroics, none of that 'he surrendered' baloney from before. You hear me, Detective?"

"Loud and clear, sir."

"Good. Look around, then get out. We'll let SWAT clear the building."

"Copy that!" Emily said, glancing at her prisoner. "Listen, kid, you've been really cooperative," she said. "Keep it up and I'll talk my boss out of pressing charges on the striptease. Meaning there's no jail, and you'll have a great story for your buddies. How 'bout it?"

The kid's eyes said yes-yes-yes, but his lips felt compelled to add, "And the money?"

She didn't have the heart to explain Branch would seize it as evidence. "By all means, keep it," she said. "Buy yourself some underwear." She locked the car, though it wasn't really necessary. The kid's eyes gleamed with beer and adoration. He wouldn't miss this for a boatload of rubbers. She pulled her Glock, then stared in horror as her backup trundled into the light.

"Well, if it ain't the Vagina Monologue," Sheriff's Sergeant Rayford Luerchen sneered. "No wonder everything's screwed up around here."

Emily made a sour face, wondering what god she'd offended to merit this as backup. "We're going in," she snapped. "Stay to my right so I know where you are—"

"Uh-uh," Luerchen interrupted, pointing to the chevrons on his sleeve. "I outrank you. I'm in command. Don't worry, hon. I'll be sure to mention you in my report."

"This is my case," she growled, sticking her face in so close she smelled his onion breath. "This lunatic is after me. If you have a problem being backup, *hon*, I'll wait for my own people."

Luerchen scowled. "Hey, you wanna take the bullet 'stead of me, be my guest," he said. "What is this present, anyway? The dispatcher didn't say."

Instead of replying, Emily keyed her microphone. "We're entering the library now."

"Affirmative," the shift commander said. "Be careful."

She tightened her grip on the Glock as sirens filled the heavy air. "Sergeant," she murmured as she eased through the front entrance, "I believe the Unsub's left us a . . ."

EMILY AND BRADY

Chicago
August 1971

"Hold the peanut still, and he'll come get it," Alice Kepp whispered. "He won't bite you. Animals are our friends."

Brady's face torqued into total concentration as he pinched the peanut between his thumb and index finger. The gray squirrel advanced slowly but was unafraid, conditioned by the nut trails they laid out while Dwight was in Atlanta hosting an insurance convention.

"Come on, buddy," Brady whispered. "I've got your treat right here." The squirrel tiptoed to the boy's hand and lifted its mouth to the nut, like a friendly dog accepting a Milk-Bone.

"He's got it," Alice said, relieved her lesson about being nice to animals was paying off. "Let go so he can eat."

The boy flicked the nut straight into the squirrel's eye, causing it to screech and dart away.

"Brady!" Alice scolded, slapping the boy's hand. "Why did you do that?"

"I don't like squirrels," Brady said, looking wide-eyed at his mother. "Why did you hit me, Mom? That's Father's job. He doesn't like it when we don't follow his rules."

Alice enveloped Brady in her slender arms. About a year ago her son had started using his slingshot on the squirrels, raccoons, and cats wandering their double lot. She confiscated it. He threw rocks instead. When she asked why, he replied, "I dunno." She mentioned it to Dwight, but he only chuckled. "Good for him," he said, waving his hand in dismissal. "Goddamn things dig the hell out of my gardens." Alice said it seemed to go deeper than that. "Brady just seems so furious when he does it, honey. Maybe we should talk to the pediatrician." The suggestion earned her a ringing slap. "All boys throw rocks at animals," he growled. "They're warriors, not florists. My son is perfectly normal and doesn't need his head shrunk."

"Mommy didn't mean to hit you, baby," Alice said, rubbing Brady's thick hair. "You didn't do anything wrong. Mommy made a mistake and feels bad. You're a good boy, and Mommy loves you." His silence encouraged her. "Let's not tell your father about this, OK? It would only make him angry. We don't want him angry at us, do we?"

"No," Brady said. "My behind hurts when Father gets angry."

"Then you won't say anything, right?"

"I won't, Mom. I promise." His half smile filled her with unease. It was almost like her son knew the value of this information and intended to hold it over her. But that was crazy! Brady was six years old!

She hugged him close, not knowing what else to say.

CHAPTER 11

Tuesday, 4 A.M.
Fifty hours till Emily's birthday

"He won't hide this present," Emily decided after a quick glance around. "It'll be in the open. He wants me to find it." She trained gun and flashlight on the string of chairs in the back of the cavernous reading room. "That's where we'll begin. Let's go."

"Should I turn on the room lights, Commandant?" Luerchen said, voice dripping sarcasm. "So we can actually see something?"

"Switches are on the wall behind you," Emily muttered.

Luerchen vanished from her peripheral vision. She white-knuckled the Glock, heart thumping in her ears as she crept forward. *What am I doing here?* her inner civilian screamed as she moved deeper into the gloom. A proper building search involved head-to-toe body armor and snuffling German shepherds.

Blam!

She yelled as her Glock bucked in her hand, blowing a neat little hole in the carpet. The sudden flash of the bright overheads was so startling, she had accidentally pulled the trigger. She slapped her ears to make the ringing go away.

Luerchen snickered as he slid back on her flank. "Glad you insisted on going first. If I'd been in front, you'd have shot me in the ass."

Emily blew out her breath, furious with herself. "I didn't realize my finger was on the trigger," she said, watching blue gun smoke curl toward the windows.

"No kiddin'. You see anything yet?"

Emily stared into now-bright nooks and crannies. "Negative."

"Me neither. Keep looking. And keep your fuckin' finger off the trigger."

She carefully surveyed the room. Tons of books, miles of shelving, computers, magazines, DVDs, videos. Nothing she'd deem a "present." The sirens grew louder as the ringing in her ears faded. *SWAT will be here any second, take over. The Unsub doesn't want that. He clearly means for me to find it. That's the whole point of delivering the birthday card.*

She spotted a thatch of hair, brown and spiky with gel, peeking over the back of the centermost reading chair—the only one turned away from the entrance doors. "That's the present!" she hissed, pointing with her Glock. "Cover me!"

"Backup's only seconds out," Luerchen objected. "We're waiting right here for SWAT—"

"Cover me!" Emily snapped, barreling ahead, Glock darting left-right-left as every nerve ending begged the Unsub to appear so she could dump all eighteen rounds in his miserable face. "I've got your back, Emily!" she heard Annie cry behind her. Luerchen was barking into the radio, "Dispatch, we found the present!" Emily spun to clear the area of threats, then yelled, "It's a man! Checking for vitals!" She looked over the top of the chair, gagged. *Run!* her mind screamed. *Let the real cops deal with this!* She ordered her feet to stay put—*you are a real cop, act like one!*—and wiped her sweat-drenched hand on her shirt. She placed two fingers on the man's carotid artery. No pulse. She shifted her fingers. *Yes!* "He's alive!" Emily shouted.

"The man's alive, repeat alive!" Luerchen barked. "Hustle those paramedics!" He ran to the chair, waving his shotgun like a magic wand. "What do we have here. Oh shit!"

Emily's mouth was so dry, she couldn't speak. Instead, she prayed the balding middle-aged man with the purple gym shorts would survive. It didn't look promising. The double-edged silver dagger was shoved in to the handguard. It split his left breast in two, its ropelike handle covering his nipple and its razor-sharp tip protruding from his back, below the shoulder blade. Blood leaked from both sides. *Not nearly enough for such a grievous injury*, some detached part of her brain noted. *Drained elsewhere, dumped here.* Silver handcuffs hung from his hands, which were folded in his lap. "Holy Christ," Emily heard Luerchen breathe. She followed his stare, and her eyes widened at the rolled-up card protruding from a hole drilled through the man's right shinbone. Her entire body shuddered.

"Aw, you're not gonna heave, are you?" Luerchen said, quickly backpedaling.

"No!" Emily coughed, doubling over, feeling like she'd drank sewage. "No way I'm—"

Too late. She blasted Luerchen with pizza, potato chips, and coffee. His cussing was explosive, and she burned with humiliation. Avoiding Luerchen's murderous glare, she spit coffee grounds from her teeth and grunted into her radio, "Dispatch, advise responding units that . . . never mind." She waved at the Whitman's Sampler of cops, SWATs, and firefighters charging her way. "I felt a pulse!" she cried. "He's alive!"

A Viking of a paramedic ran up, equipment jangling. He clomped a stethoscope to the man's chest, bellowing, "Alla ya shut up! I can't hear!"

The hubbub stilled. The SWAT lieutenant motioned his black-clad troops to the children's library in the basement and fanned the uniforms across the reading room. Annie hustled up, examined Emily top to bottom. She squeezed her shoulder, then wheeled off after Luerchen, who'd retreated to the front entrance. Emily turned back to Viking, who was listening with closed eyes. Five excruciating seconds later, he opened them and shook his head.

"I felt a pulse!" Emily insisted. "I did, in both my fingers!"

"Could have been your own you felt, Detective," a new voice said.

She turned and saw Chief Cross. No surprise there.

What did shock was his appearance. Stubbled face. Torn jeans, wrinkled navy sweatshirt. Beat-up Nikes without socks, badge flopping crooked from a neck chain. Submachine gun pointed at the ceiling, sleep sand crusting his bloodshot eyes. She'd never seen Cross less than perfectly kempt. The effect was unnerving. He'd clearly been asleep when all this erupted.

"That happens when you're under stress," Cross continued. "You think it's the victim's pulse, but it's really your own because your heart is hammering and you want it so damn bad."

"I'm not doubting what you felt, uh, Emily is it?" Viking said. "But the man's gone."

She bit her lower lip, ordered herself to look at the corpse. *Do your job,* she told herself as she took in the man's terrible wounds. *Clear-eyed, dispassionate, iron grip on emotions.* Like Branch. Like Benedetti. Most of all like Cross, the patron saint of coolness under fire. Look for clues, connect the dots, and you'll find the Unsub.

Heated voices made her turn to the entrance doors. Annie was shoving Luerchen. Emily excused herself and went over.

"You froze!" Annie hissed. "You did nothing while your partner was in danger!"

"Bullshit!" Luerchen sputtered. "I was with her every second."

"Emily was already with the victim when I came in. You were standing right here with your thumb up your ass." Annie pushed her face into his. "You were scared."

"Go fuck yourself, Bates!" Luerchen said. "I backstopped your pal one 100 percent. You tell that lie to anybody else and I'll kick your ass into next week."

"Yeah, right. I'm only gonna say this once, Ray," she said, her tone so chilling Luerchen backed up several feet. "Stay away from this case. You're a walking, talking disaster, and I won't have you endangering my friends."

Luerchen went white with fury. "You haven't heard the end of this," he muttered, backing toward the parking lot. "Neither of you."

Annie blew him a kiss. He gave her the finger and stomped out. "Great job," she said, turning to tousle Emily's hair. "You responded exactly the way you should have."

"Thanks," Emily said, blowing out her breath.

"As for the hole in the floor, here's what we're gonna do."

"Hole? What hole?"

Annie snorted. "Ray already ratted you out, dear. I, uh, counseled him that nobody likes a tattletale, least of all me." Wide grin. "But he's a weasel. He'll find Halfass and make a preemptive strike on you in revenge. A complication you don't need right now. So I'm telling him, I did it."

Emily stared. "Lie to Cross? Are you out of your mind? He'll hang us both!"

"No guts, no glory." They talked several minutes. Then Annie waved over the chief, who'd come into the room from a fire exit. He limped their way.

"You like waving red capes in front of bulls?" Emily demanded.

"Just nod when appropriate. I'll handle the rest."

"Annie, please, don't get yourself jammed up for me."

"Nonsense. This is what family does."

Emily sighed. All she could do now was play along.

"Chief, I have a problem," Annie said, arranging her face into an Oscar-winning look of contrition. "I accidentally discharged my weapon into the floor."

"What? You're kidding," Cross said.

"Afraid not, sir." She held out her submachine gun, pointed to the floor near the reception desk.

"You're SWAT," Cross said. "And an army sniper instructor. How could that happen?"

"Carelessness. I entered the reading room just as Detective Thompson reached the victim. My finger was on the trigger, ready to engage targets, because she was exposed to attack. Somehow the overhead lights flipped on, engaging my startle reflex. Kablam."

Cross surveyed the room. "Where was Detective Thompson's backup in all this?"

Annie tapped the floor with her foot. "Right here. While Emily put her life on the line, Sergeant Luerchen guarded the entry doors to thwart any escape by the Unsub."

Long pause, then, "You know, the first rule of guns is you never put your finger on the trigger unless you intend to shoot."

"I know that, sir. I feel like a stupid rookie."

"That's not true," Cross said. "You're a very good officer who made a mistake. It happens." He looked at Emily even as he spoke to Annie. "You understand that bullet could have taken your partner's life, Sergeant?"

"Crystal clear, sir," Annie replied. "From now on, finger off the trigger till I need to shoot."

Cross sighed. "All right, all right. Since you'll punish yourself worse than anything I can dream up, there's no reason to pursue this further. Excellent job in here." Cross swung his eyes to Emily. "Goes for you, too, Detective. Are you all right?"

"Yes, sir. Just a little shaken up."

"Take a few minutes to get yourself together, then go debrief Branch. He's in the parking lot."

"Sounds good, sir." She spotted Luerchen peeking through the front door, and her anger boiled. "Did he rat me out?"

Cross looked at her. "Come again, Detective? I didn't quite hear you."

The question let her compose herself. "Uh, I was wondering if you ran into my backup officer before you came in? I wanted to compare notes, but he's not in the room."

"As a matter of fact, I did," Cross said. "Sergeant Luerchen introduced himself, and we had a long conversation."

So Cross knows we're lying! His nice-nice was a trap, and Annie was snared but good. Maybe she could reduce the damage by confessing. "Chief, it wasn't Sergeant Bates—"

"Interesting man, Luerchen," Cross continued as if she hadn't spoken. "He talks so much yet says nothing of interest. I quit listening to his story halfway through. Carry on, both of you." He turned and limped toward the corpse.

Annie smiled and, when he was out of earshot, said, "Listen, I know you don't like Cross. Not without reason since he rides you like a plow horse. But he's not only a taskmaster. He's a really good guy with more than one side to his personality."

"Be nice if he showed us the human one," Emily snorted.

"He just did," Annie said. She waved at the coroner on the other side of the room. "Now tell me everything that happened."

Emily did, finishing with the Vagina Monologue crack.

"That's pretty creative for someone with brains of Play-Doh," Annie said. "Maybe Ray's the Unsub. He hates you enough."

"I thought of that. But he's too stupid, and Lucy was dead before I met him." Emily said. She bade Annie good-bye, then walked over to Cross. "Thank you, Chief," she said to his back.

"I wouldn't thank me just yet, Detective," Cross said, turning to look at her. "You and Sergeant Bates will serve one-week suspensions for lying about the shooting."

Emily stared.

"Luerchen's an idiot," Cross continued. "But he's also right. You shot the floor. Sergeant Bates is fanatic about cleaning her weapons after every use, and there was no gunpowder smell in her submachine gun. Therefore, she never fired it." He pointed at her. "Your accidental discharge was entirely understandable, and I would not have disciplined you for it. The lie is not acceptable. I cannot be misinformed about anything in this case. Hence the suspension. Not for the mistake, but the cover-up."

Emily wanted to argue, but what was the point? "Yes, sir," she mumbled. "Starting now?"

"Hardly, Detective. I can't afford to be without two officers right now. I'm suspending the sentence till the Unsub's safely behind bars."

"Uh, yes, sir," Emily said, knowing a break when she saw it. She turned, straightened, and pushed through the entrance doors toward whatever came next.

CHAPTER 12

Tuesday, 5 A.M.
Forty-nine hours till Emily's birthday

"Neither rain nor sleet nor gloom of night," Branch cracked as Benedetti strode up to the library entrance.

"Har, har," Benedetti said. "Sorry I couldn't back you up. I got two flat tires on the way over."

"I don't see your car. Where'd you park?" Branch asked.

"Next block. Too many cop cars here, so I dumped it behind Anderson's Bookshop." Benedetti stretched his arms over his head. "I changed the first tire quick enough. A mile later the second pops. Had to roust a deputy to bring me a third. Poor old Love Shack is showing her age."

"Love Shack?" Emily asked.

"Pet name for my car. You'll know why when you meet her."

"That thing's gonna kill you, man," Branch said. "Time to junk it."

Benedetti shook his head. "What self-respecting man

dumps his sweetie because she's old and gray?" He looked at Emily. "So, you OK?"

"Yeah," she said.

Branch rubbed his eyes. "Detective Thompson figures if she has to work in the middle of the night, everyone should."

"Detective Thompson," Benedetti mused. "Gee, Branch, it seems like only yesterday she was an officer. They grow up so darn fast. . . ."

Emily smiled. "You know, Branch," she said, struggling for the studied nonchalance of a homicide veteran, "if this guy keeps it up, he might very well start ticking me off."

"Me, too," Benedetti said. "Do we know the victim's name?"

Branch jerked his thumb at the library. "Arnold Harrison Soull. Double *l*. He lives in DeKalb."

Where I finished college, Emily realized.

"The local cops are checking him out."

Benedetti scratched his chin. "DeKalb's a half hour away. Being dead and all, I wonder how he managed to get himself here?"

"First thing I'll ask Mr. Unsub," Branch said dryly.

Emily told Benedetti what was in the victim's shin. The commander growled a dozen compound expletives. "Power-drill a guy just to plant a clue?" he asked. "That's cold. Was his wallet there?"

"Yes," Emily said. "Everything intact, just like Lucy's homicide."

"What's our game connection?" he said, pulling his notebook.

She explained the Boggle reference scrawled on the birthday card.

Benedetti stopped writing. "Your birthday? That's where all this is heading?"

"Yup," Branch answered. "That card tells me the Unsub intends to play the final game on her fortieth birthday. The day after tomorrow." He looked at Emily. "Please tell me you were born during Johnny Carson. We need every hour we can get."

"No such luck," Benedetti answered. "Emily greeted the world at 6:02 A.M., according to her birth certificate. Giving us only forty-nine hours to run him to ground." He shook his head. "There isn't a thing this creep doesn't know about her."

Emily looked at him. "Actually, Commander, how'd *you* know?"

"Yeah, Marty," Branch chimed in. "How'd *you* know?"

Benedetti flushed. "Couldn't sleep last night thinking about these game connections. So I swung by NPD and borrowed, uh, Emily's personnel file." He looked everywhere but her face. "Figured I should familiarize myself with it. For the, uh, you know, case."

"That's a good, uh, you know, idea," Branch said. Emily said nothing, enjoying Marty's discomfort.

"Geez, you take a little initiative . . ." Benedetti mumbled, color deepening. Then, changing the subject, "How'd Soull get inside?"

"The Unsub cut a hole in a downstairs window. Wanna see?"

"Yeah. Show me the victim first, though."

Emily tour-guided. When they reached Soull, Benedetti asked a dozen questions, paying particular attention to the silver dagger. He told Emily to describe exactly how Soull looked before paramedics arrived. He touched the dagger with a gloved finger as she talked, flicked the chain linking the handcuffs. He frowned, touched the dagger handle as though taking its pulse. He cleared his throat and said, "Show me where they entered."

They passed Emily's bullet hole on the way. She didn't comment. Halfway down the stairs, they conferred with the weary CSIs tweezing the handrails for hair, clothing fibers, and other trace. A minute later they stared at the hole in the plate glass on the westernmost wall of the children's library. Emily looked around. The posters, pint-size reading chairs, and gaily painted decorations were cheerful yesterday but now served only to mock her.

" . . . Then he cut this hatch," Branch was saying. "Threw Soull inside, then climbed in. Dragged the body upstairs and planted it in the chair."

Benedetti nodded, the sharp breeze through the hole fluttering his hair like graying butterflies. "What's this, two feet across?" he asked.

"Twenty-six-point-four inches," the CSI confirmed, not taking his eyes off the fingerprint dust he was brushing across the surface. "The part he cut out is on the table."

Benedetti examined both without touching the sharp edges. "There's no blood puddle upstairs," he said. "This isn't the place of execution. It's the display case."

Branch nodded. "When he died, the coroner will tell us. As for where, who knows? Em, lay out our working theory of what happened."

"The Unsub parks his vehicle," she began, pointing to Jackson Avenue, which separated the Riverwalk from the library. "Walks up and shoots out those security lights." She pointed to the roof overhang, made a finger gun. "Ploop-ploop-ploop, one shot for each light."

"'Ploop'?" Benedetti said.

"Silencer. It was the middle of the night, but nobody reported gunshots."

Benedetti nodded, getting on his knees next to the CSI.

"He makes the hole with the glass cutter," she continued. "Retrieves Soull from the vehicle, tosses him inside. Goes in himself, drags Soull upstairs by the ankles."

"How do you know that?"

"I saw carpet fibers in Soull's hair gel."

"Good catch," Benedetti said.

"Thank you. Then the Unsub arranges my 'present' and exits through the hole."

The CSI frowned at his brush, headed upstairs to get more powder.

"We know some interesting things about this perp," she continued.

Benedetti looked up.

"Don't say perp. Marty hates copspeak, says it's lazy language," Branch explained. "Humor him. He had a tough morning changing flat tires and all."

Emily crinkled her eyes. "The Unsub, then, is a meticulous researcher. This was the only possible place he could enter the building without setting off an alarm."

Benedetti twisted his head through the hole, looked around. "No sensors on the windows," he said. "Only on the doors. This spot is camouflaged by the retaining wall, shrubs, and roof overhang. And it's dark as a cave when the security lights aren't shining."

Emily nodded. "Those lamps are small. Recessed into the concrete overhang. If he misses, the ricochet hits him or the alarmed door. He's a marksman, though—three shots, three lights."

Benedetti stood and smacked powder off his knees. "What else?"

"Soull weighs at least two hundred pounds," she said. "Heaving that much deadweight without touching the sharp edges of a narrow hole takes muscle. That's a good indication the Unsub is male—men have more upper-body strength then women. He's also got balls."

"Yet another indication," Branch said.

Emily smiled. "At the tavern, the Unsub had no problem talking a stranger into stripping in a public parking lot. That makes him gregarious and trustworthy." She pointed at a foot-square sign over the checkout desk. "The library is videotaped after hours. Those warnings are posted throughout the building. He knew he was being watched and proceeded, anyway. Gives him a high tolerance for risk."

"Or he's so whacked out, he don't give a shit," Benedetti said.

"I was hoping to gloss over that one, Commander!" she said. "Anyway, once the lab analyzes the security tape—"

"He stole that," Branch interrupted.

Why am I not surprised? "That's everything this crime scene tells me," she said, adjusting The Mule Train to ease its weight on her hips. "What am I missing?"

Benedetti held up his hand like he was swearing on a Bible. His latex fingers glittered in the CSI's floodlights. "Did that dagger look real to you?"

Emily shook her head. "Now that you mention it, the dagger did strike me as weird. Like it'd been painted or something." She sucked in her breath. "That's what's on your gloves—paint. It came off when you touched the dagger."

Benedetti brought them to her face. "Correct. Now tell me what color."

"Silver," she said.

"Darker."

"Uh, pewter."

"He painted the dagger pewter," Branch agreed. "Why would he do that?"

"He wanted it to look fake even though it was real," Benedetti said. "Like a toy. A prop."

"A game piece!" Emily said. "There's two games represented here! Boggle and something else." She ran through her collection, but nothing fit. Branch did likewise. They shook their heads.

"Mr. Soull, with a dagger, in the library," Benedetti prompted. "Colonel Mustard, with a candlestick, in the conservatory—"

"Clue!" Branch and Emily said.

Benedetti raised a thumb. "Nixon was in office the last

time I played a board game. So I found a Web site that describes the hundred most popular in excruciating detail. The main character in Clue is a murder victim named Mr. Boddy. Our murdered character is—"

"Mr. Soull," Emily said. Boddy and Soull. I get it."

"Double *d*, double *l*, to make sure we don't miss the point," Branch mused. "Might also explain why Soull lived in DeKalb."

"It's an unusual enough surname that nobody local had it," Emily ventured. "The Unsub needed a 'Soull' to make this game connection work, so he kidnapped the closest."

"Phone, utility, and auto registrations will tell us," Branch said, flipping open his notepad. "Any other connections to Clue?"

"Three," Benedetti said, stifling a yawn. "Soull was killed with a rope-handled dagger. That's an official Clue murder weapon."

Branch scribbled. "Next?"

"The handcuffs. They appear in the game when one player is ready to accuse another of being the murderer. Soull's wrists were shackled with pewter-colored handcuffs." The commander held out the paint-splotched fingernail that had flicked the chains. "Same paint job."

"That's two connections," Branch said. "What's the last?"

"The hole in the shinbone."

Emily recalled the cylindrical wound. Her stomach bubbled again. "I don't get it."

"Remember the rooms in the Clue mansion?" Benedetti said. "Library, conservatory, study, kitchen, what have you? They're connected by secret passages." He cleared his throat. "I believe the Unsub drilled a hole through Soull's shin to represent those passages."

"Oh, man, that's a stretch," Branch objected. "Maybe he just enjoys inflicting pain."

"I don't think so, boss," Emily said. "He's done nothing

for laughs. At all three crime scenes, every single thing reinforces the game message he's sending." She tapped her shin. "If he only wanted to inflict pain, he would have done it without filling a drill with Soull's DNA."

Branch considered the analysis, landed an "atta boy" roundhouse on Benedetti's arm.

"I can't take the credit," Benedetti said. "Games would never have occurred to me without Emily's saying so first. She's a natural at this business." He flicked his handlebar mustache. "Fire her, fire her now before we're both out of a job."

Emily basked in the praise, finally starting to feel like an equal partner. Then the good feeling vanished. "Gotta get some air," she gasped, lunging for the fire door. Branch grabbed her wrist. "CSIs aren't finished," he reminded her. She turned and sprinted for the stairs.

Thirty seconds later she was hyperventilating in the predawn chill. Her eyes locked on Chief Cross huddling with the SWAT team. "We'll never find this guy," she whispered. "He's going to kill me!" She started rocking, raking her bottom lip with her teeth. Branch, who'd stepped off the curb to join Cross, shot Benedetti a warning look. Benedetti moved in front of her and said something she couldn't hear through the blood roar in her ears. She saw the Unsub's face and smashed her fist into it. The blow shook her from fingers to shoulder blade, and she dimly realized it wasn't the Unsub she'd just punched but Marty's breastbone. Heart pounding to pop her chest, she tried to smile, show she was all right. It felt weak, simpering. She gave up and concentrated on breathing. In. Out. Deep. Slow. The panic faded, her knees sagged, and she wiped her face with hands so shaky they felt like paint mixers.

"Who said women have less upper-body strength?" Benedetti grunted. "That hurt."

"Marty," Emily breathed, staring at the blood smearing his bulletproof vest. "God, I'm sorry."

"It's OK."

"I don't know what came over me," she said. "I just lost it—"

"It's all right, Emily. Honest," Benedetti said, gripping her shoulders. "This maniac's making you crazy, and you needed to let it out." He rubbed his chest. "Trust me, you did."

Emily emptied her lungs, dizzy. "That was . . . I don't know. . . ."

"Don't worry about it," Branch said. "We've all been there." He looked at Benedetti. "So, can my detectives throw a punch or what?"

"Next time I'll take 'or what,'" Benedetti said, cradling Emily's hand to examine her bloody knuckles. The touch filled her with warmth. She gently rubbed his thumb. He looked up and into her eyes, smiled softly, then let go.

"It's only a scrape," he said. "If something was broken, you'd have screamed when I pushed."

"Only thing broke is your pride," Branch snorted. "Even Luerchen didn't get beat up by a girl."

Emily tried to laugh but couldn't quite manage. She massaged her neck instead. "Where do we go from here?"

Branch high-signed Cross, got waved over. "The birthday deadline changes everything. Let me tell Ken." He returned ten minutes later. "You hungry?" he asked Benedetti.

"Always. Why?"

Branch's faint smirk became a Buddha smile. "Seems the mayor just called the TV stations from her car. SWAT scanners picked up the transmission. She said they're missing a blockbuster at the library and should route their news choppers from the fire." He blew a kiss at the mayoral Mercedes clearing the barricades. "This place is about to look like the fall of Saigon."

"Kee-rist," Benedetti groused. "Will you please get that mayor of yours potty trained?"

Branch laughed. "The good news is that most of the troops have dragged themselves to the station. They're sicker than dogs but insist on working 'cause one of our own is under attack."

"The chief can put them to good use," Emily said, voice cracking a little.

"Indeed, he can," Branch told her. "But there's not enough cruisers for everybody. Or radios. So drop yours off at the station, and ride with me to Grandma Sally's. Marty will meet us there, and we'll eat." He grinned at her look of confusion. "Ken wants you out of the way till the choppers leave. We'll use the opportunity to compare notes."

Benedetti pulled his jacket away from the blood. "Sounds good. We can order doughnut omelettes, seeing we're cops and all." He nudged Branch. "Just make sure you drive, pal. Mood Emily's in today, she'd try to run me over."

EMILY AND BRADY

Chicago
September 1974

"Half my friends are going out for gymnastics, Daddy," Emily sighed as she watched the final minute of *Dragnet* from the floor. Mama was in the kitchen washing supper dishes. "The rest want me on the basketball team. I don't know what to do!"

"How about both?" Gerald Thompson suggested from his easy chair. "You're a good athlete for age nine. You could handle two sports with no problem."

"It's too much," she said. "I already have school, homework, church, and Volunteer Club."

"Well, Princess," Gerald said, arching an eyebrow, "I suppose we could end the Thompson Family Game and Ice Cream Festival. We've been doing it for seven years, and maybe that's enough. It would free up your Saturday nights for—"

"No way!" Emily shrieked, bouncing around to look

Daddy square in the face. "It's my favorite thing in the whole world, and you know it!"

He smiled, and she realized he was teasing. "I could give up catechism," she countered. "That'd save three hours a week."

"Nice try," Gerald snickered. "Sounds like you need to choose one sport instead."

"I suppose," she sighed. "Tell me what to do, Daddy. I just can't decide."

Gerald shook his head, nestling her close. "The only real freedom any of us have is making our own decisions. I wouldn't dream of taking that away from you."

"Which means you don't want to choose," Emily pouted.

"You got that right," he said, getting up to turn off the set. Time for homework. "Let me know what you decide."

CHAPTER 13

Tuesday, 7 A.M.
Forty-seven hours till Emily's birthday

The Greek diner on Ogden Avenue bustled with mail carriers, garbage collectors, and other early-to-risers. "Hell with doughnuts, give me bacon and ham," Benedetti decided. "Preservatives are a cop's best friend."

Branch grinned from the other side of the booth and flagged the waitress. "Meat-lovers omelette with cheddar, please," he ordered. "Biscuits and gravy on the side."

"Make it two," Benedetti said.

"Three," Emily said. "With Egg Beaters, no cheese, and dry wheat toast."

"Sissy," Branch teased as the waitress disappeared. "Naperville detectives eat steel and shit nails."

Benedetti snorted. "I heard it was eat shit and steal."

Branch waggled his eyebrows. "Speaking of eating, you've lost weight since the library. Where's your vest?"

"She got it dirty," Benedetti said, blotting sweat from his forehead. "What's your excuse?"

Branch grinned. "I'm Superman. Bullets bounce off me."

The joke wasn't all that funny, but they guffawed, anyway. Benedetti's gaze rested on Emily's cheek several heartbeats longer than strictly business. He looked away and began dissecting the crime scenes.

Six coffees and a second, full-fat, omelette later—*Forget the thighs, I'm hungry!*—Emily shook her head. "There's no link in these cases but me."

"Give it time," Branch said. "We just started digging into Soull's life." He answered his phone, listened, said, "See you in fifteen." Then, to Benedetti and Emily, "Senior staff meeting."

"About?" Benedetti asked.

"The feds are coming."

Benedetti rolled his eyes.

"You got that right," Branch said. "FBI wants a piece of this. As do Homeland Security, the Secret Service, and the Bureau of Alcohol, Tobacco, Firearms and Explosives. You know, we might have the dreaded Islamofascists."

"Any excuse to stick their nose in."

"Yup. So Ken's forming a joint task force, headed by me. That way we control the investigation, and they provide federal resources. They won't like it, but tough." He crumpled his napkin. "You guys finish breakfast. I'll swing back when I'm done, pick up Emily."

"Back to Neuqua High?" she guessed.

"Back to bed."

She sputtered. "With all this going on?"

"You've worked twenty-four straight hours," Branch said. "You need shut-eye."

"No way!" Emily said. "I want in on this!"

"Who's arguing? But first you're going to rest. You're no

good to anyone this exhausted. Call me after you've gotten eight hours—"

"Four—"

"—and I'll tell your where to meet. It's still eight."

Emily knew he was right. Her fear and exhaustion had prompted that attack on Marty. She needed sleep. She still didn't like being left out, though, and shook her head.

"That's an order, Detective," Branch said.

"Yes sir, captain sir, chief of detectives sir," she grumbled, saluting.

Branch slid to the end of the booth. "Pour her some decaf, would you, Marty?" She stuck out her tongue as he threw a fist of tens on the table. "Back as soon as I can."

Benedetti moved to the other side. "Now what, Mr. Babysitter?" Emily said grumpily.

"Sleeping sucks when everything's popping," he said. "I know. But you gotta rest. You don't, you'll screw up bigtime." He raised his hands at her glare. "Yeah, yeah, shut up, Marty, or I'll pound you again."

"Couldn't have said it better myself," she said, somewhat mollified. "You know, the chief can't be pleased the FBI's involved."

"For damn sure." Two decades ago, an overly adrenalized FBI agent emptied his shotgun at Cross, then a Las Vegas Police undercover officer, who was chasing the violent bank robber they were jointly trying to capture. Cross dived behind a truck, but his backside didn't make it. The heavy lead buckshot tore off his right buttock. Cops being cops, Cross was tagged "Halfass" by fellow undercovers once they knew he'd live. He emerged from the hospital with a permanent limp, a career switch into management, and a lifelong distrust of feds. "They never did admit they were wrong," he said. "Not to this day."

"I didn't know that," Emily said. "Wow. That's so darn grade school."

"For some people life is grade school," Benedetti reminded, picking at his eggs. "You don't cuss much, do you?"

Emily reminded herself that Marty was a sharp observer. "You noticed."

"Hard not to. It's unusual for a cop. Especially rookies, who think they have to cuss like dockworkers to be tough. Are you offended by swearing?"

"No. Not at all."

"What then?"

"I made a promise about that when I was a kid," she said. "Still honoring it."

"Huh," he said, mulling that over. "How'd you feel going in there?"

"Where? The library?"

He nodded.

"Well . . ." She picked at a green pepper, recalling the fear that had turned her knees to putty. She'd known Marty a whole, what, twenty-six hours? Could she trust him? She played with the pepper some more, hoping it would provide some sort of guidance. Onions worked no better. So she looked up and said, "I was scared to death." Bitterness tinged her voice. "Yessir, nobody holds a candle to Emily Marie Bambi Child Thompson when it comes to courage."

"All those names, you must be Catholic," Benedetti said. "And being scared annoys you somehow?"

"Of course!" she barked. Heads turned, and she lowered her voice. "I hate being scared, Marty. I wanted to be brave, and all I did was shoot a hole in the floor." She explained her wayward trigger finger.

Benedetti raked his fingers through his locks. One flopped over his eyes, giving him a boyish look, which contrasted with the toughness of his angled facial planes. "Brave doesn't mean 'fearless,' you know. It means doing the right thing even if you're frightened."

"Don't remind me."

Benedetti chuckled. "I'm just getting started, Ossifer. You start the day with dead animals. An hour later you're kicking Ray Luerchen's butt. Poking through a decomposing Lucy Crawford. Finding severed heads in your mailbox. Subduing a naked kid by yourself, entering the library without hesitation. Charging across a shooting gallery to save Arnie Soull even though SWAT's a minute away and your partner's AWOL. You've worked twenty-six straight hours and could legitimately beg off from exhaustion. But the only thing you want to do is beat me up and get back on the street. Navy SEALs don't have that kind of moxie."

"And all this tells you what?" she asked, amazed at what Benedetti knew. "That I'm stupid?"

"Or reckless or brave, and the first two don't count."

"Thank you."

"That's not all. You're not only smart, not only courageous, you're . . ." He held up the breadbasket like a shield. "You sure you want to hear this? I don't want you hitting me without my bulletproof vest on. I'm delicate."

"I'll decide when you're done . . . Commander."

"Aw, geez, we're back to my rank," he groused, rolling his eyes. He dropped the basket, picked up his cup, and said, "You're pretty. Really pretty. Athletic. Smart. Brave. Nice." He pointed to her empty plate. "And you eat like a truck driver." He grinned at her withering glare. "Compliment. Too many women pick like little damn sparrows 'cause they're worried about what people might think if they eat normal. Branch is a big fan of yours. Points in my book because he's a superb judge of character. And another thing . . ."

Emily realized she was clenching her fists. This conversation was entering territory she wouldn't have dreamed possible yesterday. But she was interested. Very. She'd been asked to countless movies, concerts, dinners, and beds in the decade since Jack died. She felt nothing for the men—and several women—and kept saying thanks but no. After awhile she began hearing she was a "lez." The thought amused her. She liked men fine. She just felt still married and therefore was not dating.

"So anyway, Emily, I guess I'm saying I like you a whole damn lot. So what do you think about us having dinner sometime? . . ."

OK. There it is. Now what do I do about it?

"Say something wrong?" she heard him ask, and forced herself to pay attention.

"Wrong?" she parried. "What do you mean?"

"You're working that wedding ring like a twist top." His eyes crinkled in amusement as she whipped her hands apart. "I say something to make you nervous?"

"Of course not!" she said, the denial making her even more so. *You're not in grade school. This shouldn't be so difficult!* "How could I be nervous? You just said I was brave, right?"

"Mm-hm."

She started twisting again. "It's just that . . . well . . . I . . ."

"You're still married," he said. "And you don't want to cheat on Jack."

She stopped mid-twist. "Yes," she said, surprising herself. She'd never explained herself to anyone. "That's exactly how I feel. Ridiculous, huh?"

He raised his eyebrows a fraction. "Well, it has been ten years. When will you—"

"Get over it?" she snapped, throat constricting with anger. She hated people saying that! To think she'd thought Marty different! "Am I on a timetable? Did God come off the mountaintop and say, 'Two weeks to grieve, kid, then forget Jack existed'?" Silverware jumped as she slammed the table. "You have no idea what it's like to lose someone you love, Marty! No idea at all!"

Benedetti glanced at the hopping forks, went back to her face. The manager started over, concerned. Marty waved him away. She found herself not wanting to finish the tirade, after all. So she limped it home with, "Anyway, that's how I feel."

Benedetti finished his coffee with a long slurp. "So I gather."

Emily looked at him closely, hoping his feelings weren't hurt. She hadn't wanted to wound his pride. More selfishly, if she ever reentered the romance market—not that she would, of course—she might give Marty a whirl. He was Old Spice, not Chanel. Strong. Sure of himself. Tender under the brontosaurus hide. Said what he meant, meant what he said. Had a clumsy charm she found endearing. Good at what he did, obviously loved it, had the respect of people she admired. Listened, really listened, a trait she treasured for its rarity. But, of course, she wasn't interested in romance any more . . . She was married . . . She was faithful . . . She'd buried those feelings with Jack. . . .

"Let's wait outside for Branch," she said.

Benedetti phoned to tell him where they'd be. She paid the bill, and they walked to the back of the parking lot. They got to his car, and Emily stopped, staring. The black Trans Am was as rusty as a Louisiana garbage scow. Its back bumper hung crooked to the left, front bumper crooked to the right. A spiderweb of cracks crazed the rear window. Roof and hood were ragged as cat-clawed silk. Dents warped the passenger door so out of true, it was hard to open. Handle chrome dug into her palm. "Where'd you find this thing?" she demanded. "A flea market?"

Marty grinned.

She yanked the balky door just wide enough to squeeze inside. It proved no better, with sun-blistered dash and carpeting thin as paint. The upholstery reeked of fast food. She planted a heel to steady herself, and a ragged square of sheet metal popped off, providing a bird's-eye view of the lot.

Benedetti slid in and started the car with a surprisingly

silky *vroom*. "Never judge a book by its cover," he said. "Or beauty's only skin-deep, pick your cliché." He flipped on the heater to take off the chill. A half dozen cars and a white minivan queued up to turn onto Ogden Avenue, their slots instantly filled by waiting vehicles. Grandma Sally's hopped now that the sun was up. "A heroin smuggler owned this. He lost it to the county in a raid."

"The engine's smoother than I expected," Emily conceded. "Did the smuggler soup it up?"

Benedetti goosed the accelerator, jumping the car like a pogo stick. "I did. This is my race car."

Emily blinked.

"I drive the amateur racing circuit," he explained. "County fairs, horse tracks, what have you. If it's got prize money, I'm there." He grinned. "If it doesn't, I'm there, anyway. Beer's free."

"Racing, huh? How did you get into that?"

"I was pretty burned out eleven years ago. Needed a hobby to get my head straight." He adjusted the mirror. "I've loved muscle cars since I was a kid, so I figured why not? Me and Love Shack won our first race together and never looked back. We're three-time champs of the Midwest League."

"Cool!" Emily said, stretching her shoulders loose. "But why Love Shack? You a ladies' man?"

Benedetti's laugh was a buttery-rich baritone. "Sad to say, I never quite got the hang of that. It's the name of my sponsor. A good-ol'-boy tavern run by a fishing buddy."

"Don't sponsors want their names on their investments?"

Benedetti hooked his thumb toward the back. "Magnetic signs. I attach them for races, take 'em off for work. Shack's particularly useful in robbery stakeouts, where high-speed chases aren't unknown. There's so many horses under this hood, the bad guy's fucked before his panties are down." He put his hand to his mouth like he'd sworn in church. "Oops. I shouldn't encourage your terrible potty mouth."

She punched his shoulder. He faked wincing. "Listen, I'm sorry I yelled at you," she said. "I get kind of defensive sometimes."

"No kidding," Benedetti said, patting his chest. "But what I was trying to say back there was, When will you ever know you're ready?"

The black notes under the question made her ask her own in the form of a reply. "I don't know, Marty. Does anybody?"

He shook his head. "It's tough. But you've got to move on."

"Why?" Emily pressed, not to argue, but to find out if he had an answer for the question that had plagued her since Jack's funeral. "Why should you have to move on?"

"Because living in the past is no damn good," he said. "We've got to keep our eyes on the future, because that's where the . . . well, future is." He shook his head. "Gee, Marty, that's profound." A cell phone rang. Emily's hand drifted to her belt.

"Mine," Benedetti said, answering. "Hey, Branch." He listened, face darkening, then handed her the phone.

"What?" Emily said.

"He just paid another visit."

"No!" she gasped. "Where?"

"You know those woods east of Neuqua? Separate the school from the strip mall and Y?"

"Uh-huh . . ."

"Your police card was tacked on a tree branch. Apparently, the Unsub parked at the mall, shot a fireman hauling ladders to the east wing of the school, then fled. A TV cameraman stumbled across the body a few minutes ago."

Emily found it hard to breathe. "Where are you?"

"Leaving the station. I'll be there in ten minutes."

Emily closed the phone, handed it to Marty, and pressed her eyes with icy hands. "Another innocent person is dead," she groaned. "They'd be alive if it wasn't for me."

"Wrong!" Benedetti snapped, backhanding her forearm so hard she yipped. "Some brain-dead scumbag murdered those people, not you!" Softer, "You are not the subject perpetrating multiple illegalities upon the populace, Detective Thompson. The Unsub is."

"I suppose you're right." She blew out her breath. "He tell you about the fireman?"

"Poor guy," Benedetti sympathized. "All he wants out of life is to play with his hoses and ladders, and he goes and gets himself shot." His face lit up. "Hey!"

"Chutes and Ladders!" she yelped, getting it.

"Monopoly, Duck Duck Goose, Boggle, Clue, now Chutes and Ladders," Benedetti said, counting on his fingers. "That's five. What's left?"

"Operation, I Spy, and Timebomb," she said. "Unless Neuqua counts as Timebomb, which we won't know till the arson investigation's finished." She began speculating on the Unsub's next move, but it came out a yawn. "I need some sleep," she mumbled.

He nodded. "Branch will run you home. I'll fill in the sheriff, then rejoin you."

"Yeah," she said, the word "home" banging around in her head. She desperately needed the rest but couldn't stand the thought of reentering the empty log cabin. It represented security, which was enormously appealing right now. Comfort and familiarity, equally so. But it also meant cooking for one. Laughing at her own jokes. Scratching her back with doorknobs, needing only half the king-size bed, and then only to sleep. The manless, childless, puppyless existence she'd cloaked herself in since Jack's death just wasn't enough anymore. "You know what, Marty?" she said. "I never did answer your question."

"Which was?"

"Did I want to have dinner sometime?"

"Oh," Benedetti said. "That. I completely forgot."

"Yeah, right." She paused to gather her thoughts. "Jack was a telephone engineer. With Bell Labs here in Naperville. I was the office manager for a small insurance company in Chicago. I ordered some new equipment, and he arrived with the crew to troubleshoot. Our eyes met, and I fell pretty hard." She groped for just the right words. "His classiness, his confidence, the way he moved and dressed, being older and wiser . . . I was hooked. Guess he felt the same way, because he asked me out to dinner the day the installation was finished. One thing led to another. We got married and moved here." She waved toward downtown Naperville. "The log cabin was his wedding present to me."

"Beats a vacuum cleaner," Benedetti said.

She laughed. "Jack would never do that. Gadgets weren't his style. He was high-tech at work, but when it came to real life, he was happiest in the 1800s. He greatly admired that period—the simplicity, the values, the social certainties."

"The good old days."

"Uh-huh. But he was fun, too. Not stuffy like you'd assume for a history buff. We had some great times. Then he died." She drew a deep breath. "Jack wasn't buried twenty minutes when his best friend hit on me. I said no. I've been saying no ever since." She worried the wedding ring again. "Marty, it's been ten years. A quarter of my entire life! But I have no idea if that's 'too long,' or 'not long enough.' I visit Jack every day—the cemetery is the halfway point of my morning run—and so far I haven't let anything intrude on that." She moved her hands apart. "Not until now."

Delight creased Benedetti's face. "So you do want to have dinner with me?"

"I think so," she said. "Buuuut . . ."

"Buuuut . . ." Benedetti mimicked without a hint of condescension, "it might be cheating on Jack. But you like the idea, anyway. But you want it strictly dinner because anything else is just too complicated right now. But it's been ten

years, so the idea of dinner and, uh, dancing appeals enormously. But you can't, not yet, anyway, and would I have any
chance of understanding all that since I'm just another piggy
guy who wants only one thing?"

Emily patted his shoulder. "You're even smarter than
Columbo."

"Damn straight. But seriously, all I want right now is dinner."

"Really?"

"Yeah." He paused, and the earlier black notes resurfaced.
"I've got things, too."

"Your wife?" she said, recalling Annie's report.

He nodded once, small. "Late. Like Jack."

"Oh! Marty!" She clutched her knees. "I had no idea. I'm
so sorry."

"Me, too. Bone cancer. I watched her shrivel away. She
was a terrific gal and didn't deserve it." He stared at the
steering wheel. Her heart ached for him, and she asked if he
wanted to talk about it.

"No," he said. "There's enough bad topics on our plate.
Let's save that conversation for dinner."

Emily closed her eyes. "It's been forever since I cooked.
Hope I remember how."

"Cooked," Benedetti said. "Like at your house?"

"Mm-hm," she said. "I make a lamb curry so spicy even
your battery-acid tongue can taste it."

"Sounds great," he said. "All right if I bring the kids?"

Annie hadn't mentioned that! "I didn't know you had
children."

"Yup. Four. Fortunately, they're housebroken."

She blinked. "As in—"

"My beagles," Benedetti said, popping his off-kilter grin.
"Moe, Larry, Curly, and Branch."

He likes animals! This is getting better and better! "Dinner with the Five Stooges," she enthused. "This is gonna be one terrific date."

"Uh-uh!" Benedetti protested, waving his hands. "No date! Just dinner!" The grin turned sly. "Though maybe we ought to find a restaurant, not tempt fate. We hang out at your house, there's no telling what we'll have for dessert."

"Well, maybe you're right," she said, feeling like she was sixteen. "But I want to hear about your wife, and it's hard to do that in a restaurant. You come over. Definitely bring the kids."

"You don't mind hair on your furniture?"

Emily shook her head. "I adore dogs, Marty. I'll get some nice bones from the butcher."

"Get the fat, too. They like that," Benedetti said, beaming. "I'll pick up a '65 Bordeaux. It's an exceptional vintage."

"That's the year I was born," Emily mused. "1965."

Benedetti drew so close, she could smell the warm spiciness of his skin. "I know. I read your personnel file."

He began tracing her jawline. She closed her eyes, brought her face to his. He brushed her lips with his fingers. She kissed one callused tip, then the next, flushing from sudden warmth. She moved her lips toward his for the kiss.

"Dum-da-dum-dum," he murmured, gently pushing her away.

"Branch just showed up, right?" Emily said, eyes still closed.

"Uh-huh."

"Aw, let him get his own date." She opened her eyes and brushed her hair into place, hands shaking from the fire of the almost kiss. They exited Love Shack and waved over the unmarked car. Branch pulled up and rolled down his window. He detailed the firefighter's shooting, they did likewise on Chutes and Ladders, then Benedetti purred off to see the sheriff. Branch and Emily rolled west on Ogden Avenue. "Nice breakfast?" he asked as they passed Washington.

"Exceptional," she said as they passed Royal St. George Drive.

Branch arched an eyebrow. "Something you want to tell me, Detective?"

"No." She relaxed into the stiff cop-car seat. "Well, maybe. Branch, can we stop by a forest preserve? That one on River Road maybe? I need to uncurl my brain, and I do it best with trees. Then I'll go sleep, promise."

He called their location into dispatch and a few minutes later slowed for the turn into McDowell Grove Forest Preserve, several hundred acres of hardwoods, meadows, and hiking trails watered by the same DuPage River that edged the bottom of Emily's hill. He wasn't turning fast enough for the car on his bumper, and the driver blasted her horn while popping both middle fingers so vigorously it looked like juggling. "Probably flipping me off with her toes, too," Branch laughed. He waved an apology. "You like Marty, don't you?"

"I like him a lot," she murmured.

"Sorry, didn't catch that," Branch said, cupping his right ear.

"Just clearing my throat," Emily said.

The car went silent. Emily searched for something to fill it, some inanity about the weather perhaps, as a half dozen clouds pregnant with rain drifted into view. She hoped they'd keep moving since the CSIs didn't need more aggravation—raindrops wiped out evidence like industrial solvents. Several cars followed them into the forest preserve. The place was bustling for the early hour, but then again school was out for one of those unfathomable "teacher institutes." The clouds hovered. A small enameled sign on the bridge arching the river announced CAUTION! SLIPPERY WHEN WET!

Branch eased though the hairpin turn into the parking lot. Little girls scrambled along the riverbank, giggling and throwing sticks and leaves. Emily envied their carefree abandon. She glanced at the long wooden picnic table where a half dozen animated moms poured coffee from a stainless-steel thermos. Steam curled and danced in the cool riverside air. In the Kodak moment of life without monsters, she felt her anxieties tumble away.

"Want to take a walk?" Branch said, shutting off the engine. "Talk about it?"

Emily nodded. The river was a broken mirror of clouds and sunlight. Shoreside daffodils were starting to bud. In a few weeks they'd trumpet their full yellow glory. The pregnant clouds dipped low, merged as one. The girls sang something about a bear going over a mountain to see what he could see, and she was seized by a hunger for Marty so intense, she hadn't realized how hard she'd been suppressing it. The bear went over the mountain, the moms poured more coffee, the clouds drifted.

She exited and walked behind the car to join Branch, who was fiddling with the gas cap. A white minivan rolled through the hairpin. She kicked a leaf gob off the crusted mud flap. The van slowed. She glanced its way. It looked familiar. Branch muttered, banging the cap with a knuckle. The van stopped, and the driver's window inched down. An alarm began ringing in Emily's head. She stared openly. The van *was* familiar. She'd seen it at Grandma Sally's, waiting for traffic to clear. A sun shaft poked from the clouds to illuminate the driver's bulbous face . . . shiny . . . helmetlike hat pulled low on his forehead . . . strawberry birthmark on his left lower jaw . . . Hey, didn't the naked kid at the library say the birthday-card man had a strawberry . . .

"The Unsub! It's him!" Emily screamed, reaching for her gun.

The driver's hands snapped up, lighting the gloom with the stutter-flash of submachine-gun fire. Girls screamed as moms dove on them, blood and coffee drenching the picnic table. Emily shoveled her Glock in front of her face, no time to think just fire-fire-fire. Branch joined in with his Colt .45, roaring "Police, don't move, don't move!" Emily knew that she was screaming because she felt it in her throat, that she was firing from the jerk-jerk-jerk in her fist. She couldn't hear shots, couldn't hear anything, but watched orange flames spurt from the Glock's steel snout—*one-two-three-nine*—and bullet holes pock the van and the Unsub's cherry Windbreaker. But he wasn't falling, just sitting there, calm, turning the deadly stream their way. Emily crouched for the protection of the engine block, then remembered Branch wasn't wearing his bulletproof vest and instead leapfrogged sideways, arms flailing over her head, trying to stretch herself larger. A laser gunsight lit her midsection. Then a million sledgehammers slammed home, pounding breath from her lungs. "Ahh," she hissed, all her joints melting. The Glock skittered across the parking stripes. Her head cracked off the blacktop, and, vision fuzzing, she splayed herself over Branch's limp body. She absorbed the bullet stream but felt several thwock Branch's exposed hip. She begged her arms to grab the .45 from Branch's unmoving hand, but they refused—her muscles were frozen solid from the shock wave. Helpless, she watched the Unsub hop out of the van, run to her, rip her father's bayonet from her boot sheath and her handcuffs from her gun belt, jump back in the van, throw her a sloppy kiss, and roar up the driveway to freedom.

Uhnnnnnnnh. She was shot to pieces, unable to move, unable to feel, dying like Daddy, like Mama, like Jack, like Lucy and Arnie and firefighter and birds. Black fog shrouded her head, and the bagpipes chanted "Amazing Grace." Then the music faded, and the fog began lifting. "Why are you doing this?" she screamed at the lingering wisps of exhaust. "What do you want from me?" A strangled "wuhhhhh" was all that emerged. A tear slid as she realized how perilously close to death she was and what little she could do about it. She managed to gargle to the form under her, "Branch . . . talk . . . me." No reply.

A mom bleeding from both arms ran over. "Officer!" she screamed. "Do something!"

Emily tried bending her neck, but it hurt too bad. "Call 911," she gasped. "Hurry."

"Omigod! You're that cop from TV!" She tried Emily's phone, but it was cracked and useless. She ran to the picnic table and grabbed a purse the size of Detroit, dumping the contents, running back, dialing 911. "Hello! Hello! Hello!" she shouted. "There's been a terrible shooting! Get here quick! Hurry!"

"Hold . . . phone . . . so I talk," Emily said. The mom squatted, held out the phone with quaking arms. "Who . . . this?" Emily asked, jamming her ear into the phone.

"This is Naperville 911—"

"McDowell Forest Preserve!" Emily yelled, throat burning. "Parking lot!"

"Emily? Is that you?" Jodi said. "What's happening?"

"Officers down! Unsub! Mayday!" Emily stopped as coughs racked her body. The mom pulled her into a sitting position. "Automatic-weapons fire! Civilians shot! We need help!"

"Police and fire enroute Code 13," Jodi reassured her. "Are you injured?"

Emily's lungs screamed as she forced out the Unsub's description. She heard the alert tones of ISPERN, the Illinois State Police Emergency Radio Network, which every cop in the state monitored. Jodi was sending in the marines. "We need paramedics. Lots."

"Are you hit, Emily?" Jodi demanded.

"Yes . . . hit. Branch hit, too," Emily said. "Oh, he's hit real bad." She listened for sirens, heard none, felt as alone as the day Mama died. "Jodi?" she asked, despising the anxious squeak in her voice. "Is anybody . . . coming . . . to help?"

"The whole world's coming, Detective," interrupted a voice she didn't know. "Lay down and relax, and I'll take care of you. Police, paramedics, and a medevac helicopter will reach your location in five minutes." Pause. "Who was shot? Tell me everyone who's shot."

"Me," Emily mumbled. "But I'm not bleeding. I was wearing my vest." Her vision fuzzed a second time. "Branch shot, too. He's next to me. On ground. Not moving. Then some moms." She looked at her helper, who held up three fingers. "Three moms hit. They're still alive. Some little girls, too"—the mom flashed zeroes—"but they're OK. Not hit." She recognized the new voice. Chief Cross. She knew now Branch would live. Chief did everything perfectly. He'd save Branch. Save everyone. He would, he just *would*. "We came here to clear our heads. Not goofing off, Chief, coming right back to work."

"I know that," Cross said. "You just hang tight, Emily. We'll be there in four minutes."

Emily. She was absurdly pleased at Cross using her first name, and now she could hear sirens. "I'm going to check out the chief, Branch—"

"Emily!" Cross interrupted. "I want you to lie down. You're difficult to understand. You might have a concussion. Did you hit your head?"

She didn't know. It happened so fast. "Look at my head?" she asked the mom. "See if I'm bleeding."

The mom patted somewhere Emily couldn't feel, displayed her palm. It was red with blood and gravel bits. "Blood on my head," Emily reported. "Doesn't hurt. I have to wake up Branch. He's still not moving . . . oh God." Panic body-slammed her back twenty years to Mama's paralysis. She struggled to focus. "Chief, he might be dead—"

"Don't talk anymore," Cross said. "Save your strength. You've done everything you can, Emily. Let me take it from here. In three minutes there'll be all the help you need. OK?" No answer. "Emily! Will you let me take care of you?"

"Roger wilco over and out," she mumbled, the phrase popping into her consciousness from one of the cop shows she'd watched from Daddy's lap. The mom stripped off her orange cable-knit sweater and shoved it under Branch's head. Her expression clearly said, "This guy's a goner," but her mouth said, "I'm sure he'll be all right, Officer. Is he your partner or something?"

Emily twisted her ring. "He's . . . he's my . . ." She struggled to her knees, pain hitting like an armored car. The mom grabbed her arm. "The sirens are close," she said. "You should lie down."

"No. Just help me with him."

"OK, Officer, whatever you say." The mom positioned her, and Emily put her fingers on Branch's neck, willing her hand not to tremble. She pulled back, panting, motioning for the mom to try. She did, nodded excitedly. "He's still alive, Officer! What should I do?"

Emily pointed to the picnic table. "Go take care of them. Keep the cell phone. Chief Cross will talk you through anything else you need to do."

"But what about—"

"Go help your friends!" Emily commanded. "Those girls cannot lose their mothers like this, understand? You can make sure they don't. Now go!"

The mom hesitated, then hurried away. Emily turned back to Branch and examined him. No obvious bleeding, but who knew what was under his clothes. "Oh, Branch, you should never have taken off your vest," she sniffled, stroking his ashen face.

"No kidding," Branch groaned back.

"Oh!" she gasped.

Branch opened his eyes, grinned weakly. "Em. Are you hit?"

"My vest saved me," Emily assured him.

"Saved me . . . too. Thank . . . thank you."

"Enough of that," Emily said, squeezing his arms. "How do you feel? Try to move."

Branch's face pinched. "Can't. Muscles are screwed up. Getting hard . . . to breathe . . ."

"All right, don't talk," Emily said. "Save your strength." The first police cruiser skidded sideways through the hairpin. Emily, alarmed, looked to the splintered table. "Get everyone inside the picnic shelter!" she shouted. "Now!"

"Why?" the mom yelled back. "Help's here. We're perfectly safe!"

"A hundred cops will arrive in the next few seconds, and one of them will plow into you by accident." A second black-and-white screamed in—*thank God, it's Annie!*—then several more. "Do it now! Hurry!" The mom saw how far the cars were sliding and grabbed an armful of girls.

"Good . . . idea," Branch croaked. "Don't need . . . anyone else . . . dying."

"You're not going to die! I won't let you!" Emily snapped as the first ambulance raced into the lot, spitting gravel. She heard rotor blades beat air overhead. "The medevac's here, Branch," she said. "You'll be at the hospital in two minutes."

"It's Channel Seven," Annie Bates growled as she ran up. "Dammit to hell." She keyed her radio. "News choppers on scene. Can you clear them out so the medevac can land?"

"Working on it," Cross replied. "But negative on medevac. Grounded with rotor problems. I rerouted another flight, but it won't reach your location for nineteen minutes."

"Too long," Annie said.

"Doesn't matter," Branch grunted, sweat pouring off his

face. "Emily won't let me die. Did somebody call my . . . call my wife? . . ."

"Awk!" Emily gagged as a geyser of blood blasted her square in the face. "Help!" She fought desperately for air, gagging and coughing to clear her lungs.

"Rupture!" Annie shouted, ramming her hands atop the flood. Blood sprayed sideways through her fingers. "Right thigh! Femoral artery's torn! I can't stop it!"

Emily roared like a wounded grizzly, knocked Annie's hands aside, and plunged her fingers deep into the bullet holes. Warm pulpy tissue sucked in around them, forming a seal. "Is it stopped?" she shouted, feeling Branch pulse against her fingers. "I can't see a thing through this blood!"

"Slowed! Not stopped!" Annie said. "Work your fingers toward me, Emily. That's it, keep going." Blood arced high over their heads. "Too far! Pull back! Good, little more my way. Halt. Perfect. Bleeding's stopped. Don't move."

Emily's hands were already cramping. "This won't work too long," she groaned. "Get him to the hospital!"

"We'll take it from here, Emily!" shouted Viking, the paramedic from the library, as he ran their way. "Move out of the way. Give us room to work!"

"I can't," Emily wailed. "A bullet ripped his femoral artery! If I move, he'll bleed out!"

Viking dropped to his knees. "She's right," he announced as the ambulance backed their way. "OK, everyone, we'll patch the rest of Branch's wounds to prevent further bleeding. Then Emily pulls out her fingers. I clamp off the artery and pack the femoral hole. It'll hold just long enough to get him to Edward." He looked pointedly at the driver, who replied by goosing her accelerator.

"Good. Emily, don't move till I tell you. Rest of you, hop on those wounds."

Emily nodded, biting her lip as the paramedic cloud

swarmed. "Transport begins the instant he's stable," the driver radioed. "We cannot, repeat, cannot stop for any reason."

"Understood," Cross radioed back. "Don't take Washington Street. It's jammed with rush-hour traffic. I've shut down River Road. Go into Edward the back way."

"Copy that. I will take River Road."

Viking put his surgical clamps next to Emily's fingers. "Ready?"

Emily gritted her teeth as the arm spasms moved into her shoulders. "Ready."

"On three, pull your fingers out. One, two, three."

"Ahh!" she screamed, falling backwards, fingers popping out like wine corks. Blood sluiced into the air as Viking's metal clamps disappeared into the hole. Moments later the bleeding stopped. Three other medics poured in Israeli Army instant-clot drugs, then packed the bloody wound with gauze.

"Go! Go!" Viking commanded. Branch's gurney shot up like an elevator, two dozen cop-car sirens kicked on, paramedics piled in back, and nine seconds later the ambulance was howling through the hairpin and out of the forest. Viking turned to Emily, who was curled sideways under a blanket, with Annie stroking her hair and face. "How do you feel, Detective?"

Emily's body was one giant cramp. "Yeah!"

"Wrong answer. How do you feel?"

"Oh! I'm all right!"

Viking nodded noncommittally, glanced at the vitals monitor the other medics had attached. "Blood pressure's a bit low. How 'bout a ride to the hospital?"

She groaned, trying not to weep from the vicious pain stabbing from everywhere.

Viking motioned for a gurney, held up thumb, index, and little fingers. "How many do you see?"

She squinted. "Three."

"What month is this?"

"April."

"When's your birthday?"

"May 1."

"How old will you be?"

"Forty."

"Who is Hercules Branch?"

"Don't call him Hercules. He hates that."

Relieved grin. "Let's get you to Edward. . . ."

A couple minutes later the ambulance doors flung open. Emily peered under her armpit at an endless sea of cops weaving and undulating like blue prairie grass. Marty Benedetti sprinted her way like a man possessed. *Why on earth is he covered in blood?* she wondered. News choppers darted like metal dragonflies. She wanted to give them the finger but couldn't lift her arms. White coats cut off her uniform as they wheeled her through the blue grass. "I kept him alive," Emily mumbled as they flew into the emergency room. "Don't you let him die . . . don't let . . . don't let . . ."

Then the world faded.

CHAPTER 14

Tuesday, 11 A.M.
Forty-three hours till Emily's birthday

The angel walked closer, the bright light from above burnishing its halo. Emily tried to see its face, but her eyes hurt too much to keep them open. Her chest burned with each breath.

"Am . . . am I dead?" she asked. "Are my parents here? Jack?" She forced her lids apart. She had to know.

The angel shook its head. A muscled arm descended, and a long, polished finger touched her lips. She felt a tingle where it touched her cracked flesh.

"Am I dead?" she repeated. "Is this . . . heaven?"

The angel shook its head more insistently, then put a finger to its lips.

"Shhhhhhhh," the angel breathed. "Shhhhhhhhh . . ."

Emily blinked once, twice, and then the world faded again.

CHAPTER 15

Tuesday, 3 P.M.
Thirty-nine hours till Emily's birthday

"Where am I?" Emily croaked as she fluttered awake. Her body throbbed. Machines by her bed pumped fluid into the back of her hand, sucked it from under her green gown. She tried to sit up.

An alarm sounded, and a pretty brunette with caring eyes hurried into the room, stethoscope bouncing. "Welcome back," she said, reading the monitors. "We missed you."

Emily, dizzy, sank back into the pillows. "What is this place?"

"Edward Hospital. Intensive care unit."

Emily stared. "Who are you?"

"Dr. Barbara Winslow. Chief of the trauma unit. I'm your doctor."

Emily's heart churned as she recalled the angelic vision. "A real doctor?"

"As opposed to what?" Winslow said. "Action Medical Barbie? I'm the real thing, Detective."

Emily sighed in relief. "Thank God. Last time I opened my eyes, I saw an angel. I was afraid I was dead."

Winslow's eyes crinkled. "That 'angel' was probably a nurse giving you an injection. Or one of the ten million police running through here during your eight-hour blackout." She smirked. "Plus one sneaky TV reporter trying to get an exclusive. I bounced him good and hard, let me tell you—"

"Eight hours?" Emily gasped, wrenching upright. "I've been unconscious that long?" A machine squawked in protest.

"Mm-hm," Winslow confirmed, placing a lightly freckled hand on her arm. "Please relax. Budgets the way they are, you break my heart monitor, they won't give me another."

Emily tried laughing, but it came out a hack. "What's your name again?"

"Winslow. Dr. Barbara Winslow. What should I call you? Detective, Emily, or Miss Thompson?"

"Missus," she said automatically, squinting against the overbright room. "But call me Emily." She winced at the spasms in her rib cage. "God, I hurt."

"That's actually good news," Winslow explained, walking to the sink. "A couple inches either way with those bullets and you'd be having this conversation with St. Peter, not me. Ergo, pain is good."

"Ergo?"

"Catholic education. What can I say?" She dried her hands, untied Emily's gown, and worked her fingers around. "Good," she murmured, each press eliciting a gasp. "Very good."

"Easy for you to say," Emily groaned.

"It's extremely easy," Winslow said, rolling Emily to check her backside, "considering you were shot twenty-four times."

Emily's toes curled at the unbelievable number.

"We counted the bruises," Winslow explained. "Your bulletproof vest did its job keeping the bullets from penetrating, but the shock waves beat you badly. In essence, there were two dozen hammers, and you were the nail. You'll ache for several weeks."

Emily gingerly pressed one, which was as black as a week-old banana. She clamped her jaw against the radiating pain. "Any permanent damage?"

Winslow redraped the gown. "None. You're incredibly lucky. You've got the body bruises. Several cuts, but they're shallow. No plastic surgery indicated. You don't have an infection or rib fractures." She pointed to Emily's skull. "You banged your head awfully hard, so we did a CAT scan. There's no concussion or fracture."

"But I blacked out," Emily said. "Why did that happen if I'm not badly injured?"

"Your chief told me you hadn't slept since dawn yesterday," Winslow said. "You desperately needed rest, and your body seized the opportunity."

"I don't remember it."

"There's no sensation of time passing when you're unconscious."

"I see." She didn't, actually, but was too weary to care. "How did I get here?"

Winslow walked back to the sink. "You arrived in an ambulance," she said. "After the shooting. You passed out, I worked you up, and now you're awake." She washed and dried again.

Emily ran her tongue over her teeth. "When can I go back to work?"

Winslow picked up a clipboard, wrote as she talked. "Not for awhile. You'll stay three days for observation and physical therapy. Then you'll rest at home till the bruises get lighter."

"I don't have three days," Emily said, explaining the birthday deadline.

"Oh, dear," Winslow said, frowning. "Nobody told me. Doesn't matter, though. You need to stay. Sometimes injuries take several days to manifest themselves, and I want you here if that happens. We have excellent security, Emily. You're safer here than on the street."

Emily shook her head. "This Unsub is exceptionally dangerous," she said. "Your security can't handle him. I don't even know if we can. If I stay here, he'll kill doctors, nurses, and patients to get to me. He'll kill anyone." The thought of more innocents dying cemented her determination to leave as soon as possible. "Don't make me check myself out."

Winslow was clearly unhappy. "I can't hold you against your will—"

"No. You can't."

"All right. If you insist on leaving, at least let me prepare you."

"How?"

"I'll get physical therapy up here right away to get you out of bed and moving. Soon as you can walk normally, you can go. You'll have pain from the bruises, but everything else should be all right." She wrote the therapy order, stuffed it in her pocket. "Any questions about your treatment? About anything?"

Emily shook her head. The room swayed. "Nothing right now."

"I'll stop by later and check on you. But you're going to recover just fine." Winslow headed for the door. "By the way," she tossed over her shoulder, "what you did for Branch was magnificent. We're all proud of you."

"What do you mean?"

Winslow turned and stuck her tongue out. "C'mon, don't be modest," she teased. "The paramedics told me how you saved his life. Take the bow—you deserve it."

"I'm not being modest. I don't know what you're talking about."

The doctor's brows beetled. "You don't remember putting your fingers in Branch's thigh?"

"These?" Emily replied, staring at her hands. "They're clean, Doctor. How could they have been inside someone?"

Winslow walked to the bed. "You were attacked this morning at McDowell Forest Preserve on the city's north side. Detective Captain Hercules Branch was shot at the same time, as were several civilians."

"Branch . . ." Emily murmured, scrunching up her face to think. "You mentioned that name. It sounds familiar."

"Your friend. Your boss," Winslow prompted. "Hit by submachine-gun bullets. Started geysering blood from his femoral artery. You thrust your fingers into the holes and plugged—"

"Branch! Omigod!" Emily shrieked, the incident roaring back in Technicolor. "Is he all right? Tell me, Doctor. He's got to be all right—"

"He's alive," Winslow interrupted, dropping the clipboard and taking Emily's hands. "But he was critically injured. He's still in surgery."

Emily was drowning in Branch's blood. "Eight hours?"

"Yes. He might go another eight. Or twenty. Nobody knows for sure."

"Got a minute, Chief?"

Cross turned to the FBI agent. "Sure. Make any sense out of those case summaries?"

"More than you might think," the agent said, flipping to a yellow Post-It. "Operation is one of the girl's games, right?"

"She's not a girl," Cross said.

"Whatever. I think there's a connection between your

Unsub and the murder of that Massachusetts trooper last Christmas. . . ."

Five minutes later Cross slapped the agent's back, stopped at the auditorium to order the task force to nail down the connection, then headed for the hospital.

Emily felt tired beyond anything she'd ever known. "I promised Branch he wouldn't die," she whispered. "I killed everyone else I ever loved. I'm not going to kill Branch, too. I won't!"

Winslow's pager buzzed. She read the message, frowned. "I'm sorry, Emily, I have to deal with this. Try to get some sleep, and we'll talk later." She headed out the door, and Emily closed her eyes, murmuring the only prayer she could remember from catechism—"The Lord is my shepherd, I shall not want"—but was interrupted at "the still waters" by a buttery baritone voice.

"Branch is gonna make it, you know. He's too damn ugly for heaven."

"It's you!" she peeped, eyes popping open. "Thank God, it's you!"

"In the flesh," Benedetti said. "Damn, you look fantastic!" He rushed to the bed and enveloped her, careful not to touch the bruises. Her eyes leaked tears, and he dried them with his thumbs. Then picked up her hands, kissing each passionately.

"Hurts," Emily groaned.

"Oh, geez, sorry," Benedetti said, dropping them like hot rocks.

"It's OK. It's just everything feels like I went fifteen rounds with Godzilla."

"You did," Benedetti said, scooting over a chair. "But you won. You're alive." His voice was husky with worry.

She reached up and stroked his cheeks. "You're alive,

too," she whispered. "Thank God, you're alive . . . uh . . ." *Oh, no.* Her memory was so fried she couldn't even remember the name of this wonderful man she'd just decided . . . *Wait! It's Marty! Martin Benedetti! Don't forget!*

They talked, touching each other's arms and hands, till Emily's eyelids sagged. "Hospitals suck," she murmured, shifting for the umpteenth time. "I can't wait to sleep in my own bed."

"That'll be awhile," Benedetti said. "You're going to a safe house when you're released."

Emily flushed, anger trumping exhaustion. "You mean hiding."

"Tomato, tomahto. But we'll talk about that later. First, we need to—"

"I could kill Branch for not wearing his vest," Emily whispered. Her eyes leaked again, but she had no strength to wipe. "I could just kill him."

"Me, too," Benedetti agreed, handing her a Kleenex. They sat quietly, thinking private thoughts. Then Emily forced herself to remember. "He stole my knife, Marty," she began, fragments appearing out of the fog. "The World War II bayonet of Daddy's that I carry in my boot. The freak walked right up and took it. I couldn't stop him because I couldn't move."

Benedetti jotted notes. "Your handcuffs are also missing. Did he take those, too?"

She shrugged, having no idea. "You know what's weird? My gun. Why didn't he take that? It was on the pavement, right in front of him. Why only my knife and cuffs?"

"Guess we're gonna find out."

She touched a bruise to make sure she was alive. Pain said yes. Her mind flicked to the strobe light of bullets flying from the Unsub's weapon. "He shot so fast, Marty. What was it?"

"A Heckler & Koch MP-5 submachine gun," Benedetti

said. "Serious weapon. Expensive and hard to get unless you're in law enforcement."

"Ammunition?"

"Nine-millimeter ball. U.S. military surplus."

"He's a soldier?" she said, stirring. "Marty! Maybe the Pentagon can tell us—"

"Doesn't mean squat," Benedetti said, tugging at a sideburn. "Millions of civilians buy military surplus for target practice. It's cheap and available worldwide. We know the manufacturer from the ejected shell casings. He'll provide the distributor, who'll give us the retailer. Maybe we'll get lucky."

"Smart as this guy's been?"

He didn't contradict.

She shifted uncomfortably. "If Branch got shot so many times, why isn't he, uh, you know—"

"More injured?"

She appreciated his choice of words. "Right."

"Because of you. Your vest shielded his head, chest, and major organs, so the bullets struck only his lower body."

"Uh, the femoral artery, right?"

He intertwined his fingers in hers. "Hey, your memory's coming back!"

"Hardly. Dr. Winslow told me," she said. "I don't remember any of it. From what she says, it's a miracle he's alive."

"You're Branch's miracle, Emily. You're a hero. Especially to me." He held her eyes a long time, electrifying her. Then sadness washed over his face. "But he's got a long way to go."

"I know," she said, sensing his anguish. "I'm so sorry, Marty. I know he's a good friend."

"Best I ever had. The peckerwood."

She closed her eyes. "Tell me about his condition."

Benedetti cleared his throat. "He took six bullets. Four punched straight through, not touching anything important.

High-speed puncture wounds, basically. One fractured his right hip. Docs already replaced it with titanium. Another tore the femoral artery. Docs fixed that, too. Cleaned out your fingernails while they were at it." Grin. Fade. "Several deep lacerations but nothing stitches can't handle. The repair of all that stuff is going unbelievably well." He fell silent, looking away.

"What stuff isn't, Marty?"

A long silence, then, "The bullet that broke his hip kept going. Into his spine."

"Spine . . . oh God!" Emily slapped a fist to her mouth. "Does that mean he's—"

"Yes."

Hope leaked like a punctured tire. "Is it permanent?" she asked, trying not to cry.

"They don't know yet. It sideswiped the vertebra, didn't hit directly. So they're hoping the paralysis is only temporary." He tapped his foot several times. "Christ, it better be. Branch would rather eat his gun than be stuck in a wheelchair, shitting his diapers—" He cut himself off. "Aw, goddamn, your mom. I'm really sorry I said that."

"He'll beat this, Marty," she said. She couldn't live with any other outcome. "Because he's—"

"Too ugly for Heaven. Right," Benedetti said.

"I was going to say he wouldn't pass up the opportunity to tease us."

Benedetti raised his eyebrows. "You told him about you and me?"

"I was going to. That's why I asked him to stop at the forest preserve. But he'd already figured it out."

"I'm not surprised. He's always been a great detective," Benedetti said. "Much better than me. But don't tell him I said so. I'll never hear the end of it." He smiled crookedly. "You up for seeing Ken?"

She tugged the blanket to her neck, looking around. "He's here?"

"Playing ringmaster to the media circus in the lobby."

She thought about it. "The chief would be fine," she decided. "But nobody else. Especially no press." She tried primping her hair, gave up. "I'm a wreck."

"You're a vision," Benedetti said, pulling out his phone.

A few minutes later Cross limped in. "Now this is a sight for sore eyes," he said, with more feeling than she'd ever remembered. "How do you feel?"

"Pretty well, sir, considering." She tried to sit up, but back spasms stopped her. "As long as I don't move too fast."

"Physical pain goes away quickly," Cross said. "The department's trauma counselor will stop by tonight to help you cope with the rest." He looked her over. "You're a hero, Emily. A hundred cops want to shake your hand."

Emily looked at the ceiling. "I'm not. I had the Unsub in my sights, and I couldn't get the job done."

Cross dragged a chair to the bed. "It wasn't from lack of trying," he said. "You hit him several times, according to the witnesses. But criminals buy body armor, too. His was probably a full combat package, helmet to boots, since your bullets didn't faze him."

Emily recalled the Unsub's hat covering everything down to his eyes. "So that's why he didn't stop when I hit him. He wore bulletproof . . ." Her eyelids dropped to half-mast.

"Let's go, Marty," Cross said.

"Just give me a minute to rest, sir," Emily mumbled. "Wanna hear about the attack . . . gotta get back to work . . . fix up my house . . ."

Cross smiled. "Don't even think about that, Detective. You're on fully paid medical leave till this is over. Public Works will maintain your house and yard, and Finance will handle your checkbook. Recovery is your only assignment. I expect you to give it your usual 110 percent."

Emily forced her eyes open. "I appreciate that, Chief. Please thank everybody for me. But I don't need more time off. I'm fine. I've slept eight hours, and I'm ready for duty. Dr. Winslow will confirm I have no medical restrictions."

Cross shook his head. "No dice, Detective. I understand how you feel—"

"No, you don't."

Benedetti threw her a look that said, "Don't push it," but she was on a roll. "Chief, my head is on perfectly straight, and I have no intention of hiding. This man gunned down two cops in broad daylight. Shot up a crowd of civilians. He's a killing machine. If I vanish, he'll murder more innocents to flush me out. I can't let that happen." She slumped into her pillow, panting.

Cross looked at Benedetti. "She's right," he said.

"Unfortunately."

"Can we protect her well enough?"

Benedetti nodded.

"All right then, Detective. You're on the task force," Cross said. "Under two nonnegotiable conditions. First, you overnight at the safe house to regain your bearings. Second, you don't complain about the twenty-four-hour SWAT protection you're getting. Not one peep. Till we catch the Unsub, all independent movement is null and void."

"Done." She took a deep breath, released. "Has the task force learned anything yet?"

Cross shifted to his other hip. "Yes. The blast at Neuqua High was no accident."

Benedetti's eyebrows flew up. "When did BATFE determine that?"

Emily looked confused.

"The Justice Department's Bureau of Alcohol, Tobacco, Firearms and Explosives," Cross explained to her. "BATFE. What used to be ATF before September 11." Back to Benedetti. "Judy Stephens called on my way up here. The soil where the natural gas pipeline meets the school foundation contained plastic-explosive residue."

"What kind? Semtex?"

"Judy thinks so. Her lab is still running tests. She theorizes the Unsub shimmied up the construction trench, set the bomb, and packed around enough dirt to ensure nobody found it. FBI and Homeland Security are ruling out terrorism, making our Unsub the most likely culprit."

"Then it was Timebomb," Emily said. She counted on her fingers. "The sixth game."

"Seventh, I'm afraid," Cross said. "The Operation game may be connected to last December's torture slaying of a Massachusetts state trooper. Do you remember that case?"

"No," she admitted. "My memory is very spotty."

"Trauma batters the brain," Cross said. "Makes hash of your memory. It happened to me when I got shot. The good news is it comes back. Not tomorrow, maybe not for weeks or months, but eventually, you'll remember everything." He looked at Benedetti, who took up the story.

"They found the dead trooper in a wall tent. It was set up like a MASH unit, a detail they withheld from the media," he said. "There was an operating table, lights, air tanks, scalpels, saws, everything you'd find in an operating room. Their Unsub handcuffed the trooper to the table and surgically removed ten organs—heart, solar plexus, rib, stomach, knee—"

"Oh, that poor man!" Emily breathed, feeling herself shiver under the blanket.

"Yeah," Benedetti said. "Turns out the trooper's organs match the plastic versions contained in the Operation game— Broken Heart, Bread Basket, Spare Ribs, Butterflies in Stomach, Water on the Knee, what have you. Nobody could have known then that it was a game, or that the two Unsubs are actually the same man. One of the FBI guys made the connection and told Ken."

Cross popped a throat lozenge. "This killer is far more cunning than we realized. To that end, I've asked the State Police to reinvestigate the deaths of your parents and husband."

Emily's mouth fell open.

"They may not have been the accidents they seemed at the time," Benedetti explained.

Cross turned his palm over and back. "It's unlikely, I admit. But forensic science is far better than two decades ago. Especially DNA. We'll run each case from scratch, see what we find. Because your birthday is so near, we and the feds agreed to leave out the usual interagency backstabbing. An FBI lab team is working with our CSIs, and Homeland Security will funnel our data through its worldwide intelligence networks. Dr. Marwood's already working up a criminal profile."

"Marwood? Who's that?" Emily asked.

"Ellis Marwood. An industrial psychologist who worked on the Massachusetts case. He created their profile, so he's familiar with how their Unsub thinks. He flew in several hours ago."

"Why not a profiler from the FBI?"

"They're swamped with terror assignments. They've contracted with Dr. Marwood many times and highly recommend him. Plus he can stay as long as we need." He looked at Emily. "I'm running the task force personally and named Marty my chief investigator."

"Only till Branch is back," Benedetti said.

"Goes without saying," Cross said. "Local, federal, state, and county law enforcement are all on board. The University of Illinois made its supercomputer available for data crunching. As I mentioned, there's the profiler. Anybody I'm forgetting, Marty?"

"Me," Emily answered.

Cross smiled. "Couldn't do this without you." He pulled a badge from his pocket and placed it on her blanket.

She stared. It was gold instead of silver. "Detective" instead of "officer." Her eyes filled. "Thanks, Chief," she whispered.

"You earned it," Cross said. "Any more questions?"

She strained to remember the shooting scene. "I think there was a white minivan?"

"Yes. It was stolen from long-term parking at O'Hare Airport, abandoned in a subdivision near the forest preserve entrance. We assume the Unsub had a second vehicle prepositioned."

"Where did he leave my police card? In the van?"

Benedetti surprised her by saying, "He didn't leave one. And the scenario doesn't match your games, or any on that Web site. I don't think this was part of his master plan. It was spur of the moment, a twist he hadn't scripted."

Emily nodded as another fragment shook loose. "The Unsub couldn't have known to stash a getaway vehicle, Chief. We didn't know we were going to McDowell till we reached River Road."

"Damn. It was inside the van," Cross said. "Had to be."

"Something small," Benedetti agreed. "Bicycle. Motorcycle. Dirt bike."

"Electric scooter," Cross guessed. "Doesn't stand out, because they're so common. Allows him to wear helmet and goggles to cloak his appearance, detour through fields or parking lots. He drives outside the roadblock zone and transfers to a third vehicle." He pursed his lips. "This man is well prepared."

"But not invincible," Benedetti said. "If he'd made just one mistake at the parking lot . . ."

"That's his Achilles' heel," Emily said. "He left the script because of his obsession with me, and he'll do it again. That's when we'll get him." She thumbed her morphine button, felt the velvet hammer of the opiate soothe her joints. "What . . . now?" she croaked, wondering who'd stolen her voice.

Cross looked at her with fresh concern. "You rest. When you're discharged tonight, you go to the safe house." He pointed to the SWAT cops crowding her doorway. "These are your new best friends, Detective. Sergeant Bates leads your protective team. She's at the safe house already."

"We'll keep you nice and safe, Emily," a SWAT reassured from the hall. "Like Robin and the Seven Hoods."

"More like Snow White and the Seven Dwarfs," Benedetti cracked.

"Yeah, Commander, you're just jealous of our snappy uniforms. . . ."

"Can't they guard me at home?" Emily asked. "I'd kill for my own bed."

"Forget it," Cross said. "That log cabin of yours is too tough to secure. With all the media attention, too well known. Besides, the profiler wants you on neutral ground."

"What profiler?" She saw Cross and Benedetti trade glances, didn't know why.

"Dr. Ellis Marwood," Cross repeated. "He did the profiling on the torture-murder of that Massachusetts state trooper. Remember we were just talking about it?"

No, she thought. "What does a profiler do? Like that TV show?"

"Except for the stiletto heels and shoot-outs," Benedetti said. "Dr. Marwood will figure out what kind of person is targeting you—loves his mommy, wets his bed, works manual labor, hates cops, sleeps in a coffin, whatever. Then he'll create a personality portrait, hoping it'll suggest someone. If we have multiple suspects, the profile can narrow the field."

Cross popped another lozenge. "Since the Unsub's obsession is you, the person Dr. Marwood will work most closely with is, naturally—"

"Me," she said, already hating the invasion of privacy it implied. But she'd promised not to complain. "Make sure he talks to Annie," she urged. "She was right there. She helped me stop Branch's bleeding."

Benedetti frowned. "That was me, Emily. Not Annie."

"You?" Emily said, astonished.

He nodded. "Annie was responding, but her car broke down. I got to you first. You knocked my hands aside to do the finger-in-the-dike—"

"God, Marty, I don't remember!" Emily wailed. "I'd have sworn on a stack of Bibles you were Annie Bates! My head is so messed up!"

"That's why you're going to the safe house," Cross said. "A good night's sleep in a totally secure environment will help. Dr. Winslow prefers you stay at the hospital, and normally, I'd agree. But it's too open for us to guarantee protection against an Unsub attack. At the safe house, we can. You'll get a good night's sleep and start fresh in the morning."

Emily wanted to say she could start right away, but her traumatized nerves were sending missile strikes into her body. "Now that I think about it, Chief," she said, melting back into her pillows, "a night off isn't the worst idea I've ever heard."

Cross smiled. "Glad to hear it, Detective. We'll be in touch." He pivoted and limped out.

Emily punched the morphine button and drifted into space.

EMILY AND BRADY

Chicago
October 1974

"Weakling!" Dwight Kepp screeched, hammering his son with the leather belt. "You wet the bed again! Nine years old and you keep wetting your fucking bed!"

Brady chewed his tongue to keep from screaming. While proud that he could take anything Father dished out, he had limits. Sobbing, begging, or other displays of "sissy-ness" would double the punishment, and his butt couldn't take it after last week's "correction" for a B on a spelling test instead of his usual A.

"I buy nice things for my family, and all you do is wreck them!" Dwight swung so fast that sweat sprayed Brady's back. "What the hell kind of a son pisses all over his father's love?"

*   *   *

"Bastard," Gerald Thompson seethed, turning to stare at the house they just walked past. "That isn't right, beating the crap out of a kid like that."

"Some parents use harsh discipline," Alexandra pointed out. "Sad but true—"

"A normal kid would holler, beg the old man to stop," Gerald interrupted, fists bunched. "This one isn't saying a word. He's scared he's gonna die. I'm gonna stop this."

Alexandra linked her arm into his. "You can't just barge in there, Gerry," she said firmly. "I see a police car at the corner. Let's tell the officers."

"I'd rather grab some boys from the mill and beat this guy till Easter. See how he likes it."

Alexandra shot back, "You head the biggest steel union in Chicago. Bring a gang to duke it out with this idiot and the police will wind up arresting you. It'll appear in the newspapers, and you'll get fired."

Gerald snorted. "Boys would elect me pope if that happened."

"It's still not worth it, honey," she said. "That's what the police are for. Let's tell them."

"Oh, no," Alice Kepp gasped, running for the house. She'd heard screaming a half block away, and two policemen were headed for her front door. She darted around the side of the house, entered through the back, dumped the groceries, and rushed toward the front.

The doorbell chimed a half dozen times, halting Dwight's arm mid-swing. "Chicago Police!" he heard two men bellow. "Open up!"

"All right, boy, make yourself presentable," Dwight hissed.

"I've got to take care of this. No whining to those coppers—they're not part of our family." He looped his belt in his trousers, calmly opened the front door. "Hello, Officers," he said. "What can I do for you?"

"We heard someone beating his kid," the senior cop said. "That you?"

Dwight put on his best salesman expression. "Officer, all I can say is—"

"Darling, what do the policemen want?" Alice asked, slipping her arm through his.

"They heard me punishing our boy," Dwight said, sounding embarrassed. "I guess I got carried away with the theatrics we decided to employ."

Alice nodded. "I'm so sorry we put you to any trouble, Officers," she said, blushing. "I've been trying to help our nine-year-old quit wetting the bed. We've talked to him till we're blue in the face, put rubber sheets on the bed, everything. I've even tried spanking, but it doesn't take. A woman just isn't strong enough to handle a big active boy."

"So she asked me if a good old-fashioned belt whupping, same I got from my old man when I misbehaved, would work for little Brady," Dwight said. "I thought it might."

"That's your son's name?" the junior cop asked. "Brady?"

Dwight nodded. "We tried all that Dr. Spock nonsense, and it didn't work."

"Who the hell is Dr. Spock?" the senior cop said.

"He wrote that fancy book on raising kids," junior said. "My wife swears by it."

Alice looked at Dwight. "I was at wit's end and asked my husband to try the only thing left." Her blush deepened. "Brady wets his pants at school," she said, so soft the cops strained to hear. "You know how cruel kids are at this age, Officers. He's teased mercilessly. We just wanted to end the wetting so our boy won't be so miserable. Father Snowe wants Brady to go out for football, but he's petrified of wetting himself in front of the other boys. So we did what we thought was right, and it got out of hand. We're so sorry."

The cops' expressions softened. "I understand, ma'am," senior said, recalling the lickings he'd taken from the old man. And he'd turned out fine! This was a nice couple in a good neighborhood of churchgoing people. No previous police calls to this address. The husband talked educated, looked like a successful businessman. The wife was pretty, slender, and as graceful as a ballerina, clearly wanting the best for her family. Like any good parents, they simply made a bad judgment call.

"Would you like to see Brady, Officer?" Alice offered. "To make sure we're telling the truth?"

They're not trying to hide anything, senior decided, following her. *I'll check out the boy. Then we'll take off.*

Junior, meantime, escorted Dwight to the front porch. "Listen, Kepp," he said as soon as the door latch clicked. "Raising kids is tough. Especially boys. You gotta smack the fresh out of them sometimes. But you were outta control, and we can't have that."

"Hello," Brady said, sitting up against his Chicago Bears headboard.

"Hello yourself, son," senior said, smelling the urine. "How are you this evening?"

"Fine," he said, looking at his mother in bewilderment. She patted his head and said, "This is a police officer, Brady. He wants to ask about your father's punishment."

The boy's eyes widened. "Are you going to arrest me for wetting the bed, Mr. Policeman?"

"No, lad, nothing like that," senior assured, kneeling to the boy's level. "It's just your father was hitting you, and I wanted to make sure you were all right. Did he use something besides his hand?"

"His belt," Brady said, wincing. "It made my bottom sting. But I promised Father I wouldn't wet the bed anymore, and he stopped hitting me right away. I'm OK now." He paled. "Please don't arrest Father, Mr. Policeman. He loves me, and I love him. He'd never hurt me for real."

"The yelling was mostly theatrics," Dwight explained, looking ashamed. "To reinforce the spanking. I figured I could scare the boy into behaving where my wife couldn't. But I went a little too long with that belt. I'm sorry."

"It's OK," junior assured, taking Dwight's elbow. "We've all been there, believe me. I have four boys myself." He tightened his thumb into the elbow nerve, making Dwight gasp. "But if we have to come back here, my partner and I will drive you to the station house for a chat. Only three blocks away, but it'll take forty minutes to get there." He pushed deeper yet. Dwight blanched from the lancing pain. "Do we understand each other, Kepp?"

"I wonder how it turned out?" Alexandra said as Gerry hung their jackets. She adored these "just us" after-supper walks with her husband of eleven years. Both late bloomers socially, they didn't meet and marry till their mid-thirties. She'd wanted only one child so she could keep her career as a legal adviser to poor women. Gerry said fine, the choice was every bit hers as his. And meant it. The man was a treasure—brave, sexy, and intelligent, and still in good enough shape to play league softball. He tramped the North Woods every deer season with Tommy Lutz's nephews and approached Saturday night's family games with optimism, even though their daughter skunked both of them regularly. She and Emily, whom Gerry dubbed "Princess" in affectionate teasing of her tomboy ways, were his worldly treasures, his shining lights. Who could ask more from a man, husband, and best friend?

"Don't know," Gerald said, shrugging. "I hope they broke the shitbird's kneecaps."

Alexandra laughed, and they went to check Emily's homework.

"You put the fear of God in him?" senior cop asked junior.

"He got our message loud and clear," junior assured him.

"Good lad," senior said, punching the kid on the shoulder. This rookie was going to make a fine copper, because he already knew justice isn't always served in a courthouse.

"Did I do good, darling?" Alice whispered, praying Dwight's anger at their son had cooled. She stroked his arm. "I didn't want you in police trouble."

"You did great," Dwight assured, patting her cheek. "I'm proud of you. But Brady still needs to learn not to wet the bed. Maybe some time in the closet—"

"No, please," Alice begged. She hated when he wrapped Brady in the urine-soaked sheets and locked him in the broom closet till he "learned his lesson." "If the police find out, they'll haul you to jail, and we'll never see you again!" She knew how to distract him. It would hurt, but sometimes a mother had no choice. "It was my fault, all of it. I allowed Brady to drink a can of pop right before going to bed. I knew better and did it, anyway, forcing you to beat him when it was really my doing." Her husband's breathing became shallow, and she knew she had him. "Discipline me, Dwight, not the boy. Correct me so I can be the wife you deserve."

Dwight smiled, pointed to the basement stairs. She descended, mouth dry. They walked into the root cellar, which Dwight had soundproofed several years ago for the express purpose of disciplining his family without alerting neighbors. "You scream too loud when you force me to discipline you," he'd explained when she asked why he'd bought the truckful of insulation and Sheetrock. "So I'll handle it down here. It's nobody's business what goes on between a man and his family." He'd been religious about using the cellar but was so eye-popping furious at the stench of urine—he'd just returned triumphant from Manhattan, having brokered millions of dollars of insurance for a new skyscraper called the World Trade Center—he beat Brady right in the bed. As the police response proved, that was a mistake he dared not repeat.

Dwight locked the door and removed his belt. "All right, dear," he said. "If you insist on this discipline, I'm happy to oblige."

"Yes," Alice muttered. "I insist." She tugged her flowered dress over her head, hung it neatly on an armchair. Dwight paid a lot of money for her clothes and didn't like them wrinkled. She removed her white bra and panties—any other color made her look cheap, Dwight said—locking her eyes with his. "Ready, darling?" she said, noting the bulge near his fly. Good. His anger was already draining. She cupped her small breasts and rubbed the nipples stiff, the way he liked.

"Bend over," he directed.

She leaned over the chartreuse davenport she'd inherited from her grandmother. She pushed her breasts deep into the cushions and thrust her buttocks in the air, standing on tiptoe and spreading her legs wide. Dwight liked to see "everything" as he worked, in order to hit the "right spots." She dreaded the cellar. Her slender body had so little fat that every blow was torture. But Brady had had nightmares for two months after his last closeting, so she did what she had to do. Dwight formed a loop in the belt, snapped it till she flinched. He drew back his arm. She closed her eyes and tensed, praying he'd tire before his usual twenty-five.

Bam!

"That's one, Father," she gasped, determined not to scream. "May I have another?"

Bam!

"That's ... two ... Father. May I ... have another?"

Bam!

He stopped at nineteen, wheezing. "Have you learned your lesson?" he said, slipping the leather tip back through the loops.

"Yes, Father," she croaked, burning from pelvis to knees. Dwight's aim got sloppy when his arm tired.

"Good. I'll be in our bedroom so you can thank me for correcting you." He ran his manicured hand between her legs, sparking new agony. But she didn't even wince. For that, she was proud.

"I'll be up soon, darling. Make yourself comfortable while I clean up," she muttered through her dizziness. *Why do I put up with this?* she wondered. *Maggie says it's shameful. She says he'll kill us one of these days, and we should get out while we can. Maybe I should listen.* But her best friend didn't mind being divorced. She, on the other hand, couldn't imagine life without a husband. Even if she did find the courage to leave, where could she go? Her deeply religious parents believed "till death do us part" was an original Commandment. They'd never take her in and would, in fact, call Dwight to fetch her "so you won't embarrass your family any further." She couldn't support herself, let alone a growing child. She had no job skills because "no wife of mine will ever work." Tears brimming, she stiff-legged to the lotion she applied to keep her skin from cracking. She gingerly worked in the creamy white balm, heartsick at what she'd become.

"Don't stop now, Father. She hasn't cried," Brady mumbled, listening to the whipping through the furnace vent. "It's Mom's fault I wet the bed, not mine. You're right to discipline her. Just like you discipline me for breaking your rules." Still no scream. Disappointed, he abandoned the vent for his window, looking for the cat that visited every night.

"There you are," he whispered happily as the gangly brown feline approached. He tapped on the glass. The cat hopped onto the wide sill, staring with its one good eye, pawing the window in friendship. He'd been taming this one for weeks, and tomorrow it'd surely accept the bowl of milk he'd put on the back porch. He'd smack the cat with the hammer as it drank, carry it to the woods. He'd already hidden fresh gasoline and matches in the tree crotch and couldn't wait to see how big a fire this animal would make.

He giggled. The puppy he'd stolen from the truck when the dogcatcher wasn't looking had screamed insanely when it burned, making his pee-pee go stiff in his pants. "You and I will have lots of fun tomorrow," he whispered, waving good-bye to the cat. "Just you wait and see."

CHAPTER 16

Wednesday, 4 A.M.
Twenty-six hours till Emily's birthday

Emily threw her blanket over her head, groaning at the knock. She was in the main bedroom of a private sportsman's club southwest of Naperville, surrounded by 1,700 acres of woods, lakes, marshes, fields, and heavy-duty electric fence. They'd arrived at midnight after fifty miles of fast driving, and she'd crashed. Her brain begged for more sleep. . . .

"Rise and shine, sleepyhead!" Annie sang through the wood door. "You've got company!"

Her eyes popped open. Marty and Chief Cross were the only ones who knew the safe house location. The club manager, a retired Secret Service agent, had left last night on a department-paid fishing trip to Canada. Branch was in a coma, induced by the doctors to let nature make repairs. And Annie was so paranoid, she wouldn't let Emily near the team's cell phones or cellular laptop, lest the Unsub somehow trace the signal. *So who was this?*

She slipped the replacement Glock from her thigh holster—she wore a gun even while sleeping now—and eased herself to the floor. "What's it like outside?" she asked. "Do I need a coat?"

"No, it's warm enough for you."

Emily nodded, satisfied with the exchange. Any other meant Annie was under duress and Emily should lock herself in the bathroom. The small room was stocked with energy bars and water, was reinforced with steel panels over windows and doors, and contained full body armor, gas grenades and mask, two AR-15 combat rifles, a backpack of bullets, and a satellite phone. But since paranoia doesn't mean they *aren't* out to get you, Emily duckwalked to the bedroom door, Glock straight out, finger off the trigger in deference to the library floor. She took a deep breath and angled up to the peephole.

Looking back was a man her age. He was handsome, even with the distortion of the fish-eye lens. He wore a calm, closed-lips smile. His walnut hair was thick with no gray, combed straight back. He had a wide, square jaw with deep cleft. Narrow-set green eyes and a nose borrowed from some Roman god. No birthmarks, scars, blemishes, or ear hair. He was six feet something, broad-shouldered, and the skin around his eyes crinkled with laugh marks.

"You're the angel," Emily breathed. "From the hospital!" She pinched herself to ensure she wasn't dreaming.

His cheeks and chin were shaved blue. Sideburns ended mid-ear. Separate wide eyebrows. Tiny square ears tucked close to his overly large head, an imperfection that enhanced the package—a beauty mark on a supermodel's cheek. She couldn't see his teeth through the closed lips. His tan was light, his posture relaxed, and he looked athletic, which was easy to tell since he was dressed in . . .

Running clothes?

"Detective Thompson?" the man said. "I'm Dr. Marwood. Hope I'm not too early."

"For what?" she asked.

"Our running date."

That annoyed her. Dr. Marwood was the criminal profiler Cross had mentioned. But how could they have made a running date? This was a head game to see how she'd react. *Well, two can play at that.* She hid the Glock behind her back, pasted on her brightest smile. "Oh, right, I must have forgotten. Come on in." She unbolted the door, and Annie waved.

"Nice to meet you, Doctor," Emily said. "You coming in, too, Sergeant?" she asked, opting for Annie's formal rank in front of strangers.

"No. Chief Cross authorized one-on-one," Annie said, clearly unhappy. "I'm heading back to the kitchen." She handed Emily a carafe of French roast. "Need anything else, holler."

"Will do. Thanks." She swung the door wide, set the carafe next to the faux leather La-Z-Boy.

Marwood stepped over the threshold. His smile faded when the gun appeared from behind her back. "Taking no chances, I see," he murmured.

"Would you?"

"Hell, I'd carry a bazooka given what's happened. Want to see my ID?"

Emily nodded, and Marwood eased his wallet from his fanny pack. The half-moons of his fingernails were clear and bright, she noted. The man paid attention to his grooming. But he wasn't vain enough to clearcoat the nails, either. He underhanded the black calfskin onto the double bed, and she rifled the contents.

New York State driver's license. Homeland Security photo ID. British Airways frequent-flier card. A dozen others, dog-eared from use. Ditto the wallet, which was flannelled from folding and carrying. Another point for authenticity—most criminals forgot to "age" their documents with the lint and grime of life in a pocket. That he was here at all meant Marwood had run the Cross-Bates-Benedetti gauntlet, plus a federal background check. She holstered the Glock. "I'm Emily," she said, sticking out her hand.

"Ellis." They shook, and she picked up a faint scent of bay rum aftershave. She swallowed. That had been Jack's favorite. "Coffee?" she responded, pointing to the carafe.

"Only if it's leaded," Marwood said, stuffing the wallet in the pack. "Decaf's a joke this time of morning." He pointed to the running clothes draped over the stuffed moose guarding the bathroom door. "After that, I'd like to join you in a six-miler. Or as far as you can go."

"So you know I run. I thought you only profiled the bad guy."

Marwood shook his head. "Can't do a jigsaw puzzle without sorting the pieces first. So I check out everyone and everything connected to the case. Separating the edge pieces from the centers early on makes the game go a lot faster when it counts." He grinned. "Sorry for the tortured analogy, but most of my clients are CEOs. They understand game references best because they all think they're players."

"It's OK. My life's a game right now, so you fit right in," Emily summarized, then waggled a finger at the moose. "How did you know I wouldn't be dressed and running already?"

"Ken said you go out at sunup. Our interview ended a little after two. He and I grabbed a bite. Then one of the SWAT guys drove me down. I wanted to get here before you left."

Explains his bloodshot eyes. "You really should have gotten a few hours' sleep," she chided, remembering Branch's admonitions. "This could have waited till noon."

A look of something, she didn't know what, crossed Marwood's face. "No rest for the wicked," he said. "So if you don't mind . . ."

"Sure, let's run," Emily agreed. "There's a path around the lake. Help yourself to coffee while I change." She shot her chin at the carafe, then trotted into the bathroom. The armored door closed glacially, allowing her to see that rather than pouring, Marwood was quietly pulling her dresser drawers. "Hey!" she snapped. "Cream's in the fridge, not under my panties."

"Sorry," Marwood said, his chirpy tone indicating he didn't mean it. "But you might as well get used to it. I'll be in your face all the time. No avoiding it if you want to stay alive."

That jarred her, and she backed off. "Rummage away."

"Ten-Four, Ossifer."

Thoughts of Marty's affectionate twist on "Officer" hit hard, and she wished she could call him. But Annie made that impossible. "Be out in a few minutes," she said. She shut the door, turned on the sink faucets, tiptoed back to the peephole to see if he was behaving.

Marwood was in the recliner, sticking out his tongue and wiggling his fingers, with thumbs in his ears. Knowing she would look.

She couldn't help laughing. Ten minutes later she was back in the bedroom, pouring her own cup. "Hope you like to sweat, Doc," she announced. "The lake's got hills."

"Actually," Marwood said. "We're going back to Naperville."

"For what?"

"We're doing your fun run. Annie's warming up the cars."

Emily stopped mid-gulp as her good feelings vanished. Mining her head for clues was one thing. Trespassing in Jack's was another. "Run to the cemetery?" she repeated. "From my house?"

Marwood nodded.

"No."

He tapped his knee with the cup. "I need to participate in your rituals, Emily. It's important."

"No," she repeated. "Some things are just too private."

"Nothing's private in a serial murder," Marwood said. "It's a fact that—"

"I don't care about your facts," she snapped. "Or what you think you know about me. I have no intention of taking you to see my husband."

"Why? What are you afraid of?" He waved dismissively. "Ah, right, it's obvious. You'd rather cower in a safe house than face the Unsub."

Emily steamed. "The only reason I'm here is direct orders from Chief Cross. You don't believe me, confirm it with Sergeant Bates."

"My orders supercede yours," Marwood said, stepping closer. "We're doing the fun run."

Emily delivered a stare to boil wet cement. "Shove your orders, pal."

"Wrong answer, Detective," Marwood shot back. "When I say jump, you ask how high. I say run, you ask how far. Because when I understand what makes you tick, I understand the Unsub." He folded his arms. "We've got twenty-four hours to stop this man. So we're going to your house, and we're going to run. Cross and Benedetti have already signed off, so quit stalling."

Emily stared, not answering. Marwood gazed back with the faint, closed-lips smile she'd seen in the peephole.

"This is some kind of reverse psychology, isn't it?" Emily said. "You jab and punch till I'm so angry at you, I won't have time to be afraid."

Marwood's toothy grin said she'd hit Bozo Bucket No. Six.

"Well, guess what? It worked," she continued, snatching her bloodstained Nikes from the antlers. "I'll tell you what you want, and I'll do what you say." She knelt and laced, swallowing hard. "Just get him."

CHAPTER 17

Wednesday, 6 A.M.
Twenty-four hours till Emily's birthday

"If I'm answering all these questions for you," Emily grunted after several miles of chilly silence, "how's about we split your fee?"

"Sure," Marwood agreed, following as she swung onto Washington Street for the straightaway to Naperville Cemetery. "Half of nothing is still nothing."

"You're not charging for this?"

"Only expenses."

The answer surprised her. Private consultants generally mooched off taxpayers like Bluto worked a cafeteria line. "How do you pay the rent?"

"I'm an industrial psychologist," Marwood said, hopping a winter-fractured sidewalk. "CEOs pay me obscene amounts of money to ensure their hires aren't thieves, perverts, embezzlers, con men, or other such negative revenue enhancers."

Emily winced. "I thought cop language was stilted."

"It is. But CEOs talk worse, believe me." He huffed as the elevation sharpened away from the Riverwalk. "I interview executive candidates in office and social settings. Conduct FBI-grade background checks. Analyze finances, credit, lifestyle-income ratios, personal and professional relationships, dozens of other matrices. I run the results past my lie detectors—a detective sergeant in the NYPD fraud unit, a U.S. Treasury agent, and an Oxford University psychology professor—then tell the CEO who's the best bet for the job. And who the cops should visit." He scratched his neck. "Kinda dull, but it pays the bills."

It actually sounded interesting to her. "What's your track record?"

"I turn down several hundred corporate assignments for every one I accept," Marwood said. "I'll never bat a thousand—nobody does, a determined enough sociopath can sneak past the most sophisticated firewalls—but I do very well." He coughed. "But that's only money. Police cases I take pro bono."

"Why?"

"They're fun."

Emily touched her rib cage. She'd tried to sprint out her back door as usual, but the bruises demanded a slower approach. They walked the first mile, jogged the second. Once she was thoroughly warmed up, the pain became tolerable. "I'd hardly call it that."

"Satisfying, then. I love getting killers out of circulation. Same reason you do your job—some things are more important than money."

"I hear you." Personal satisfaction was the single most important attraction of being a cop. The pay and working conditions mostly sucked. "Did Cross call you?"

"Other way around. I'd done what I could in Massachusetts—"

"That's right!" Emily interrupted, recalling where she'd

first heard his name—on Newsradio while showering Lucy Crawford out of her hair. "You were their profiler."

"One of several on the task force, right," Marwood confirmed. "But all our leads fizzled, so I headed back to Manhattan to catch up on laundry."

Emily snorted at the just-folks touch but didn't call him on it. "You live in Manhattan?" she said. "I thought everyone moved out after . . . you know . . ."

"I have to admit I was tempted to leave," Marwood said. "But I was born and reared in Manhattan. Running away lets the terrorists win. So I stayed."

She looked at him, nodding.

"Your case made the crime boards on the Internet," he continued. "My chief of staff e-mailed me in Boston, thought I'd be interested."

"Guess you were."

"I met Ken a few times on the rubber-chicken circuit. I called to say I was free. He said come on out." Sweat dripped from his nose. "Nothing's harder than digging into a killer's head, Emily. Nothing's more satisfying, either. And, Lord, it generates good PR for my business." He winked. "The bonus is my FBI pals have to buy drinks whenever I catch one before they do."

"Win-win," Emily said. She spied her husband's grave on the distant hilltop and hummed a little. While part of her still resented Marwood's presence, another part wasn't all that unhappy about it. First, he was her get-out-of-jail card. The safe house wasn't Stateville Prison, but she wasn't free to leave, either. Second, Marwood took her seriously enough to blow his stack when she balked, instead of going to a boss. Third, while the task force had done an eye-popping amount of work in its few hours of existence—alibiing every one of her arrestees, stalkers, neighbors, and friends, tracing the Unsub's ammo to a Las Vegas gun shop that burned to the ground years ago in a still-unsolved arson, exhaustively computer modeling every crime scene and victim—there still wasn't a live suspect. That's where Marwood and his profile came in.

"What?" she asked, noticing his stare.

"Just thinking."

"About?"

Marwood's head ticked back and forth. "How much I invade people's privacy. I know this stuff gets personal, Emily. I won't pry more than I have to."

"Baloney," she countered. "You're going to turn me inside out. And you're not one bit sorry."

"Annabelle Patricia Sampson Bates!" Cross sang as Annie walked into roll call. He limped over to refill her empty coffee cup. "Lovely to see you!" he enthused. "Your husband's well? The children? Your little white horse named Spitzer?"

"Aw, man." Annie plopped herself on a table. "Whenever you make nice, I know I'm going to hate myself for saying yes."

"Sergeant! Have I ever buttered you up for a favor?"

"Does a bear shit in the woods?"

Cross patted her knee. "You still know how to reach your friend in Iraq?"

"Which one? I've got lots of friends over there," Annie parried.

"You know who I mean."

"Why?"

"At the hospital, Emily asked if the Unsub was a soldier."

"Because of the military surplus ammo he used, right," Annie said.

"Marty said no, surplus is far too common. I agreed. Now I think she's onto something."

She sipped her coffee, pulled at her narrow chin. "You think the guy's a soldier?"

"A commando."

Annie stared. "Shit," she groaned, slapping her head. "I should have known that right away. This guy's done too many things too well to be a civilian."

"Or even a regular soldier," Cross said.

"Uh-huh. The precision of his attack on Neuqua proves it."

"Exactly what I thought. Our FBI and Homeland Security liaisons agree and asked the Pentagon for a list of Special Forces personnel so we can cross-match with the computer models and Dr. Marwood's personality profile. No luck. Pentagon refuses to release."

"They won't without a gun to their heads."

"I woke up our congressional delegation for just that. But it'll take time we don't have."

Annie waved her hands in protest. "C'mon, Chief. I'd do anything for Em, and you know it. But not this. It isn't fair to Cap." She stared at him. "Or me."

Cross nodded, filled his cup, sat next to her. "You're right. It isn't fair. I certainly wouldn't blame you for saying no."

Annie pursed her lips. During her last Reserve call-up to Iraq, she'd been downing beaucoup Heineken with the Baghdad-based Navy SEAL captain who coordinated her sniper-school assignments. Halfway through bottle eight, he'd professed deeper-than-the-ocean love for her. "Aw, Cap, that's sweet," she'd replied, meaning it. She liked the quiet commando a great deal. "But I'm happily married." The captain smiled at what he presumed was pro forma protest, and she shook her head. "I'm serious. My husband is the prince all those fairy tales promise us frogs." She smiled at his expression, which clearly said, "You ain't no frog." "If he wasn't the best man for me, I'd be all over your gnarly ass. I would. But." The captain nodded, held up his green bottle in salute. "If you love him that much, Annabelle, I won't pursue this. But you're the finest woman I know." She was touched and said so. "E-mail me if you ever change your mind," the captain sighed, handing her a card. "I'll probably be stuck in this stinkin' desert till retirement." She'd never written after returning to Naperville, not even a casual hello, meaning what she'd said about her husband. She had, however, confided the tale to Cross last summer after one too many beers at a departmental bash.

"It's a lot to ask, goddammit," she growled.

"Too much," he agreed.

They held up their cups, drank, and Cross left her to her laptop.

Marwood shook his head. "Nobody will know what you tell me unless it bears directly on finding the Unsub," he declared. "My goal is not to strip you naked before your friends. It's to figure out how you think. What you do or don't care about, where your feelings are strongest, how you react in any given situation."

"Put your head inside mine," she ventured.

"Exactly. And when I do, his ass is mine." Grin. "Well, ours. I'm just creating the profile. You've still got to find him."

"No kidding," she said. "What have you figured out so far? Besides most serial killers are male?"

Marwood kicked at a goose in their path. It hissed, then stomped away. "The naked kid at the library described a 'good-looking dude with a movie-star smile,'" he began. "You reported a nondescript pudge with gapped hillbilly teeth. The kid swore the Unsub's strawberry birthmark was on his neck. You said cheek. So our man's an expert in disguises." He hurdled an upthrusted piece of cemetery service road. "He's white. Born and raised in the United States. Six feet, 170 to 200 pounds. Unusually strong, but not freaky-muscled like a bodybuilder. He's handsome, with straight white teeth and immaculate grooming. No potbelly or bad breath. Clean-shaven except maybe a moustache."

"Mr. July on a firefighter calendar," she suggested.

"You've got it."

Emily listened to the rest, hoping her damaged brain would absorb the flow.

"Full head of hair. Traditional men's cut, nothing feminine. He's between thirty and fifty, most likely thirty-five to forty." He mopped sweat off his neck. "He's intelligent, with an animal cunning off the scale. Enjoys risky sports—scuba, skydiving, big-game hunting. A charmer, can talk his way through any situation. Confident as hell, lots of admirers." He trotted sideways to look at Emily. "And he's pure evil, Detective. An absolute psychopath. Killing people means no more to him than swatting a fly, and he's set on your complete and utter destruction." Long pause. "Because he loves you."

"Cap, it's great to hear your voice!" Annie gushed, feeling like a worm.

Emily felt like she'd hit a tree. "Love me? He can't love me! He's trying to kill me!"

"Hate is love in disguise," Marwood explained. "And he's got it for you bad. You don't expend this kind of emotion on someone you don't care about."

"That just isn't possible! I don't even know who he is!"

"Probably not. But he certainly knows you." Her pained expression made him hold up his hands. "I'm sorry, this is upsetting you."

"Very much," she agreed. "But keep going. I need to know everything." She told Marwood about the alarming gaps in her memory. "Maybe this'll fill some of the blanks in my head."

They headed cross-country through the tombstones. "Our Unsub is financially secure. Possibly wealthy," he continued. "Long-term research is expensive, and so are his hobbies."

"Where'd he get his money? Rich family?"

Marwood shook his head. "He's too independent to take orders from a rich daddy, so he's self-made. The only time he obeyed anyone but himself was in the armed forces."

She blinked rapidly. "I mentioned the military angle to Marty," she said. "He wasn't interested."

Marwood frowned. "I wonder why not? It's one of the first alleys I'd explore." He let the question hang, then added, "Of course, Marty's ex-military himself."

"He is?" Emily said. "I didn't know."

"Air Force pararescue. That's what Ken told me," Marwood said. "Maybe Marty refuses to believe a comrade-in-arms is going after you. Or maybe he . . . never mind."

"What?"

"It's nothing. Stupid thought."

"Come on, Doc," Emily pressed. "Share and share alike." She caught her breath as his point became clear. "No way!"

"I'm sure you're right," Marwood backpedaled. "There's millions of veterans and only one Unsub. Why assume he's from your particular family?"

"Exactly!" she emphasized. "I'd trust Marty Benedetti with my life. I'd trust any of them." Still, her brain churned. Annie was a decorated Army Reserve master sergeant, a sniper instructor blooded in Iraq and Afghanistan. As a SWAT, she routinely carried one of those MP-5 submachine guns. Branch pulled two hitches in the marines, Cross likewise in the navy. Branch and his wife Lydia knew everything worth knowing about her and Jack. Cross was a cop in Las

Vegas, where that gun store burned. Maybe he torched it to destroy records of a particular military surplus ammo purchase. Maybe his Captain Queeg routine went deeper than keeping a fresh-baked rookie out of trouble. Her hands turned clammy. What about Annie's "car trouble" on the way to the forest preserve? Engine problem? Or establishing an alibi? She despised the traitorous thoughts but was unable to stop them. *Cross runs the entire show. He could easily manipulate events! And what about Marty? I know nothing about him, really. Marwood said the Unsub is charming. So is Marty, in spades. And he's the one that called me to the cemetery the morning I found the birds. . . .*

"It's not possible," she insisted.

"I'm sure you're right," Marwood repeated. "Not worth thinking about."

She shot him a look that said, "Don't patronize me."

"All right, it's possible," he said. "I don't know anyone here except by reputation. I have no idea what motivates your colleagues or how they feel about you."

"That's comforting."

"You want comfort, get a pet," he said. "If it's one of your own people, we need to know."

"It's crazy talk, Ellis," she muttered. "Let's get back to the Unsub."

"That's the first time you've used my name," Marwood pointed out. "I appreciate the confidence that implies."

She stopped to pull up her socks. "I have to trust you. Who else is left?"

He grinned, and they resumed running. "The Unsub shoots accurately under pressure, steals cars, picks locks, plants explosives. Murders people without raising alarms, sweet-talks a kid into stripping naked in front of cops. That kind of expertise practically shouts 'commando.'"

"Makes sense," she said. "Plus he'd learn to kill in Special Forces."

"Kill professionally," Marwood corrected. "Any moron can kill. Commandos kill objectively and dispassionately. They're every bit as professional as doctors, lawyers, and accountants."

"Except they hurt people and break things."

"Tools of the trade in an uncertain world," Marwood said. "Of all the commando units in the U.S. military—Delta Force, Navy SEALs, Army Green Berets, Marine Force Recon—his specific skills suggest Green Berets. They blow up stuff like all the others but also have to blend in with their targets for years at a time. Anywhere on the planet, under any conditions. That makes them experts in human psychology. This guy is long haul, Emily, not quick hit. So I say he's a Green Beret. That narrows our search considerably."

"But that's an elite unit, Ellis. Crème de la crème," Emily argued. "Wouldn't he be tested? You know, psychologically? How could he get into any commando unit if he's a psycho?"

"Yes, yes, and not easily," Marwood replied. "But it's not impossible, either. Here's why."

"Son of a bitch," Cross groaned when Benedetti dropped the *Chicago Sun-Times* atop the mountain of reports on his desk. "I thought this task force was leakproof."

24 HOURS TILL CHECKMATE!
KILLER ISN'T 'SORRY'—MAYHEM
TIED TO COP'S BOARD GAMES!

Benedetti shrugged. "It is. I think the Unsub called the *Times* to ratchet up the pressure on us. We'd better catch this man fast."

Cross leaned back. "Gee. Now I know why I made you chief investigator."

"Hey, I could have said, 'We're pursuing any number of promising leads, and we're confident an arrest is imminent,'" Benedetti shot back. "But then you'd fire me, and I'd miss

out on all this fun." He sobered. "There's tons of good people on this task force, Ken. Any one of them can do my job.
I'm renewing my request to join Emily's bodyguard detail."

"Denied. Again."

"Goddammit, why not?" Benedetti said. "It won't take
long to train my replacement."

"Because you like her too much. That's why."

Benedetti stared. "You know?"

"It's my job to know."

"How could you? I don't even know—"

"Yes, you do," Cross said. "It's all over your face, tough
guy. You light up like a Christmas tree whenever her name
comes up."

"Bullshit!"

"Don't kid a kidder, Marty. You like Emily a lot. Which is
great. She's a damn good woman, and, well, you're OK for
an old fart." He motioned for Benedetti to sit. "I won't put
you on the bodyguard team. You're too anxious to protect
her from everything, like the other night in her basement,
when you were unhappy she volunteered for the midnight
shift. Your judgment is impaired when it comes to Emily. In
a good way, but still impaired."

Benedetti slumped into the chair. "I guess you're right. It
shows, huh?"

"Worst-kept secret in the building. So forget bodyguard-
ing. The Unsub provides all the risk I need right now." He
smiled. "Besides, someone's got to do my shit work."

"Commando units attract men a little on the edge, anyway," Marwood said. "Who else would volunteer for such
life-threatening jobs? As for psychological testing, a determined enough psychopath—"

"'Can break through any firewall,'" Emily said, quoting
him. "My memory's not so bad you have to repeat every sin-

gle thing. Shelby!" Her heart soared as the beloved neighborhood yellow Lab emerged from behind a family mausoleum. "C'mere, boy!"

"You know this dog?" Marwood said, slowing to a jog.

"Sure. Shelby's my favorite guy in Naperville besides you." She squatted to clap and whistle. The big dog charged her way. "He belongs to one of my neighbors, but everyone's family to him."

Marwood clapped his hands. "Come here, boy! Let's play!" He sounded so awkward, Emily laughed. "Not much experience with dogs, huh?"

"None. Except for those yappy little dust mops, Manhattan's not exactly dog country," he said. He clapped louder. Shelby slowed, cocked his head.

"He usually likes strangers," Emily teased. "He must sense you're up to no good."

"Au contraire, Detective," Marwood said. "He knows all about Calamity Em, and he's not getting near either of us." Shelby woofed a couple times, then disappeared.

"Can't blame him," Marwood said, sniffing theatrically. "If your bad karma didn't get him, your armpits would."

"Said the pot to the kettle," she said. "Onward, Doc."

"Right. Our Unsub is an only child. If not, then firstborn, the most independent of the clan. He grew up in a northern state, speaks American English perfectly. He spent time in Naperville doing research. Might even have landed a job on a local police department—clerk, dispatcher, something anonymous to the public—to gain an insider's perspective on you." He kicked a loose stone. "Crooks profile us, we profile them. Helluva world."

She told Marwood how Sheriff's Sergeant Rayford Luerchen acted toward her at the cemetery and library. "Then again," she said, "Luerchen might hate me only because I embarrassed him."

"That's probably it. I talked to the man, and frankly, he's

not smart enough to pick his own nose. But let's have Commander Benedetti roust him, anyway, make sure it's not an act." He scratched his head. "Hmm. That's the same Benedetti who claims—"

"I don't want to hear it," Emily warned.

Marwood shook his head, flinging drops of sweat. "Defending your friends is admirable, Detective, but everyone's guilty till proven otherwise."

"Including you," Emily challenged.

"Of course, including me," he replied. "Everyone knows if the butler didn't do it, the shrink did."

"You can't be the Unsub," she said, pointing out Jack's tombstone. "You weren't in the military." She grinned at Marwood's startled expression. "I had nothing else to do waiting for physical therapy, so I profiled you, too. Now tell me how you deduced all this nonsense."

Cross pointed to the printouts in Benedetti's arm. "Good news from Iraq?"

Benedetti nodded. "I took the download on my own computer and encrypted it so deep that God couldn't source it to Annie's friend."

"Excellent. How fast can we sort through the names?"

"That's the bad news. He sent the complete personnel abstract of every American soldier since the Civil War. Not just Special Forces, but everyone."

Cross winced. "That's millions of names. The captain really does love Annie."

Benedetti nodded. "This business sucks sometimes."

"Yes. But you know the stakes. Annie, knew, too, or she wouldn't have agreed." He took the printouts, fanned them like a deck of cards. "Let's sort these by distance from Emily's home addresses," he suggested. "Nearest to farthest away, every place she's lived."

"Because she'd more likely know someone from the old neighborhood than from Fairbanks or Guam," Benedetti agreed. "I'll get the computer guys on it. One other thing. I'd rather Marwood not know we have this."

Cross looked surprised. "Why not?"

"I know he's your guy and all. But he's not a cop and doesn't have to play by our rules." Benedetti tapped the newspaper as case in point. "Soon as these are sorted, we'll call her in. She finds a name, I'll tell the doc so he can add it to the profile. Till then, let's keep it to ourselves."

Cross considered that. "I'm trusting Ellis Marwood with Emily's life, Marty. But she trusts you with hers. Handle it as you see fit."

"Naperville's a white city," Marwood explained, running backwards a few yards, then turning. "Which means the Unsub is."

"White man scopes out a residential neighborhood, and everyone assumes he's a builder looking at teardowns," she said, following his reasoning. "Black man does it, and the neighbors call 911."

"Correct. That's also why he's from the Midwest or another northern state. The y'all speech pattern of Dixie would stick out like a sore thumb here."

The heel strikes of her fast gait sparked her bruises like tiny cattle prods. She slowed. "Why do you think he's retired military?"

"If he was active, he'd be overseas hunting Osama. So our guy's retired. Honorable discharge, of course. Anything less would have limited his career options too much."

Her brain grappled with the overload of information. "You said he hunts," she said, recalling her own Winchester-toting weekends with her father. "What? Deer? Birds?"

"Big game. Grizzly bears, Cape buffalo, warthogs—animals that bite back. Even better, banned animals, like elephants and hippos. Eluding the poaching police adds to the rush."

"Like this guy needs more adrenaline," she said.

"He does, actually. To practice controlling it. Going after dangerous animals is the best way to mimic hunting a cop—you miss, you die. That's also why he climbs mountains. Successfully managing the adrenaline rush bolsters his confidence."

She looked at the popcorn clouds, not knowing what to say.

Marwood slowed to match her pace as they crested the cemetery hill. "The naked kid is most interesting. When you were his age, didn't you assume adults were always on the up-and-up?"

"Sure."

"Me, too. But that's changed. Today's youth assume a con job unless proven otherwise."

"But the naked kid said yes," Emily said.

"Uh-huh," Marwood said. "That makes the Unsub normal-looking, probably handsome. If he was short, fat, ugly, bald, crippled, or cross-eyed, had crooked teeth, bad breath, or acne, the kid would've told him to get lost. We all avoid doing things for people we don't like. Conversely, if the person's good-looking, muscular, intelligent, and mesmerizing, we do what he or she asks. We like to please the people we're attracted to."

"I arrested a con man once," she said. "He could charm the scales off a snake."

"Their livelihood depends on earning the trust of their victims," Marwood said. "So they work hard at being attractive, charming, and helpful. Ask the women who survived Ted Bundy. They wanted to bring him home to meet the folks."

The Unsub was becoming more alive. "Someone mentioned classic markers of a serial killer," she said, irritated she couldn't recall who said it. "What are those, and how do they fit this guy?"

Benedetti closed the interrogation room door and dialed Emily's cell phone. Hardly the stuff of the gritty homicide dick he prided himself on being, but he didn't care. He needed to hear her voice.

He got voice mail.

"Dammit," he grumbled, recalling that Annie had confiscated Emily's phone on the way to the safe house. "I miss you, toots," he said after the beep. "I hope you're all right."

Marwood stretched his arms back. "Virtually every serial killer did three things when they were boys," he said. "Wet the bed, set fires, tortured animals."

"What kind of animals?" she said, anger welling.

"Puppies, kittens, mice, squirrels. You name it. He feeds them rat poison and watches them convulse. Clubs them with baseball bats. Sets them on fire. Sticks them in a microwave till they explode. If real animals aren't available, he catches flies and rips off their wings. Drops goldfish into gasoline. Crushes the backs of ants to see the front ends squirm."

"Gross!"

"Sure is. But show me a little boy who does all three things consistently—tortures animals, wets the bed, and set fires—and I'll give you a future serial killer."

"If it's so obvious," Emily objected, "then why aren't these monsters stopped early?"

"Because we don't see little Hannibal Lecter eating corn-flakes at the kitchen table. We see little Johnny in a sailor suit, rehearsing his lines for the Easter pageant. The rare times we notice something disturbing about their behavior, we say boys will be boys, we all played with matches, I wet the bed myself, no big deal, he'll grow out of it. But a psychopath doesn't. Not without early, forceful intervention, and even then it's only fifty-fifty." Marwood tacked in behind her. "The man behind us doesn't look familiar," he said. "He's one of ours, right?"

Emily whirled to the figure half blocked by a tombstone. "That's not a man, you goof," she chided. "That's Annie!" She tried not to flinch at the long-barreled Remington in Annie's hands.

Marwood moved back to her side.

A minute later they reached Jack's grave. "This is it, Ellis," she wheezed through pounding ribs. "The goal of my fun run. Hope it's everything you wanted." She grabbed her ankle to stretch, turning her head to hide the sudden tears.

"Why did you decide to become a cop?" Marwood asked.

Not trusting her voice, she inspected Jack's headstone. She spotted a spiderweb inside the first *K*, dug it out with her little finger. She wiped the sticky thread on her T-shirt, brushing the Glocks underneath.

"Well?" he prompted.

"Um, well, I . . ." The question had come up before. She always blew it off with a chirpy "'Cause I look so good in blue." The truth was, it just sort of happened. She'd been sitting at the kitchen table, hair drying from her post-run shower, idly scanning the local *Naperville Sun* and wondering what to do with her life. The "poor me" voice inside her head was driving her crazy. As were her office mates, who griped ceaselessly about friends, rivals, parents, spouses, kids, lipstick, and weather, their lives never-ending tragedies. The more Emily heard, the more she wanted to scream, "Shut up! You have no idea how good you have it!" She needed to find something else to do. Then she saw the article tucked between the ads.

POLICE TEST TODAY

She read it twice, then set it aside for housework. She dusted, vacuumed, and scrubbed, but the inexplicable excitement grew stronger. She called Branch to see what he thought—Lydia and Jack worked together at Bell Labs, and all four of them had become close. She'd loved Branch's police stories but never imagined one happening to her. He encouraged her to go for it. "The worst that can happen is you don't pass, and that's where you are right now." She drove to Neuqua High and took the written exam. The questions were harder than she'd anticipated, and she left the auditorium dejected.

Several weeks later she wandered out her front door, played with Shelby, then waved to Joey the mailman as he motored away in his box truck. She leafed through the mail. Electric bill. *Ooh!* American Express. *Ahh! Runner's World's* shoe issue. *Oh, catch me. I'm faint!* Heart research, lung research, cancer research, siding manufacturer, Naperville Police Department, immediate response requested.

She tore the cream-colored envelope and was astounded to read she'd scored in the uppermost percentile and would she please arrange an interview. A dozen physical, mental, and medical hurdles later, she scissored off her long hair and reported to the police academy for training. . . .

"I really have no idea, Ellis," she said, running her hand through her wet hair. "Office work seemed tedious and police work didn't. So I became a cop."

Agreement and contradiction danced across Marwood's face. "Maybe," he said. "But maybe you were telling them off."

She cocked her head.

"Mama. Daddy. And Jack." Marwood shook his fist.

"'You abandoned me!'" he cried in a mimic of her voice. "'I'm gonna get even by becoming a cop! I'm gonna wrestle killers and rapists, and if you don't like it, you can kiss my dimpled ass! It's payback time!'"

Emily stared, not believing her ears. *Revenge?* That couldn't be why she'd joined the department. Couldn't be! "Who can say?" she said, trying to shrug it off.

"You can," Marwood said, his gaze direct. "Your family abandoned you. Left you alone. Shattered your existence. You hate them for doing that. Hate!"

"I don't hate them," Emily whimpered. "I . . . I can't."

"Just a few more minutes till the list is sorted," Cross said over the encrypted cell phone connection. "Pray the Unsub's there, because we're almost out of time."

Annie blew a sweat ball off the tip of her nose. "I know."

"Don't worry," Cross said. "Marty encrypted the file with Level Nine. . . ."

She listened to the particulars, alarmed at the body language Emily displayed through the high-powered binoculars. Hands bunching and releasing her shirt. Nostrils flaring. Head shaking, eyes darting. *Come on, girl, I know you're hurting,* she thought. *But hang in there. We're almost at endgame. Show Marwood what you're made of.* "Cap thought I'd changed my mind," she responded when Cross finished. "It was a lousy thing to do to him."

"You didn't do it. I did."

"No, Chief, it was me."

"Both of us then. How's Emily handling the emotion of this fun run?"

"Fine," Annie said. "She's a trouper."

"I'll call the instant Marty's finished," Cross said.

* * *

"Are you all right?" Marwood asked.

"Fine. Fine," Emily muttered. "Some bad memories is all." She was drowning in the moment Jack's mahogany casket disappeared into the grave. She'd hurt so bad, she wanted to jump in and inhale dirt till she died, too, but somehow managed to remain calm. *Just like now,* she thought grimly.

"We gonna pull her soon, boss?" Flea asked, refocusing his binoculars. "She's lookin' awfully bad down there."

"She looks calm and collected to me," Annie said.

"Right. That's what I meant."

Emily hugged herself to get on track. "We've wasted enough time on my problems," she grunted, pushing to her feet. "Let's go."

Marwood shook his head. "Tell me about your folks first."

"What do you want to know?" she said, picking grass off her backside. "That a pickup truck hit Daddy so hard, his face cracked the sidewalk? Or that Mama couldn't take a dump without somebody coming to measure?"

"Both. Everything."

"Sure. You free the rest of the century?" She plopped back on the grass and crossed her legs, the image of her brutalized parents sparking incredible fury. Fury was good. Fury she knew. Fury she could handle. "Daddy was big," she began. "Not fat, just big. Muscular. He was a steelworker, took great pride in his strength and physique. He wasn't book smart—he barely graduated high school—but he was the most intelligent man I ever knew." She patted her hair. "These henna highlights aren't from any bottle, Doc," she said. "Daddy had a full head of electric-red hair."

"Ken mentioned that in our briefing. Was it wavy like yours?"

"No. That I got from Mama." She thought some more. "He smelled like Clubman. You know, the aftershave?"

"Barbershops and locker rooms," Marwood said. "My favorite after bay rum."

"Mine, too," she said. "What else? He was easygoing, didn't have a cross word for anyone but stupid bosses. But he was a grizzly when provoked. We were at a White Sox game when I was seven. Some drunk pawed my boobs. I didn't know what it meant. Daddy did. He stomped the guy unconscious."

"You inherited his tough-guy gene, I see."

Emily shrugged. "I don't let anyone push me around, Ellis. Daddy taught me that." She conjured more happy memories. "The neatest time I had with him," she said, watching herself sprint barefoot across the green shag carpeting and leap into Daddy's lap, "was watching TV together after supper. Just him and me, Mama in the kitchen doing dishes. We sat in his lounger." She crinkled her eyes. "It was a nineteen-inch Quasar—"

"His lap?"

Emily chuckled. "We watched cop shows. *Kojak, Mannix, Dragnet, Adam-12,* first runs, reruns, it didn't matter. He liked them all. Said he would have loved being a copper, but steelwork paid better, and he had a family to think of. We watched just one show a night because the nuns piled on the homework. When the show ended, I hit the books, and he and Mama took a walk. Every night, just the two of them. It was their alone time. All my friends thought it was so sweet." Her eyes misted over.

Marwood looked sad. "How did your father die?" he asked. "I know hit and run, but what can you tell me about it?"

Emily explained what neighbor Goldie Abrams had said that long-ago night, then told him what she remembered about Mama. "I lived in the family bungalow till I met Jack," she finished. "Sold it to move here. And now I'm by myself again. Full circle."

Marwood rubbed his knees. "I'm sorry for your loss, Emily," he said. "Losses. You loved and admired your family, and they adored you. I'm sure they're watching from the penthouse suite."

She nodded, not trusting her voice. "Time to leave," she finally said. "I'm starting to stiffen up."

The profiler hopped to his feet. "Want to say good-bye?"

Her eyes widened at the thoughtfulness. "Yes. I'd appreciate that."

Marwood jogged off. Emily murmured her love to Jack, caught up. She pointed out the quarry beach, bell carillon, skateboard park, and covered wooden bridges, feeling so energized she could handle a thousand Unsubs. She couldn't wait to rejoin the hunt.

Annie's phone rang. She answered, hoping the list was ready—this graveyard gave her the creeps. She listened, and her face turned stony. "Rapid extraction! Now!" she barked, thrusting an arm at Emily. SWATs ran full-out. She raised her rifle, scanning for targets.

Emily's face drained as bodyguards stormed from the woods. "What's happening?" she asked, pulling up her shirt to expose her Glocks. Flea grabbed her left arm, another SWAT her right. The rest of the team encircled and moved her to the service road. Annie ran up.

"Bomb threat at Edward Hospital," she panted. "Too dangerous to go there now. Cross wants you at the safe house."

Emily cocked her head. "Why were we going to Edward?"

"Branch is out of the coma," Marwood said, waving his phone. "Winslow just called."

Emily shrieked, clapping her hands. "He's awake! What's he saying?"

Marwood shook his head. "The doc says it'll be hours before he's coherent. I'm heading there now to pick up what little I can for the profile."

Emily tensed to shake her captors and join him, but Flea tightened his grasp. "Don't even think about it," Annie warned.

"All right, I'll behave," Emily grumbled. "But, Ellis, tell Branch I'm thinking about him and I'll visit the moment I can."

"You got it." He turned toward Edward and ran, and Annie pushed her into a waiting cop car.

CHAPTER 18

Wednesday, noon
Eighteen hours till Emily's birthday

"A whole buncha ninjas and a psycho killer, too," Emily grumbled. "My life's a country song."

"Yeah," Flea said from his observation post at the safe-house kitchen window. "Dead Skunk in the Middle of the Road."

Everyone cracked up at the black humor, stirring a body-guard napping by the fire. He snorted and fell back asleep. Emily smiled, went back to the profile. "Ellis thinks he's a Green Beret," she said as Annie typed. "Maybe we can get a list of commandos from the Pentagon—"

"It's noon," Annie interrupted. "Time to check the in-box." She switched the laptop to secure mail, motioned for Emily to look.

Subject is fully awake. Subject vital signs look good. Four hours till hospital fully secured. I'll let you know when to leave. E.M.

"E.M. and Em," Annie said. "Awwwwww."

"It'd be cuter over a latte on Michigan Avenue."

"Quit griping," Annie said. "This is the plushest campout you'll ever have." She tapped her watch, and the team headed out to switch places with the woods crew. "I did some more snooping on that commander of yours. Did you know they offered him the job of sheriff and he turned it down?"

Emily shook her head.

"Eleven years ago. A motorcycle gang was pulling a series of home invasions. Marty went undercover. He looks like a biker when he's grungy and knows his way around a Harley. Two of their toughest whack jobs took him on. He broke all four of their arms, made 'em cry for their mommies."

"No way!"

"Way. The gang bought it and made him their chief enforcer. He went on to put every one of 'em in Stateville."

"Wow." Emily tried to square that with her vision of Marty.

"At the time, the sheriff was retiring with no electable replacement in sight. The politicians asked Marty to run and said they'd guarantee his victory. Marty wanted to say yes— he'd wanted that job since he was a rookie—but turned it down. Too much time away from his wife, who was dying of cancer."

Emily recalled Marty's sadness when she mentioned his wife in the car. "What happened?"

"They were furious," Annie said. "Nobody tells them no. They said take the job or kiss it off forever. 'I guess it's forever,' Marty said. 'Thanks, anyway.' One of them accused Marty of using the dying wife to extort a bigger salary before saying yes. Marty walked, and that was the end of it." She stood, adjusted her trousers, sat. "How many people walk away from a dream for someone who's gonna die anyway? Your man's a real mensch."

Emily put her chin in her hands.

"Hey, hon, you feeling all right?" Annie said, looking closely at her face. "You look pretty down. Is it what happened during the fun run? You want to talk about it?"

"Yes," Emily said, rubbing her tired eyes. She stifled a yawn, and another popped out. "But I don't have the energy all of a sudden. Rain check till after supper?"

"You got it. Go take a nice long nap."

"Aw, why bother?" Emily grumbled. "Soon as my head touches the pillow, we'll have to leave. Didn't Ellis say four hours till the coast is clear?"

"That means eight. Minimum. Edward's a huge place to search. Go on, get all the shut-eye you can. I'll keep the coffee hot."

Emily stretched. "All right. Since you insist."

"Adamantly. Sweet dreams."

EMILY AND BRADY

Chicago
November 1974

"Guess what?" Emily whispered to her third-grade classmates as they stood in line for meatless hot lunch. "My parents heard a father whip his son!"

"No!" a girlfriend squealed as the others crowded in. "Where? When?"

"Last week sometime. Mama and Daddy were taking their walk and heard a man screaming at his son inside a house. Then he smacked him with a belt!" A dozen kids squirmed, having been there themselves. "I don't know where it happened," she continued. "They walk through different neighborhoods every night. But Daddy told the police, and they went to the house. Right in the middle of the whipping!"

Brady Kepp froze, not daring to breathe.

"Sure they weren't messing with you?" a boy asked skeptically. "My dad makes up stuff all the time to 'prove' what he's saying. Mom calls it 'poetic license,' whatever that means."

"No, it's definitely true," Emily insisted. "Because they didn't say it to me. They were talking during Johnny Carson. I'm usually asleep, but a bad dream woke me up, so I heard everything. Daddy wanted to beat up the father, but Mama said no, he'd get arrested. So they found some policemen, who ran to the house and pounded on the door. That's when my parents left."

"Your ol' man," the boy murmured admiringly.

"He stepped in boiling steel to save his friend," Emily bragged. "He helps everyone!"

"That's really cool, Em," the boy enthused. He kind of liked this pretty tomboy who was afraid of nothing. Maybe he'd ask her to the Valentine's Day dance. "It takes a whole lotta balls to do that—*ow!*"

"We do not say 'balls' at St. Mary's Elementary," the nun scowled, twisting the boy's ear like a dead bolt. "It's disrespectful of the young ladies present, not to mention Our Jesus, who died in horrible agony for you." She waved her ruler. "There's enough swats in this for everyone," she warned. "So quit fooling around, and get your lunches." She frowned at Brady. "Are you all right, Mr. Kepp? You look ill."

"He probably wet his pants again, Sister," the boy snickered. "It makes his dinger itch.

"We do not say 'dinger,' either," the nun said, bouncing the ruler off his rump. Boys winced and girls giggled as sister whapped him to the principal's office. "Oh, hey, I forgot to tell you," Emily said, looking around carefully for more penguins. "Daddy gave Mama this cool new board game for her birthday. It's called Chutes and Ladders. . . ."

CHAPTER 19

Wednesday, 2 P.M.
Sixteen hours till Emily's birthday

Emily padded back from the bathroom, gazing at the bedroom window. It would be so simple. Just unscrew the steel plate with her all-in-one tool, raise the window, hang off the sill, drop to the ground, race through the woods, hitch a ride to Naperville, and fall into Marty's arms till happily ever after. She could definitely do it.

"But I won't," she said. With her luck, she'd start to drop, change her mind from guilt, and lack the strength to pull herself back inside. She'd have to yell for help, and Annie would throttle her before the Unsub got his chance. So she snuggled back under the covers, turned the pillow to the cool side, closed her eyes, and drifted.

"Hey! Em! Get up!" Annie yelled through the door.

Emily jarred awake. "What's wrong?" she yelled back, heart thumping.

"Marwood called! We're heading back to Naperville!"

"Really? OK, I'm up!" She rolled out of bed and opened the door. Annie held out a cheese sandwich, which Emily snatched happily. "What about the bomb threat?" she said, munching.

"False alarm," Annie said. "Some jerk kid playing dial-a-cop. Get dressed so we can get out of here."

Emily heard the distant boom of thunder, raised an eyebrow.

"Big storm headed our way," Annie said. "If we don't leave now, we'll be stuck here."

Emily finished the sandwich in three bites and ran for her clothes.

CHAPTER 20

Wednesday, 4 P.M.
Fourteen hours till Emily's birthday

Cross had suggested they stop at Edward before going to the station, and Emily murmured an "Our Father" when she spied Branch's room. She crossed the threshold and saw his familiar face. "Branch! You're awake!" she choked. She ran to the bed and hugged him carefully. "You look so good. I came as soon as I could."

No reply.

She let go to examine him. His skin was a sickly yellow, his normally lustrous hair oily and matted. He smelled like old bacon, and his bruises had merged into a giant black oil slick. He bristled with tubes, hoses, monitors, and bandages. His stockinged feet pulsed when the pressure cuffs kicked on. But his jaw was firm, his gaze clear and straight into her eyes.

Blink.

"Oh my God," Emily whispered. "You can't speak. You're paralyzed. Like my . . . my . . ."

Blink.

"Dammit, Ellis," Dr. Winslow barked as she charged into the room. "Didn't you warn her?"

Marwood shook his head. "I assumed she knew, Barbara," he said. "Commander Benedetti said he told her about the paralysis."

"But her memory's playing tricks. She might not even recall that conversation."

Emily's nerves pulsed. "I'm sure Marty told me, Doctor. I just don't remember."

Winslow squeezed Emily's arm. "Give me a minute to finish up a patient, and I'll answer all your questions." She pantomimed sipping. "I'm stopping at the cafeteria. Anybody need a drink?"

"Me," Marwood said, stifling a yawn.

"Coffee?"

"Nah," Marwood said, eyes flicking to Branch. "I'll take a nice cold pop."

"Regular or diet?"

"Any pop will do as long as it keeps me awake. . . ."

Branch is paralyzed, and you're discussing soft drinks? Emily nearly screamed as they debated the wake-up effects of Coke, Mountain Dew, and Winslow's "all-time favorite during residency, Cherry-Ola Cola spiked with No-Doz." But Winslow dealt with tragedy all the time. Marwood, too, she supposed. They weren't heartless. Just inured.

"How are you, Emily?" Winslow asked when she reappeared. "Annie says you're a little sore. Don't worry. That's to be expected." She placed her pop can on a tray and ran her fingers over Emily's ribs. "How does this feel . . . good . . . now here . . . excellent," she said. "You're healing nicely."

Emily pointed to Branch. "He's healing nicely, too? He's coming back from this?"

Blink, Branch said.

"Yes," Winslow agreed. "The bullet sideswiped a vertebra, making it swell like a balloon against the spinal cord. That's why he's paralyzed. When the swelling decreases, so will the pressure on the cord, and with it the paralysis. His speech will return then, too."

Thank God! "When will he be back on his feet? Memorial Day? Thanksgiving?"

"We don't know. The body heals when the body heals."

"But he'll recover completely."

"Well," Winslow said, taking a sip. "Naturally, our goal is 100 percent—"

"What?!" Emily objected.

Winslow sighed. "Branch will walk and talk again. How completely, there's simply no way to predict right now. He may come back only 90 percent. Maybe 80. Perhaps as low as—"

Blink-blink.

Winslow touched Branch's arm. "Still insisting on one hundred, are we?"

Blink.

"You're prepared to do everything the therapists say? No matter how painful or exhausting? Sixty days or six years, you'll stick with the regimen to the bitter end?"

Blink.

"OK, then, Hercules," Winslow said, breath catching a little. "I won't let this killer beat you. I'll get you that 100 percent."

Blink.

Emily swallowed hard, thinking of Mama. "He understands what we say?"

"Every word. Mind's not affected, just his body."

"So"—she swung her eyes to Branch—"you can talk by blinking?"

Blink.

Emily blew out her breath, knowing that Mama somewhere, somehow, was helping Branch out. "Can you spell out words? Sentences?"

Blink-blink.

"One blink or two," Winslow said. "Yes or no. That's all we'll get for awhile. His eyelid muscles go into spasm if he works too hard."

"I remember," Emily said, tucking her hands in her armpits for warmth. "Mama never could semaphore. Only yes or no." She glanced at Marwood, who hadn't said a word since snapping open his pop can. "Semaphoring is how you spell words with blinks, Ellis," she explained. "One blink means *A*. Two equals *B*, three *C,* and so on. Given enough time, you can blink out *Hamlet*."

"Mm-hm," Marwood said, sipping.

Emily looked at Branch again. His expression was a little off center, like ice cream melted and refrozen. "You will get back to your old charming self, right, Captain?" she pressed. "So Lydia won't have to wait on you hand and foot?"

Blink.

"I couldn't have said it better myself," Winslow said.

Emily noticed Branch staring at Marwood. She realized he might not even know the profiler. Or had completely forgotten, if his memory blanks were as bad as hers. "Do you know this man?" she asked, pointing.

Blink-blink.

"Then please meet Dr. Ellis Marwood, the criminal profiler Chief Cross brought onto the task force," she said. "Remember telling us about the task force at Grandma Sally's?"

Blink.

"Ellis is an industrial psychologist," Emily continued. "His clients are large corporations and federal law-enforcement agencies. He's born, raised, and still lives in Manhattan, so he's an arrogant so-and-so"—quick grin—"but we forgive him because he's so dedicated to hunting."

Blink-blink.

Blink-blink.

Blink-blink-blink-blink-blinkblinkblink-blinkblink-blinkblink . . .

"Doctor!" Emily gasped. "Do something!"

Winslow shook her head. "He's just falling asleep."

"No, he's not. Look at him! He's in pain!"

"Branch is fine," Winslow assured. "He's fighting to stay awake for you. When his body can't take it anymore, his eyelids start to spasm. A minute later he falls asleep, to regain his strength. It's been happening since he woke."

Blinkblinkblinkblinkblinkblinkblinkblinkblinkblinkblink-blinkblinkblinkblink . . .

"Cross wants us back ASAP," Annie called from the hallway. "Let's go."

Emily squeezed Branch's hand, then headed out.

They drove to Jackson Avenue so she could change, then headed for the police station. Emily drove her own car, Marwood her sole passenger at her request.

"So what was that about?" Emily said at the first red light.

"What?"

"You didn't talk to Branch during the visit," she said. "Not once. What gives?"

"What should I have said to the man, Emily? 'Gee, pal, your life sucks. Bummer.'"

She stomped the accelerator at the green. "How about a simple, 'I'm happy you survived, Captain?' Or maybe, 'We're gonna get this scumbag, Branch. Let me tell you the profile I created.'" Her volume climbed. "A little something to acknowledge he's a living, breathing human being and not just a piece of your puzzle."

"Yes, I could have," Marwood said. "I chose not to."

Emily passed Safety Town, turned into the patrol-car lot. "Why?"

No answer.

She nosed into a space. Annie glided by. Emily held up a finger—*one minute*—then turned to Marwood. "Tell me, or my cooperation with you is finished."

Marwood glared at her. "All right, Detective, if you insist," he said. "This nightmare isn't happening to Joe Citizen. It's happening to you. A member of the tribe." His expression was hostile. "Meaning Branch, Cross, Bates, Benedetti, and everybody else around here are too emotionally distracted to make their usual sound judgments. I certainly understand that. Hell, if family doesn't go to bat for you in a crisis, who will? But someone needs to see the bigger picture. To stand at arm's length and point out where emotion is clouding judgment."

"And that's you?" Emily snapped.

"Damn straight. I'm the designated driver for this punch-drunk outfit." Marwood's body was a coiled rattler. "Ken Cross knew exactly what would happen to his department when word leaked you were the target. That's why he brought me in. To be his profiler, sure, I'm good at it. But most of all, to be the one set of eyes and ears without an emotional stake in this." He poked Emily's shoulder. She slapped his hand away. "I start caring too much about things like whether Branch walks again, I become less objective. Meaning less effective. So I let others play those roles. I play mine."

"Professional detachment, huh?"

"Yup."

Emily slumped back. "All right, I get it. Sorry I keep blowing up at you."

"Don't be sorry, dammit!" Marwood raged. "Just quit pissing on me all the time!"

"Ellis—"

"I have very good reasons for what I do!" he said. "So

quit the sniping and second-guessing. It's a distraction neither of us can afford!"

She touched his forearm, letting her hand linger to say, if not sorry, then thanks. Marwood released his door handle and smiled. "You ready to meet the task force?"

EMILY AND BRADY

Chicago
January 1975

"Any idea how this got started?" the Chicago Fire Department engineer yelled over the howl of sirens.

"Not a clue!" the battalion chief replied, ordering hose teams down the alley to knock down floating cinders. What had started as a routine garage fire—two trucks, one hose, back in time for the Bulls game—had exploded into a three-house conflagration when flames hit the drum of stove fuel the homeowner stored under the workbench. The chief waved over a cop. "Still too close," he said, pointing to the wide-eyed kids watching the fire. "Push 'em back another hundred feet so they don't get hurt, OK?" The cop nodded and ran off.

"Always count on the neighborhood boys turning out for us," the engineer said, waving his sooty helmet. They waved back, thrilled to be noticed by their heroes.

"Good thing they do," the chief agreed, saluting the boys

himself. "Half our guys joined the department because they saw a fireman scale a wall or save a kid." The kids cheered the arrival of the snorkel truck, prompting its driver to toot the air horn.

Brady Kepp saluted back, his dick harder than he'd ever known. This fire was his best yet. He'd never dreamed of an explosion, too! A shame he couldn't light the whole city on fire . . .

CHAPTER 21

Wednesday, 5 P.M.
Thirteen hours till Emily's birthday

Emily was halfway into the auditorium when Marty grabbed her arm from behind. "There's something new in the case, Detective," he growled, steering her into an interrogation room and shutting the door. "Something you need to know now."

His slate-hard expression unnerved her. "What?" she asked.

"This," he said, wrapping her in his arms and kissing her lips.

"Ohhh, Marty." She returned the kiss, trying to grab all of him at once. He was warm, solid, reassuring. "I'm so glad to see you!"

"Me, too, Emily Marie," he said, stroking her hair and ears. " 'Nother?"

She closed her eyes.

He kissed softer but longer, matching his breath to hers.

She leaned into him, heat lightning sparking from every place they touched. He backed off after awhile but kept his face close. "You scared me, darling," he whispered, eyes bright. "I thought I'd never see you again."

Emily's legs wobbled. "A big ol' tough guy like you?" she teased. "Scared?"

"Out of my mind."

They embraced without saying anything. Then Benedetti sighed. "I'd comfort you right on this table if we had time. We don't. Take my IOU?"

"I'm cashing it in the minute we catch this guy. Plan on calling in sick for a week."

"Happily, Miss Nightingale. But till then it's strictly business between us." He kissed her again, massaging her head with both hands. "Agreed?"

"Agreed . . . Commander Benedetti," she said.

"Good." He pointed to a double stack of printouts. "Dig in."

"What is it?" she said, combing her hair into place.

"Personnel roster from the Pentagon. Our Unsub's in there somewhere."

Emily lunged for the treasure trove. "Ellis predicted he was military!"

"So did you," Benedetti said. "Remember asking if military ammo meant the Unsub's a soldier?"

She looked at him.

"Never mind. Bottom line is the Unsub's a veteran, and he's on one of those sheets. Read fast."

"Are you serious?" she said, thumbing the stack. "There's thousands of names here!"

"Millions," Benedetti corrected. "But I sorted them by home address, nearest to farthest from the three places you've lived—Naperville, college dorm in Wisconsin, childhood bungalow in Chicago—"

Emily gasped as a memory surfaced. "Marty! I quit playing games when I buried Mama! I didn't start again till Lucy was murdered!"

Benedetti's eyes widened as the meaning hit home. "You know the Unsub from childhood. Because you stopped playing games at twenty-one!" He paced. "Did you tell anyone about those game and ice cream nights? I mean, after your mother died?"

"No."

"Are you certain?" he pressed. "Your memory's fragged."

She thought hard. "After Mama died, even thinking about game night turned me into Niagara Falls. So I never told anyone." A chill swept her body, and her hand darted to the closest thing she had to a rosary—the handcuff key taped to the back of her neck. "The only adults I ever told are Jack, Branch, Annie, and you. Though I assume Branch told Cross and Ellis."

Benedetti pulled out a chair and gestured at it. "Em, you just cut the suspect list by two-thirds. Now find a name. Take all the time you need, of course, but the quicker we find the guy . . ."

Emily sat and picked up the first printout. The scent of the predator was heavy in her nostrils.

CHAPTER 22

Wednesday, 8 P.M.
Ten hours till Emily's birthday

"I'm never gonna find this clown," Emily groaned, rubbing her burning eyes. The first name she'd looked for was Daddy's. She'd turned light-headed when she saw it pop from the end of the page—*THOMPSON, GERALD FLANDERS*—and quickly moved on. The hunt was tedious, and so far fruitless. She'd waded through the navy, air force, and half the army and still wasn't done with Illinois. Nobody knew for sure the Unsub was in fact ex-military. Criminal profiles were educated guesses, not facts.

KEPP, BRADY MAURICE. Captain, U.S. Army. Born 23 January 1965, Chicago. Inducted into service 23 January 1982, East St. Louis. Final posting USSOCOM, MacDill AFB, Tampa. Separated from service 06 June 1990 . . .

"Get the commander!" Emily hollered through the door. Marty charged into the room. "I know this name," she said, breathing fast. "I went to grade school with a Brady Maurice Kepp."

Benedetti read over her shoulder. "USSOCOM. That's United States Special Operations Command. It fits. Do you remember him?"

She screwed her eyes shut, willing Kepp to appear. "No," she complained bitterly. "My memory is so—"

"Just relax," Benedetti said, studying the information. "Tell me about Kepp. He's your age. Lived in your neighborhood." He frowned. "Wait, that doesn't fit. His house was more than a mile from yours. That's two neighborhoods away at least."

"I attended Catholic school," she said. "The parish boundary might have stretched wide enough to include both houses. I could know him from school but not from the neighborhood."

Benedetti leaned against the table. "Makes sense. Were you friends with this boy?"

A little of Brady floated back. "He didn't have many friends, mostly kept to himself. He played baseball. Maybe football. I think I liked him. I don't know why." She thought hard. "There was something about his family. Something unusual. I don't know what."

Benedetti paced. "We'll search newspaper archives and police reports. All Kepp's government records. If there's anything there—"

Emily jumped to her feet. "I beat him up once."

"You did? When?"

"In eighth grade. Brady asked me to a dance." She closed her eyes, concentrating. "I blew him off for some reason. He got mad and called me a cunt."

Benedetti tapped her elbow with his notebook. "Ah. Like Ray Luerchen did at the ditch."

"Same result, too—I went after him. Brady fought back.

He got in some good licks. But I was quicker and whaled on him from every direction." She made a face. "All the kids gathered 'round, chanting, 'Fraidy Brady, beat up by a girl! Bed wetter! Retard!'" She felt mildly embarrassed. "Kids were pretty stupid back then."

Benedetti wrote fast. "Em, that could be his motive. Revenge."

"It was a school yard fistfight," she argued. "No big deal. I had them twice a month. So did my friends. Fighting came with growing up on the Southwest Side. How could anyone be so angry about a meaningless little dustup"—she counted on her fingers—"twenty-eight years later?"

"Hey, tinfoil can jump-start a wacko," Benedetti pointed out. "That's why they're wackos. Plus this kid was a bed wetter. Do you know if he tortured animals or set fires?"

She shook her head.

"We'll find out." Scribble-scribble-scribble. "Did your school have yearbooks?"

Emily shook her head. "We had class photos, though. I threw them in the trash when I left for Madison—big, tough, unsentimental college girl, you know—but Daddy fished them out. I found them in the basement after he died, along with a note. *Your children will want these, Princess. Don't cuss too much. Love, Daddy.*" Her skin prickled as an image of Brady Kepp took shape in her mind. Stocky build, big puppy eyes, bright yellow hair, and dandruff. Handsome except for the ears sticking out like dinner plates. Eager to please in grades one through four, moody in fifth, surly till graduation. Her hatred for this man was building like a runaway train, and he wasn't guilty of anything but his name. *God help him if he's the Unsub!* "Maybe the FBI can age his school photos with their computers," she suggested. "See what he'd look like at twenty, thirty, and now. If it matches his official photographs—"

"Passport, driver's license, military ID—"

"We'll at least know we're dealing with the same Brady Kepp."

Benedetti summoned a computer tech and two detectives. He told them what he needed, Emily explained where she kept the photos, and they headed out. He dialed his cell phone. "She found a name, Ken," he reported. "I'm coming up." He disconnected, slapped the printouts. "Finish Illinois. Make sure there's nobody else. Then join us in the auditorium. We've got a lot of work to do in ten hours."

CHAPTER 23

Wednesday, 9 P.M.
Nine hours till Emily's birthday

Finding no more names, Emily walked into the police station auditorium, a quarter acre of tiered seating, tables, computers, paperwork, and personal belongings. Everyone wore a badge. Most carried guns. Tall windows filled one wall. Corkboards of crime-scene photographs, diagrams, and notes filled the others. She wrinkled her nose at the wooly smell—too many people working too-long hours. A stained banquet table mounded with sandwiches, bagels, fruit, chips, pop, bottled water, and coffee was shoved in a corner. She looked around for familiar faces, heard somebody crow, "Hey! Look who's here!" She didn't recognize the plump man or his uniform but waved, anyway. Everyone turned, moved in, started talking at once.

"Emily! You look great!"

"Terrific job at the forest preserve! Against a machine gun yet!"

"We're gonna find this asshole and fuck him up!"

"You want coffee? How 'bout coffee? I'll get ya coffee!"

A tall, lanky-limbed woman in short heels offered her hand. "I'm Judy Stephens," she said. "Head of the Chicago office of BATFE. Good to finally meet you."

"Same here," Emily said. "You're the one who determined Neuqua was a bomb, right?"

Stephens nodded. "We traced the plastic explosives to Eastern Europe. . . ."

A half dozen such conversations later, Emily's stomach rumbled, reminding her the last thing she'd eaten was a Velveeta sandwich. She excused herself from a Naperville narcotics detective whose name she didn't remember and worked her way to the buffet, accepting more handshakes. She stabbed an arm between two state troopers and snatched a cinnamon raisin bagel, closing her eyes in worship. *God, if you're God, make this a doughnut! I've got a sugar jones that bagels can't possibly fix!*

But it'd likelier turn into wine, she knew. Cross hated the Doughnut Cop stereotype so much, he vowed his first day on the job that his officers were going to lose their potbellies or else. He learned in a grievance letter that the union contract specifically prohibited physical fitness as a condition of employment. Cross retaliated by banning doughnuts from the station, jail, cruisers, and all departmental functions, and to this day the only doughnut at NPD was for hemorrhoids. She scraped the bagel through strawberry Philly, filled a cup with steaming coffee, and backed away.

"Ow! Watch where you're going!" someone carped as her heel mashed a toe.

"Oops, sorry," Emily said. Then she saw who it was. "Gee, Ray, did I hurt you?"

"Hell, no!" Rayford Luerchen snapped.

"Too bad." She slurped an inch off the top. "What are you doing here?"

Luerchen grinned. "Funny you should ask. Sheriff got first dibs on Branch's replacement. I'm it. And I've got you to thank, hon. If you weren't such a crummy shot at that forest preserve, Branch wouldn't be wetting his sheets at the hospital, and I wouldn't be named to the hottest task force in . . . Yeow! Shit!"

"Oops," rumbled the narc. "Clumsy me, bumping Emily's elbow. What with her holding hot coffee and all." His face was picture-perfect with concern. "Didn't burn yer pecker there, did I, Ray?"

Luerchen's eyes watered as he fanned his crotch. "You did that deliberately!"

"Not me, Bubba. I just heard what you said and damned if my hand didn't slip. By accident." He held out a pink cocktail napkin and smiled. "Want me to pat yer crotch for ya, hon?"

Luerchen flushed. "Outside, you and me, right now—"

"OK, people, take your seats," Cross boomed. "There's an important development."

The narc balled the napkin and bounced it off Luerchen's leg. "You really oughta dry yourself, Ray," he stage-whispered. "Don't want the bosses thinkin' you wet your sheets."

Emily sat near a window so she could see the front of the police station, fire department headquarters, the animal control building, the pint-size skyline of Safety Town, and Lake Osborne, the retention pond with the grandiloquent name. The view made her happy. She'd sworn to defend Naperville, and this Public Safety Campus was ground zero for doing it. But the view also made her anxious—the city she loved was a deadly menace to her. Maybe sitting here wasn't such a good idea after all. . . .

Benedetti entered the auditorium with Annie, who shooed cops from each side of Emily to plant herself and Flea. Benedetti conferred briefly with Cross, then took the microphone. Everyone in the room stole curious peeks at

Emily. She shifted, uncomfortable in the center of this three-ring circus.

"We have a suspect," Benedetti said without preamble, thumping the mike. "He's Brady Maurice Kepp, age forty. Retired Army Green Beret and a grade-school classmate of Detective Thompson's. She just confirmed she knows him. Our FBI liaisons are downloading Kepp's military dossier. You'll get copies shortly." The hollow-eyed exhaustion of the room vanished, and a dozen hands shot up. Benedetti waved them down. "We'll do updates first, starting with Lucille Crawford. Sergeant Luerchen, go ahead."

As Luerchen sprang to his feet, Emily looked outside to see children marching into Safety Town from long yellow school buses. Fourth-and fifth-graders, with their clean, scrubbed looks, staying up past bedtime to enjoy their treat for getting straight A's in school—a bonfire and ghost stories in Safety Town. Preceded, of course, by Safety Town's real mission, teaching them how to safely cross streets and railroad tracks, avoid rivers and retention ponds, use crosswalks, and escape burning buildings. The kids looked happy, pointing excitedly at police cruisers, geese waddling up from the lake, a prisoner truck rumbling toward the jail entrance. A hook and ladder backing into the firehouse burped its siren. The kids waved NPD ball caps. A FedEx driver ran inside with a carton, then drove off. Luerchen cleared his throat, and she reluctantly turned back to the meeting.

"The sheriff's CSI team discovered a hair in the stolen Porsche," Luerchen began, tugging his polyester jacket over the wet spot. "It is a scalp hair. It does not belong to the deceased." Marwood snapped to attention, and Emily felt a catty grin slide across her face. *So you* don't *know everything, huh, Mr. Designated Driver?* "It does not belong to the owner of said stolen vehicle, nor to anyone the owner says rode in said vehicle, nor to official personnels at the scene." Emily cringed at the sodden language, having a new appreciation for Marty's hatred of copspeak. "Therefore, there is an excellent chance it belongs to the perpetrator. When we deem a suspect, we can use the DNA possessed in the hair's root to link said perpetrator to the wrecked subject vehicle and therefore to Ms. Crawford." He detailed the rest of the lab results, then said, "Put all that together and it spells *h-o-m-i-c-i-d-e*."

"Jesus Christ, he actually spelled it," a cop behind her moaned. "What a moron."

Benedetti nodded. "Thanks, Ray. Good brief." He drained his foam cup. "Next up, BATFE on the Neuqua High bombing."

The chief's cell phone burbled. He answered it, frowned, whispered to Benedetti. Then hustled up the auditorium stairs and out the rear exit. Dozens of eyeballs followed, snapping back only when Judy Stephens began speaking.

"Our analysis indicates the Unsub breached the safety fence around the construction tunnel and shimmied up the natural-gas main into the school," she said. "When he reached the foundation wall, he attached two packages. Each consisted of plastic explosive, detonator, and timer. The first was a cutter charge, which sawed the pipe in half. Natural gas leaked for hours, saturating the soil and foundation. Then the second package detonated, igniting the gas." Nods and murmurs indicated they all remembered the strike on Neuqua. "Lucky for us, he decided to limit the damage."

"Are you kidding, Judy?" someone in back sputtered. "He crushed it like a pop can!"

"If the gas had ignited during school hours, we'd be shoveling several thousand children along with the debris," Stephens replied. "So, yes, the Unsub chose to limit his damage. He wasn't interested in mass murder, only in recreating the Timebomb game from Detective Thompson's collection." She glanced at her notes. "We recovered enough fragments to determine the particular timer used. It's a relatively new design, developed by NATO for use in Iraq."

The auditorium's back door slammed open, making more than one cop reach for a gun.

EMILY AND BRADY

Chicago
April 1975

"Boooooooo!" Dwight Kepp shouted as the umpire called a third strike on his son. "That pitch was ten miles off the plate! I'll double whatever Blessed Martyr's paying you!"

"This is a charity game," Alexandra Thompson reminded the boor from nine rows back. She'd looked forward to this annual fund-raising event with Our Lady of the Blessed Martyr, and this idiot was ruining it with heckling. Not to mention distracting the players! "Why don't you be quiet so we can hear what's going on?"

The man whirled as the crowd clapped its approval. "I bought my ticket like everyone else, hon," he growled. "And a hundred raffle tickets to boot. I have every right to question bad calls—"

"She ain't your hon," Gerald Thompson said, plunking

himself next to the hemorrhoid. "And the kids play great without any help from us parents. Give it a rest, friend."

Dwight whipped around. How dare someone question his right to speak! Then he noticed the stranger's break-you-in-half physique under the Cream of Wheat expression. "Aw, I guess you're right," he said, donning a mask of sheepish apology. "I get carried away seeing my boy play. I travel a lot on business—I'm the regional president of Chicago Life and Casualty—and rarely make his games."

"I understand," Gerald said, realizing where he'd heard this voice before—the jerk-off beating his son last fall. "We all want our kids to do well. But you're distracting them." He offered his hand. "But, hey, it's a nice day out. Let's start fresh. I'm Gerald Thompson." He nodded at the diamond. "The pitcher's my daughter, Emily."

"Oh, she's a great one," Dwight enthused. Inferiors were so easy to manipulate with a smile and false praise. "Her pitches swoop in like a pro. You should be proud." He pumped the big redhead's hand. "The name's Dwight Kepp. My boy, Brady, hit that three-run homer in the first."

"He's the left fielder?"

"Right!" Kepp enthused. "I mean, correct! This here's my wife, Alice. Honey, meet Gerry." She said a faint hello and went back to her scorecard. Gerald made small talk as he kept shaking hands. "You know, Dwight," he said, squeezing harder. "My wife and I take a walk every night after supper."

"That so?" Kepp said, trying not to flinch.

"Yup. We stretch our legs while Emily does her homework." He leaned in so only the hemorrhoid would hear. "Thing is, Dwight, I heard you beating the snot out of your kid. We don't put up with that garbage around here—a child abuser is the worst kind of scum." He heard knuckles crackle and smiled to himself. "I run a steel union. My buddies from the mill can be at your house ten minutes after I call. You know what that means." He paused to emphasize the next point. "Now you might think you're tough, beating up a kid and maybe your wife, too. But we're tougher, and the cops around here look the other way when it comes to kicking a child abuser into pudding. So here's the deal. I hear one more scream like I did that night, and you're gonna wish you'd never been born. You follow?"

Dwight's lean face was as white as chalk. Gerald released the hand. "It's good meeting you, friend," he said. "You, too, Mrs. Kepp. Stop by the house sometime. Emily probably knows Brady from school." He walked up the bleachers to rejoin Alexandra, humming "Dragnet."

"What'd you say to him?" she asked, kissing his cheek.

"Just the facts, ma'am," Gerald said, thumbing a mustard glob from her Vienna hot dog, which she'd accessorized the Chicago way with raw onions, sliced tomatoes, hot peppers, dill pickle spear, yellow mustard, bright green relish, and two shakes of celery salt, all stuffed into a steamed poppy-seed bun. He took a bite from the back end.

An inning later the game was over, Brady Kepp's tumbling dive catch preserving Emily's shutout. She tried high-fiving him, but he'd already turned to meet his parents. So she trotted to the opposing team's bench to find Blessed Martyr's catcher, who'd kicked dirt and grunted ethnic slurs at St. Mary's players when the ump wasn't paying attention. She saw him unbuckling his shin guards and pasted on her snottiest grin. "Gee, Beaver," she said. "Don't you hate getting whipped by a girl?"

"Kiss my ass, Thompson," the catcher snapped.

"I can't. Your head's already up it." She laughed along with the catcher's teammates. "Face it, shit-for-brains, you're just a sore loser. You deserve getting your ass kicked by twelve runs for giving me and my friends so much fucking . . . Whoa!"

"You're headed for the showers," Gerald grunted, tucking his daughter under his left arm like a loaf of bread. He marched Emily into the dusty field behind the bleachers, not stopping till they were clear of eavesdroppers. He dropped her, stared down into her wide eyes. "What was that about?" he demanded.

"What?"

"The cussing. The gloating. The snotty attitude. And did I mention the cussing?"

Emily met his eyes. "That boy had it coming, Daddy. He called Marcy a kike, Lawrence a wop, and Stan a Polack. Stuff nobody should say!" She put her hands on her hips. "Nobody else would tell him off because he's so big. So I did."

Gerald knelt so they were face-to-face.

"Listen, Princess, don't get me wrong. I'm proud you stood up for yourself and your teammates. It takes guts, which I'm glad you have. But that doesn't give you permission to rub someone's nose in your success. Only poor sports do that." He sat on the grass, motioned her to do likewise. "As for the cussing, you should never do that around people you don't know."

"Why not?" Emily said, clutching her knobby knees to her chest. "When you fixed the boat motor and skinned your knuckles, I heard words I never knew before!"

"Yes, I did," he admitted. "But I didn't know you were listening. I would never cuss at you or around you. It's disrespectful, and I won't do it."

"You would if I was a boy," she said, pouting.

"Wrong," Gerald countered. "I don't cuss in front of kids. I also don't cuss around neighbors, acquaintances, or strangers. I don't know if they appreciate salty talk, so why would I offend them? You're a bright girl. You know there's lots of ways to make a point without cussing."

Emily crinkled her face. "But I do cuss, Daddy," she said. "I can't help it sometimes. When someone picks on my friends, I jump in, and those bad words just come out. Sometimes I even say . . . uh . . ."

"Go ahead."

"'Fuck' because it sounds cool."

"Yeah, I heard."

She looked away, embarrassed. "How do I stop?"

"Aye, there's the rub," Gerald muttered.

"What?"

"Never mind. Here's what we're going to do. You're going to cuss only with me."

Emily's eyes widened.

Gerald shifted to his other hip, allowing him to see Alex waving from the bleachers. He pointed at the station wagon, mimicked steering. She nodded. He turned back to Emily.

"That's right. I'm going to allow you to cuss your head off. But only in front of me," he explained. "Whenever you feel the need, you tell me. We'll wander down to the basement, go fishing, whatever, and you can let 'er rip."

Emily sat up taller. "Really?" she asked. "I can say anything?"

"That's right. 'Shit' or 'ass' or 'fuck' or whatever you can dream up. I won't teach you any dirty words, but if you find them on your own, you can ask me what they mean. I'll give an honest answer." He smiled. "And anything else you feel like asking about, like boys or kissing or sex—"

"I should go right to Mama."

He laughed. "You're pretty smart for nearly ten," he said, rubbing her hair with great affection. They chattered till Mama rolled up, and Gerald helped his daughter to her feet.

"Just remember our deal, Princess," he warned, escorting her to the back door. "No bad language around anyone but me. Especially not around Mama. She doesn't like your using bad language, and you will respect her feelings. Break that little rule and your butt's gonna wear some blisters."

Emily grinned. "I promise, Daddy. By the way, that man hollering from the bleachers was right. The umpire did have his head up his ass."

"So far up he'll eat shit for supper."

They laughed themselves silly, climbed into the station wagon, and she replayed for Mama all the way to the Dairy Queen "the best gosh-darn game of my career."

CHAPTER 24

Wednesday, 11 P.M.
Seven hours till Emily's birthday

The slamming door was Cross reentering the auditorium. His grim expression made Emily's stomach lurch. "Brady Kepp just delivered a message," he announced. He pulled a jewel box from the FedEx carton under his arm, handed it to Benedetti. "It arrived a short time ago, addressed to Detective Thompson. The bomb squad ran it through X-ray and sniffer dogs. No explosives. They put it in a DVD player, called me after seeing the first screen."

Benedetti popped his head from the projection control room. "Cued up, Chief."

Cross stabbed "play." The lights dimmed, and the video came to life on the wall-size screen behind the podium.

EMILY AND BRADY

Chicago
April 1975

Emily stared wordlessly at Brady Kepp, whose face was falling like one of those California mud slides on TV. She'd just finished delivering party invitations to her classmates—*Games festival for my tenth birthday! Pizza! Prizes! My house, three weeks, be there or you've got cooties!*—and hated leaving Brady out. But Mama was firm, and Daddy backed her up. All her girlfriends concurred, saying Brady had gotten really annoying this year.

But she kind of liked him, anyway. Brady was good-looking, even with those ears. He got straight A's and was a superb athlete because he lifted weights after practice while the other boys horsed around. But Brady was awfully moody, she had to admit. He'd kept entirely to himself after the softball game with Blessed Martyr. She'd tried to congratulate him the following Monday—a ploy to make sure he'd come to her party, where maybe they could move beyond the longing looks he gave when he thought she wasn't looking—but he curtly brushed her off.

Oh, well, she said to herself, walking back to her desk. *He can't say I didn't try.*

CHAPTER 25

Wednesday, 11 P.M.
Seven hours till Emily's birthday

The first image on the screen was a photograph of a note typewritten on Xerox paper.

Dear Chief Halfass—
  You and the task force are to watch this DVD presentation. Do NOT preview. Everyone must watch it together, without interruption, immediately upon receiving the FedEx package. If you don't follow my rules, if you don't watch my entertainment exactly as I specify, if Emily leaves the room even once—I'll know. And the innocent children of your community will pay with their lives.

                            Sincerely yours, Brady Kepp

"Screw you," a cop snarled.
"He just did," Cross responded.
The DVD played on.

EMILY AND BRADY

Chicago
February 1977

Brady Kepp, having rehearsed this speech till every syllable was perfect, screwed up his courage and began walking
her way. He'd finally decided to ask Emily to the Valentine's
Day dance, figuring if she said yes, then Father would have
to approve. Brady had no idea why he was supposed to hate
the Thompsons—it was grown-up stuff that didn't interest
him. He just wanted to dance with this cute, smart girl and
run his fingers through the long hair that sometimes invaded
his dreams.

"Emmy and Brady, sitting in a tree, *K-I-S-S-I-N-G*,"
Emily's girlfriends sang as they hung from the monkey bars
in the playground behind St. Mary's. "Boyfriend at six o'clock."

"He's not my boyfriend," Emily said. "He's ignored me
for two years now, and I'm sick of him. The heck with Brady
Kepp."

He arrived at the monkey bars, screwing up his courage.

He hated to pop the question in front of the other girls but heard himself say, "Emily? Can I talk to you a minute?"

"Go right ahead," Emily said, not looking at him.

"Uh, how 'bout over there?" he tried, pointing to the cinder-block incinerator near the alley.

Emily swung through the bars and dropped to the pea gravel. "We have nothing to talk about, Brady Kepp," she declared, hands on her jutting hips. "Ever since that softball game, you've treated me like measles. I suppose you want to ask me to the Valentine's dance, right?"

Brady's face burned as the other girls giggled at Em's brazenness. "I . . . well . . ." He found his tongue. "Yes, I do. Will you go to the dance with me, Emily?"

"I might," she said, sweeping her long chestnut ponytail to the side. "If you get down on your knees and apologize for being mean."

Brady stared.

"Well?" Emily demanded, tapping her patent leather shoe.

Brady's guts heaved. Apologizing went against everything he'd been taught by Father. But he found himself on the ground, arms wide, palms up, knees a half inch from the gravel—if they didn't actually touch, maybe it wouldn't count. "I apologize, Emily," he said in a soft, pleading voice he'd never heard before. "I shouldn't have ignored you all this time." He felt like throwing up. "Will you go to the dance with me?"

Emily smiled. "No. But it was nice of you to apologize, anyway."

The girls exploded with laughter, attracting kids from swings, teeter-totters, and dodgeball. Brady sprang to his feet, mortified. "What do you mean, no?" he demanded.

"Exactly what I said. I'll go with anyone but you."

"Then why did you make me beg?"

"Because you've been a jerk, that's why," she said, holding tight to her promise not to cuss. "I did exactly what you've been doing to me for two years. How do you like it?"

Brady shook with rage. Part of him wanted to skin this girl alive, make her scream like that poodle he'd gutted last week at his riverside place. But most of him liked her even better for sticking up for herself. Emily Thompson was nobody's pansy. "Have fun with whoever then," he said, choosing the worst thing he'd ever heard Father call Mom. "You stupid cunt."

Emily's face went rigid. "What did you call me, Brady Kepp?"

"Cunt," Brady sneered. "Big, fat cunt with a capital—" *Woof!* Emily's uppercut caught him off guard, tripping him. She landed on him like a TV wrestler, pinning his shoulders with those sharp knees of hers and grinding her butt into his chest to keep him from tossing her off. Which he had no intention of doing. Her plaid uniform skirt had hiked up so much, her white cotton panties were doing the rubbing, exciting him. He wrestled hard enough to make Emily think he was fighting back—even socked her a few times, taking care to aim at flesh, not bones or joints—but otherwise allowed her to smash and claw as she wished. He'd taken far worse beatings in the cellar.

"Never call me that awful word again, Brady Kepp!" Emily shouted, splitting his upper lip with a middle-knuckle shot. "Not ever! It's gross and disgusting, and I won't have it!"

"Cunt! Cunt!" Brady yelled. He tried to throw her off, but she rode him like Willie Shoemaker, bruising both his eye sockets with punches. Time to end this. She'd stuck her thumbs in her fists, and one more solid hit would break her hand. He grabbed her forearms, heaved her overboard.

"Children! Stop it!" the nuns shouted, running over to break up the fight. One dragged Emily back, and two others hauled Brady to his feet. "What's all this about?"

"Nothing," he mumbled. Emily said likewise, earning her still more respect from Brady.

"Perhaps Father Snowe's paddle will convince you to follow the rules against hitting girls, young man," the flinty-eyed nun from the lunchroom scolded as she hauled Brady to the principal for correction. Another, younger, nun walked Emily to an office to call her parents, whispering that was a jim-dandy uppercut, but rules were rules, and she'd be suspended the rest of the week.

Brady bit his lip as Father Snowe applied the "board of education" to his cotton boxers. He'd get it a hundred times worse if his actual father found out a girl had blackened his eyes, but that didn't matter. Those few seconds under Emily's heaving body made all the misery worthwhile.

CHAPTER 26

Thursday, midnight
Six hours till Emily's birthday

"That's Nichols Library!" Luerchen barked over the *Jeopardy* theme song. "That man! With his face covered! It has to be Kepp!"

"Footage from the security videotape he stole," Benedetti agreed.

Kepp, wearing boots, coveralls, gloves, hat and face-covering balaclava, pitched a clearly dead Arnold Soull through the hole in the library window. He followed on fingers and toes, then stood and waved at the camera.

"Showing off," Annie muttered from Emily's right. Kepp, meantime, wedged Soull's feet under his arm and galloped toward the stairs, his victim's head bumping along behind.

Quick cut.

Emily, in running clothes, on the Riverwalk. Brown grass dusted with snow. Bare trees. Glassy river. Winter. She high-stepped the icy pavers, planting each foot squarely. "Jeopardy" became "Charlie's Angels," prompting snickers from several jaded cops. "That's enough," Cross warned as Emily sank into her seat.

Quick cut. Kepp again, roping Soull to the reading chair. Unsheathing a pewter dagger. Twirling around like a matador, weapon high above his head. Tippy-toeing to Soull, plunging the dagger through his chest and out his back. Emily knew there'd be no blood because Soull was drained elsewhere, but that didn't lessen the horror. Curses rippled across the auditorium. Kepp bowed to all four corners of the library. More curses.

Quick cut. Front of Emily's house. Windows open. Curtains fluttering. Summer. "Charlie's Angels" becoming "Mannix," camera zooming in on picture window. Emily, staring off into space, idly playing with the gold rope around her neck.

Startled, she recalled Mama's wake. It was just before the funeral director let the crowd into the flocked-wallpaper viewing room. Goldie Abrams had slipped the eighteen-karat rope necklace off Mama's powdered neck and put it around Emily's, fumbling with the filigreed clasp. "Your daddy gave this to your mama the day you were born," Goldie said, sniffling. "Right in the hospital room where he first met you. Give it to your daughter someday, darling. That's what they'd have wanted." Emily wore the heavy rope whenever she wasn't at work.

"Look at my hair," she whispered. "I didn't cut it short till the academy. He's been making this movie for at least a year." Annie passed a note to Benedetti, who scowled.

Quick cut. Emily unloaded groceries from her Saturn. Stacked firewood on the backyard hill as snowflakes whistled across the cast-iron sky. Charged downhill in the start of a fun run, placed her weekly bouquet on Jack's grave, play-wrestled with Shelby on the back porch, under the picture window that flooded her kitchen sink with light. Wrote parking tickets. Inspected fender benders. Argued with teenagers smoking in the Riverwalk pavilion.

Click.

Emily jumped at the sound of a gun hammer being cocked. But the screen had gone black. "Where are we?" a high-pitched female voice was pleading. "Who are you? Omigod! What do you want?" No reply. "You're from the garage where I work! You came inside and said your car kept stalling and your puppy wasn't feeling well and you had to get to the vet! Then something touched my arm, and I passed out! It's OK though mister, I won't say a word to anyone! Take whatever you want, just don't hurt me! If you want sex, I-I-I'll do that, too, honest. My husband says I'm really good in bed. . . ."

Emily's thighs squeezed so hard, the tendons spasmed.

"Please, mister!" the voice screeched. "Say something! I've got cash! Credit cards! I'll take you to my ATM, and you'll be rich!" She was bawling openly. "Just don't kill me. I've got a wonderful, beautiful son I love so much *please*—"

The gunshot was deafening.

The video portion came back, and there was Lucy Crawford, slumped in the driver's seat of the wrecked Porsche. Blood pulsed from the holes in her head. The camera stayed tight on her face till her heart quit beating—the tub-emptying gurgle at the end so sickening, even Annie turned away— then widened to take in the entire cemetery. A train rolled across the background, engineer whistling "shave and a haircut." Camera tilted up. The Man in the Moon stared, omniscient and silent. Camera tilted down, bouncing in rhythm to "Kojak."

"The jerk-off's dancing!" Flea seethed, pounding the table. Emily could barely breathe. They watched the incognito Kepp hide the boot in the weedy hole, then toss the dead puppy onto Normantown Road, where Emily would find it several hours later.

Quick cut. Kepp crawling in the pipe tunnel to blow up Neuqua High. Unlike the full color of the previous clips, this was only shades of green. "Night vision equipment," Annie murmured to Emily. "Allowed him to record without turning on lights." *Quick cut.* Kepp aiming his submachine gun at the back of a fireman silhouetted by arching flames. *Quick cut.* Kepp waving at the camera, then moving close, filling the lens with the fake hillbilly teeth she'd seen at the forest preserve. *Quick cut.* Jack knotting his tie in their master bedroom. *Quick cut.* Emily scrubbing the kitchen floor. *Quick cut.* Jack and Emily, glistening from the shower, walking hand in hand to the king-size bed . . .

"Oh man," Annie whispered. "He bugged your house."

Emily nodded, wishing she'd die right now. This monster had quick-cut her most secret intimacies into steaming, bite-size morsels and served them to the world.

"The hell is this?" Annie muttered as dancing hot dogs and spinning cups of pop appeared.

The next slide explained.

Dear Chief Halfass—

    Never let it be said I'm without pity. This slide will remain on the screen for thirty minutes so you can take a potty break. Make sure you're back in time to watch the rest. It gets two thumbs up from Satan himself! Same rule—everybody watches or kids die.

                    Sincerely yours, Brady Kepp

Fade to black except for a clock ticking down by seconds . . . 1,799 . . . 1,798 . . .

Emily slumped in her chair and tucked her head in her arms.

"Take the break, everyone. Return in twenty minutes in case he starts early," Cross said.

EMILY AND BRADY

"Home already?" Alice Kepp asked. Her football-crazy son insisted on staying an hour after every practice to correct any weaknesses his Summer League coaches noticed. "How did it go?"

"OK."

"OK," she grunted in affectionate mimic. "There's pop in the fridge. Leftover cherry pie, too, if you can't wait till supper."

Brady shook his head. "I'm not hungry."

Alice looked up from the roaster chicken she was flouring. Her thirteen-year-old son was so big and hardworking on the field that college scouts were already chatting up Dwight about scholarships. Brady was always ravenous! "Are you all right, honey?" she said.

No answer.

"Please tell me," Alice urged, wiping her hands on the

hen-and-chicks apron around her waist. Brady hardly ever confided in her, preferring his father's "man-to-man" counsel. But Dwight wouldn't be home till midnight. He was flying back from Los Angeles after firing a manager caught diverting policy premiums into some bizarre investment scheme involving computers the size of bread boxes. And the Defense Department and "Net" hookups and all kinds of crazy things that sounded like science fiction to her. "You look sad. Maybe I can help."

"Well . . ." Brady hesitated, then plunged ahead. "There's this girl at school, Mom. I've been thinking about her all summer. She's really neat, and I'm pretty sure she likes me."

"Well, she should! You're a wonderful boy!"

"Aw, geez, Mom," he said, embarrassed.

Alice patted his cheek with great affection. "I take it you like her, too?"

Brady nodded, face alight with a joy Alice hadn't seen since he was little. *My boy likes a girl! And she likes him! Finally!* He'd never shown much interest, alarming Dwight so much, he'd dragged the boy to a poker game at the VFW, forcing him to stay for the stag film afterwards. Thank God she could report Brady was all-American!

"I'm thinking of asking her to the homecoming dance in September," Brady continued. He'd never mentioned Valentine's Day, telling his parents instead that his black eyes and split lip came from "clobbering three guys for calling me a sissy." Which made Father so happy, he'd solicited Brady's advice on which model aircraft "they" should build next. "I think she'll say yes."

"That's great, honey," Alice enthused. "So what's the problem?"

"Father won't approve," he said, staring at the kitchen table.

Alice abandoned the chicken to rub her son's shoulders. "Of course, he will, darling," she cooed. Brady was hard as nails emotionally, made that way by a hammering father who insisted "my boy can't show weakness—or even feel it. The predators will smell it and eat him alive." Occasionally, though, Brady showed the briefest flash of a normal child's love and compassion. Which, she believed, came from her. "Your father will be so pleased you want to ask a girl to a dance," she said. "Who is the lucky lass?"

He looked up. "Emily Thompson."

"Colonel Mustard, in the library, with a dagger?" Emily tried.

"Wrong!" Alexandra cackled. "Which means I win! Bwa-ha-ha!" She loved daughter and hubby to distraction but was happy to whip their fannies at game time. Games brought out her competitive streak, and Emily had gotten so sharp over the years, she was practically unbeatable.

"Aw . . . shoot," Emily grumbled, just catching herself. Daddy smirked, and she kicked him under the table, making it wobble so much the game pieces slid around like tiny hockey pucks.

Oh, no. Emily was that pretty young pitcher whose parents objected when Dwight razzed that umpire. Her husband's face pinched like a crab claw every time he brought up Mr. Thompson's name, which was at least once a week, even after all these years. "Why do you say that, Brady?" she asked, not knowing what Dwight had told him. "Why wouldn't your father approve of your seeing Emily?"

"He ordered me to stay away from her, Mom," Brady said. "After that softball game with Our Lady. I can't even talk to her at school. He said Emily and her parents are jealous of our success. That they're blue-collar trash and they want to make big trouble for our family."

Not knowing what Brady meant, she asked, "What did the Thompsons do—"

"I don't believe it, Mom! Emily's great!" Brady interrupted, frustration pouring out. "She's supersmart and plays baseball as good as I do. She's beautiful. And she doesn't take crap from anyone, not anyone. She keeps trying to talk to me, Mom. Even after I ignore her and treat her like garbage. Why can't I talk to her, maybe help her with math or something? Why won't Father let me ask her to the dance? It's not fair!"

"*Kojak's* on!" Emily squealed, prompting the fast break from the game table to the TV set. Mama darted to the kitchen for the ice cream, Daddy tuned the channel, and Emily pushed Mama's rocker next to Daddy's chair. Mama passed out bowls of French vanilla as Emily plopped onto the shag carpet, sitting up against Daddy's shins. She was too old to sit on his lap—"Those sharp elbows just poke me to death," he teased—and this was the next best thing. They spooned in unison as the theme song played. "Ahhhh," Daddy moaned after the first swallow. "I'm telling you, ladies, the French do everything right! Maybe we'll fly there when Emily graduates college. I'll show you my D-day beach and all the places I visited after I personally plucked out Hitler's mustache."

"Oui, oui, monsieur," Mama said, rubbing his thigh. "And we'll find those French doctors who kept you alive after being shot. I want to thank them for all the years we've had."

"Shhhh!" Emily shushed. "Kojak's gonna say it . . . now!"

"Who loves ya, baby?" they shouted in unison.

* * *

Alice fumed as Brady turned to hide embarrassed tears. Why should her boy have to worry about the simple act of asking a girl to a school dance? Why should he have to worry about anything at age thirteen? *And why, in fact, should I?* As Dwight's career stalled, thanks to that investment scandal in L.A., the "corrections" of his family were getting worse. After he locked Brady in a closet for an entire weekend, she'd said she wanted the family to seek professional counseling to learn how to not anger Dwight so much. Instead, she couldn't leave the house for a week lest neighbors notice the staggering gait that came from her kidneys being punched till she threw up. Thanks to his high income, winning personality, and soundproof root cellar, everyone believed Dwight was a fine, upstanding family man who doted on his son and wife. Which he did, actually, in between "punishing" and "correcting" and "guiding to greatness." He was handsome and articulate, with a keen eye for clothes, cars, and artwork. He was a stallion in bed and didn't fool around on the side as far as she knew. Professionally unstoppable until the scandal, he provided a beautiful home in a safe neighborhood, with all the modern conveniences a wife could want. He never forbade her girlfriends from visiting and was garrulous even to strangers, greeting them as "friends I haven't met yet." More than one wife had confided to her during a coffee klatch that they'd kill for such a great husband.

But those were trappings, she'd finally come to realize, and they just weren't enough any more. Death or crippling shouldn't be the tax she paid for Dwight's love. Her best friend, Maggie, said she'd take them into her home in Wisconsin "for as long as it takes," so food, clothing, and shelter were covered. She could get a job at a tourist boutique, work her way up, maybe attend night school and start her own business. She'd make it, no matter what. The real problem was Brady. He worshipped Dwight. Like a slave loves his cruel master perhaps, as Maggie so sourly put it, but that didn't mean it wasn't real.

As for Dwight, she had a pretty good idea how he'd react. Which is why she'd decided to flee while he was out of town. Maggie would arrive any minute from Lake Geneva, they'd throw in the suitcases she'd already packed, and their new life would begin. If losing his family jarred Dwight into seeking help, maybe one day they could return. Despite his abusive ways, she still loved him, and Brady still needed a father. But she couldn't keep assuming their son wouldn't die in one of Dwight's frenzies. Accidentally, of course, but that wouldn't make the ground less cold or the darkness less eternal. She owed her child this chance to keep living.

"Honey," she said, stroking her boy's butter blond curls. "I've got some fun news. Aunt Maggie called while you were at practice. She wants us to come visit. Would you like that?"

"Sure!" he said, brightening. "Aunt" Maggie was his overwhelming favorite of Mom's friends. He loved the hills, forests, and endless blue water of her home in Lake Geneva, where he could swim, fish, and hunt to his heart's content. "With that rifle Father bought me for my birthday, I could shoot enough rabbits to feed us for a week," he said. "Could we stay that long?"

"Maybe even longer," Alice said, smiling. "And honey, we can leave right now. . . ."

"Holy cannoli!" Gerald barked. "That's the ugliest Mr. Potato Head I've ever seen!"

Emily held up her gnarled, sprouting creation. "It looks like Father Snowe!"

"Now, Emily," Alexandra admonished as she scooped

more ice cream into the bowls. "You shouldn't say mean things about people."

"Even if it's true?" Gerald asked.

"Truth is entirely beside the point, dear," Alexandra said, squishing a glob of French vanilla on his ski-slope nose. He crossed his eyes like Crazy Guggenheim, trying to lick it with his tongue, making Emily fall off her chair giggling.

"Finally," Dwight grumbled as the baggage carousel rumbled to life. "The one time I catch an early flight, the luggage takes forever." He grabbed his blue Samsonite, walked outside to hail a taxi, headed for the Southwest Side.

"No way! We can't leave Father!" Brady said, shocked at what Mom said when he asked why she'd packed so many suitcases. "He loves us. We love him!"

"That's true, darling," Alice said. "But we're not leaving your father. We've giving him time to deal with his problems."

"He doesn't have any problems!"

"Yes, he does," she said. "He beats us senseless when he's angry. Makes you do push-ups till you vomit, then punches you for dirtying the floor. He burned your foot with that cigarette—"

"I deserved that, Mom! I didn't run fast enough to make the catch! I lost us the championship—"

"And he forces you into that little closet. Wrapped in your own wet sheets. Remember that?"

Brady's shudder made her pray Maggie didn't get a flat tire. "He'll beat you so badly one of these days, you won't recover. You wouldn't be able to play football or go to college. You might not even be able to walk."

"Father would never do that!" Brady howled, springing from the chair. "Never! We're his family!"

The Yellow Cab turned onto Dwight's well-lighted street. "Hey, Mr. Kepp, didja run into any of them Hollywood star-lets on your trip?" the cabbie inquired.

"I sure did, friend," Dwight said. "There were several at the dinner party the L.A. boys threw for me last night. Liz Taylor even stopped by."

"Hoo-wee!" the cabbie said, mightily impressed. "So didja . . . you know . . . get lucky?"

"Didn't try," Dwight said, clapping the bony man's shoulder. "The only starlet I want lives right there in my house. I've been away from her and my boy much too long." The cabbie pulled to the curb, retrieved the suitcase from the trunk, grinned at the huge tip. "Wow! Thanks!" he enthused. "Any time you need a ride, you ask for me personally, Mr. Kepp. I'll take real good care of you."

Dwight nodded, then headed to the front door, suitcase in one hand, Chinese takeout in the other. He had the cabbie stop on the way. His family would celebrate tonight. He'd managed to convince Los Angeles prosecutors the firm had zero knowledge of the office manager's deceptions and should be held criminally blameless. That would put him back on the fast track. He'd also quietly put a chunk of his own savings into this midget-computer thing. If it worked out half as well as he thought it might, forget CEO—he'd own the damn company.

"Hey, remember that guy?" the senior Chicago cop asked his junior partner as Dwight disappeared into the white brick house. "Kepp?"

"Yeah," junior said. "We rousted him for beating his kid? Three or four years ago?"

Senior nodded, jinking the cruiser around a pothole. "Guess it worked," he said. "He's been a good boy ever since. Hope his son's doing OK."

"I hope Mama's OK," junior said, fondly recalling the lithe beauty of Kepp's wife.

"Don't let your old lady hear that," senior laughed. "She's a pistol. She'll mount your pecker over the fireplace for sure!"

"Beautiful night for a walk," Alexandra said, linking her arm through her husband's.

"You say that even when it's twenty below and I'm freezing my balls off."

"But you love how I warm them afterwards," Alexandra teased. Gerald winked, then pointed to the Kepp house, the turnaround point of tonight's meander. "Not a peep," he said, nodding to the cops driving by. "Guess old man Kepp listened to me."

Alexandra snuggled closer.

Emily washed the Jell-O bowls as her parents took their "constitutional." She found herself thinking of Brady Kepp in his tight orange football uniform. Their little cold war had started thawing after she beat him up, and they'd come to like each other. She knew they'd never be boyfriend-girlfriend or anything—their parents' dislike made that impossible—but they might get away with going to homecoming together. If Brady didn't ask her by the first day of school, she'd bicycle over to his house and pop the question herself.

*   *   *

"Yes, Brady, we are leaving," Alice said firmly. They still had five hours before Dwight's plane landed, and Maggie had called from a gas station to say she was thirty minutes out. "I'll call him from Aunt Maggie's and explain what's going on. When he gets help for his problem, we'll come home."

"This is all my fault!" Brady raged, pacing the kitchen like a caged tiger. "I tell you I like Emily, and now we have to leave! Forget Emily, Mom! I don't want to see her anymore! Or her stupid family! Never! Just don't make us leave home! I want our family the way it is!"

"What are you talking about, boy?" Dwight snarled, flinging the egg foo young as he stomped into the kitchen. "Who the hell's leaving home?"

Alice wheeled in panic. Brady wheeled, too, overjoyed Father was home to stop this crazy thing. "I told Mom I want to take Emily Thompson to homecoming," he explained. "Now she says we have to go live with Aunt Maggie, and we can't see you till the doctor says you're better!"

Dwight backhanded Brady across the butcher-block table. "How dare you tell such lies about your mother! After all she's done for you!"

"Leave him alone!" Alice shrieked, planting herself between husband and son. "He's not lying, Dwight! You're sick and you need help! You're going to kill us with your beatings, and I can't take it any longer! Maggie's picking us up, and we're living with her till you're cured!"

Dwight roared and flung himself at his wife.

Gerald swore a blue streak as shrieking erupted from the Kepp house. He waved his arms at the cops, who'd already pulled a U-turn and flipped on lights and siren. "Kepp's killing his family!" he yelled as the cruiser screeched to the curb. "Stop him!"

Dwight's belt slashed to bone, but Alice refused to abandon Brady. "You'll never leave me, you cunt!" he screamed as the sterling silver buckle filleted her back. "Never! Never!"

The cops pounded on the door. Two more cruisers spilled reinforcements. "This isn't our fight anymore," Alexandra said, tugging her husband away. "The law will deal with Mr. Kepp."

Alice's head spun, her body burning like napalm. Dwight was so berserk, he'd already cracked half her ribs. If she passed out, there'd be no one to shield her son.

She crawled to the counter, drawing Dwight away from Brady. Spitting broken teeth, she stood, absorbing his pummeling fists, feeling for the big china bowl behind her. "Stop it!" she screamed, flinging bloody chicken and flour into Dwight's face. She smashed the bowl on the cast-iron sink, waved a foot-long shard. "Get out of this house!" she ordered, his snarling image swimming out of focus. "Brady and I are leaving, and you can't stop us! Get out of my way, Dwight, or I'll cut you to ribbons!"

"No!" Brady wailed, seeing blood spurt from where Mom gripped the shard. He exploded from the floor and grabbed it from her hand so she wouldn't get hurt more. His feet scribbled on wet chicken, and he fell, the razor-sharp edge slashing hard across her neck. Arterial blood exploded, and Alice crumpled, eyes staring into her horrified son's. Dwight made a strangled cry and snatched the shard from Brady. "Why the hell did you do that?" he croaked.

"I was protecting her!" Brady cried. "I didn't want anybody to get hurt!"

"But you did, boy! You did! You killed your own mother!"

Over and over he kneed Brady, who absorbed the ruthless blows without complaint.

The front door imploded, and cops raced to the kitchen. "Drop the weapon, motherfucker!" senior roared, leveling his Smith & Wesson as junior sprinted to the woman in the pool of blood. "Drop it now or I'll shoot!" Dwight opened his hand, and the shard hit the floor.

The boy on the floor stared at them. "This is all my fault," he wailed.

"Shut up!" Dwight shouted. "It was me, Officers, I did this! She wanted to leave me. She was taking my son away from me. Forever! It made me insane, and I just snapped—"

"Save it for the judge, asswipe," junior growled, handcuffing Kepp's wrists behind his back.

"Brady, the police officers will watch you till I get back," Dwight instructed as more cops flooded the house. "Don't say anything until our lawyer arrives. Understand?"

"Yes, Father," Brady said, sniffing.

"You're a good boy," Dwight said. "The best son a man could ever have." Brady's eyes filled with tears. "They're taking me to jail now. I'll be out as soon as our lawyer pays the bail. Then I'll take you home. None of this is your fault, son."

"Shaddup, asshole," senior growled, ordering Kepp removed.

Dwight Kepp surveyed the enormous holding cell at Cook County Jail. It stunk like dead alewives and was packed with lice-ridden desperados. He hitched up his trousers—the cops had confiscated his belt as evidence—and bumped someone to his left. "Sorry about that, friend," he said, slapping the moon-faced fellow on the back. "It's so crowded in here."

The fellow nodded, saying nothing. Then drove a fist of tattoos into Dwight's Adam's apple, fracturing his throat and flooding it with blood.

"What . . . why . . ." Dwight gurgled, legs turning to baby food. He slumped to the urine-slopped floor. "Why did you do this to me?"

The moon-faced fellow shrugged. "Never did like being touched."

Senior and junior escorted Brady to the empty roll call room. They handed him a can of pop and seated him at a brown oak table scarred by ten thousand interrogations. "I've got bad news, son," senior said, hating to hurt this boy more, but someone had to tell him. "Your dad is dead."

Brady stared, gripping his knees.

"He was in a jail cell, waiting for his lawyer," junior explained. "Another prisoner punched him in the throat. Your dad died on the way to the hospital. The head nurse, Mrs. Hoffmeyer, just called to inform us." He cleared his throat as tears welled in the kid's eyes. "We'll charge the man with murder, of course, and . . . well, the state's attorney has decided to drop all charges against your dad. He's been punished more than the state can ever do. You've suffered enough, too, losing both your parents this way. It's a tough break, but you're a big, strong kid. I know you can handle it."

Brady didn't reply. His mind was instead crystallizing on the cause of his devastating misery—Emily Thompson. She'd stolen his family just like that, and someday, somehow, he'd get even. "Where will I go now?" he said.

"Your Aunt Maggie is here," senior said. "We'll let you see her as soon as we're finished."

"She's not my real aunt, you know," Brady snuffled. "She's Mom's best friend. We just call her aunt."

"We know," junior said. That was the problem. Maggie wasn't blood. And none of Brady's relatives would take him.

They had "enough problems with our own kids" without adding a "homicidal teenager" to the mix. Which meant Brady was headed for the state home for boys in southern Illinois. Junior drove a kid there once and spent a couple hours nosing around. The place was nice enough, with rolling terrain filled with what every boy needed—lakes, forests, and fishing holes. The social workers tried hard, the odor of piss and fried perch was less strong than at other such places, and the military-style high school had a ranked football team. He explained Brady's new reality, and senior added, "The government takes fine care of kids like you. If my boys lost me and the missus, this is the place I'd want them to live. . . ."

The cops waved good-bye as Brady disappeared into the government station wagon idling at the curb. "He'll be all right," senior remarked. "The boy's tough—didn't cry. And he's smart enough to know his relatives are pricks, so this is the best thing for him." He smacked his hand in his fist, enthused. "Let's visit Brady sometime. Go fishing, play a little ball. You know, encourage him. A boy like that would make a good policeman. Yeah, we'll visit in the fall, after he's settled in, tell him a few war stories, nudge him toward a copper's life. . . ."

Junior nodded, knowing they wouldn't. But it was nice to think so.

CHAPTER 27

Thursday, 1 A.M.
Five hours till Emily's birthday

Benedetti rubbed Emily's back as the task force filed out. Luerchen walked past without comment, then turned at the front door to stare. Annie glared from the back of the auditorium. Luerchen snickered, then waddled out to the front lobby.

"You didn't do anything wrong," Benedetti said. "It's gonna be OK." He offered his handkerchief. She took it, wiped her brimming eyes. "Go back to work, Commander," she said, handing it back. "Remember what we agreed about staying professional."

"Forget our deal—"

"No." She pushed him away. "We have to catch him by sunup, and we won't if your head's not in the game." She breathed deep, and the rest spilled without thinking. "I can't look over my shoulder the rest of my life. It'll interfere with my loving you."

"Loving," Benedetti said. "Me."

"Yeah," Emily said. "Isn't that crazy?"

Benedetti smiled. "No crazier than my loving you, too, Detective. Let's get the bastard." Then walked into the lobby without looking back.

Emily just sat, watching the "clock" tick down, amazed how horrific and utterly joyous the same set of seconds could be.

EMILY AND BRADY

Thursday, 1:30 A.M.
Four and a half hours till Emily's birthday

Kepp's video resumed with a lonely stretch of highway. Two lanes ran on each side of a wide grass median. The setting sun poked fiery red fingers into purple cotton balls. Rain wands wove gently in the distance. Except for the concrete and implied presence of a camera, there was nothing but corn and sky. "Where are we?" Annie whispered. "What are we looking at?"

Emily's anxiety clicked like a Geiger counter.

A speck appeared on the horizon. Far lane, headed for the camera, which was up high, as if it sat on a viaduct. A rock zipped across the image and struck the interstate, bouncing like a hailstone. A second rock skidded like a major-league curveball, clipping leaves from a roadside maple. Cops murmured. A dozen more rained down as the speck grew big enough for Emily to recognize a boxy, older Jeep Cherokee, high off the pavement like a leggy colt on all fours, speeding along just this side of reckless.

"No!" she gasped, cracking her knees on the table as she bolted to her feet. "Turn back!"

More rocks flew and the driver swerved. Inner lane, outer lane, median, back. The right tires lifted as the driver wrestled for control. The windshield shattered. The driver skidded into the median, swerved back. Skid, control, wobble, control, control.

A rock center-punched the driver. The Jeep careened, then flipped, skidding along the pavement, orange sparks shooting out the back. Emily bit her lip so hard, she tasted blood. The Jeep grew in the unblinking lens till it slammed into the viaduct below. The camera lurched.

"Jack," Emily whispered. "Jack."

"Goddammit, Chief, that's Emily's husband!" Annie raged. "Turn that thing off!"

"Can't," Cross answered. "We see it through, or Kepp starts killing children."

A deep orange fireball erupted as the gas tank exploded. The Kojak soundtrack merged into the thumping beat of "Disco Inferno." Emily whimpered like a deer in a jaw trap. "Prom," she mumbled.

"What does that mean?" Annie asked.

"Disco Inferno," Emily replied. "It was the theme of my high-school prom—Disco Inferno. Kepp knew it. He knows everything."

The video froze on a photo of Safety Town. The music stopped, replaced by the harsh tick of the intermission clock. "I Spy," Emily said, suddenly realizing the video clips were the last of her eight games. "The video represents I Spy."

"I know," Benedetti said from the aisle. "I figured it out, too. I already sent CSIs to your house to find the cameras."

Two paramedics charged down the stairs. Benedetti turned

to meet them. They stopped like they'd hit a tree, stared at the screen. The rest of the room followed.

A mushroom cloud was erupting from the photo of Safety Town. Flames shot from every window and door. Crudely drawn stick figures, each in navy blue with a shiny badge on its "chest," hopped like fleas on a griddle, then dissolved in a blinding fireball. Emily blanched, realizing what was about to happen. "Get down everybody!" she screamed, throwing her arms over her face. "It's gonna—"

Blue-white lightning turned the dark auditorium Saharan. A millisecond later the blast wave hit, breaking windows, toppling the lectern, knocking cops over chairs. Emily scrambled to her feet. Annie pulled her down. Lobby cops shouted over the Klaxons braying throughout the station, "Safety Town! It's exploding! The kids are still in there!"

"Lunatic!" Emily screamed at the screen. "You already did Timebomb!" She scrambled outside with the rest of the task force to see the miniature city dissolve in sheets of fire, schoolkids run for their lives. "Evacuate her, Annie!" Cross bellowed. "There may be more bombs—"

A high-pitched squeal choked off the command. They whirled on a wide-bodied sheriff's deputy staggering up the driveway, burning like acetylene. "Medic!" Annie screamed. A firefighter aimed his hose, and the deputy fell sideways. A crisp ear popped off.

Bodies smoked everywhere. One teetered faceup on the fence, legs and arms missing. Beneath it lay two lumps, big curled around little, smoke tendrils hissing from all four eye sockets. A police dog protecting his human handler to the death. Emily burst into tears at the raw horror.

"We got most of them out!" Cross shouted in her ear, arm tight across her shoulders. "As soon as Kepp made his threat, I ordered Safety Town cleared! Six at a time so he wouldn't notice if he was watching. Three-quarters were safely evacuated when the bomb—"

"Ken!" It was the BATFE director, emerging pink and hairless from a billow of smoke. "One of the chaperones said the blast came from the top of the covered bridge. Kepp chose a spot the sniffer dogs couldn't reach. Say the word and I'll bring in Delta Force to neutralize this goblin." Her expression made clear "neutralize" did not mean "arrest."

A throbbing noise made everyone look up. "Here come the locusts," Cross muttered as news helicopters filled the horizon. SWATs surrounded Emily, training gun barrels up and out. Fire hoses shot thick arches of water onto the inferno, creating obscene rainbows in the floodlights. Cross marched away, barking orders. Emily held her breath as the miniature police station inside Safety Town collapsed.

"How are you bearing up?" Marwood said, slipping inside the protective circle.

"Fine," Emily said in a low voice. No more tears. She was going to kill Brady Kepp and had to stay alive long enough to do it. "Take me to my house. I want to see how he did it."

Marwood looked at Annie, who flagged a cruiser. Marwood hopped in the passenger side, Emily in back with Flea and Annie. Nobody spoke over the screaming siren. Six minutes later they spotted Marty Benedetti in the driveway, phones jammed against both ears. A news chopper was landing at the end of Jackson to disgorge reporters. Annie popped her air horn, and Benedetti signaled the barricade crew to let Emily and her companions pass.

"Fiber-optic cameras with wireless transmitters," Benedetti said when they reached him. He held out a clear bag of electronic parts. "Kepp hid them well. I couldn't spot one till a CSI pointed it out."

"How many did he plant?" Emily asked.

"Dozens." He tossed her the bag. "Psycho turned your house into a TV studio."

Emily examined the camera, shocked at how much it looked like an ordinary nail. The shiny head was the lens, the long shank the transmitter. They were hidden in plain sight in ceilings, floors, and millwork. She offered the bag to Marwood.

"I'm familiar," he said, waving it off. "CEOs use them to spy on employees. With this particular model, the master recorder is within five hundred yards."

"We found it," Benedetti said. "Tucked in a tree crotch on the Riverwalk. It allowed Kepp to download the images without breaking into the house each time."

Emily watched firefighters drag ladders across her lawn. Shelby barked when one veered too close to the ankle-twisting hole of a rotted-away fence post. The firefighter rubbed Shelby's neck in gratitude. "How many children died, Marty?" she asked.

"Lemme find out." He called Cross, listened, disconnected. "Only two, thank God. But a dozen have third-degree burns. They're only gonna wish they died."

Emily shivered, knowing exactly what he meant. When she was seven, she defiantly planted her hand on the new electric Hotpoint when Mama turned to wipe a skillet. Partly because the ring glowed a pretty cherry red, but mostly because Mama said not to. Emily screamed as her palm charred. "I told you a million times not to touch hot stoves! Why didn't you listen?" Mama wailed as Daddy sped to the emergency room. Emily learned the hard way that third-degree burns were healed by scrubbing the crusting scabs with a bristle brush, bringing even the most stoic patient to howling weepiness.

"Commander!" a CSI hollered from the second floor. "I'm done mapping the master bathroom. Wanna see before I dig 'em out?"

They took the stairs two at a time.

The CSI stood on an aluminum stepladder, floured in Sheetrock debris. The floor below was dented from dropped tools. Emily looked at the delicate china sink where she'd piled her cut-off hair. It was cracked and filthy. "This makes thirty," the CSI was saying, tugging the camera from its spot over the toilet. "He got the volume discount."

She followed Marty into the master bedroom, looked out the south window. CSIs swarmed the hill like carpenter ants, dismantling her woodpile, running metal detectors along her foundation, peering under the back porch. Jack was so proud of this wedding present, so excited to explain the significance of each peg in every plank. *I'm glad you'll never see this,* she told him silently.

"Thanks, Lieutenant," she heard Marty say. "Chief Cross will call himself soon as he gets the chance." He shut the cell phone. "Chicago Police," he explained. "They searched your old family bungalow at Ken's request. Guess who left a note in the fridge saying hello?"

"Is he living there?" Emily asked, knowing full well Kepp wouldn't make it that easy.

"Uh-uh. It's furnished but uninhabited. Chicago's tracing the electronic fund transfers that cover taxes and maintenance, but those'll link to a false bank account."

"It's a trophy, isn't it?" Emily said, scowling. "My house."

"Serial killers love their keepsakes," Benedetti agreed, answering his ringing phone. "Hey! That's great! Let me know!" He signed off, buzzing with new energy. "Branch is awake and blinking. Doc Winslow thinks he's trying to say something. Ken's going over to find out."

"Maybe the paralysis is ending!" Emily said, clapping her hands.

"Could be random nerve patterns," Marwood warned as he joined them. "Don't get your hopes up."

Benedetti paced. "Neither of you get the point. Branch knows something about Kepp. Something important. He's sure to have seen the news"—he pointed to the circling choppers—"and wouldn't bother Ken in the middle of this shitstorm unless it was vital."

Emily breathed shallowly. "Maybe Branch knows . . ." She groaned, unable to finish.

"You don't look so good," Benedetti said, taking her arm. "Did you get hurt in Safety Town?"

"No," Emily mumbled, laying her head on Marty's chest. "I'm so tired, I can barely stand."

"You can sleep on the way to the safe house." He tapped his watch. "It's nearly daybreak. Kepp undoubtedly has something planned for your moment of birth. The farther away you are, the safer you'll be when it happens."

Emily was too exhausted to argue. "Let me grab a few things," she said as Annie issued instructions to the protective team.

"Take five minutes," Benedetti said. "If I see you in ten, I'll arrest you for real." He jogged downstairs to answer a shout.

Emily trailed on leaden legs, glancing through the octagon window to the front yard. Shelby was prancing near the mailbox that had started this disaster, wagging his tail at admiring emergency workers. "I'm glad you're happy, big fella," she mumbled. "I'll never be again."

Marwood passed her on the stairs, walked outside. A minute later he poked his head back in. "Annie says I'm driving," he announced.

"Why?" Emily said.

He pointing to the fire engines blocking in the SWAT vehicles. "Those aren't going anywhere. And my car's a rental. Kepp won't know to look for it."

She turned to stare at Marty's thick back—*Be careful. Be safe. I love you*—then dragged herself to the rented Lincoln Town Car, every bruise pulsing. Annie handed her a Kevlar helmet and lap blanket to augment her bulletproof vest, helped her belt in. Flea crawled into the backseat with a submachine gun and satchel of ammunition. Annie joined him with her scoped Remington, radioed dispatch they'd drive north on Illinois 59, the prearranged code for "heading southwest to the safe house." Marwood crawled the Town Car past the rubbernecks thronging Jackson Avenue, picked up speed on Washington Street. "I don't see any chase cars," he said as Naperville faded in the rearview. "We're not making this drive by ourselves, are we?"

"Got no choice," Annie said. "Most of my guys are demolitions experts, so they're searching the campus for more booby traps. The rest are at the safe house doing pre-check. That leaves me and Flea." She patted her rifle. "And Baby makes three. Don't worry, Doc. We'll keep your powder dry till we get to the lodge." Flea slapped Marwood's back and began the SWAT swivel—look right, left, front, back, repeat.

Emily fell asleep.

"Sniffer dogs swept her place three times," she heard Annie say when she blinked awake. "No explosives, but Ken's not taking chances. He boarded up her windows and doors and evacuated the neighborhood. Jackson Avenue's deserted now except for the cruiser in Emily's driveway."

"How'd the school shutdown go?" Marwood asked.

"No problems. That was a good suggestion you made, shutting down the system in case the bastard wired a school."

"Well, if he's got more kids in mind, what better place to find them. . . ." Marwood fell silent, then asked, "You have enough troops to handle everything on your plate, Annie?"

"Shit, Doc, the Chinese Army isn't big enough for a plate like this. But we'll make do." She heard Emily yawn and rubbed her shoulders from behind. "Hiya, sleepy. I was just telling Ellis about Marty's latest e-mail." She recapped their conversation. "The safe house is ready for our arrival. It's raining hard there, but the main road's passable. We'll get through."

Emily hugged herself. "I hope the guys have a fire going. I'm freezing—"

"Behind us," Marwood warned.

Annie and Flea whirled. "What? That green SUV?" she demanded. "It wasn't there ten seconds ago." She glanced at Flea, who confirmed with a head shake.

"It just pulled out of that gravel road," Marwood said, gripping the wheel. "I saw one the same color on Jackson Avenue. What should I do?"

"Drive steady and straight, exactly like you're doing," Annie ordered, pulling a satellite radio from a thigh pack. "No heroics unless combat driving was an elective at that shrink school of yours. Pull over at the next crossroad, and we'll let him pass." Flea switched his submachine gun's fire selector to AUTO. Emily pulled her Glock, unbelted herself, turned toward the back. Marwood withdrew a small black pistol from his jacket. "Hey, Doc," Emily kidded. "Only three Wyatt Earps per vehicle."

He pulled the trigger, plunging a small finned dart into Emily's exposed tricep.

"Matter of fact, Annie," she heard Marwood say as he whipped around to sink two darts each into her and Flea's unarmored butts. They flopped sideways, unconscious. "I'm an expert at combat driving. I learned it in the Green Berets."

Emily lunged for Marwood's throat but didn't move an inch. Every muscle in her body was paralyzed. All she could do was breathe and blink. "Yooooou," she gargled as she melted into her seat, steel bands tightening on her chest.

Marwood smiled till his eyes disappeared. "That's right, Princess," he said. "It's time to play our final game." He whipped the Town Car into a hard U-turn, darted her again. Emily's eyes leaked rain, and the world faded to black.

EMILY AND BRADY

October 1990
Desert Shield, south of Baghdad, Iraq

Brady Kepp staked the feral dog to the desert floor, belly-up and spread-eagled, and turned to stare at the captured Iraqi missile commander. The Iraqi stared back. For two hours he'd refused to answer the American infidel's demands for the map coordinates of his Scud missile battery.

"All I want is the location," Kepp said in the Iraqi's native dialect as he secured the dog's last paw. "Say it and I'll release you unharmed."

The Iraqi remained silent.

"Oh, well," Kepp said. "I guess you're just too tough for me." He waved at his companions, dressed like their leader in the loose robes of desert nomads. "Hey, fellas, lunch?" They waved, spreading the coals they'd fired thirty minutes ago. Kepp pulled a knife and slid the tip into the dog's upper chest. It howled, eyes bulging.

"You can join us," Kepp told his captive as he flayed the

dog alive, one furry strip at a time. "You need strength to walk home." Muscle, tendon, and sinew jerked and spasmed under the relentless blade. The animal barked itself hoarse trying to bite its tormentor. Kepp dismembered its jaw and vocal cords, turning it as silent as the Iraqi. He warmed his hands over the steam emanating from the cuts—the desert was cold this time of morning. "I admire your bravery," Kepp said. "But the war will be here soon. Why die now when battle glory is so near?"

Still no reply.

Kepp dissected out the dog's internal organs, humming as it vomited a beery froth. He filleted steaks from its thighs and flanks. One of his companions plopped the fresh meat in the pot suspended over the glowing coals. Kepp smacked his lips at the gamy aroma, then cut out the dog's beating heart. "I need the coordinates of your missile battery," Kepp said, wiping the spurting organ across the officer's bushy mustache. "Your precise orders, the structure of your unit, and whether you stock nuclear, chemical, or biological weapons. If you do that, I swear to Allah, you will walk free from here." He carved the dog's throat into a clown smile, then drew the gore-flecked knife over the Iraqi's bare left knee. A blood creek bloomed, and the Iraqi wet himself.

"Oops, sorry," Kepp said. "Didn't mean to scare you that much." A few more slits exposed the kneecap. The Iraqi howled, black eyes bouncing like pinballs. "Tell me what I want, and I'll set you free," Kepp repeated. "With water, food, and directions to your front lines. You'll be with your woman by tonight." He sighed. "If you keep refusing, however, we'll eat you for lunch. We're hungry from killing your countrymen, and this skinny dog won't fill our bellies. It's time to choose." He pointed to the distant sand dunes, then the carcass of the dog. "Talk, or die." The other CIA men snatched up their golden brown doggie steaks and stuffed them in their mouths, licking the spurting juice. The Iraqi was too shocked to answer. Kepp, whistling, put the point of the knife on the exposed bone and pushed.

"Yes!" the Iraqi screamed. "Yes! I will tell you!"

Kepp withdrew the knife, and the Iraqi spilled his guts. An agent translated responses for the Navy SEAL team on the other end of the radio.

"Excellent job, my friend," Kepp said when he was done. "You're a man of your word. As am I. Here are the water, food, and map I promised for your journey home."

The team medic untied him and bandaged his knee. The radioman helped him into fresh desert clothing and handed him a rucksack of provisions. Kepp gave explicit directions to the Iraqi front line, waving till the grateful man reached the crest of the first dune. Then he pulled a silenced 9-millimeter Beretta and put two holes in the Iraqi's skull.

"Nice, boss!" the medic enthused as the others sped off to retrieve the precious supplies. "You hit the X ring at a hundred yards! Annie Oakley couldn't shoot better!" He smiled. "Sure you can't stick around for Desert Storm? Be a lot of cool things to blow up."

"Nah," Kepp said, making himself a sandwich of the "doggie fillets"—chicken strips the boys slipped in the pan when the Iraqi was distracted. So much of what Kepp did was theater, the boys teased he was a Hollywood action hero, not a CIA intelligence officer. "I blew up enough stuff in Afghanistan for a lifetime of fond memories. I've got a girl waiting at home, and it's time I paid her the attention she deserves."

The medic repacked his kit as the boys returned with the gear. This "retired" Army Green Beret captain had proven himself a superb CIA field operator since taking over this team two years ago. He was a visionary leader who pitched in on the shit work just like the newest grunt. The medic would miss him. "How you gonna make a living back in the world, boss?" he asked. "Our skills aren't exactly transferable to the civilian workforce."

"Au contraire," Kepp said, sharpening his knife to restore its killing edge. "I've learned so much about human psychology over the years, I think I'll become a shrink. 'Doctor' Kepp sounds so much classier than 'Fuck you, American pig CIA eater of shit!'"

The boys laughed, then broke camp to hunt the next intelligence bonanza.

CHAPTER 28
EMILY AND BRADY

Thursday 5 A.M.
One hour till Emily's birthday

Emily awoke naked but for bra and thong. Her mouth was taped, and something was snugged tight around her neck, over her hair. She was standing in her kitchen. Not on the floor, though, unless she'd grown several feet.

She looked down as much as the neck restraint allowed and saw the game table from her basement. She froze, knowing how easily it toppled. She and Daddy crafted it one night from rock maple, a hardwood as heavy as cement. She'd protested his suggestion that she make the legs twice as thick. "I measured right!" she'd pouted. "I know what I'm doing!" She finished her cuts on the table saw, glued and screwed the legs to the top, hauled the table upright . . . and discovered it wobbled like a drunk. "Daddy, fix this!" she'd wailed, flinging her arms. "No way, Princess," he'd replied. "You insisted. You gotta live with it. . . ."

She couldn't dip her head enough to see her feet. She

moved them instead. She heard a metallic clink. She pulled on her wrists, which were secured behind her back. More clinks.

Handcuffs on my ankles and wrists.

"Good morning, Princess," Ellis Marwood said from close behind. "Have a nice sleep?"

Emily looked up. "Sweet Jesus," she whispered, shocked beyond words. The thing around her neck was a rope! Tied to a ceiling beam! She felt an urge to urinate.

"It's Hangman," Marwood said, walking around. "The last game you're ever going to play."

"Up yours, Brady Kepp," she mumbled into the tape.

"Eh? Can't hear ya, hon," Marwood said, bending at his waist and cupping his ear like an old man. It brought him into kicking range. She tried. The table fell sideways, and she gagged from the flesh-rending choke of the noose. Marwood laughed, held her legs to ease the pressure as he reset the table. "Listen up," he said, pulling her father's bayonet from the small of his back. It gleamed from fresh sharpening. "I'm going to remove the mouth tape. Behave and we'll play our game to the end. If you fight, shout, or even whisper too loud, I'll carve you up like that poor sap in Massachusetts." He planted her feet on the table. "Will you play by my rules?" he asked. "Can I remove the tape?" Emily nodded. "You'd better," he warned, flicking her kneecap several times with the needle tip. He smiled, then ripped the tape away.

"Uh, uh, uh, uh," she panted, gulping fresh air.

"Breathe," Marwood cooed, putting away the bayonet. "You need your strength to play."

"You're Brady Kepp," Emily gasped.

Marwood looked at her.

"The kid from my grade school in Chicago," she pressed. "One of my classmates."

"Yes, that was me," he said. "Little Brady Kepp, everybody's classmate and nobody's friend. Especially not yours. Not after you butchered my family."

Emily shifted, having no idea what he was talking about. "Where's Annie and Flea?" she demanded, realizing they weren't in the room. "And the officers guarding the house?"

"Neutralized."

She recoiled.

"No, not that way," he said. "They're tied up in your basement. I don't kill indiscriminately, so they're alive. Don't get your hopes up for a rescue, though. They'll be unconscious till long after you and I are done."

Emily breathed deep, trying to quash her trembling. "You drugged us. What was it?"

"Animal tranquilizer. One dart paralyzes all voluntary body functions. Two put your lights out for hours." He put a finger to his cheek, amused. "Gee, Princess, they sure are lucky to have you for a friend, aren't they?"

"Patrol Six," Jodi the dispatcher radioed as she rubbed her eyes. Third straight shift. Even her hair was tired. She popped the lid of her triple espresso and gulped two Tylenols, hoping to ease the ache in her lower back. "Six, it's time to report."

Marwood pressed the bayonet to Emily's spine and the police radio to his lips. "This is Patrol Six," he replied, mimicking the older of the driveway cops. "All quiet."

"Only place that is," Jodi replied. "You all right, Six? You sound congested."

"Ate a lot of smoke at Safety Town," Marwood said. "But I'm all right."

"Catch you at the next check-in then. Dispatch out."

"Six out." Marwood put the radio down. "I know you're

dying to ask why I'm doing all this, Princess. Go ahead. Like the nuns always said, there's no such thing as a stupid question."

"Marty!" a Secret Service agent hollered, waving a database printout. "It's not him! Brady Kepp died a month after leaving the army! Hit and run in Miami! Kepp isn't the Unsub!"

Emily sighed. "All right, Brady—"

"Ellis," he corrected. "Brady died years ago. Good riddance to the weakling."

"OK . . . Ellis," she said, filing that nugget away. "Why?"

"That answer will take awhile, so let me get comfortable." Marwood filled her Three Little Pigs mug with French roast, pulled the half-eaten carton of French vanilla from the freezer. "What's with you and France, anyway?" he said, returning to the table. "You don't like berets."

"You know good and well the French saved my father's life on D-day," she snapped. "If this is the best you can do, go ahead and hang me."

"Touché," Marwood said. "It wasn't worthy. I apologize." He ate from the carton, held it out. "Shame I couldn't preserve one from 1985 to give you now. But it was full of Daddy's teeth."

Emily gasped. "You . . . you killed . . ."

"Yeah, Princess, I did," he said, sipping the coffee chaser. "Your folks were your twentieth birthday present. Jack was your thirtieth."

"Where the hell am I?" Annie mumbled. She could barely move, her wrists and ankles hog-tied behind her. She used her tongue to probe the tape over her mouth. It wouldn't budge. She wiggled her nose and face. The tape over her eyes wasn't nearly as tight. She worked herself to her knees, then scraped the loose tape against the concrete wall she'd been smelling since she woke. The left end stuck, then popped off. She cursed and tried again.

"You killed Jack, too! You psycho!" Emily raged.

"Shut up," Marwood warned, chopping a bruise with the bayonet handle. "I meant what I said about noise."

She whimpered from the pain, fell silent.

He leaned against the refrigerator. "I used an air gun of my own design to launch the rocks. It adjusts for windage and angle, so hitting Jack's Jeep was no challenge."

Emily's lips curled off her teeth. Not being able to kill this man hurt worse than the bayonet.

"I wanted the cops to think they were thrown by kids," he continued. "They did. Stupidity isn't confined to state troopers, either. The Chicago cops who investigated your folks' hit and run in 1985 had no clue what they were up against." He sat and ate more ice cream. "Now it's your fortieth, and I'm fresh out of family. I guess I'll have to kill you." He pointed at the noose.

"You tried at the forest preserve," she spat. "See how well that worked out."

Marwood flipped his spoon in the sink. "It worked out fine. I knew from the spy cameras in your bedroom that you always wear your bulletproof vest. So I directed my bullets between your boobs and hips, to make sure they stayed on your vest. I wanted you immobile, not deceased."

*   *   *

"Kepp isn't dead," Benedetti snapped. "Keep looking."

"Waste of time," the Secret Service agent argued. "We've traced his entire life—"

"Born in Chicago. Raised on the Southwest Side. Attended Catholic schools. Parents killed in 1979," Benedetti recited from memory. "Lived in a state home in East St. Louis till 1982. Joined the army. Honorably discharged in 1990—"

"And killed in Miami by a drunk driver," the agent said. "The Dade County coroner confirmed Kepp's identity through records provided by the army. Kepp appears on the Social Security death index. His driver's license renewals stopped after 1990."

Benedetti raised an eyebrow, grabbed the army list from his briefcase.

"His obituary appeared in the St. Louis papers. And so forth." The agent shook his head. "Chasing this further is a waste of time, Marty."

Benedetti plucked a page and waved it like a flag. "He's alive. This proves it."

Bliiiiiiiink.

"See how long it takes now, Ken?" Dr. Winslow warned. "He's right at the edge of spasm."

"I know. But the sun's about to rise." Back to Branch. "Do you want to stay awake? Take some sort of drug?"

"Ken!" Winslow said. "He can't handle that!"

"Emily's living on borrowed time," Cross shot back. "Branch knows that. So do you." Back to Branch. "Your call, Captain. Do you want to sleep?"

Bliiiiiiiink . . . bliiiiiiiink.

"Or do you want that stimulant?"

Bliiiiiiiink.

"It's too dangerous," Winslow insisted.

"He said yes, Doctor," Cross said. "He's mentally and emotionally qualified to make that decision. Let's get cracking."

"Branch is held together by spit and nylon," Winslow argued. "There's no way to predict what a stimulant will do—help, kill—it's a coin flip." She pushed Cross into the hall to prevent any undue influence from his presence, then brought her face to Branch's, searching his eyes for any sign of equivocation. "You're gambling with your life, Hercules," she whispered. "Do you want this injection, knowing it might injure you further? Or kill you?"

Bliiiiiiink.

"Are you lying to please the chief? To prove how macho you are?"

Bliiiiiiiink . . . bliiiiiiiink.

"This is important enough to make Lydia a widow?" she pressed. "Deprive your kids of a father? Because that's what we're talking about here. Not just your life. Theirs, too."

Bliiiiiiink.

"OK," Winslow said.

"Why did you shoot us?" Emily asked, eyes roaming the kitchen for a means of escape. "I couldn't find that scenario in any of my games."

"Think of it as a special edition," Marwood said. "After our first conversation, I knew Branch would be trouble. He's far more intelligent than I expected for a suburban flatfoot. Could have posed a threat to my timetable, given enough time. I had to remove him from the game."

"Jerk," Emily seethed.

"He certainly is," Marwood said, twisting her condemnation to his own purpose. "The big lug takes all those bullets and lives? What are the odds?" He drummed his fingers on his chest. "As for shooting you, I had no choice. You were trying to kill me. So I immobilized you, allowing me to kill you properly now."

"Or vice versa."

"Highly doubtful," Marwood said. "But theoretically possible, I suppose. I did leave that darling little knife in your bra to give you a shred of hope." He blew her a kiss. "Though I did remove the spare handcuff key from your ankle. I may be crazy, Princess, but I ain't stupid."

"Quit calling me Princess!" Emily snapped.

"Mmm . . . nope," Marwood said. "But ask nicely and I'll tell you why your family's dead."

"Don't bother. I don't care."

Marwood laughed. "Bluffs don't become you."

She blew out her breath. "All right," she whispered, her naked shivers increasing. "Why did you kill my family, Ellis? Why?"

He retrieved the spoon from the sink, humming a tune she vaguely recognized from oldies radio. "Banana Nana Fo Ferley," something like that. He ate a few more bites, put the carton back in the freezer, washed the spoon, put it in the strainer.

"Because you killed mine," he said.

Benedetti slid the list into the projector. "Brady Kepp's personnel summary says he was 'honorably separated' from service," he said. "Everyone else on this page was 'honorably discharged.' Why the discrepancy?"

A dozen cops frowned, trying to recall their own military discharge papers.

Benedetti scratched his chest, which itched from caked sweat. "Because only the name is dead," he said. "The body is alive and under new identity. I believe Kepp was transferred from the Green Berets to another, unnamed, federal agency. The transfer was hush-hush, and the appropriate records doctored, but you know what happens in big bureaucracies—not everybody gets the word. In this case, some associate deputy assistant clerk typed 'separated' instead of the cover designation of 'discharged.'"

"And the error wasn't caught because higher-ups don't proofread clerical work. Especially work to which outsiders have no access," Secret Service agreed. "Meaning you obtained this information by, uh, stealth."

Benedetti's grin was brief but telling. "Next step is finding Kepp's new agency."

"CIA," said Judy Stephens, the BATFE chief. "Has to be."

"Explain," Benedetti said.

"My husband was an Air Force major," Stephens said, adjusting the scarf on her burned-shiny head. "When he was killed in Desert Storm, he wasn't wearing a uniform. He was a CIA spook, recruiting Kurds to rebel against Saddam Hussein."

"Shit," the cops groaned in unison.

"He'd officially retired from the Air Force six months earlier," she said. "The certificate on our bedroom wall says 'honorable discharge.' But a letter from Pentagon accounting, the one in our safe-deposit box, certifies that since he was 'honorably separated' to work for 'another agency within the federal retirement system,' pension credits would accrue per usual."

"Then Marty's right. Brady Kepp went into the CIA," said Secret Service. "Now he's in Naperville, with a new identity. Presumably, a new appearance. How do we find out what it is? Call the CIA?" He glanced at the FBI liaison.

"Don't look at me," FBI said. "Easier to squeeze blood from a turnip than get a straight answer from Central Intelligence."

* * *

Emily tried to ignore the throbbing from the tight ankle cuffs. "Killed your family? I have no idea what you're talking about."

"Don't play stupid," Marwood growled. "You know exactly what you did. Pretending you don't is an insult to Father. Keep up your filthy lies and I'll gut you."

Rattled at his venom, she moved on to the "tenth birthday" he'd mentioned. "What's that about, Ellis? Why would I remember something from that long ago?"

"Some things you don't forget," Marwood said.

"I thought you wanted me to know everything," she tried.

He glowered, then began.

"You decided to throw a party," he said, words clipped, expression menacing. "To play those board games you loved so damn much. The ones you played every Saturday night with your parents. You invited your classmates to your house. To play. To have fun. You invited everyone. Except me." He whipped the Three Little Pigs mug against the basement door, the crash startling her so much, she wrenched her back staying upright.

"That day is still so clear," he continued, folding his arms. "You made party invitations from typing paper. Colored them real pretty with Crayolas. Pasted on candles and birthday cakes you scissored from construction paper. Put the finished product in little white envelopes—"

"Like mine at the library," Emily said, the significance of that "birthday card" now thundering.

Marwood's entire body was a spring under tension. "You brought the invitations to school. Chatted with each kid individually to make sure they could attend. I sat in the back corner, where the penguins always stuck me before I became Mr. Touchdown. Waiting. Hoping. Excited. Everyone else was invited, why not me? I could be your friend. Why not?" He hissed like an angry goose. "But you stopped when you got to my desk. You looked at me a long time, then turned around. I was the only one in the room not invited! And everybody knew it!"

"I'm sorry," Emily said, wishing she could recall the incident. But it was three-quarters of her life ago! "I just don't remember . . ."

Then she did.

"But, Mama," she'd argued, "he'd be the only one left out. That's not right, is it?" Mama stroked her long hair but wouldn't yield. "I'm sorry it seems unfair, honey, but your father and I don't want you associating with Brady Kepp. He's a troubled boy from a troubled family." She stuffed Brady's invitation in her apron, went to the fridge to begin supper. "You're sweet wanting to include everyone, but someday you'll understand why we're doing this."

"Oh," Emily said in a little voice, astonished at her twinge of sympathy for this monster. "I couldn't invite you. My folks wouldn't let me. I-I'm sorry."

"You're sorry, all right," Marwood snarled, twisting her words again. "Oh, you were tough enough in front of your friends, giving me those black eyes when I asked you to the Valentine's Day dance. But you wouldn't stand up to your parents!" He trembled from the acid of childhood humiliation. "I heard all about it Monday. The games were a blast, the cake yummy! Everyone got a present! Emily's so cool, she's our new best friend and . . . and . . ."

"It was thirty years ago, Brady—"

"It was yesterday!" he growled. "And don't call me Brady, you stinking cunt. Brady's dead. My name is Ellis Marwood."

Branch's pupils danced as Dr. Winslow's powerful stimulant took hold. Sweat leaked from his matted hair, and he looked on the verge of passing out. . . .

Blink-blink.

Blink.

Blink-blink-blink-blink.

"He's semaphoring," Winslow whispered, stunned. "That's not possible!"

"Two, one, four," Cross interpreted. "*B-A-D.* Bad. You know the bad guy's name."

Blink.

"We know it already, Branch. It's Kepp. Brady Kepp."

Blink-blink.

"No?" Cross said, shocked. Winslow blotted Branch's face, murmured encouragement. "Then who?" he tried again. "Give me his name. First letter, come on—damn!"

Branch was in full spasm.

"Easy does it," Annie muttered, the eye tape finally sticking to the wall. "Easy . . ." She pulled it off centimeter by centimeter, batting her eyelids to restore her vision. She knew where she was. Emily's basement. She and Lydia Branch had helped install the forty-gallon water heater in the corner a couple months ago. "Yo! Chicks rule!" Emily had shouted when her blowtorched copper connections didn't leak. She couldn't see what was hog-tying her hands and feet behind her back, but it felt like rope. Good. She looked around for cutting tools. None. Then spotted a long curl of sheet metal jutting from the base of the heater. She recalled Emily promising to snip it flush the next day so nobody got sliced. *God bless procrastinators!* She inch-wormed to the heater on kneecaps and forehead, rubbing them raw. She turned backwards and pushed against the makeshift blade. Something stabbed her tailbone. She wiggled her hips till a little red hotel popped out. *Monopoly.* She shook her head, resumed rubbing rope against metal.

* * *

"Patrol Six, report," Jodi crackled.

"All quiet," Marwood replied, glare-warning Emily. "Any update from Safety Town?"

"Nothing new. Coroner's still matching up body parts."

Marwood coughed. "We had some good friends in there. I hope this maniac resists arrest."

"Emily's got dibs," Jodi said. "Hey, you want me to send over a paramedic? Your throat sounds worse."

"No, no," Marwood replied. "They have better things to do. Soon as this is over, I'll swing by the hospital, get checked out."

"Understood," Jodi said. "By the way, that thunderstorm keeps gathering strength. Weather Channel says it'll hit Naperville in an hour."

"Peachy. I love standing guard in a typhoon."

"I hear ya," Jodi said. "Dispatch out."

"And it was important Brady understood the people he would kill, Emmy," Marwood continued, circling the table, voice becoming childlike. "So he learned all about the human mind, why people do the things they do." His eyes gleamed. "Brady was a Green Beret and led secret missions. He killed a ton of people, Emmy."

Emmy. You called me that the first time we met because you couldn't pronounce Emily.

"Important people, all around the world. America's enemies became Brady's enemies, and he dispatched them ruthlessly." Pace-pace-pace. "Brady was wonderful at searching and destroying. His bosses were very pleased. Then he got a visit from a man he didn't know. 'We have a job for someone with your special talents, Brady,' the man said. 'But it's extremely dangerous. We'll destroy your identity when you're finished and provide a brand-new one. One you'll create from scratch, that only you will know. Only a handful of people on this planet could do this job, Brady, and you're one of them. We'd like to offer you this very special chance to serve your country.' Brady loved killing, Emmy. So he transferred to the CIA and did the job they wanted. Two more after that. Powerful people, heads of state. The CIA gave Brady that new life. Brady Kepp went to heaven."

"And Ellis Marwood was born," Emily said.

"Right," he spat, snapping back to the present. "You might be interested to know, I named myself after the two most prolific public executioners in British history—Arthur Ellis and William Marwood."

"British? Why?"

"To honor your British heritage, of course. Something Jack would have appreciated. Lucky for me, you never shared his fascination with history, or you might have outed me sooner." He cackled, seamlessly shifting between man and boy. "The only thing Brady carried to his new life was Emily's belittling. The birthday party. The black eyes. Making him beg on his knees. And even that wasn't enough, so you made him an orphan. An orphan!" His eyes bugged out. "That's why Brady chose a military life, Emmy, so he could learn the best way to take his revenge on the Thompson family. For their heartless murder of Brady's entire family."

Emily floundered for understanding. *Is this a vanished memory? Is Marwood hallucinating? Is it actually true? Does it matter?*

"Scared?" Marwood sneered.

"Cold," she lied. "I left my fur at the station." She pursed her lips in disgust. "Did you do me when I was unconscious? Or just play with yourself?"

Marwood reared back. "I didn't touch you!" he barked. "I have no interest in you that way. None. You're unworthy of a man like me." His expression turned malicious. "You're naked so I can watch your body respond to Hangman. It's the last of the nine games you didn't let me play thirty years ago.

Operation was the first, my dress rehearsal played in Massachusetts. Monopoly was the second, played with Lucy Crawford. Clue was the third, played with Arnie Soull—"

"And fourth is Chutes and Ladders, played with the fireman," she interrupted. "Save your wind, I don't want to relive ancient history."

Marwood poured coffee into a new cup and detailed, anyway. Exactly as she anticipated.

The blood-soaked rope finally parted. Annie eased her sliced-up feet and hands from behind her back, wiggled her toes and fingers to restore circulation.

"They're overdue, Commander," the safe-house SWAT warned Benedetti through the fearsome static. "Can't raise them on radio, cell phone, or laptop."

"Us either," Benedetti said. "Storm's screwing up communications. We'll have to do this the hard way. You and one backup stay at the lodge. Send the rest north along Annie's route."

"That's gonna take awhile," the SWAT warned. "Secondary roads are washing out already, and the storm's trained back to Kansas City."

"I know," Benedetti said. "But I have no choice. Boys are gonna get a little wet."

"Hell, they can't wait. They're still young enough to think this shit's fun." He waited out the earsplitting crackle. "Maybe they got a flat tire and can't reach us through the interference."

"I sure hope so," Benedetti said.

"Roger that, Commander. Heading out now."

"Good luck." He raised the State Police and FBI helicopters surfing the roiling sky—"We'll search till the storm forces us to land," both pilots assured—then ordered the station SWATs to drive south.

Emily was exhausted by the time Marwood reached I Spy. "When did you hide those cameras?" she asked.

"Right after your wedding," he replied. "Lucky Jack. You sure were randy back then."

Annie climbed the carpeted stairs, pinning her shoulder against the wall to avoid stepping in the middle, which would be more likely to squeak. The pipe wrench and hammer she found weren't the greatest weapons, but Marwood had taken everything else.

Cross stood in Branch's line of vision, ready to interpret. "Welcome back, Captain," Winslow said, flooding his IV with stimulant. "Ready to spell us that name?"

Blink.

Annie eased her ear to the six-panel door. She heard Emily and Marwood clearly, meaning they were just on the other side, in the kitchen. She wouldn't have to run more than twenty-five feet, which she could cover in two seconds. Praying Marwood hadn't wedged a chair under the knob, she began turning the solid brass cylinder.

Emily bit her lip in frustration. With her hands cuffed behind her back, that bra knife might as well be on Mars. Marwood was out of kicking range, the bayonet kept her from yelling, the neighborhood evacuation meant nobody would hear her, and the submachine gun and rifle by the back door ruled out everything else. Even if she miraculously escaped the noose, she couldn't run, thanks to the cuffed ankles.

"Wait a minute, Ellis," she said. "Trooper O'Brien said the walls were breathing. Why?"

"Oh, that. I built a MASH unit inside an army-surplus wall tent," Marwood said, relishing his cleverness. "It was windy the day of the kidnapping, and the canvas walls flapped. That's why he told Bertha the walls were breathing."

"Bertha?"

"The Boston 911 dispatcher who fielded my call. As for the organs I removed, they were Broken Heart, Bread Basket, Adam's Apple, Spare Ribs, Butterflies in Stomach—"

"Sadist!" Emily snapped.

"Nah, there's no 'sadist' in Operation," Marwood said. "I piled his organs in order of removal, for easy identification. But those imbecile cops couldn't find the tent. I wound up calling Boston back with directions."

"They weren't imbeciles. You were simply smarter," Emily said, switching to ego massage to keep the conversation going. An escape plan was tugging at her subconscious, and she needed time for it to jell. "What was the first game you played, Ellis? I mean, the one that started all this? Was it Operation?"

Marwood pantomimed a steering wheel. "Bumper cars. Get it?"

"I'm worried about the guys at Emily's house," Jodi said.

"Why?" Benedetti asked, alarmed. "Security breach?"

"No, everything's quiet," she said. "But one of them is raspy from smoke inhalation, meaning the other is, too. He claims they're fine, and they probably are. But I'd feel better if we—"

"Send the next available paramedic unit," Benedetti said. Branch said Jodi was the sharpest knife in the dispatching drawer. If she thought the house sitters needed TLC, they did.

"Bumper cars! You're a filthy piece of vomit!" Emily fumed.

"Hey, you asked," Marwood said. "I had leave coming from the army and decided to visit the old neighborhood. I hitchhiked to Chicago and stole a pickup truck. I swung by your house on your birthday, hoping you'd be visiting for the occasion. No such luck, but your folks were walking back from the store with ice cream. I seized the moment."

"I don't want to hear this!"

"Too bad. I squashed them like armadillos and got back to my motel before the first ambulance arrived. But the kill wasn't perfect." Marwood put his chin in his palm. "Having been a soldier for several years, I assumed I could smite anything in a single blow. Wrong! Mama survived to love her precious Emmy another full year. That was simply unacceptable, so I volunteered for the Green Berets. I wanted to learn to do these things right."

"Yeah, it takes real brains to kill middle-aged people carrying ice cream," Emily taunted.

"Damn straight," Marwood retorted. "Nobody else in that fucking school of ours could have done it. Not the nuns. Not you. Not anybody. Only me." He sauntered to the coffeepot. "The psych courses and hands-on field training I got in the Berets were infinitely more useful for my purposes than sitting in a classroom bored out of my mind. I retired with a doctorate in knowing what makes people tick. But I needed university credentials to form my practice and build my reputation as the go-to guy for law enforcement. The friendly database hackers at the CIA were happy to help." He stroked his squarish ears. "As was the plastic surgeon in Bombay who altered my physical identity. I killed him afterwards, of course." His smile was chilling. "I profiled you between corporate assignments and hunting trips."

"Always the big-game hunter," Emily said, quoting from his criminal profile.

"You don't know the half of it, Princess," Marwood said. "There are sixty-seven unsolved murders across these United States with my name on them. Not counting the bodies right here in River City."

"Sixty . . ." she breathed, stunned.

"Practice makes perfect. They were inferiors—runaways, crackheads, prostitutes. People nobody cared about. If I left a clue by mistake during practice, I wanted to ensure no cop would give enough of a shit about them to do anything beyond file paperwork." He kissed his fingers, savoring his own brilliance. "I visited Naperville regularly over the years to update your profile."

"And shoot your video," Emily said.

"I've always wanted to direct," Marwood said. "Then you met Jack and became happy with your life. Started putting your parents' tragic deaths into perspective. So naturally, it was time to take that away." He chuckled. "Ah, the poor sap never knew what hit him."

Emily's eyes roamed as Marwood described the fiery explosion under the viaduct. That mental tug meant something. What was it? What had she missed? What hadn't she considered?

Wait! The noose is looped over *my hair, not under!*

Maybe, just maybe, Marwood never found the key taped to my neck!

* * *

The knob quit turning. Annie cracked the door just enough to prevent relatching, then cranked back the pipe wrench and hammer.

"You blinked thirteen times," Cross said. "That's the letter *M*, correct?"

Blink.

"All right then. Next letter."

Blink.

"One," Winslow said. "The letter *A*."

Blink.

"Did that mean yes or the letter *A*?"

"Single questions only, Ken," Winslow reminded.

"Oh, right. Branch, was that the letter *A*?"

Blink.

"Good. Third letter."

The pause was so long, Winslow checked Branch's vital signs.

Blink-blink-blink-blink-blink-blink . . .

"*R*," Cross said when he finished. "*M-A-R*." His eyes widened. "I don't believe it," he whispered, incredulous. "Marty? Marty Benedetti is the Unsub?" He whipped his head toward Winslow. "First or last name, Barbara?" he demanded. "Which did we ask Branch to spell?"

She stared. "I don't know. I don't remember!"

"Shit!" Cross groaned. He started to ask Branch for clarification, but the captain's eyes had already glazed over.

Emily relaxed her knees and let a soft moan escape.

"Finally sinking in that you're going to die, Princess?" Marwood asked.

"Only in your dreams," she said. "And stop calling me

Princess. Your tongue isn't fit to clean my father's behind, much less use his nickname for me."

"I thought Princess was Jack's nickname for you."

"They both used it. Not that it's any of your business, you hair ball."

"Behind. Hair ball." He snickered. "You know, Princess, it's just not the same. I really miss the old potty-mouth Emily. Too bad you promised Daddy about swearing." His voice turned reminiscent. "Remember third grade? When you cussed a streak so filthy, the penguins washed out your mouth with laundry soap? What a stitch. Then in fifth grade when you . . ."

She wiggled her scalp as he yakked on, trying to feel the handcuff key. Marwood confiscated the one on her ankle because the I Spy cameras in her bedroom recorded her attaching it. The neck key might still be there because she taped it at the police station, out of camera range. *Thank God for superstition!* But how would she get her hands on the get-out-of-jail card when those hands were behind her back?

"Why did you switch names?" Emily tried, hoping to extend Remember When. "Was Kepp too many letters for your pea brain to remember?"

Marwood laughed. "A new identity is a must. After they find you dead, every cop in this country will hunt Brady Kepp till the end of time."

"Which is almost here, you know," Emily said. "Benedetti and Cross know we've disappeared because Sergeant Bates stopped checking in. They'll figure out you came here to play the final game. You're too obsessed not to, and they know it." She shifted to ease the cramp in her left calf. "Just surrender, Ellis. You could plead insanity and get away with it. Lord knows, I'd testify you're nuts."

Marwood laughed. "You don't get it. This place was scoured by the feds and your own SWAT team. Every door and window is boarded tight, and I check in every fifteen minutes. We're out of sight here, out of mind. Your colleagues aren't going to save you, Princess. Neither are guns, batons, helicopters, SWATs, task forces, and all the other bullshit you cops wave like magic wands. You're the only one who can save your life, Princess, by winning our final game. But you aren't good enough to beat me. Not then, not ever—"

Annie kicked the door and heaved the wrench at Marwood's head, screaming. With the reflexes of a cat, Marwood dodged it and the hammer to his abdomen, then flung Emily's bayonet deep into Annie's stomach. The SWAT went down howling, Marwood on her like a mongoose. "A for effort, Sergeant," he said, stunning her with a vicious hand chop to the neck. "But no reservist beats a Green Beret." He broke Annie's pelvis with a heel stomp, and she fell unconscious. He placed the bayonet on her carotid for the killing thrust, then reconsidered. "I know! I'll slit your throat when I hang Emily. You can watch each other die. That'll be fun, won't it?" He cuffed Annie's wrists, removed the bayonet, duct-taped her wound—"Can't croak till I say so, Ossifer," he said—and hurried to the basement door. "One peep from you, I'll come up and fillet her to bone," he warned Emily. "So don't get stupid on me."

"Not Martin. Marwood!" Winslow insisted. "Commander Benedetti isn't capable of murder!"

"Everyone's capable given enough motivation, Barbara!" Cross said loudly, over the snoring captain, desperately trying to think through this dilemma. If he wasted even a minute hauling in the wrong man . . . "I'm positive I told Branch to spell his first name! Not his last name, his first! So it has to be Marty! Not Marwood!"

"We drugged this poor man up to his eyeballs," Winslow shot back. "And Branch is human. He misunderstood our directions. Or believed he was spelling Marwood's first name. Or something else entirely." She clapped her fists together, burning off adrenaline. "To hell with logic, Ken. Who do you *believe* committed these crimes? Ellis or Marty?"

Cross closed his eyes, weighing what she said. He opened them a minute later and pulled out his cell phone. "Marty? Ken. We've been suckered!" he barked. "Marwood is the Unsub. Repeat, Dr. Ellis Marwood is the Unsub."

"You killed Flea, didn't you?" Emily growled, sickened by her certainty at what this monster just did in the basement. "All of them."

"Of course, I did. I don't need more fucking surprises." Marwood wiped the bloody blade on Emily's legs, slipped it in his belt. "What were we talking about?"

"Your CIA identity," Emily said, seeing Annie stir.

"Ah, right. Those political assassinations I did were on presidential orders. So if you believe the CIA will hand my new identity to your people, you're crazier than I am."

"The courts will make them."

Marwood snickered, fluffed his hair. " 'Golly, Judge, the paperwork on this Kepp fellow you ordered us to produce?' " he falsettoed, mimicking a bewildered CIA lawyer. " 'It's disappeared. We're looking high and low, Your Honor. We'd never disobey an official court order.' " A harsher laugh. "Nothing about me will leak. Kepp is dead, long live Marwood." He bowed in admiration. "Nice gambit, though, Princess. You're playing the game brilliantly."

"I told you not to call me that."

"You're in no position to dictate rules," he said. "I'll call you whatever—" He darted for the submachine gun, slicing a finger across his throat. "There's noise on your back porch," he whispered. "Say one fucking syllable and I'll shoot you. Annie, too. Savvy?"

Emily nodded, hoping whoever it was carried grenades and heavy weapons. She'd gladly die in a SWAT assault if it meant taking Kepp with her. It was one thing to terrorize her for the crimes he imagined she'd committed against him. Lucy Crawford deserved no such fate. Neither did the other lost souls, especially Mama, Daddy, and Jack, whose only crime had been to love her. She prayed for a lightning entry and instant annihilation.

But the only "assault" was a light scratching on the door, followed by thumps. Not in the middle, where people put their hands, but way down at the bottom.

"It's the neighbor's dog," she whispered. "The yellow Lab from the fun run."

"Shelby," Marwood whispered back.

"Right. He's come over to play. Probably heard Annie scream and wants to join the party."

Marwood peered through the puffball curtains. "All right. Just keep your mouth shut," he ordered, hooking the submachine gun on the doorknob. "Animals are stupid. If Shelby doesn't hear anything for sixty seconds, he'll get bored and leave."

The porch noises faded. It was time. This escape plan was desperate, practically suicidal. But Marwood held every other card. "Please, Shelby, don't go!" she blubbered. "Don't leave me with this bad man!"

"I told you to shut up, Princess!" Marwood snarled, pulling the bayonet.

"And I told you not to call me that, you lunatic!" Emily shouted.

"That's it, Princess!" Marwood thundered, eyes bulging. "Time to hang you by the neck till you're dead-dead-dead! Not by snapping it quick and easy, nosirree. I knotted that rope so you'd strangle! Your face will turn purple. Your tongue will sag, and your eyes will bulge. At that point I'll cut your cunt pal's throat, and you'll watch each other die. Then I win our final game! After thirty years of plotting and rehearsing and dreaming of this—"

"We didn't play Hangman at my birthday party, you idiot!" Emily screeched, going for broke, praying Shelby hadn't wandered too far. "There were only eight games! Not nine! Thirty years and you're still a pathetic loser—"

"Hangman was my game!" Marwood thrust the bayonet like a picador. Blood spurted from her thigh. "It's the game I was bringing to your party, if only you'd invited me!"

"There's no way I'd invite you, Fraidy Brady! You're a loser! A bed wetter! The kids at school laugh because a girl beat you up! Your father whips your sorry butt because you're such a disappointing son! You're weak! Pathetic! A disgrace to your family! Your underwear's always wet! Boo-hoo-hoo, better run to Mommy and have her change your widdle—"

Marwood howled, pulling back his leg to kick the game table away.

"Shelby! Help!" Emily screamed as the burly Lab blasted through the pet flap she'd installed so many years ago. "Bad man, Shelby, get him! Help me!"

The dog yowled, ears flat to his skull. He rocketed across the kitchen and sank his teeth deep into Marwood's left arm. The profiler screamed, the bayonet clattering under the refrigerator as Shelby tore muscle and tendon. "Let go of me, goddammit!" Marwood shouted, punching Shelby's head with his free fist while straining to reach the guns. Shelby dragged him back, eyes glowing, frothy slobber turning the pine floor into a skating rink.

"Good boy! Attack! Kill!" Emily prepared for the high-school gymnastics move she prayed would save her and Annie. "That's right! Get him! Get the bad man. Awk!" Shelby's butt knocked the table away, dumping her sideways and jamming the noose deep in her throat. "Do it!" she screamed at herself, panic overwhelming her nervous system. "Do it now or die!"

She moved her wrists as far apart as the handcuff chain allowed, lifted her knees to her chin, kicked her feet back behind the chain, then dropped her legs all the way down. The "dislocation" made her shoulders squeal in pain, but it moved her hands where she needed them—from the back of her body to the front.

"Gotta land, Commander," the FBI pilot warned by radio. "Air's too unstable. We'll go back up at first break."

"Understood. Thanks." Benedetti turned to Cross, who'd just dashed up from his car. "The storm's grounded the choppers. Nothing from the road search. Marwood's got nine lives—"

"He thinks we're stupid, right?" Cross interrupted, panting. "Dull-minded pencil pushers who couldn't hack it in the big leagues, so we're stuck writing parking tickets in the suburbs? As opposed to his superior, world-class self?"

"Yeah . . ."

"So where would such a genius bury his treasure? Where X marks the spot? Or somewhere he knows for certain we'd never look because we're too retarded?"

Benedetti realized what Cross meant. "No way, Ken," he protested. "Emily's house is too risky even for that maniac."

"Because it's right downtown," Cross pressed. "Because it's boarded up tight. Because the cops check in every fifteen minutes. Because a starving rat would never risk a trap to steal the cheese. Right?"

Benedetti recalled Jodi's concern over the team's raspy voices. "Right!" He grabbed his radio to flood Jackson

Avenue with firepower, but Cross touched his hand. "If Marwood hears the cavalry coming, he'll kill her on the spot. Where's your race car?"

They broke into a dead run.

Bearing her full body weight suspended from her neck, Emily saw stars explode in the approaching black clouds. Only seconds of consciousness remained. She raised her shaking arms, clawed her bra, pulled out the knife Marwood had condescendingly allowed her to keep. Heart pounding fast and thready in her ears, she thrust the knife over her head and sawed at the rope. Marwood and Shelby wrestled across the slick pine. "Let go! Let go!" Marwood screamed, hammering Shelby's skull. Shelby growled and held on tight. Eyelids fluttering, Emily sawed as hard as her numbing hands allowed.

She hit the floor like a sack of hammers. She rolled to her side, gasping and retching, reaching under the noose to find the taped handcuff key. Her heart pounded so hard from the fresh oxygen, she thought it'd explode. She glimpsed Shelby's eyes rolling and knew it'd be only a moment before Marwood freed himself to finish his deadly obsession.

There it is!

She ripped the tiny key off her neck and shoved it at the ankle cuffs. It scraped past the lock hole. She steadied herself against a cabinet, then eased the key into the hole, willing her hands to quit trembling. "Shoot this mongrel! Then you!" Marwood howled, dragging the ragged dog toward the guns. "You'll never get away!"

Click!

"I'll come back! I won't abandon you guys!" Emily croaked, her legs popping free. She flung the bra knife at Marwood—dizziness made her aim so bad, it clanked off the stove—and tossed the key into Annie's lap. Gathering the last of her strength, she stood, picked up the game table, and heaved it at the window over the sink. The heavy rock maple shattered the glass, and Emily dived face-first through the jagged hole, still-cuffed hands shielding her eyes. Marwood fired a long burst, but she was already through, her body whomping onto the shards littering the porch. Groaning, she rolled to her feet and limped down the hill.

"We're coming, Emily! Hang on!" Benedetti yelled as he tromped Love Shack's gas pedal to the floor and blasted through the garage.

"There's his rental car!" Cross shouted as the air bags deflated. "They're here!"

Marty grabbed his shotgun from under the passenger seat and rolled out the door.

Marwood chased her down the hill, raising the submachine gun.

Annie unlocked the handcuffs, moaning at the pain in her pelvis and belly. She heard the shuddering crash from the front of the house and arm-crawled to the sniper rifle. She grabbed it and headed out the back door. Shelby was already down the hill, inching toward Emily.

Emily zigzagged down the steep slope, dodging Marwood's first two submachine-gun bursts. The third came so close, she heard the bullets' angry buzz. She could barely see through the blood sheeting down from her forehead cuts, but a decade of fun runs had burned this route deep in her muscle memory. "Thirty-seven, thirty-eight, thirty-nine!"

she cried as her bare feet hit familiar depressions. "Forty, forty-one, jump!" She soared headfirst over the woodpile, exactly forty-two strides from her back door, intending to roll to her feet on the other side to keep momentum. But her foot caught a jutting log. She crashed face-first into the ground as Marwood's fourth burst thudded into the thick birch logs. "Go-go-go!" she huffed through her broken nose, aiming at what she hoped was the path through the woods. She screamed as a bullet drilled her left calf, stumbled hard but recovered.

"Got you now, Princess!" Marwood sang from not nearly far enough behind.

"Never!" she screamed, abandoning her zigzag for a fourth-and-inches plunge. The submachine gun ripped a fifth time, but she was safe in the tree line.

Annie sprawled sideways, pointing the rifle downhill, careful not to disturb the duct tape—if it became unstuck, she'd bleed out in seconds. Benedetti appeared from the side of the house as Cross blasted out the back door. "Annie!" they shouted together.

"Marwood's chasing Emily!" Annie shouted back. "He's got Flea's submachine gun!"

"I'll catch them!" Benedetti said, tossing the shotgun to Cross and charging down the hill.

"Who's that?" Cross yelled, swinging on the figure about to vanish in the trees. "Can I fire?"

Annie replied by pulling the trigger.

"Noooooo!" Marwood howled as the rifle bullet shattered his left elbow into a fog of blood and bone. He wheeled around and emptied the submachine gun at the smoke puff near the porch.

* * *

Benedetti slammed to the ground to avoid the bullets pouring uphill. Coughing out dirt and grass, he scrambled to his feet at the first lull and kept running.

Bare feet bleeding from rocks and glass, Emily sailed out of the woods, across the Riverwalk bricks, through the weedy shoreline bramble, and into the churning river. She couldn't swim because her wrists were still cuffed. "You can't escape!" Marwood howled from the trees.

She splashed into the water as far as she could, then latched onto a floating tree branch, letting the current pull her downstream. Naperville was still rain free, but Wisconsin had been deluged, turning the sedate DuPage River into a blender of foam, waves, and hidden boulders. She slammed into one and spun, silted brown water flushing down her throat. "Awk," she gargled, the branch floating away. She clutched onto a moss-covered tree stump, holding it with shredded fingernails. The bramble was dense here and would hide her. She looked around for weapons. None, and she'd thrown the bra knife at Marwood. But now she saw what was causing such pain in her left breast—a nine-inch shard of window glass. If she could get it out intact, maybe she could use it as a spear. But it was so slender! It couldn't possibly hold up long enough to reach a vital organ! She hunkered in the mud, looking for another plan, another place to run. . . .

"Forget it," she growled as a feeling of utter calm settled in. "You want me, Doc, give it your best shot. I'm tired of running."

Annie screamed as Cross fell on her. "Bastard clipped my legs," he gasped. "I can't stand."

"He got me, too," she said. She racked in a fresh cartridge and searched for Marwood. "You've got to help me here, Chief."

Cross didn't reply, his breathing labored.

"I can't steady the rifle by myself," Annie said. "Crawl in front of me, and I'll use your neck as a barrel rest. Hurry!"

Cross grunted, inching forward.

Emily stared at her pursuer through the bramble. His gun was moving in tandem with his head. "Come out, come out, wherever you are," he sang. "I killed your daddy and crushed your mama. I burned Jack like a witch at the stake. Crippled Annie and paralyzed Branch. When I'm done with you, I'll find Marty and gut him like a trout."

She freed herself from the mud, gripping the shard she'd extracted from her breast. Its jagged edges sliced deep into her palm. But she no longer cared about pain. About past or future. Only about ending this madness.

"You're naked, cold, and bleeding," he said. "Shock will get you if blood loss doesn't." Six feet from the river, four feet, two feet, one, so close she smelled bay rum. "Surrender to me, Princess! Right now! If you do that, I'll leave Marty alone. I'll let him live, I promise. Just one quick bullet to the brain and you'll join your family. You'll be happy forever! Come out, come out, wherever you are."

Emily exploded from the river and jammed the shard between his legs. "Ahhhhhh!" Marwood screamed. "You stinking cunt—"

"Nobody calls me that, Brady Kepp!" Emily screamed, shattering Marwood's left kneecap with a river rock. He flopped sideways, squealing like a stuck pig. She flattened his nose, then raked his face with her fingers, trying to pull his eyes out. He counterattacked, hurting her bad with every punch. He was insanely motivated, and she was half-dead from the rope.

Benedetti burst from the tree line, closing the gap to the boiling water.

"Perfect, Chief. Don't move," Annie commanded. Cross lay facedown, fingers stuffed in his ears, elbows and legs splayed so she could sandbag the rifle barrel on the back of his neck. It was a crude but effective platform to launch what she prayed would be the killing shot. She adjusted the telescopic sight for range and bullet drop, then welded herself to the black stock. "They're next to the river," she said, controlling her breathing to allow an instantaneous squeeze of the three-pound trigger. "Fighting. Too close together. Soon as they separate, I'll fire. Don't move an inch, Chief. Don't even breathe."

Emily jumped behind Marwood and jammed the handcuffs against his carotid arteries. "Bad guy passes out instantly or double your money back," the academy instructor had bragged about the choke hold. But Marwood dropped his chin to block the choker, reached up, and grabbed Emily's hair with his good right arm. He body-slammed her into the mud like a pro wrestler, then dropped on top. All her injuries squirted fire. He kneed her till she went limp, then seized her throat with his huge right hand. "I'm going to strangle you anyway, Princess," he gloated, muscling them both to their knees, keeping their faces so close their noses touched. "You should have known you could never win against me. This isn't child's play. It's winner take all."

"You're so right!" she croaked, reaching down for the shard still in his crotch. She wiggled till her palm ran red with their commingled blood. The pressure on her throat eased. She yanked on the glass till it snapped and watched pink drool run from Marwood's mouth. His face turned pasty, and his head lolled to the right.

Annie's finger twitched. Her rifle thundered.

"Emily! Duck!" Benedetti screamed, launching himself like Superman.

"Ahh!" the psychologist gasped as his left eyeball exploded. He released one more breath, then flopped to the ground. The bullet slowed from punching through his skull but didn't stop.

Emily was drowning in mud. Her attacker jumped on her back, and her fury turned atomic. She bucked him sideways, then pounced, stabbing desperately for his face.

Annie clutched Cross's arm in horror. "No! No!"

"He's dead, Emily. He's dead!" her attacker was shouting. "You stopped him! You're safe!"

"Marty!" Emily blurted, hands snapping back like bungee cords. "I thought you were Marwood! Thank God you're all right!"

He grimaced, shaking his head. "I'm shot."

Emily frantically checked him for bleeding. None that she could see. "Where, baby?" she demanded, panic rising like helium. "Where were you shot? Tell me!"

"My cheek."

Her hands flew back to his face, but she saw no blood or holes.

"My other cheek, Detective," he groaned. "Marwood left the rifle in your kitchen. Annie and Cross found it. Their bullet hit Marwood in the head, but I guess a fragment caught me."

Emily ripped away his muddy trouser seat, ran her hands everywhere. She found the wound nestled in the fine hair of his lower right cheek. It was a shallow crease, not an entry hole. Raw but not life-threatening. She told him, then started giggling, all the fear and tension of the last three days transforming the oxygen into laughing gas.

"You find something funny about this?" Benedetti demanded.

"No sir, Commander sir, not me," Emily said, trying to control herself. That made it worse. "You'll need a new nickname, though. Since Halfass is already taken, we could call you Half and Half. Sir." She fell to the ground, laughing so hard she couldn't breathe. Benedetti scowled.

"How did you find me?" Emily finally said, gulping air like a landed tuna.

"Hang on," Benedetti said, glaring at Marwood's lifeless body. He got to his feet, grabbed Marwood's arms, and dragged him several yards downriver. Then stumbled back and flopped into the mud next to her, draping his arm over her naked waist. "That's better. We came here because of Branch. He figured out Marwood was the Unsub."

Emily stiffened, thunderstruck. "How did he know?"

"Remember when you guys visited him on the way back from the safe house?" Benedetti asked. "He was paralyzed but wide awake, listening to everything?"

She wiped mud off Marty's nose. "I remember."

"At some point Marwood asked for cold pop. Doc Winslow returned with a few cans. A couple minutes later you told Branch that Marwood was born and raised in Manhattan."

She shook her head, not following.

"New Yorkers call soft drinks 'soda,'" Benedetti continued. "Chicagoans call it 'pop.' Very distinct regional dialects. It suggested to Branch that Marwood was lying about his roots and, therefore, might be our wolf in sheep's clothing."

"Incredible," she said. "But how did Branch tell you? He was paralyzed."

Benedetti shifted with a soft moan. "The doctors said it was impossible for Branch to semaphore the news. But he did. He broke through the paralysis."

"To save me," she breathed, starting to tear up.

Benedetti kissed her cheek. "Yeah. He spelled out *M-A-R* before going into spasm. We couldn't find you on the road, so Cross thought Marwood might bring you back to the house."

"Because of his obsession."

"Right. And here's the rest." He stopped to catch his breath, then leaned over and kissed her full on the lips.

Smiling through her tear-filled vision, Emily kissed back, then pulled Marty as close as her wounds allowed. She heard Cross bellowing at cops to get paramedics down to the river, then put up crime-scene tape. Always the martinet. But if Cross hadn't griped and bullied her into thinking under pressure, she'd be dead, and Marwood gone with the wind. She owed him.

She kissed Marty again, then asked about Shelby, fearing the worst.

"Tough little hombre," Marty replied, admiration in his voice. "He was halfway down the hill when we arrived, trying to get to you. Couple of cops rushed him to the animal

hospital on Main Street. He'll survive, Em. Battered but un-
bowed."

Emily wiped her eyes, explaining how Shelby and Annie
had tried to rescue her, and how the cops in the basement
had paid the price. "It was Hangman, Marty," she said, shiv-
ering in the frigid mud. "Our final game was Hangman.
Marwood—Kepp—told me everything while I was hanging
in that noose. It all started in grade school—"

"Plenty of time for that," Benedetti said, removing his
shirt and draping it over her. "The task force will take your
statement after the hospital fixes you up. Just relax."

Emily nodded, turned her gaze to the river. The wind had
whipped the surface into frothy whitecaps. Towering purple
clouds raced across the French vanilla sky. Lightning flashed
not too far away—*1,001; 1,002*—followed by kidney-
shaking thunderclaps. It looked like the long drought was
ending. She looked at Marty, who was wincing himself into
a new position. *Yes,* she decided, stroking his mud-riven
back. *The drought is finally over.*

"Jesus Christ, Ken," Viking puffed as he ran up to Cross.
"Can't you stay in your office and play with yourself like all
the other chiefs?"

"I'd tell you to kiss my ass," Cross groaned. "But I ain't
got one." Viking dropped to his knees to examine the leg
wounds. "They're not too bad," the medic declared. "One
bullet in your left thigh, two in the right. No broken bones
and the bleeding's only seepage. Surgeons will dig them out,
and you'll be fine." He replaced Annie's duct tape with bandages, splinted her broken pelvis, and ordered them to the
idling ambulance.

As they slid inside, Cross reached over and squeezed
Annie's hand. "You done good, Sergeant," he murmured.

She squeezed back. "You, too, Chief. You, too."

* * *

Emily started as the oddest thought struck her. "I'm still suspended, aren't I?"

"What on earth are you talking about?" Marty asked, cringing as paramedics swabbed disinfectant on his butt.

"Annie and I got suspended. By the chief. For my shooting the library floor. Annie tried taking the blame, but Cross caught us. We each got a week's suspension for lying."

Benedetti raised his eyebrows. "And you're thinking about this now because—"

"So I don't have to think about the rest." She fell silent. "That's a week of income I can't afford to lose, Marty. With my house destroyed and all. Maybe he'll forget about it."

"Would you? If you were chief?"

She thought about that, looked at her feet. "I guess not."

"And for good reason," Benedetti said. "It keeps maniacs like you from shooting poor old innocent carpets that never hurt no one." She stuck out her tongue, and he smiled. "Actually, Detective, Ken said you owe him a week after the Unsub's safely behind bars."

"I just said that, Marty," she said. "Soon as Dr. Winslow clears me, I'll serve it."

"You're not listening," Benedetti said. "Ken said you'll serve your suspension when the Unsub's safely behind bars. Until then, he needs you out on the street."

She stared, then got it. The Unsub would never be safely behind bars because he was dead. Ergo . . . "So the chief isn't suspending us."

"Correct."

"But he said he was."

"Also correct."

She shook her head. "Why say one thing when he means the opposite?"

"It's what us management types do."

"I see. So if I said I hate you . . ."

Benedetti grinned. "Happy birthday, Emily. With many more to come."

"And many more together," she said, closing her eyes and smiling.

Blink, her Mama said.

Special Bonus! Here is a preview excerpt from *Cut to the Bone*, the heart-pounding new thriller by Shane Gericke, coming from Pinnacle in 2007.

On June 29, 1972, the state of Illinois strapped an innocent man into the electric chair and threw the switch, executing him for a crime he didn't commit. Now, more than three decades later, Naperville Police Detective Emily Thompson may pay the price for that tragic miscarriage of justice—as she becomes the target of a serial killer obsessed with payback.

"Glad you came?" Emily Thompson asked.

"Oh, man, this is great," Martin Benedetti groaned as the attendant shoveled another layer of steaming mud onto his chest. "I feel like the marshmallow in the hot chocolate. I should have done this years ago."

Emily reached across the tub-for-two to pat his face. They were spending the morning at a high-tone "mud spa" on Ogden Avenue in Naperville. She'd been asking Marty for a while to try it with her. He kept insisting he wanted nothing to do with "toenail polish and dulcimer music." Then, on her forty-second birthday, he handed her a gift certificate for two, agreeing to join her.

Emily settled herself deeper in the 104-degree mud, a "mystic Zen formula" of "precious minerals and botanicals" that "detoxified and cleansed" the body. The attendant's description was just sales puffery, she knew—it was peat moss and volcanic ash. She didn't care. Its clinging heat whacked her stress like a hitman. Having Marty next to her in the deep redwood tub was a bonus—they could make fun of everything tonight as they snuggled up in bed.

The attendant poured them flutes of Soy-Carrot Infusion Juice, then offered to swaddle their eyes with citrus-misted cucumber slices. "So your inner child stays cool," she murmured in a breezy Jamaican lilt. Emily tilted her face to accept them. Marty muttered about needing a testosterone patch. Emily pinched his leg, making him yelp. The attendant giggled, shoveled on the final thick layer, said she'd step out to let the mud "work its magic." After the door closed, Marty cleared his throat.

"You can't tell anyone about this, you know."

"About what?" Emily smiled into the lemon-scented darkness.

"About me. Parking my ass in a tub of goo."

"And liking it," she reminded.

"Don't rub it in."

Emily pushed her hand through the slurry, threaded her fingers through Marty's. "Don't worry, tough guy. I wouldn't dream of blowing your cover—" Her eyelids popped open so fast the cucumbers flew. "What was that?"

Marty was already struggling to his feet. "Gunshots," he said, his buttery baritone turned hard and flat. "Three. Nearby."

Emily fought to sit up. Marty pulled her wrists, sucking her torso out of the hot mud. She heard voices shrieking, "Omigod! Help! Help!"

Their attendant raced into the mud room, slamming the

door so hard the frosted glass cracked. "Somebody shot Leila in the lobby!" she screamed, eyes wide. "Hide or he'll kill us all!"

"Call 911!" Marty roared, bounding out of the tub. "And get our clothes!"

"No time for that!" Emily shoved her heels against the bottom until she popped out of the mud. She swung her legs over the side and lunged for their guns—she went nowhere unarmed since the serial killer Ellis Marwood had knotted a noose around her neck and hanged her in her own kitchen. She slipped on the cornflower tiles and fell sideways, banging her head off the wall. "Ow! Dammit!" she yelped.

"Emily! You all right?"

"Go! Go! I'll catch up!" she gasped.

Marty knotted a bath towel around his waist. Emily reached over her head and yanked her knockoff Coach tote from the wall peg. She fumbled with the zipper then pulled out a pair of .45-caliber Glocks.

The attendant shrank into a corner. "Don't hurt me," she begged, covering her head with her mud-streaked arms. "Please, miss, I'll do whatever you say."

"We're the police!" Emily said, thrusting Marty's black pistol over her head like the Statue of Liberty's torch. Marty snatched it and bolted through the door. A moment later he stuck his head back in, pitched her a belted terrycloth robe and took off.

Emily grabbed the pitcher of Infusion Juice and poured it over her head, gasping as the icy slush chilled her warm body. The bells fell silent. She scrambled to her feet, jammed her arms in the over-large robe, wrapped her muddy hands around the checkered butt of her gun, and ran down the hall to the lobby.

"Oh Jesus," she breathed, absorbing the horrific scene. Blood slopped the walls as though a tomato can had exploded. The room stank of burnt gunpowder. Marty was on his knees, blowing air into a short, slender woman. Ugly holes were torn in her chest and forehead. Her face was white as cake flour. Blood fizzed from the holes when Marty blew. Emily knew instantly the CPR was not going to help her. She scanned the handful of onlookers.

"Naperville Police! Which way did he go?" she said, primed to pull the trigger if the shooter was in the crowd. "Is he here? Did he leave? Talk to me!"

A manicurist, slender as a willow whip, pointed to the centermost of the lobby's five doors. "He went that way. He didn't say anything. Just started shooting!" she said, tears splashing down her cheeks. "He killed Leila and ran!"

"Parking lot," Marty said, looking up. "Watch yourself, detective. I'll be there as soon as someone takes over." He surveyed the crowd. "All right, who knows CPR?"

Emily charged into the lot, robe flapping, eyes flashing. Nobody was fleeing. Nobody sauntered nonchalantly. Nobody jumped in a Dumpster or darted behind a store.

Breathing fast, she searched the nearest row of parked cars. Nobody hiding. No tailpipe exhaust. Ditto second row, third, fourth.

She heard an engine turn over. *He's out there. Go get him.* Her bare feet flew over pavement, litter and broken pop bottles. She still saw nothing. "Police!" she screamed. "Come out with your hands up!"

"Look behind you!" Marty yelled.

Emily whirled to see a black Grand Prix bear down on her like a runaway locomotive. Shooting wouldn't save her—the car was too close. She jumped straight up, desperately clawing air to clear the bumper—

"Aaaah!" she screamed as her body flew up over the hood. She smashed into the windshield, heard a sickening crunch. The driver jammed the gas pedal. His acceleration flipped her onto the roof. She windsurfed until a sharp swerve bucked her off.

She slammed into a rust-bucket SUV and tumbled to the pavement. She started rolling as soon as her shoulder touched, to avoid breaking her neck. Her Glock skittered out of her hands. Dizzy, she rolled to hands and knees and crawled after it, skin on fire from pavement scrapes.

A gun behind her barked. The Grand Prix's rear passenger window shattered. Energized by Marty's counterattack, she struggled to her feet, scooped, aimed and fired three quick .45s at the driver's door. Holes appeared but did no good—the car careened onto Ogden Avenue and disappeared into eastbound traffic.

Emily yelled out the license plate. Marty fed the information into a cellphone. She tightened her robe and took off, running diagonally across the lot, hoping to catch the Grand Prix before —

She fell to the pavement, clutching her leg in agony.

"Officer down!" Marty bellowed as he ran up. He flung the phone and knelt to check her for bleeding or broken bones.

"It's the scar!" Emily said, groaning. She'd taken a submachine gun bullet in her left calf two years ago during her wild escape from Marwood's noose. The thumb-sized wound healed well enough for her to pass the medical exam and return to work. But sometimes it spasmed when she pushed herself too hard.

"Dig into it, Marty!" she begged. "Use your knuckles! Oh God it hurts!" She heard sirens and prayed one was a paramedic bearing Vicodin.

"I've got you, Emily," Marty reassured, clamping her leg between his knees and drilling for oil with both fists. "I've got you, I've got you . . ."

The spasms eased as the first Naperville Police cruiser zoomed into the lot.

She clutched Marty and pulled herself into a sitting position, breathing four-seconds-in, four-seconds-out. "Is . . . that woman . . . dead?" she wheezed.

Marty nodded.

"Who shoots . . . a little old lady . . . at a day spa?"

"Dunno," Marty said, hugging her close. "But we're sure as hell gonna find out."

The shooter wheeled onto Sherman Avenue, then into the strip-mall parking lot, keeping a tight rein on his fear. In all his executions, this was the first time anybody had fought back. It rattled him harder than he'd anticipated. *Don't panic!* he told himself. *Panic brings paralysis! Do what you planned and you'll be fine!*

He looked around for witnesses. None. He whipped the Grand Prix into an empty space in the back of the lot and turned off the engine.

Hands shaking from the adrenalin dump, he looked again. Still nobody. He relaxed a fraction. As he'd learned from his practice runs, this medical-office strip mall made an excellent place to switch cars—just thirty seconds from the spa to get him off Ogden fast, with a wall of storefronts to screen him from responding cops.

Though that wouldn't last if he dawdled.

He peeled the fake beard from his wide cleft chin, rubbed off the rubber-cement residue. He stuffed the disguise into the glove compartment, along with the Chicago Bulls cap that camouflaged his head. He looked around a third time. Frowned.

A mommy van was pulling next to the curb.

He couldn't leave now. Couldn't risk her telling the cops about the maroon Taurus that peeled rubber when the sirens came. He had to wait, each tick of the cooling engine as loud as a gunshot. *Get out of here, goddammit!* he screamed silently. *Thirty more seconds and I'll have to leave! I'll have to shoot your stupid ass! Move it!* But she was still in her car, and his right hand gripped the .357 Magnum in his belt. *Five seconds.* His left hand grabbed the door handle. *Three seconds.* He'd walk up to the driver, empty the gun in her head, retreat as quickly as possible. *One second . . .*

A little girl in pigtails hopped out, ran inside one of the offices. The mommy van made a three-point turn and exited the lot.

He slumped, panting.

Then got moving.

He slid out of the Grand Prix, threw the keys down the storm drain. Hopped into the Taurus, started the engine with a gas-heavy "Vroom." Nosed onto Ogden Avenue, quickly moved to the middle divider to let a police cruiser scream past. The cop made a little wave, "Thanks." He waved back.

He drove the speed limit to Wisconsin Avenue, cranked the wheel in a quick hard right, and began his escape from the city.

"Enough already, guys," Emily groaned, shooing away the paramedics who'd been poking, prodding and painting her antiseptic-yellow the past thirty minutes. "We gotta get dressed."

"Before CSI bags our clothes as evidence," Marty agreed. He grasped his towel with one hand, offered Emily the other.

She grabbed his fingers and pulled herself to her feet. The movement shook up her vision like a snow globe. She blinked, then walked toward the spa, planting each foot firmly before lifting the other. She'd feel silly falling in front of the Fire Department.

"Hey! Wait up!"

Emily turned to see a muscular blonde spill from a black-and-white. It was Lieutenant Annabelle Bates, commander of the Naperville Police SWAT team and Emily's best friend besides Marty. They stopped to let her catch up.

"We were serving an arrest warrant when we heard the 'officer down' call," Annie said, eyes searching Emily for injuries. "We just got back. Are you all right?"

"A little banged up," Emily said. "But nothing's broken."

Annie blew out her breath. "I heard we spotted the car?"

"A patrol officer found it a few minutes ago," Emily said. "In that medical mall on Sherman. We know it's his because Marty shot out a window."

"For what good it did," Marty said. "Canine units are searching the neighborhood in case he's on foot. But I'm guessing he stashed an escape vehicle and got out of Dodge before roadblocks went up. He's long gone." He rubbed at a scratch on his arm. "Unfortunately, nobody at the mall saw anything."

"The mall have security cameras?"

"Plenty," Emily said. "Inside the offices. Nothing aimed at the lot."

"We're never that lucky," Annie said. She touched Emily's arm. "Are you sure you're all right, hon? Branch said you got run over."

"Well, sort of," Emily said.

"The bastard rammed her all right. But she bounced off," Marty explained. "She got to her feet and started chasing him. Might have caught up except for the charley horse."

Annie's eyes dropped to Emily's scarred calf. "Again?"

Emily nodded, disgusted the two-year-old injury was still getting the best of her. She wanted every shred of Ellis Marwood out of her life, and it just wasn't happening quick enough.

"Well, you're standing now," Annie said. "Took three hours to do that last time your calf went nuts. Progress." She looked Marty top to bottom, and her lips curled into a wide, catty smile. "And what, pray tell, are *you* supposed to be?"

she purred, reaching up and peeling a long shingle of mud off his shoulder. "A hot fudge sundae?"

"No. And there's a perfectly good explanation for this," Marty grumbled, face turning as pink as the towel around his waist.

"I'm all ears," Annie said.

Their affectionate teasing made Emily want to join in—with all that shiny mud on his six-six body, Marty *did* look like a giant ice-cream treat! But there'd be hell to pay if a TV camera caught them looking any way but serious. "We need to get to work," she said, dipping her head at the Fox Television van bouncing into the lot. "Right now."

Annie agreed they should move inside. "But you don't think you're working this case, do you?"

"Why not?" Emily said. "I'm a detective, aren't I?"

"You're also a participant," Annie pointed out. "You're involved."

"I tried to apprehend a suspect," Emily argued. "That's all. I have nothing to do with this otherwise." She grasped at another straw. "It's like back at the station—first one to answer the phone catches the case. I *was* the first one here." She ran her fingers through her matted chestnut hair.

"And your calf?" Annie pressed. "You can walk and kneel and do all those other crime scene things?"

Barely, Emily thought, feeling the lobster pinch when she put weight on it. But she wasn't going to miss handling a homicide case because of a stupid cramp. "I'm fine," she said. "Besides, I already talked to Branch. He's inside with the victim."

Annie's faint smile said she knew Emily was tapdancing—talking to Branch wasn't the same as getting approval from Branch—but would ignore it because she'd do the same thing. "Well, hell, why didn't you say so?" she said, aiming Emily at the spa. "Let's get your clothes so you can get right to work." She looked over her shoulder at Marty, cranked the smile to full wattage. "You go finish your bath, dear. You missed some dirt behind your ears."

His reply was blacker than the mud.

"What the hell *happened?*" the shooter screamed as he zoomed down Interstate 55, riding the adrenaline wave now that he was safe. "Who was that fucking *woman?*"

The family in the Volvo next to him stared openly.

He glared back, peeling his lips away from his square yellow teeth.

Dad cut off a semi moving over a lane.

"That's right! I'm nuts!" he screamed over the trucker's horn, smacking the steering wheel like it was on fire. "Tell all your fucking friends!"

Wait. Keep this up and someone'll flag down a cop. Can't have that. Not yet. Not till I'm finished. Nothing can interfere with the plan. Get ahold of yourself, goddammit.

"Everything's fine," he said, forcing himself not to blink. "You escaped. You changed cars. You took side streets to the interstate. Nobody saw you. Nobody's following you." The rearview was smudgy from all the times he'd made sure. "Sit back and relax. It's an easy drive to St. Louis. Your flight's not till tomorrow. You'll have a nice supper and get a good night's sleep, fly to Arizona in the morning. You'll go kill the rest of them, return to Naperville and finish. You're fine. Just follow the plan. The plan is everything." He liked the little pep talk. His muscles leaked tension—

"Shit!" he hissed, neck cords re-popping. "She saw me! She can identify me!"

He breathed hard awhile, decided maybe not. The woman had hit his windshield only an instant before blowing onto the roof. Not enough time to focus, let alone identify. Plus he'd been wearing the camouflage cap and beard, which he'd dumped in various fast-food-joint garbage cans. He'd kept gloves on throughout to ensure leaving no fingerprints. The Grand Prix and Taurus were rentals, would trace back to fake drivers' licenses and credit cards. The car he drove now was his own, with real license and credit. He was doubly— triply!—removed from the spa execution, with no way for anyone to connect A to Z.

Still . . .

He punched in the radio pre-set. After the weather, sports and an advertiser puff-job disguised as a feature story— "And now, another product made in Chicago!"— the news report began. He turned it loud. The announcer said a man shot a woman in west suburban Naperville. Said the woman died. Said cops found the getaway car and launched a man-hunt. Said a police detective was inside the spa and heard gunshots. Said she chased the shooter but got run over. Said the detective wasn't seriously injured. Said her name was Emily Thompson. Said she'd killed a man two years ago for trying to hang her.

Killed a man . . .

He tingled with cold sweat.

The announcer didn't give a description. If she'd seen him they'd have aired it for sure. He was safe.

Then again, he hadn't gotten this far taking chances.

He put on his turn signal and pulled to the shoulder. Trucks whizzed by inches from his door, their windshear rocking the car like a hobby-horse. He didn't care. His hands were steady now.

He pulled a spiral notebook from his sportcoat. It was pocket-size, with a canary cover and light-blue page rules. He clicked a pen and added the name in red ink, with neat lettering that touched neither rule.

Emily Thompson.

He smiled. The cop was as dead as all the rest of the names.

She just didn't know it yet.

* * *

Emily sniffed cautiously as she entered the spa's lobby. Before, the woman was so freshly slain she had no odor. Now, feces and urine had drained from her bladder and bowels. The odor of her wastes joined the waxy copper odor of the blood puddle congealing around her body. There was chlorine from the whirlpools. Jasmine and sandalwood from the mood candles. The palpable fear of the traumatized employees and clients, who couldn't leave this wretched place till detectives took their statements.

Which Emily couldn't do till she knew some basics.

"What's her name?" she asked the large man bending over the small corpse.

Hercules Branch didn't look up, but raised an index finger to indicate, "With you in one minute."

"OK." She turned to a uniformed cop. "Please tell me you brought Vapo-Rub."

"I don't leave home without it," he said, pulling a flat tin from his pocket.

Emily smeared a gob under each nostril and breathed the menthol fumes that would mask the stench of death. She murmured thanks and turned to examine the room.

The building was an old Chinese buffet restaurant reincarnated as an elegant day spa. This was its ornate lobby— what management called the "client welcome center." Its high ceiling came to a series of peaks, reminding Emily of a circus tent. Fringed Oriental rugs softened the white granite floor. Sheetrock walls, rag-rolled in sky blue, held a series of oil paintings that were colorful but indefinite. Dark red curtains covered the windows. A dozen chairs, lacquered the same black as the picture frames, surrounded a low, round table filled with women's magazines. The manicurist who had directed Emily through the front door occupied one chair. Next to her sat their attendant from the mud bath. A cappuccino maker steamed in one corner. A water dispenser gurgled in another.

"Leila Reynolds," Branch said.

Emily watched the Naperville Police Department's chief of detectives push to his feet with the help of a black thornwood cane.

"I got her information from the manager," Branch continued. "Before he became too shaky to continue."

Emily recalled the white-faced young man being helped to the ambulance by the paramedics. "And the other witnesses?"

"Those two insisted on staying with Leila till her children arrive," he said, pointing to the chairs. "The rest are out back. The squad's taking their statements. Soon as we're done, go help." He took his notebook out of his jacket and started his recitation.

"Leila Clarice Reynolds, age seventy-seven. She's a retired bookkeeper for a Chicago auto dealership. She lived in Old Farm"—a subdivision on Naperville's south side—"and was widowed four years ago. Started working here a year after her husband's funeral. She has two grown children, a daughter in Milwaukee and son in Miami. I already called them. The daughter will get here first, obviously, so keep an eye out for her arrival." He stopped to write himself a note.

"Why was she working?" Emily asked, taking her own notes. "If she'd already retired?"

"Leila got bored," the manicurist piped up. "You know, living by herself after her husband died. We're glad she took the job—she was so much fun." Her lower lip trembled. "She wasn't supposed to be here today."

"Why not?" Emily asked.

"She had a cold. I told her to go home, I'd cover the desk. You know what she did?"

Emily shook her head.

"She patted my face. You know, like a grandma? Then she said, 'It's OK, dear. I'd rather work. It's better than sitting around the house feeling sorry . . . for . . . my . . .'" The manicurist's face crumpled as the floodgates opened.

"Why don't you take her outside?" Emily told the attendant. "Fresh air will do you both good. I'll come find you when I'm ready."

The attendant put her arm around her sobbing friend and led her out. Emily glanced at the uniformed cop.

"I'll keep them from leaving till you get there," he said.

"Thanks." She moved to join Branch at the body. Marty touched her shoulder from behind.

"Find your clothes?" she asked, reaching back and taking his hand.

"And a shower," he said. "Listen, I'm gonna go back to my shop and write up my report." Marty was chief of detectives for the county sheriff's police. "I'll send over a copy soon as I'm finished."

"Will it contain anything you didn't tell me in the parking lot?" Branch asked.

Marty shook his head.

"No hurry, then," Branch said. "Get some coffee, take your time."

"Nah. Might as well get it over with. If I think of anything I didn't tell you, I'll call."

Branch gave him a thumb's up, and Marty swung his attention back to Emily. "Want me to stay over tonight?"

She nodded her head back against his chest. "I'll call you when I'm done," she said. "No idea when that will be, though."

"Doesn't matter. You just call." He rubbed her shoulders, then gently pushed away.

"Aw, Marty, tell her you wuv her," Branch said.

"I'd better not," Marty said. "She'd fling her arms around

me then you'd have to fire her for sexual harassment and we'd all be embarrassed . . ."

Cop humor, Emily thought as the two men laughed. Like these two homicide veterans, someday she'd be an expert at whistling past the graveyard.

But not today.

Not with Leila Reynolds staring at her.

Emily turned her attention to the short, slender victim. She lay face up, her legs straight out and arms at her sides. She hadn't fallen that way—Marty had to reposition her for the CPR. Her wrinkled hands were cupped, as though she was holding water. Her black wig was sharply askew, exposing white hair so thin that the overhead lights sparkled on her scalp. She had large green eyes with perfectly shaped brows. She wore an expensive yellow sundress, an alligator belt with silver buckle, and brown sandals with medium heels. Bra and briefs—Emily saw the telltale lines—but no hose. Toe and finger nails looked freshly manicured, and painted the same shade of pink.

She finished cataloging Leila, then studied the holes in her chest and forehead. Each was the size of a pencil eraser. Her forehead had flame-charring, but her chest didn't. That suggested the chest shots were fired several feet away, then the shooter moved up close for the insurance shot. "What caliber do you think, Branch?" she asked. "A .38?"

"Maybe .357 Magnum—there's lots of damage on the wall that caught the bullets after they exited Leila." He tugged at his chin, considering. "Both are revolver cartridges, so that's what the shooter used."

"Unless it's one of the few semiautomatics that do," she countered. "I should look for ejected shell casings to make sure."

"Unless he picked them up to fool us."

"Marty and I were right behind—he didn't have time. So

if I find casings, he used a semiautomatic. If I don't, he used a revolver."

Branch smiled. "Very good, Detective. Go ahead."

She mentally divided the room into three-foot squares. She tucked her gloved hands behind her back and examined them in order. She worked her way across the floor, reached the door to the parking lot.

She stopped, cocking her head in confusion.

"What?" Branch asked.

"There's a pair of burnt matches on the floor."

"Que?" Branch said, raising an eyebrow.

She squatted to study them, wincing at the ripple in her calf. Wood. One-eighth-inch square, two inches long. Large kitchen matches—Ohio Blue Tips or a generic clone. Available anywhere.

She closed her eyes and visualized scraping one against its sandpapery lighting strip. The bulb head flared yellow. The flame crawled down the stick. The flame died when it ran out of wood.

She opened her eyes, compared reality to the visualization.

The heads were indeed charcoaled. But the burn ended right under the bulbs—the sticks were untouched. Suggesting the matches were lit and immediately blown out.

She relayed the information.

Branch pointed to the mood candles.

"I've been at this spa enough," she said, "to know they light their candles with butane torches. Like you'd use on a Weber grill."

"That's not it, then. Do they allow smoking?"

She pointed to the large warning sign over the cappuccino maker. "No. They're pretty militant about it. They even called the police when a guy waiting for his wife wouldn't put out his cigarette. And he was out on the sidewalk."

"Ah, the cigarette Nazis," Branch said, shifting his grip

on the cane. "Interesting where you found those matches, eh?"

"In a corner *behind* the door," she agreed. "Where nobody stands. I think it's a clue."

"Almost certainly."

"But what on earth does it mean?"

"Hey, you're the detective," Branch said. "Find out."